Our Fair Lily

Dilly's Story Series
Dilly's Sacrifice
Dilly's Lass
Dilly's Hope

The Days of the Week Collection
Mothering Sunday
The Little Angel
A Mother's Grace
The Blessed Child
A Maiden's Voyage
A Precious Gift
Time to Say Goodbye

The Precious Stones Series
The Winter Promise
An Orphan's Journey
A Simple Wish
A Daughter's Destiny
A Season for Hope
A Lesson Learned

Rosie Goodwin is the four-million-copy bestselling author of more than forty novels. She is the first author in the world to be allowed to follow three of Catherine Cookson's trilogies with her own sequels. Having worked in the social services sector for many years, then fostered a number of children, she is now a full-time novelist. She is one of the top 50 most borrowed authors from UK libraries and has sold over four million copies across her career. Rosie lives in Nuneaton, the setting for many of her books, with her husband and their beloved dogs.

Rosie GOODWIN
Our Fair Lily

ZAFFRE

First published in the UK in 2024 by
ZAFFRE
An imprint of Bonnier Books UK
4th Floor, Victoria House, Bloomsbury Square, London, England, WC1B 4DA
Owned by Bonnier Books
Sveavägen 56, Stockholm, Sweden

A CIP catalogue record for this book is
available from the British Library.

ISBN: 978-1-80418-304-5

Also available as an ebook and an audiobook

1 3 5 7 9 10 8 6 4 2

Typeset by IDSUK (Data Connection) Ltd
Printed and bound in Great Britain by Clays Ltd, Elcograf S.p.A.

Zaffre is an imprint of Bonnier Books UK
www.bonnierbooks.co.uk

This book is for my beautiful children and grandchildren.
Never forget I love you all to the moon and back xxx

Chapter One

July 1875

High on the hill overlooking a valley in Galley Common, a small mining village on the outskirts of Nuneaton, stood Oakley Manor, a large, imposing house surrounded by acres of landscaped gardens that had been the home of the Bellingham family for many generations.

On this beautiful summer day the youngest member of the Bellingham family, Lady Arabella, stood before her grandmother in the old lady's bedroom with her chin on her chest as sobs wracked her body.

'Oh, Arabella!' Lady Bellingham said wearily. 'Do you realise that your whole future is now at risk? Should Lord Lumley hear a whisper of this he will end your engagement and the family will be disgraced.'

'I don't care,' Arabella said defiantly, raising her chin to stare back at her grandmother through striking blue eyes. 'I never wanted to marry him in the first place. He is almost old enough to be my father! I only agreed to the engagement to please you, and Mama and Papa, but that was before I met Freddie. And I *love* him!'

'Love, *huh*!' the old lady said grumpily, leaning heavily on her ebony-topped walking stick. 'You cannot die from love but you *can* die from cold and starvation and Freddie is as poor as a church mouse. Do you *really* think love will put food on the table and pay your bills? He is merely a captain in the army, whereas Lord Lumley is one of the richest men in the county. Married to him you will live like a queen. So put this young captain from your mind.'

Her grandmother paused and examined her granddaughter. 'How many courses have you missed?'

Arabella sniffed. 'F-four.'

'Then the child should be due early in December. We have no time to lose.' Lady Bellingham tapped her chin thoughtfully. 'Go away, child, and leave things to me. Oh – and be sure to tell no one else, especially not your parents. Do you understand me?'

'Y-yes, Grandmama.'

'Well, what are we to do now? The silly, silly girl!' Lady Bellingham said when the door had closed behind her.

Her maid, Hudson, who had served her for more years than she cared to remember, frowned. She had long since discovered that although her mistress could strike the fear of God into most people, her bite was actually nowhere near as bad as her bark.

'It's unfortunate but the girl *has* made it known from day one that she didn't want to marry Lord Lumley. Happen it were only a matter o' time before she met someone she fell in love with, and the young captain seems to be the one.' She spoke as she would to one of her own class.

'*Rubbish!*' Her mistress scowled at her as she tried to think of a way to save the situation. Some minutes later, she said thoughtfully, 'Hudson, the Moon girl, the one that just got promoted to parlour maid. What do you think of her?'

'She seems a nice enough girl,' Hudson answered as she tidied her mistress's bed. 'Well thought of by the housekeeper, apparently, and from a respectable family in the village.'

'Hmm, well I have an idea. Go and tell the girl I wish to speak to her immediately.'

With a long-suffering sigh, Hudson went off to do as she was told.

They returned soon after, and Lily Moon bobbed her knee respectfully. 'You wished to see me, ma'am?' Her heart was thudding uncomfortably as she wondered why she had been summoned.

It was the first time she had ever been this close to the old mistress and, as everyone had told her, she was certainly a flamboyant character. Her face was heavily powdered and rouged and her grey hair was piled high on her head with feathers sticking out of it. Her gown was a deep lilac satin covered in lace and frills, and jewels seemed to sparkle on every inch of visible skin, reflecting the sun that poured in through the windows.

Lady Bellingham narrowed her eyes and stared at her. The girl certainly looked respectable enough. 'How old are you, Moon?'

'Nineteen, ma'am.'

'Hmm.' So, she was the same age as Arabella and very similar in looks with her fair hair and blue eyes. The idea she'd had just might work.

'I have a proposition to put to you, Moon. But before I tell you about it, I want to know how trustworthy you are.'

Lily blinked in surprise. 'I-I believe I am very trustworthy, ma'am.'

'Good, and can you promise to keep everything I am about to tell you to yourself? It's imperative that no one else ever learns of it.' Lily nodded solemnly and the old woman continued. 'Good. I have just discovered that my granddaughter Arabella finds herself in a, er . . . delicate condition.'

When Lily looked confused, she said, 'She has had, shall we say, a most unfortunate affair with a totally unsuitable young man and she is with child, but, as you may be aware, she is betrothed to Lord Lumley. What I am proposing is to send her away for a few months to have the baby and once it is born, I shall have it fostered and she can return home to continue with the plans for the wedding.'

'But won't people find it strange if she goes away for so long?' Lily asked sensibly.

'Not if we tell them she needs time to prepare herself and rest. But let me worry about that side of things. What I want to know is, would you be willing to go with her and look after her, acting as her maid?'

Now Lily really was shocked. 'May I ask where we would be going and for how long?'

'I should think until sometime in December, and as to where, I was thinking I could rent a cottage somewhere out of the way for you both to stay in. It wouldn't do for her to bump into anyone we know. Oh, and I would double your salary for the time you are gone, of course.'

'I see.' Lily's teeth nipped down on her lower lip before she said, 'I would have to speak to my parents about it, but I would tell them it was to accompany Miss Arabella on a holiday, as you just told me.'

'Excellent. Then you may take a couple of hours off to go and see them immediately and meanwhile I shall make enquiries to locate a suitable place for you both to go. Thank you. Off you go, my dear, and remember, not a word!'

Lily curtsied again and hurried downstairs to collect her shawl. She had no doubt her mother would be as surprised as she was at the offer, but she doubted she'd object. Robbie, however, might be another matter. They had been walking out together for over a year now and she knew he would have married her tomorrow had she agreed to it, so he definitely wasn't going to be too pleased at the idea. Still, she thought, she was being well paid to go, and how hard could it be?

Because she lived so close to the manor, she didn't live in as most servants did, and soon the little terraced two-up, two-down pit cottage in Valley Road, which had been the only home Lily had ever known, came into sight and with a spring in her step she hurried in to tell her mother about the proposed holiday.

'A holiday before the wedding, you say?' Sara Moon paused from rolling the pastry for the rabbit pie she was making and raised her eyebrows. 'And what does Lord Lumley think of that idea? Most young ladies would prefer to stay at home an' be involved in the plans fer their weddin'.'

4

Avoiding her mother's eyes, Lily shrugged. She hated lying to her mother but she had promised to keep the secret, and she was a girl of her word.

'An' furthermore, what do you think your Robbie will think o' yer being away all that time?' Sara went on. 'I can't see 'im bein' too pleased about it neither.'

'Well, it's not as if I'm goin' away forever, is it?' Lily pointed out. 'I'll ask 'im tonight if you've no objections to me goin'.'

'All right, love.' Sara nodded.

Walking back to the manor, Lily thought about what she would say to Robbie. She wasn't looking forward to the conversation, but if truth be told she was quite relieved to be going away. Most of her friends were already married and some even had children. Robbie was a lovely chap and she should have jumped at the chance of him putting a ring on her finger, but every time he suggested it, she managed to come up with some excuse or another. Perhaps this break would give her time to decide if getting married was really what she wanted.

Just as she had expected, Robbie was not pleased with the idea. 'Four or five months?' He gasped. 'An' why 'ave they chosen you to go with 'er? Why can't she take 'er own lady's maid?'

'I 'ave no idea,' Lily answered, keeping her fingers crossed behind her back. 'I think perhaps she wanted someone her own age to go with her. But cheer up, it's not as if I won't be comin' back, is it? An' I will be gettin' double me salary.'

'Then I suppose I can't stop you,' he said petulantly. 'But I still don't like it!' And with that he slammed off home in a sulk.

Up at the manor that evening, Lady Bellingham sighed as she wiped her gnarled hand across her heavily powdered face. Following the death of her husband some years ago, Clarissa Bellingham had retired to the west wing, and to all intents and purposes her son and his wife now ran the estate and their many businesses – although everyone knew that old Lady Bellingham kept a very close eye on things. To most people she was a forbidding figure, including to her daughter-in-law, who was a semi-invalid. Lady Bellingham had little time for her, although she was close to her son and absolutely adored her grandchildren, Arabella and Louis. She had spoilt them both shamelessly, which was why her granddaughter had turned to her now.

'I could really do without all this stress at my age, Hudson,' she complained as her long-suffering maid strained her favourite Earl Grey tea into a china cup. 'Do you think the Moon girl will take me up on my offer?'

'I don't see why not,' Hudson replied as she added two lumps of sugar to the tea and carried it to her mistress. 'I dare say she'll let you know when she turns into work tomorrow. So stop frettin' an' get this down you else you'll worry yerself into the grave. I've no doubt the girl will agree to it so all we 'ave to do now is find somewhere for them to go.'

Over the following days, Lady Bellingham wasted no time in renting a cottage in the Yorkshire Dales and Arabella told her parents that she wished to have a few months' holiday before throwing herself into the plans for her wedding.

Neither Lord Lumley nor her parents had been too happy with the idea but as usual they had bowed to the old woman's wishes and within no time at all Arabella and Lily Moon were on their way to Yorkshire. Then, once the baby had been born, Lady Bellingham would find a family to foster it, and Arabella could put the whole sorry situation behind her.

She had done well, Lady Bellingham thought with satisfaction. She just hoped Arabella would be suitably grateful!

Chapter Two

November 1875

'Letter for you, an' it's got a Yorkshire postmark!'

'Is it from Arabella? Bring it here at once, Hudson!' Lady Bellingham held out her hand.

'Don't reckon it's from Miss Arabella,' Hudson commented, handing the letter to her. 'It don't look like her handwritin' to me.'

'Hmm.' Lifting a pair of gold-framed spectacles, Lady Bellingham perched them on the end of her nose, then opening the envelope, she took out the single sheet of paper. She visibly paled as she read, her wrinkled hand flying to her throat.

'What's up? Is it bad news?' Hudson asked with concern. 'Is it somethin' to do wi' Miss Arabella?'

'Yes . . . yes, it is!' Lady Bellingham took a deep breath. 'It appears that Arabella has given birth prematurely.'

'Crikey, the baby weren't due till the beginnin' o' next month,' Hudson gasped. 'Are mother an' baby both all right?'

'It seems that the baby is, but I don't know about Arabella. Moon informs me that she disappeared two days after the child was delivered.'

'What do you mean, *disappeared*?' Hudson frowned.

'Just that!' Lady Bellingham snapped irritably. 'Lily Moon says here that she woke up to the sound of the baby crying and when she went to check on mother and baby, Arabella was gone . . . all her clothes were gone too!'

They stared at each other in silence for a moment until Lady Bellingham said, 'Bring me a pen and paper, Hudson. I must write back to the girl immediately. The last thing we need is for her to turn up back here with the flyblow. That really would be the end of Arabella's engagement, and think of the scandal it would cause!'

'Well, I did say all this skulduggery wouldn't work,' Hudson said unsympathetically. 'You don't think her captain 'as turned up an' swept her off her feet again, do you?'

'Unfortunately, that could be a possibility,' the old woman conceded with a shake of her head. 'The little *fool*! What she ever saw in that young pup I'll never know. Not when Lord Lumley worships the very ground she walks on. Everyone knows he's one of the richest men in the county.'

'Hmm, an' he's also old enough to be 'er father,' Hudson pointed out. 'Didn't the girl tell you an' her parents from day one that she didn't want to marry him? She's in love with the young captain, that were as plain as the nose on your face!'

Now as Lady Bellingham recalled that conversation, she could almost picture her granddaughter standing before her. With her soft blue eyes, golden hair and curvy figure, at nineteen years old Arabella was a beauty, and she knew it. She could have had her pick of any number of young men and loved to flirt with them, but until she met the captain no one had interested her, which was why she had reluctantly agreed to her engagement to Lord Lumley.

But this latest development had thrown everything into disarray again – it just went to show that the best of plans could go wrong. As yet she'd not found a foster family for the baby, so it was imperative now that she get in touch with Lily to tell her to stay where she was until she received further instructions. It really wouldn't do if she were to turn up on the doorstep with a flyblow in her arms!

As she penned a reply, her arthritic old hands fumbled across the paper, but at last it was written and after sealing it in an envelope she told Hudson, 'Take this down to one of the grooms and tell him to ride into town and see that it is posted immediately.'

Hudson sighed ungraciously but did as she was told.

Once she was alone tears stung at the back of Lady Bellingham's eyes. She suddenly felt very old and frail, and it was no wonder with all the stress her granddaughter had caused her. And yet she still adored her, possibly because Arabella reminded her very much of herself when she had been her age. It was hard to remember, when she looked in the mirror, that she had once been young and beautiful too. Now her mother or even her grandmother seemed to peer back at her, despite the rouge and powder she used so lavishly. And her hands . . . She sniffed as she stared down at them. The veins stood up on the back of them like the lines on a map and even the many jewelled rings she wore did nothing to improve their appearance.

Leaning heavily on her walking stick, she stood up and crossed to the window just in time to see one of the young grooms riding hell for leather down the drive, no doubt going to post her letter. Somehow, she must find Arabella and make her see that her future lay with Lord Lumley and not the dashing young captain who had stolen her heart. Marrying for love was all well and good but it wasn't always enough. How long would it last when she was surrounded by a herd of crying children clinging to her skirts and with no money to feed and clothe them? She herself had married for love and look where it had got her!

She remembered the day she had first set eyes on Lord Montague as if it was yesterday. She had been attending a debutante's ball in London with her parents and the moment she saw him it was love at first sight. He had been tall, handsome and dashing, and ten years older than her. Within months their engagement had been announced. They had moved into Oakley Manor following their marriage and within a year her son George had been born and she had thought her happiness was complete. But soon after she had been forced to acknowledge that her husband had a roving eye and her idealistic marriage began to crumble.

It had taken her a long time to come to terms with the fact that Montague had mistresses but at least she had her son and a pampered lifestyle. Now she wanted the same for Arabella and her grandson. At twenty-one years old, Louis was the apple of her eye. He was tall, dark and handsome but as yet had shown no interest in the many suitable young ladies she and his parents had paraded in front of him. Still, she mused, he was young, there was plenty of time.

Sighing heavily, she dropped into the chair and stared sightlessly out across the manicured grounds, until a tap came at the door and her grandson entered the room.

'Good morning, Grandmama,' Louis greeted her with a broad smile as he crossed to kiss her hand, and as always, she melted at the sight of him. 'How are you on this beautiful day?'

'As well as an old biddy can be expected to be,' she answered as he plonked himself down on the chair closest to her.

'You're not old, Grandmama,' Louis told her with a cheeky grin.

'So what have you got planned for today?' the old lady asked him.

'I'm going out with Papa this morning to see the tenant farmers,' he groaned. 'But then I'm going down to the stables to help Ned groom the new horse Father just acquired. He's a beauty – a black stallion.'

'So I understand.' She smiled at him indulgently. He had always shown far more interest in the horses and was an accomplished rider. She was sure he would have lived down in the stables if he could. It was hard to imagine that one day he would inherit his father's title, Oakley Manor and all the many businesses – the Bellinghams were major shareholders in the local Haunchwood Mine, the brickworks, numerous tenanted farms on the estate, as well as many of the pit cottages in the village and yet more properties in nearby Nuneaton. So much responsibility to place on his shoulders, she thought, but hopefully that would be a long way in the future.

His face became solemn then as he asked, 'When is Arabella coming home? She seems to have been gone for an awfully long time and although I hate to admit it, I miss the little nuisance.'

'Oh I've no doubt she'll be home very soon now,' his grandmother said vaguely.

Luckily his questioning was interrupted by the sound of barking from beneath the bedroom window and Louis shot across to look out.

'Oh, it's Father and he's taking Prince and Bosun for a walk by the looks of it. I'm going to join him. Bye for now, Grandmama.' And with that he rushed away.

Out of the window, Lady Bellingham watched the young man run after his father and the two black Labradors until they were all out of sight and her mind returned to Arabella. Somehow, she must find the silly girl before she made the second biggest mistake of her life. But she had no idea how she was going to go about it, so for now all she could do was wait and see how the maid responded.

Chapter Three

It was almost a week later when Hudson entered Lady Belling-ham's room early one afternoon all of a fluster.

'What's wrong with you, woman? Pull yourself together and spit it out,' Lady Bellingham bellowed.

'It's Lily Moon,' Hudson gushed. 'She's downstairs askin' to see you!'

'She's *what*?' Lady Bellingham looked shocked. She'd been expecting a reply to her letter any day but she hadn't expected her to turn up on their doorstep.

'She's down—'

Lady Bellingham flapped her hand at her. 'I know, I know, I heard you. I'm not deaf yet!' And then anxiously, 'Is she alone?'

'Well, she ain't got the babe with her, if that's what you mean!'

The old woman frowned. 'Then go and fetch her up here at once.'

Hudson hurried away and soon returned with the girl, who stood staring at the old woman in consternation. Lady Bellingham was dressed in a burgundy satin gown embellished with beads. In her younger days, she had been a large woman but now the weight had dropped from her bones and the over-decorated gown seemed to hang off her. As usual, her face was heavily rouged and today she wore a beautiful ruby necklace around her sagging neck, and matching earrings. Her fingers were covered in rings set with gems and overall, Lily thought that she looked like a grotesque doll.

'Come forward, girl. I don't bite!'

Lily took a few tentative steps towards her.

'What a to-do, eh?' Lady Bellingham shook her head. 'You're the last person I expected to see. I wrote to you last week; didn't you get my letter?'

'No, ma'am. I had to set off back for home shortly after I wrote to yer cos Miss Arabella only left me wi' enough money fer me an' the baby to get back 'ere. She took all the rest.'

'I see.' The old woman scowled, making lines appear in the thick face powder. 'And where is the baby now – and was it a girl or a boy?'

'The baby is back at our cottage wi' me mam. It's a little girl,' Lily informed her, tossing a lock of her shining fair hair back across her shoulder. 'We 'ad a terrible journey back. Miss Arabella flatly refused to feed 'er after she gave birth so I 'ad to do me best wi' a pap bag, but on the way 'ome I could only do it when the coach stopped at an inn to rest the 'orses.'

'And Arabella?'

Lily shrugged her slim shoulders making the fringe on her shawl dance. 'I've no idea where she is, ma'am. The young captain turned up just days afore Miss Arabella give birth an' then once she had, she just upped an' left in the dead o' night wi'out a word.'

'So, she could be anywhere?' Lady Bellingham examined the maid through narrowed eyes. She was a pretty girl with a heart-shaped face and dimpled cheeks and her eyes were a lovely shade of blue. She and her granddaughter might have been taken for sisters.

Lily nodded.

'Does anyone know who the baby is?' she asked.

'Only me mam an' dad an,' o' course. I 'ad to tell them.'

'Good . . . good.' Lady Bellingham stared into space thoughtfully as an idea occurred to her.

Her thoughts were interrupted when Lily asked, 'When do yer want me to bring the baby back 'ere?'

The woman looked horrified. 'I *don't*,' she said coldly. 'I don't even know what baby you are talking about, girl!'

'Wh-what do yer mean?' Lily looked stunned. 'I'm talkin' about Miss Arabella's baby!' Then as she realised what the old woman was trying to do, her eyes narrowed. 'Don't you go tryin' to land the little 'un on me, missus! She ain't *my* responsibility.'

'Isn't she?' Lady Bellingham responded imperiously. 'I'm afraid she must be, for I have no idea why you would bring Arabella into this.'

'You know damn well that the child is 'ers,' Lily snapped, her blue eyes flashing. 'And so will everyone else when I open me trap an' tell 'em.'

'Oh, I don't think it would be in your interests to do that, my dear.' Lady Bellingham's eyes were like chips of ice. 'After all, your family lives in one of our tied cottages. And doesn't your father and one of your brothers work down the mine, and another one here in the stables? Wouldn't it be terrible if they were all suddenly to lose their jobs and you were all to become homeless.'

Lily shook her head in dismay as Lady Bellingham waved her hand towards her dressing table telling Hudson, 'Fetch me the string pouch from the top drawer.'

When Hudson had done as she was asked, the old woman checked the contents before holding it out to Lily. 'In there you will find twenty golden guineas. Quite a fortune, isn't it? More than enough to buy your silence, I believe? And more than enough to cover the cost of bringing the baby up respectably.'

'B-but this baby is your great-granddaughter. *Surely* you can't just give her away as if she was nothing to you!' Lily choked. 'And who am I supposed to tell people she belongs to? Babies don't just appear out of thin air. Won't you at least meet her and give her a name? She deserves that at least.'

'This child is nothing to me and I don't give a damn what you choose to call her. Furthermore, as from this day I don't want to

14

hear another word about her. What you do with her is up to you entirely. You can leave her on the steps of the workhouse for all I care. But just remember, should any gossip get back to me tainting my Arabella's name I shall know where it came from.'

'And what about my job 'ere?' Lily asked.

Lady Bellingham shrugged. 'You may return to work if you wish to, just so long as you don't bring the child.'

Lily knew when she was beaten and her shoulders sagged. The Bellinghams were the most influential family in the neighbourhood, and she had no doubt the old woman would think nothing of turfing the family out of their home if she were to try and get justice. Who would believe her word over theirs?

With as much dignity as she could muster, Lily automatically reached for the bag of gold. Deep down she wanted to refuse it but common sense told her that it may well be needed in the future, so after tucking it into the deep pocket of her old brown skirt she left the room without another word. How she wished she had never agreed to go with Arabella. But it was too late for regrets, so blinking back tears she descended the stairs and walked out, leaving the huge oak front door swinging open behind her.

Meanwhile, back in Lady Bellingham's bedroom, Hudson was staring at her mistress through narrowed eyes.

'You bloody planned to do this, didn't you?' she said accusingly. 'Otherwise, you'd never have had that purse o' gold ready.'

Lady Bellingham shrugged. 'What else was I supposed to do? Arabella's reputation must be protected at all costs. Lots of pit wenches like her have a baby out of wedlock, so she'll survive, whereas this would be a disaster for our family if word got out. I've no doubt Arabella will be home in the next day or so when she realises how foolish she has been. She'll soon see which side her bread is buttered after a few days on the road living rough with her captain! And then we can put this whole sorry mess behind us.'

'And what if she ain't?' Hudson asked sceptically.

Lady Bellingham pursed her lips. 'We will cross that bridge if and when we come to it. Now get about your work, woman. I don't pay you to stand about.'

With a shake of her head, Hudson left the room.

Just before Lily turned out of Oakley Manor's tree-lined drive, she paused to look back at the house. The many sash cord windows on either side of the porticoed entrance were glinting in the cold November sunshine and the arched marble steps leading to the front door shone like mirrors. An enormous fountain stood in the middle of the carriage sweep, the water it contained sparkling like diamonds. This was the home of possibly the richest family in the whole county and yet in that moment, Lily almost felt sorry for them. Their money and their reputation obviously meant more to them than their own flesh and blood.

However, now she was faced with a dilemma: what to do with the baby? She was a beautiful child and as Lily had been caring for her since she was born, she had formed a bond with her. Lady Bellingham had told her she could leave her at the workhouse, but the thought of doing that made Lily's blood run cold. Everyone knew that most of the infants abandoned there didn't reach their first birthdays. Most of the poor little souls in the nursery didn't even cry because they knew no one would come to tend to them. But what was her mam going to say?

Lily had arrived late the evening before and had been able to enter the cottage without anyone knowing she or the baby was there. Her family had all left for work by the time she had risen that morning, but what would be said when word got out? And what would Robbie say? Her heart turned over at the thought of what she could tell him. He was going to be furious, she thought,

16

rubbing her forehead. But all she could do now was tell her mam what had happened and take it from there.

'There you are, luvvie,' her mother said when she entered the small kitchen of their home. Glancing about Lily saw the baby sleeping peacefully on a blanket in a drawer and suddenly burst into tears.

'Oh, Mammy, everythin' is *such* a mess,' she sobbed.

Drying her workworn hands on the large huckaback apron tied over her drab skirt, Sara Moon rushed over to envelop her daughter in a hug as she drew her towards a chair.

'Right, you sit there while I make you a nice cup o' tea then you can tell me all about it.' Sara rushed away to swing the soot-blackened kettle across the flames and began to prepare the teapot as Lily sat glumly staring at the baby.

Soon they both sat at the table with steaming mugs in front of them.

'So come on, tell me what's happened.'

And so, between sobs, Lily told her what had happened up at Oakley Manor.

Sara's face flushed with anger. 'Why, the schemin' old bugger 'er!' She slammed her fist on the table making the sugar bowl and milk jug dance. 'What's she thinkin' of tryin' to foist the responsibility for the poor little mite on to you?'

'I don't know,' Lily told her in a small voice. 'But the question is, what are we goin' to do wi' 'er?'

Sara started to pace the small kitchen floor. 'I wish you'd told me the situation afore you went,' she fumed. 'I'd never 'ave agreed to you goin'. I thought it were strange that she was clearin' off for a holiday wi' her weddin' comin' up.'

'I couldn't tell you the real reason,' Lily said. 'Lady Bellingham made me promise I wouldn't.' Then suddenly remembering the bag of money the old lady had given her she took it from her pocket and handed it to her mother. 'She gave me this an' said it should be enough to bring the baby up an' keep me quiet.'

Sara tipped the contents of the small pouch onto the table and the sun shining through the tiny leaded window glinted off the golden guineas. 'My God . . . there must be a fortune there!' she gasped.

Lily nodded in agreement. 'Yes, twenty golden guineas. But I shouldn't have taken it. It's just, I was so upset and angry at her that I took it without thinking.'

'Hmm, well the old bugger can 'ave it back!' Sara declared. 'She must 'ave planned this was what she'd do if you turned up with the baby.' Her breath caught in her throat as something occurred to her. 'But what are we going to do if everyone thinks that the baby is yours? You must admit it looks fishy, you disappearin' fer months then suddenly comin' back 'ere wi' a babe in yer arms.'

Lily gulped. She hadn't thought of that. 'P-per'aps we could say she was a relative who'd been orphaned?' she stammered.

Her mother snorted. 'Aye, we could say that but yer know what the folk round 'ere are like fer gossipin'. An' what's Robbie goin' to say? How can yer explain her away to 'im wi'out tellin' 'im the truth, eh?'

At that moment the baby whimpered and crossing to the drawer Lily lifted her out and held her to her chest.

'I reckon the best thing we could do is give the old lady 'er money back an' take the child to the workhouse as she suggested. We've done wi' the whole sorry affair then.' Yet even as she said it Sara knew that it was going to be easier said than done. Lily was clearly attached to the child and it wasn't the baby's fault she had been born, after all. 'Look . . . let's wait an' see what yer dad 'as to say when he gets in from the pit this evenin'. In the meantime, try an' keep 'er quiet. We don't want to give the neighbours owt to gossip about till we 'ave to.'

'But what will we say to the others when they come in from work?' Her siblings were bound to ask questions when they found Lily back with a baby.

'You just leave that to me.'

Lily nodded and went to warm some milk for the baby's feed, feeling sick with worry and wishing with all her heart that she had never agreed to go with Arabella in the first place.

Chapter Four

Bridget, Lily's eighteen-year-old sister, was the first to arrive home that afternoon. She worked in the village shop, which was a hotbed for gossip, and when she saw the baby lying in the drawer with Lily sitting beside her, she raised her eyebrows. Lily was a pretty girl, but Bridget was beautiful and she knew it. Already she had broken more hearts in the village than she could count, but not one of her beaus had managed to put a ring on her finger as yet, because unknown to everyone, Robbie was the one she wanted.

'What's goin' on 'ere?'

Lily sighed as she glanced at her mother for help.

'Lily's helpin' a relative out carin' fer the baby fer a few days,' Sara told her daughter calmly as Bridget took a thick shawl from about her shoulders.

'Oh, but I thought you were away on 'oliday with Miss Arabella?' Bridget clearly didn't believe a word that her mother had told her, and avoiding her sister's eyes, Lily felt herself flush.

'Anyway, the baby bein' 'ere won't affect you none so come to the table an' get some stew,' Sara said sharply before Bridget could question her sister further. Meekly Bridget did as she was told.

'So what does Robbie think to you carin' fer a baby?' Bridget said when she was halfway through her meal.

'I haven't seen 'im yet to tell him,' Lily admitted. 'I didn't get 'ome till late last night and he would 'ave been at work today.'

Bridget turned her attention to the child and after studying her for a while she commented, 'She's got the same colour 'air an' eyes as you, ain't she?'

'So what 'ave you got planned fer this evenin', then?' her mother cut in sharply, seeing Lily squirm.

'I'm goin' up to the dance at the village 'all,' Bridget responded, all thoughts of the baby forgotten for the moment. 'In fact' – she glanced at the tin clock on the mantelpiece – 'I'd best go up an' get ready. I'm goin' to wear that new gown we finished sewin' the other night. Is there any 'ot water fer me to wash in?'

'There's a kettleful on the range.'

Bridget quickly finished the food in her dish and without giving Lily a second glance she snatched the kettle and rushed off to her room.

'That wasn't easy,' Lily said quietly and Sara nodded.

'Just leave the talkin' to me,' she insisted. 'There's nothin' I'd like more than to tell 'em all who the baby's mother is but we don't want our family to lose their jobs an' get chucked out of 'ome so fer now we just 'ave to go along wi' a few lies. The only one who needs to know who the baby really belongs to is yer dad, an' we'll tell 'im when the rest of 'em are abed. But I'll tell yer now, I'd like nothin' better than to put me 'ands round old Lady Belling'am's scrawny old neck an' strangle the bloody old bugger!'

Lily grinned but then a thought occurred to her. 'But what about my job, Mam? I can 'ardly take the baby along to work wi' me, can I?'

'I've told you, let's talk to yer dad afore we make any decisions,' Sara said firmly.

As the rest of the family arrived home, their response to the baby was much as Bridget's had been, but Sara stuck to her story, telling them all that Lily was caring for the baby for a time for a sick relative she had met in Yorkshire. It was the best she could come up with.

Bill, her husband, and Teddy, Lily's seventeen-year-old brother, arrived shortly after Bridget had set off for the dance, dressed up in her Sunday best. They both worked in the local Haunchwood Colliery, as did most of the men in the village, but whereas Bill accepted his lot, Teddy dreaded every shift. Their lives were not easy and during the winter months they became accustomed to going to work in the dark and returning in the dark after spending hours doing back-breaking work deep in the bowels of the earth. Bill had done the job for so long that no amount of washing could remove the black soot ingrained in his skin but he never complained, for he knew that with the children all working now they were a lot better off than most.

It was accepted that come Friday evening many of the miners would wind up in the Miner's Arms, or the Lamb and Flag, two inns close to the pit, where they would hand over the majority of their hard-earned wages before finally staggering home, often leaving their wives with barely enough money to feed their children or pay the rent. This was why most of the wives took in washing and ironing or found other jobs to make ends meet, but Bill had never been one of these men. Every Friday as regularly as clockwork he would come home and tip his wages onto the table.

Many of the miners were free with their fists, too, after they'd had a skinful and many a night, they would all be forced to listen to Cissie Bailey's screams through the adjoining cottage wall when her husband crawled in drunk and knocked her and the children from pillar to post. But again, Bill was a kind, mild-mannered man, and Sara knew what a lucky woman she was.

Bill beamed at the sight of his older daughter as he entered, whereas Teddy was in a tearing rush to scrub the filth from his skin and join Bridget at the village hall.

'Did yer fill the bath fer me, Mam?' he asked with barely a nod in Lily's direction.

'I did, it's ready fer you in the washhouse,' she told him indulgently.

After snatching up a towel he disappeared to scrub himself from head to toe. Sara worried about Teddy; it had always been his dream to go to sea, but like most boys his age he had followed his father down the pit. Still, she lived in hope that one day, knowing how much he hated his work, he might achieve his ambition.

'It's nice to see you back an' in good time fer Christmas an' all,' Bill told Lily as he kissed her cheek, but then his eyes settled on the baby in her arms and his smile turned to a frown.

'Who is this little 'un?'

Before Lily could say a word, Sara hurried across to him and whispered, 'I'll tell you everythin' when Teddy's gone out, if Richie ain't back.'

'Aye, all right, pet. I'll go an' wash then 'ave me dinner, I'm starvin'.'

'You're allus starvin', I reckon you've got hollow legs,' Sara teased him and when Lily saw the loving look they exchanged, it brought tears to her eyes.

They had gone through a very bad time two years previously when they had lost the two youngest members of the family to a flu epidemic that had swept through the village. Susan and Timmy had been just five and eight years old when they had been laid to rest in the little village churchyard and for a time, they had all feared that Sara would never recover from it. She still had a hacking cough that had been plaguing her since the weather had turned cold, but aside from some very dark moments, day to day she seemed to be coping much better.

Minutes later, wrapped in a large towel, Teddy reappeared from the washhouse, shivering as he headed for the stairs. 'Bye, it's enough to freeze the 'airs off a brass monkey out there,' he complained. 'Dish me dinner up would yer, Ma? I'll just about 'ave time to eat it afore I go out.'

23

In no time at all he was back, clad in his best shirt and trousers and he golloped his dinner down as if he hadn't got a second to live. His mother frowned at him. 'You'll give yerself indigestion eatin' like that, lad,' she scolded, but her eyes were soft as she looked at him. He was the double of his father, with dark hair and brown eyes, as was his younger brother, whereas both the girls took after her.

'Sorry, Ma.' He grinned at her, although he didn't slow down and in seconds his plate was empty. Snatching his coat from the back of the door he pecked his mother on the cheek and shouted 'Ta-ra, all!' then he shot out of the door, letting in a blast of icy air.

'Right, so what's to do?' Lily's father asked.

Slowly Lily told him what had happened and by the time she'd finished he was scowling. 'So what are we goin' to do about it now?' he asked eventually.

'Lady Bellingham suggested Lily leave the baby at the work-house.' His wife placed a large dish of steaming stew and dump-lings in front of him and he sighed.

'Yer do understand that if we keep the poor little mite everyone is goin' to think she's yours an' your reputation will be ruined?'

Lily nodded miserably and stared down at the child in her arms. She really was a beautiful baby with her halo of blonde downy curls and big blue eyes. 'I know, but look at 'er! None o' this is her fault an' if we leave her there, she might not survive. I know we shouldn't worry about that,' she added hastily. 'But . . . I've grown fond of her.'

'And what do you reckon Robbie will 'ave to say if you decided to keep 'er?'

They didn't have to wait long to find out, for at that moment there was a hammering on the door and before Sara could open it, Robbie burst in.

'What's this Bridget is tellin' me, eh?' he stormed, his eyes settling on Lily. 'That you've turned up wi' a babby in yer arms. Whose is it, eh? Cos sure as eggs is eggs it ain't mine and yer must 'ave been carryin' it when yer left!'

'I was not! And she *isn't* mine,' Lily shouted back indignantly.

Before she could say any more, Sara pushed forward and staring into his angry face told him, 'That's quite enough o' that sort o' talk in my 'ouse, young man. You should know our Lily better than that. That baby ain't 'ers. We 'ave relatives close to where she were stayin', an' while she were there the mother gave birth an' took ill, so Lily's brought the babe back to stay wi' us until the mother 'opefully recovers!'

'Oh aye!' Robbie sneered. 'Why, yer must think I were born yesterday and if yer think I'm taking to another man's bastard yer can think again. No wonder yer wouldn't set a date fer the weddin', not if yer were seein' someone else be'ind me back. Well, 'e's welcome to yer as far as I'm concerned cos I wouldn't touch yer now wi' a bloody bargepole!' And with that he stormed back out into the frosty night, leaving the door flapping open behind him, as Lily dissolved into tears.

'I did think this might happen,' Bill said miserably as Sara rushed to shut out the bitterly cold night. 'But it looks like yer mam 'as made 'er mind up, lass. You can go on back to work an' the little 'un will stay 'ere wi' us.'

'But that ain't fair on me mam,' Lilly said in a choky voice. 'And what will 'appen when our so-called sick relative doesn't come to claim the child?'

'Don't you go worryin' about that. We'll just say that sadly she didn't recover.' Sara sighed as she looked at the baby. Her reasons for agreeing to keep her weren't entirely unselfish. There had been a hole in her heart ever since she had laid her two youngest children to rest and she had a feeling that this poor little soul might just help to fill it. 'And I'll tell you now, our Bridget will get a clout round the ear when she comes in for openin' her big mouth like that.'

Her sister had always been a gossip, but the fact she'd told him straightaway made Lily wonder whether she had another motive. Now she came to think of it, Bridget was always hanging around if Robbie popped in, smiling and tossing her hair. 'I reckon she's got a soft spot for Robbie,' she said.

'Even if she did she 'ad no right to tell him about the baby. At least not until you'd had time to explain.'

'But I can't, can I?' Lily pointed out. 'Lady Bellingham would 'ave us out on the street and we'd all lose our jobs if she thought I'd been telling anyone that the child was Miss Arabella's.'

'That's as may be,' Sara stormed. 'But you get back up there to work wi' your head held high tomorrer, and when yer get there yer can throw that bag o' money back at 'er, the bloody old battleaxe!'

'Hold fire,' Bill warned. 'We don't want to go makin' things worse than they already are. Let's sleep on it first, then decide what's best to do.'

The conversation was stopped from going any further when Richie arrived home from work smelling strongly of horses with bits of straw tangled in his hair. At fifteen, he was one of the junior grooms up at Oakley Manor and his main job was to tend to Lord Bellingham's pit ponies. There were two teams of horses that each worked twelve-hour shifts. The first from six o'clock in the morning until six at night, the second from six in the evening till six in the morning. The poor creatures dragged the coal from deep underground to the surface of the mine each day and by the time they had finished they were always exhausted. Richie loved each and every one of them with a passion and when they arrived back at Oakley Manor, weary and with their heads hanging with tiredness, he would immediately rub them down, feed them, then settle them in their stalls one at a time, as well as tending to any wounds they may have. The second team usually arrived back at the stables as Richie arrived to start the day, and his work would begin all over again. Now, he too stared at the baby before asking, 'Whose is that?'

Sara repeated the story they had decided on, but by that time Richie was more interested in getting his dinner and accepted it without question. His mother smiled at him fondly as she placed a steaming dish of stew in front of him. Richie was a mild-mannered lad who took after his father in looks and nature with his dark hair and dark eyes. He had never caused her a day's worry and Sara had a huge soft spot for him.

Lily fed and changed the baby then settled down to work on the charcoal sketch she had started before going away with Arabella. She had always had a flair for drawing and examples of her work were dotted about the cottage walls in wooden frames that her father had made for them. For a time, she was able to lose herself in the drawing, but soon the worries began to set in again. Now that Bridget had told everyone at the village hall about the baby, it would only be a matter of time before the staff at the manor heard of it and she had no doubt the gossip would begin in earnest. Still, Lily was made of strong stuff and hopefully it wouldn't be long before they found someone else to gossip about. And so she decided she would brazen it out – she really didn't have much choice.

Chapter Five

The next morning, bright and early, Lily reported to Mrs Biggles, the housekeeper at the manor. The woman had looked mildly surprised to see her as she had assumed that Miss Arabella would return with her – Lily's going with the young mistress had caused quite a stir in the servants' hall when they had first left. Arabella's lady's maid had quite had her nose put out of joint, as had some of the more senior servants in the house. But Mrs Biggles knew her place, so she didn't comment and soon Lily was getting back into her old routine as she set about making sure the dining room was ready for the family's breakfast. She had almost finished when Louis appeared with a newspaper tucked under his arm and, like Mrs Biggles, he looked surprised to see her.

'Oh . . . Moon, I wasn't aware you and Arabella were back,' he said in a friendly fashion.

Lily flushed, unsure how to answer, so she merely inclined her head before scuttling from the room to fetch old Lady Bellingham's tray. She had the bag of money deep in her apron pocket and she intended to return it to her that morning – though she was dreading seeing her again. However, when she carried the tray into her room, the old woman barely looked at her, acting as if nothing had happened. She opened her mouth to say something, but Hudson hastily shooed her out of the room. Secretly she was relieved, but she knew she'd have to brave it sooner or later.

Not long after breakfast, there was a tap on Lady Bellingham's door and Louis appeared.

'You didn't tell me Arabella was back, Grandmama,' he scolded gently as he leant over the bed to kiss her wrinkled cheek. She looked very different without her rouge and powder.

'What do you mean?'

He frowned. 'Well, I just saw Moon so I assumed Arabella was back too?'

Hudson snorted as she began to lay out the clothes her mistress would wear that day. 'Didn't I warn you you wouldn't be able to pull the wool over 'is eyes for long!'

'Oh, hold your tongue woman,' Lady Bellingham snapped.

Louis was now more puzzled than ever. 'What do you mean, pull the wool over my eyes? Is Arabella back or not?'

His grandmother peered at him for a moment as if she was trying to make up her mind about something before letting out a deep sigh. 'Oh, I might as well tell you; you're going to find out anyway sooner or later. No, Arabella isn't back.'

'Where is she?'

'I . . . I don't know.'

'What do you mean you don't know?'

'It's plain enough to understand isn't it? I don't know.' Then realising she needed to be honest with him, she took a deep breath and told him the whole sorry story. By the time she was finished, Louis looked gravely concerned.

'So, what you're telling me is, you've dumped my sister's illegitimate baby on the Moon girl?' He could scarcely believe what he'd heard.

'What else was I supposed to do?' The old woman's faded blue eyes flashed. 'Don't you realise what a scandal it would cause if people found out that Arabella had had a child out of wedlock? Her reputation would be ruined and we could forget about Lord Lumley wanting to marry her. At least by getting rid of the baby we still have a chance of saving everything – if we can find her and make her see sense, that is! The little *fool*.'

'Do my parents know?' Louis asked, and when she shook her head he groaned and ran his hand distractedly through his thick dark hair.

'The thing is, now that you know, you could possibly save the day.' Lady Bellingham stared at him hopefully.

'Oh yes, and how do you propose I do that?'

She gave him a lopsided smile. 'You could make it your mission to find her.'

'Could I? And just how would I go about it?' Louis was exasperated.

'Well, *someone* must have seen them. You could go to where she and Moon had been staying and make enquiries. The cottage was quite isolated so she would have had to have some form of transport to get away from there.'

'But her captain could have had his own transport,' Louis pointed out.

Lady Bellingham chewed on her lip; she hadn't thought of that. 'Even so, I still think it's worth you trying,' she said obstinately. 'Please say you will . . . for me, Louis? Our whole family's reputation will be in tatters if word gets out. No one will ever want to marry Arabella – or yourself for that matter. We'll be a complete laughing stock.'

'Is that all you care about?' For the first time in his life Louis was angry with her. 'And what about that poor baby? It's our own flesh and blood!'

'It's a flyblow, born the wrong side of the blanket. How do you think your mother and father would react if they found out?'

'In a kindlier fashion than you, hopefully,' Louis ground out. But deep down he knew she was right: they would be just as horrified as she was.

After a moment he sighed. 'Very well, I'll set out first thing in the morning, but first I want to see Moon and find out what she's done with the baby.'

The old lady bristled with indignation. 'You most certainly will *not*. I expressly forbid it,' she told him in no uncertain terms. 'I have paid her handsomely to get rid of it. That's an end to it as far as I'm concerned so I don't want you interfering! You just concentrate on finding Arabella and bringing her home.'

Louis had always obeyed her in the past but as he glared back at her, she had the awful feeling that he wouldn't this time.

Without another word he turned and strode away and the old woman sagged back against her pillow.

'You can't cover somethin' like this up forever,' Hudson commented with a shake of her head. 'It'll all end in tears, you just mark my words!'

'Oh, *shut up*, woman, and get on with your work!' Lady Bellingham screeched, pulling the blankets over her head.

The Bellinghams had guests dining with them that evening so it was past seven o'clock before Lily finally set off for home. She had just turned into the lane that led down the valley to the pit cottages when the first flakes of snow began to fall and she pulled her woollen shawl more closely about her and hurried her steps. She had gone no more than a few yards when hoofbeats sounded behind her and she stepped to the side of the lane. However, instead of going past her, the rider reined the horse to a halt beside her and peering up into the darkness, she was surprised to see that it was young Louis Bellingham

'Miss Moon, I was hoping to catch you.' Louis didn't tell her that he had been waiting until he saw her leave the manor. 'I, er . . . believe I owe you an apology for the way my grandmama has treated you.'

'None o' this is your fault, sir,' she told him. 'But I wonder if you'd do somethin' for me?'

'Of course.'

Lily withdrew the small bag from her apron pocket and handed it up to him. 'Your grandmother gave me this and I took it wi'out thinkin', but I'd be grateful if you'd give it back an' tell 'er me an' me family don't want it.'

Louis weighed the bag in his hand. 'And what is it?'

'It's twenty golden guineas.' Lily glared at him. 'She thought it were worth that amount to get rid o' . . .' Her voice trailed away.

Louis frowned. 'She thought it was worth that amount for you to get rid of my sister's illegitimate child. It's all right, you can say it. She's told me the whole sorry story. But do you mind me asking, what have you done with the child? Did you take her to the workhouse as my grandmother suggested?' Just the thought of any child, let alone his own sister's, ending up in the godforsaken place made his blood run cold.

'No, she ain't gone there, nor will she,' Lily told him. 'Me mam 'as said she'll bring 'er up alongside the rest of us.'

'I see. Then your mother is a very good woman and I'd like you to keep this. You all deserve it.'

Lily shook her head. 'Thank you, but no. We might not 'ave much but we do 'ave us pride.'

'But you must have *something* towards the child's keep.'

'No, thank you.' Lily began to walk on but he wasn't finished with her yet and he kept pace with her.

'I don't suppose you have any idea where Arabella might have gone, do you?'

'I've told yer grandmother all I know,' Lily said firmly. 'Now if you'll excuse me, I want to get out o' the weather.' She began to walk faster as the snow settled on her hair and the shoulders of her shawl, but still the horse trotted along at the side of her.

'Have you, er . . . given the child a name yet?'

She blinked in surprise. 'Not as far as I know, unless me mam 'as come up wi' one while I've been at work. Why, did you 'ave one in mind?'

'Not at all,' he assured her. 'But she is my niece and—'

Lily came to an abrupt halt. 'You'd best forget that,' she advised. 'Your grandmother made it more than clear that she'll never be accepted into the family so just let us get on wi' bringin' 'er up.'

'I'm eternally grateful to you all. And should you ever need anything – anything at all – be sure to come to me.' He raised his hat to her and sat and watched until her slight figure was swallowed up by the snowy night.

Chapter Six

'How has she been?' Lily asked as soon as she entered the cottage shortly after. It was a tiny place in comparison to Oakley Manor but it was the only home Lily had ever known and she loved every inch of it.

'Good as gold. I've just fed her so she should sleep for a few hours now,' her mother answered with a smile as she carefully took a large rabbit pie with a golden pastry top from the small range cooker. There was fresh winter cabbage and boiled potatoes to go with it, which would be followed by a plum pudding.

Lily went to stand by the fire making her damp clothes steam as the snow began to melt. 'The young master stopped me on me way 'ome so I gave 'im the money to give back to Lady Bellingham.'

'Good. We don't need their blood money. I just 'ope as they can live wi' their consciences.'

'He asked me if we'd given the baby a name yet?'

'Well, I suppose we should. We'll 'ave to call 'er somethin', won't we?' Sara was in the process of laying the table but she paused to glance towards the baby asleep in the drawer.

'Miss Arabella did speak of names before she was born.' Lily put her hand into the drawer and the baby wrapped her tiny fingers about her thumb, melting her heart. 'She was going to call a boy Theodore, and if it was a girl it was going to be Anastasia.'

'Anastasia!' Sara's eyebrows rose almost into her hairline. 'That's a bit posh for a kid who's going to be brought up in a pit cottage, ain't it?'

'Not if we call her Annie for short. I think it quite suits her.'

Sara came to stand beside her. 'I suppose it does,' she admitted. 'Anastasia, or Annie, it is then. Now, you go up and get those wet clothes off afore you catch your death o' cold. Richie an' the men should be in any minute and dinner's ready to serve up.'

Lily had just disappeared up the steep narrow staircase when the cottage door was flung open and Edie Manning, their next-door neighbour, appeared holding an empty cup.

'Eeh, it's bitter out there.' She shuddered dramatically as her beady eyes scanned the room and when they came to rest on the baby, she went to stare down at her.

Sara frowned with annoyance. 'Was there somethin' yer were wantin', Edie?'

'What? Oh yes, I were wonderin' if yer could lend me a cup o' flour till the shops open tomorrer. I thought I'd got plenty but I just came to make my Walt a couple o' dumplin's to drop in the stew an' realised I'd run out.'

'Hmm.' Sara didn't believe a word of it. Edie Manning was one of the biggest gossips in the village and she'd probably got word about the baby. Even so, she took the cup and began to fill it from a big stone jar.

'It's right what I were 'earing, then? That young Lily arrived 'ome wi' a baby in tow?'

Sara handed her the flour. 'Yes, as you can see, it's true. She's my niece's child.'

Edie smirked. 'It were lucky your Lily were away all them months an' in just the right place fer 'er to bring 'er 'ome then, ain't it?'

'I suppose it is.' Sara knew what she was insinuating and was doing her best to keep her temper. 'Was there anythin' else yer were wantin', Edie?'

'Eh? Oh no, ta. I'd best be off. Bonny little thing, though, ain't she? Got a look o' your Lily about 'er wi' her blue eyes an' fair 'air, don't yer think?'

Thankfully the door opened again at that moment and Bill and Teddy appeared.

'Right, I'm off to leave you lot in peace to 'ave yer dinners. Ta fer the flour, luvvie, bye fer now!'

'What did that old nosy parker want?' Bill said with a wry grin once she'd left. 'Got word that the babby were 'ere, had she?'

Sara nodded and sighed as she poured some hot water into a bowl for him and Teddy to wash their hands and faces in. Normally they would go out into the tiny yard that housed the privy and the coalhouse, take their clothes off and whack them up the wall to get the worst of the soot out of them. But tonight, it was so cold that she didn't have the heart to make them do it.

Richie was the next to appear and soon, apart from Bridget, they were all seated around the old table tucking into their meal as the newest addition of the family slept peacefully in the drawer.

'Bridget workin' late at the shop, is she?' Bill asked his wife as he dipped a wedge of freshly baked bread into the gravy on his plate.

'She didn't say she was, but then our Bridget is a law unto 'erself, ain't she? I despair o' that girl sometimes, I really do. Goodness knows what time she got in last night. I was goin' to give her an earful for tellin' Robbie about the baby but I was in bed before she rolled in an' she set off for work early today so I ain't had chance.' Sara would keep Bridget's meal warm over a pan of hot water on top of the range although she felt it would serve the little madam right if she didn't.

They had almost finished when Bridget finally appeared.

'Oh, you've remembered where you live 'ave yer?' Sara said caustically. 'Just what time did you turn in last night, miss? An' why did yer have to break yer neck to tell Robbie our Lily were back?'

'He'd 'ave found out sooner or later anyway,' Bridget responded flippantly. 'It's all over the village already. Everyone that's been in the shop 'as been talkin' about it an' yer might as well know, they're all assumin' the baby is Lily's. Well, they would, wouldn't they?'

'You little *devil*!' Sara rose, but Bill held his hand up to stop her approaching Bridget

'Leave it be, love,' he urged. 'People are bound to draw their own conclusions. Let 'em. It'll be a nine-day wonder; they'll find someone else to gossip about soon enough. As for you, love' – he smiled kindly at Lily whose eyes had filled with tears at her sister's words – 'why don't you go an' try to make your peace wi' Robbie, eh?'

'It wouldn't do 'er much good.' Bridget grinned spitefully as she shook the snow from her shawl and hung it on the hook on the back of the door. 'Robbie told me he's finished wi' her fer good now.'

Lily shrugged, wondering why she didn't feel more upset about the fact. They had been walking out together for quite some time after all. She couldn't deny that her pride was hurt, though. She had always thought that she would be the one to end their relationship. 'That's his choice, but can we just leave it now? I really don't want to talk about it,' she said dully.

Bridget smirked and sat down at the table, so Lily rose and went to work on her latest sketch.

She arrived at work the following morning to find Louis Bellingham hovering by the servants' entrance waiting for her.

'Miss Moon.' He removed his hat as if he was addressing someone of his own class. 'I was hoping to catch you. How is the baby?'

'She's very well, sir,' she answered starchily, glancing around to ensure that no one was about.

'Good, good. And, er . . . does she have a name yet?'

'Your sister wanted to call her Anastasia so we 'ave, but we shall call 'er Annie.'

He nodded. 'I thought I'd let you know that I shall be leaving this morning to try to find Arabella.'

When she continued to stare at him coldly, he flushed. 'I, er . . . had better let you get on.' Replacing his hat, he gave a small bow and headed for the stables.

She had been in the kitchen only a matter of minutes when old Lady Bellingham's bell tinkled and cook pointed to the tray she had ready for her. 'Best get that up to the old dear, Lily. You know what she's like if she's kept waiting.'

Lifting the tray, Lily set off for the west wing where she found the old woman seated at a small table in the window still clad in her nightclothes. Lily placed the tray down in front of her before saying hesitantly, 'I thought you might wish to know that the baby is doing well and we have named her Anastasia. It's what her mother wished, but we shall call her Annie.'

'I have no idea what you're talking about, girl,' Lady Bellingham said cuttingly. 'Now get about your business!'

Lily exchanged a glance with Hudson, who was surreptitiously shaking her head, before gathering what dignity she could and leaving the room without bothering to bob her knee. *Old witch!* she thought as she stormed down the stairs. It seemed incredible to her that the baby's great-grandmother could turn her back on her own great-grandchild. Still, her loss would be their gain. Annie was a lovely baby and both she and her mother loved her already.

The day hadn't got off to the best of starts but, could Lily have known it, it was about to get worse, because when she went back into the kitchen two of the maids and the cook were standing by the sink in earnest conversation. They stopped speaking the minute she walked in and Lily knew they had been talking about her.

'There's some tea left in the pot if yer fancy a cup,' the cook told her. Then she sidled across to her and said quietly, 'Is it true what's goin' around the village? That you came home wi' a baby?'

Lily gritted her teeth and nodded as she poured some of the stewed tea into a cup. 'Yes, it is, and before you ask, *no*, she isn't mine. A relative of ours gave birth while I was away and is very ill so we're temporarily caring for her until her mother is fully recovered and can 'ave 'er back.'

'Oh!' The cook clearly didn't believe a word she was saying if the lopsided grin she gave the two young maids was anything to go by. 'And 'ow did Miss Arabella feel about yer leavin' 'er there?'

Lily hated having to lie but she had no choice. 'She wished to stay on for a little longer but she 'ad no objection to me bringing Annie 'ome to my mother.'

'Hmm. You'd think she'd be itchin' to get back to get stuck into preparations fer her weddin', wouldn't yer? Did yer get the feelin' that she's gettin' cold feet about it?'

'I've no idea what Miss Arabella feels about getting wed; I merely went with her as her maid,' Lily pointed out.

The cook frowned. 'All right, leave me 'ead on, I were only askin'. Touchy, ain't yer?'

'Not at all.' Lily drained her cup, then lifting a tray she headed for the green baize door. 'I'd best get on wi' me jobs. The family should be finished breakfast now so I'll go an' fetch the dirty pots, shall I?'

The cook watched her go with a thoughtful expression on her face. 'There's more to this than meets the eye, you just see if I ain't right,' she told the maids with a nod of her head as she plonked herself down in the chair next to the fire to have a break before she started preparing the lunch.

By the time Lily made her way home that evening, the snow had settled and was beginning to form drifts and soon the bottom of her skirt and her boots were sodden. She shivered as she made her way towards the village, trying her best to stay on the lane and not fall into the ditch. Far below, the lights in the cottages twinkled in the darkness and beyond them the ugly structures erected above the open shafts of the pit stood out like dark jagged teeth.

It hadn't been the best of days and all Lily wanted to do was get home, get warm and try to lose herself in her sketching. At least that would help her forget the fact that everyone believed the baby was hers. She had promised herself that she would brazen it out, and so all she could do was keep her head down until they found someone else to gossip about.

As she turned into Valley Road, she noticed a couple some way ahead of her. They were laughing and giggling, their arms tight about each other, and as she drew closer shock surged through her as she realised it was Robbie – and the girl he was with was Bridget.

Chapter Seven

'Are you all right, love? You're as white as the snow.' Sara eyed her daughter with concern as Lily entered the kitchen and stamped the snow from her boots.

'Y-yes, I just had a bit of a shock, that's all.'

'And what were that?' Sara was busy carrying a large cottage pie to the table and was only listening with half an ear.

'I just saw Robbie.'

'Well, he does live in the village, so what's so strange about that?'

'He was with our Bridget and they had their arms about each other.'

'*What?*' Sara stopped in her tracks and stared at her in disbelief. She had hoped that Lily and Robbie would patch things up once he'd got used to the idea of Annie being there. Plonking the pie on the table she sat down heavily on one of the wooden chairs. 'This'll be our Bridget's doin', the young bugger 'er!' she declared. 'So it seems you were right: she's allus had a fancy fer 'im. She ain't wasted much time, 'as she?'

Lily shrugged as she tugged her wet shawl off. It had been a shock to see them together, but she felt angrier with Bridget than with him.

'Eeh, I wish now you'd never agreed to go away wi' that young madam,' Sara said vehemently. 'Fancy pullin' a stunt like this over 'er own sister! She'll feel the length o' my tongue when she comes in, don't you doubt it.'

'Don't waste your breath, Mam. If she wants 'im that much she can 'ave 'im.' Lily crossed to the drawer where the baby lay contentedly gurgling. 'And how 'as this one been?'

41

'She's a little angel.' Sara came to stand beside her and smiled. 'She's as good as the day is long. She only cries when it's time fer 'er milk or she needs 'er bindin' changed, bless 'er.'

Lily went on to tell her mother about her meeting with Louis Bellingham that morning and her mother pursed her lips. 'Then let's 'ope he does manage to find 'er, cos sure as the sun will rise come mornin', if she ain't back soon that lord she's betrothed to is bound to smell somethin' fishy an' 'er name will be mud. I wouldn't count on it, though. Her an' her captain could be anywhere. It'll be like lookin' fer a needle in a 'aystack!'

Lily nodded and looked around the room. 'Teddy and Richie gone to band practice, 'ave they?'

They were both members of the Salvation Army brass band in Nuneaton and loved it. Teddy played the trumpet while Richie was turning out to be excellent on the trombone. They went to practice twice a week as well as attending the Sunday service. Each Christmas they would tour the houses of the town and surrounding villages playing their tunes and collecting for the poor, and when they came to the village Sara would almost burst with pride, although she didn't seem so happy about them attending this evening. 'It'll be a miracle if they even manage to get there with the snow comin' down as it is,' she grumbled, dragging herself out of the chair to carry the vegetables to the table.

It was then that Bill arrived home and after he had washed, they started their meal. They were halfway through when Bridget breezed in with a smile like a Cheshire cat's on her pretty face.

'An' just where do yer think you've been, young lady?' Sara asked sternly as Bridget removed her shawl and joined them.

'If you must know, Robbie called into the shop just as I was fin-ishin' work an' he walked me home.' She smirked at Lily. '*An*' he's asked me if I'll walk out wi' 'im.'

'He can't be very 'eartbroken about yer sister then.' Sara glowered at her. 'An' you should be ashamed o' yerself. Would yer
jump in 'er grave so quick?'

Bridget shrugged. 'Yer can hardly blame 'im fer dumpin' 'er,
can yer? It's all round the village that she's turned up 'ome wi' a
baby an' they're all sayin' that Annie is 'ers.'

'An' I bet you said nothin' to dissuade 'em o' the notion.' A bout
of coughing made Sara double over and Bill sprang out of his seat
and rushed around to her.

'Now look what you've done,' he bellowed at Bridget. 'Goin' an'
upsettin' yer mam like that when you know she ain't well. Shame
on you, girl!'

Bridget had the grace to flush. 'I were only tellin' the truth,' she
mumbled, before slamming off upstairs as Lily rushed to get her
mother a cup of water.

'I'm all right now,' Sara assured them as the coughing bout eased
but Bill wasn't happy.

'This damn cough 'as gone on a bit too long fer my likin'.
I reckon it's time we got the doctor to 'ave a look at you.'

'Oh, stop fussin',' Sara scolded as she squeezed his hand. 'Now
finish yer dinner while I go an' feed the baby.'

Bill reluctantly did as he was told. He knew better than to argue
with his wife but suddenly he'd lost his appetite and merely pushed
his food about his plate keeping a wary eye on her.

'Shall I plate a dinner up fer Bridget fer later?' Lily offered but
Sara shook her head.

'No, it'll not hurt her to go wi'out,' she said emphatically. 'An'
I'm right sorry about her settin' 'er cap at Robbie when you two
'ave barely broken up.'

Lily shrugged. 'It doesn't matter. He can't 'ave been that fond o'
me after all, can 'e?' It was then that she realised it wasn't Robbie she
was feeling heartbroken over, but the way her sister had betrayed

her. Not wanting her mother to guess at her feelings, she hurried away to put the kettle on.

One morning in early December, almost three weeks after her return, Lily was up at the manor clearing the family's breakfast when Louis Bellingham walked into the dining room and quietly closed the door behind him.

'I was hoping I'd catch you.' He smiled. 'I got back late last night and thought you'd like to know that I managed to track Arabella down.'

Lily paused and stared back at him, unsure how she should answer. It was none of her business, after all.

'I had no luck in Yorkshire,' he continued. 'But then I remembered her telling me that the captain was stationed at a barracks in Lincolnshire so I made my way there, and after asking a lot of different people a lot of questions I finally found her staying in the married quarters there.'

'*Married!*' Lily couldn't stop herself commenting or the look of surprise on her face.

He sighed. 'That's what she says. She told me they had been married in a little church in Grainthorpe with two witnesses present. But between you and me I don't know if I believe her. I thought before a wedding took place banns had to be read and there hadn't been time for that. It all sounded a bit fishy to me and she certainly didn't seem very happy. The accommodation she is staying in is very shabby to say the least, not at all what she's used to.'

'I'm sorry to hear that,' Lily answered, and she genuinely was. Despite what had happened, she had grown quite fond of Arabella during the time they had spent together.

'I'm just going to report to my grandmama now. It was too late to see her when I got back last night and I know she isn't going to be happy about it.'

'But none of this is your fault,' Lily answered and he grinned.

'Hmm, well here goes.' He paused when he got to the door and glanced back across his shoulder. 'Er . . . do you mind me asking how the baby is?'

Despite how she felt about the family at present, Lily felt herself warming to him. He was so nice and unpretentious. 'Annie is doing really well. I don't suppose Arabella has changed her mind about havin' her with her?'

'No. I touched on it but she said that her husband doesn't want them to have children for some time. What sort of a man must he be, eh?' Remembering who he was speaking to he gave her an apologetic smile. 'Sorry, I shouldn't have said that. Wish me luck.'

After he'd left, Lily frowned. Despite the shameful way she had saddled Lily and her family with her baby, she was worried for Arabella: something didn't feel quite right.

Upstairs, Louis tapped on his grandmother's door and entered the room, feeling as if he was entering a lion's den. She was in bed with a tray across her lap, but the instant she saw him she shoved it towards Hudson and demanded, 'Well? Did you find her?'

There was no welcome, but Louis was used to her ways now. 'Yes, I did eventually but she gave me a merry chase.' He went on to tell her what he had told Lily and by the time he was finished the old woman's face was set in a grimace.

'Something's not right here.' She scowled as she stared towards the window. 'Did you see her marriage certificate?'

Louis shook his head.

His grandmother tapped her chin with her forefinger. 'We have two weeks left before she should have been coming home. That gives us two weeks grace before Lord Lumley starts to become suspicious. Did she by any chance mention the name of the vicar who supposedly married them?'

'Yes, she did as a matter of fact,' Louis recalled. 'She said she was surprised when she met him because he looked barely older than she was. Now what was his name?' He thought for a moment, before exclaiming, 'Ah, I remember now. It was Reverend Toolley.'

'Right, so your next job is to track him down.'

'*What?*' Louis was exasperated. 'I can't just go haring off again. How will I explain it to Father? I'm supposed to be learning how to run the businesses and the estate.'

'You leave him to me,' his grandmother told him sternly. 'And remember, the reputation of your sister and the whole family is at stake. There can't be that many churches in Grainthorpe so it shouldn't be hard to track down a vicar. Start with the rectory.'

Louis knew when he was beaten. 'Very well. But what will you do if the marriage is legal?'

'We'll worry about that when and if the time comes. Now go while we still have the chance to save this sorry situation from turning into a disaster!'

'Yes, Grandmama.' Grim-faced Louis went to order the groom to saddle his horse.

Chapter Eight

When Louis finally arrived in Grainthorpe he headed straight for the rectory. It had been a strenuous journey involving two overnight stops – one in Newark and the next in Lincoln. He would have liked nothing more than to sink into a deep feather mattress and sleep for a week, but now that he was here, he was determined to get the job out of the way. After tethering his horse to the picket fence that surrounded the rectory, he approached the front door and rang the bell.

The door was opened by a plump, middle-aged lady with steel-grey hair and a kindly smile. 'Yes, m'dear, how can we help you? If it's the reverend you've come to see, I'm afraid he won't be back till late afternoon.'

'I see, then perhaps you could help me.' Louis flashed her a charming smile and bowed courteously. 'I'm wondering if I've come to the right church? I'm looking for a Reverend Toolley who is the vicar of a church in Grainthorpe?'

'Toolley?' She frowned and shook her head. 'I'm afraid the reverend of St Clement is Reverend Mason. I've been his housekeeper for years and I can't say as I've ever heard of a Reverend Toolley, and there isn't another church here.'

'I see. Then I'm very sorry to have troubled you, ma'am. Good day.' Louis bowed again and left. His next stop would be the army barracks.

Once there he asked to speak to the commanding officer and eventually, he was shown into an office with a stern-faced man sitting behind a large polished desk.

'Good afternoon, sir, and how may I help you?'

Louis took a deep breath and slowly began his story and as he progressed the officer scowled.

'Hmm, I can't say as I remember giving any of my men permission to marry.' He tapped his chin thoughtfully. 'And you say your sister is staying here in married quarters?'

'Yes, sir. Arabella informed me that the vicar who married her and Captain Frederick James was called Reverend Toolley, but I just called at the rectory of St Clement and the vicar's housekeeper informed me that she'd never heard of anyone by that name.'

'No indeed, but *I* have.' The officer rose from his leather chair and began to pace with his hands clasped behind his back. Eventually he paused and facing Louis again he asked, 'Would you kindly excuse me for a moment?'

While he waited for his return, Louis stood at the window and watched a group of young men marching up and down the large yard outside, their backs ramrod straight, while an officer barked orders.

Eventually the commanding officer reappeared with a young man in a captain's uniform behind him.

'This,' he said sternly, 'is Captain Toolley. He is a very good friend of Captain James's.' He turned to the young man. 'And this is Louis Bellingham, the brother of Lady Arabella Bellingham, and if what he says is true, I think you have some explaining to do, young man.'

The young man visibly paled, although he kept his head up and stared straight ahead as he stood to attention.

Louis frowned with confusion. 'I, er . . . don't quite understand, sir.'

'No, I don't suppose you do, sir, but I have a horrible idea that I might.' The officer stared at Toolley before bellowing, 'So what have you got to say for yourself, Captain Toolley? What do you know of what I believe to have been a duplicitous marriage ceremony?'

The young man said nothing for a moment and then he muttered, 'It wasn't my idea, sir. It was Freddie, Captain James, who put me up to it.'

'So you are admitting that you deliberately led this young woman to believe that she was being legally wed?' The officer was red in the face with rage and it was clear that Captain Toolley was quaking in his highly polished boots.

'I . . . yes, sir. But we didn't mean any harm.'

'Didn't *mean* any harm!' The officer was incensed, and striding to the door he barked, 'Have Captain James sent to me *immediately*.'

'So you're telling me that my sister *isn't* legally married?' Louis croaked. 'B-but how did you manage that?'

'We just chose a time when we knew the reverend wouldn't be at the church,' Toolley told him sheepishly. 'I found his vestments in the vestry and we got two more of our chaps to stand as witnesses while I read out the marriage service.'

'*You cad!*' Louis surged forward with his fist raised, but the commanding officer stepped between them.

'I can quite understand how you feel,' the officer informed him. 'But please let me deal with this. I assure you none of the people concerned will get off lightly. In fact, by the time I've finished with them, they'll wish they'd never been born. I cannot *believe* they would even consider bringing such disgrace on our regiment and I'm deeply ashamed of them.'

At that moment there were footsteps outside and Captain James appeared. 'You wished to see me, sir?' He saluted, but when he spotted Louis, his mouth dropped open with shock.

'*You lousy bastard!*' Louis ground out between clenched teeth. 'I know what you've done and I'd like nothing more than to knock you straight into hell!'

One glance at Toolley told Freddie that they knew everything and his shoulders sagged. 'It was your sister's fault,' he whined pathetically. 'It was *she* who insisted I should make an honest woman of her.'

'*That's enough!*' The officer turned to Louis again and extended his hand. 'Leave it with me, sir. All I can do is offer my heartfelt apologies for their disgraceful behaviour. I suggest you go and find Lady Arabella and get her away from here.'

'And what am I supposed to tell her?' Louis was red in the face with rage. 'That the man she loves, whose illegitimate child she has just given birth to, has been using her all along?'

'*A child!*' The officer looked even more shocked, but quickly composing himself he patted Louis' arm. 'I can quite understand your distress,' he admitted. 'James is a cad, but as I told you, you can rest assured he will not go unpunished. And I can also assure you that none of this will go beyond these four walls.'

Louis took a deep breath before nodding and storming from the room. He had to get out of there quickly, because if he didn't, he wasn't sure what he might do. Once outside he let the softly falling snow settle on his face as he tried to calm himself. Then, with his lips set in a grim line, he started in the direction of Arabella's quarters.

They looked even more dismal than he remembered and he steeled himself for what he had to tell her, because he had a terrible feeling that she wouldn't believe him. Once there he took another deep breath and banged on the door.

When Arabella answered it, his eyes widened with shock. Her left eye was bruised and standing out in stark contrast to her waxen face, and she looked dishevelled and grubby, nothing at all like the pampered little sister who had always prided herself on looking her best. Her gown was crumpled, as if she hadn't changed it for days, and her beautiful blonde hair hung in rat's tails about her shoulders.

'Good God above, whatever has happened to you?' He was across the step and in the room in a second and Arabella threw herself into his arms and began to sob convulsively as he cradled her to him.

'It . . . it's nothing. I slipped and cracked my face,' she whimpered after a time as she took the handkerchief he offered and tried to compose herself.

Louis didn't believe a word of it and now he saw there were bruises on her arms too and once again his temper began to rise. 'Don't lie to me, Arabella. I can always tell when you're lying. Freddie did this to you, didn't he?'

'He didn't mean to. It was my fault; I made him angry.'

'Only a *coward* hits a woman,' Louis told her sternly. 'When are you going to wake up and stop seeing him through a rosy glow?'

'H-he's my husband,' she answered so quietly that he could barely hear her.

Now he knew that she must know the truth. 'I'm sorry, but he isn't,' he told her seriously. 'The marriage ceremony was a sham. His commanding officer has confirmed that one of Freddie's friends stood in as a reverend and two of his other friends stood as your witnesses. I hate to tell you this, but it seems that he never had any intention of marrying you.'

She was so shocked that her mouth gaped for a moment before she said dully, 'So he was just using me all along?'

'I'm afraid he was.' Louis placed a gentle hand on her arm as she thudded down onto the nearest chair.

'Then that explains his behaviour,' she said almost to herself. Then it all came pouring out. 'The first couple of nights we arrived here he was so romantic and lovely. But then he started to go out with his friends leaving me with no food or heating and when he did come home, he was drunk. I complained and he . . . he hit me. He told me that my trunk containing all my gowns and possessions had got lost and never arrived, but last night I found a pawn ticket in his pocket. I think he might have pawned them all, which is why

51

this gown and my cloak are all the clothes I have now. Oh, Louis, what am I going to do? I've been so foolish!'

'I'll tell you what you're going to do: you're going to come home with me *right* now.'

'But how can I? Look at me. What would Mama and Papa say?'

'Hmm!' Louis began to pace as his mind worked overtime. 'I'm going to organise a coach to come and fetch you. I shall follow on behind on my horse and when we get home, you'll say that the carriage you were travelling in overturned in the snow and your trunk and everything in it was ruined. That will explain your bruises too. But you *must* stick to the story; Mama and Papa still have no idea about the baby or you being here. Will you do that?'

Arabella sighed as she wrung the handkerchief between her hands and gazed around the room. She had loved Freddie so much – worshipped him – and she would have followed him to the ends of the earth, but now she knew that it had all been a sham. He had never loved her and with the realisation she saw all her dreams crumble to ashes.

'Yes . . . I'll do it. There's no point staying here if Freddie doesn't love me.' Her eyes were dull and full of pain and her voice was dead as the full horror of what she had been through sank in. It hurt her brother to see her like this; she was usually so vivacious and full of life. But now his main concern was to get her away from there as quickly as possible.

Fetching her cloak from the back of the door he slid it around her shoulders. 'You sit there and try to keep warm,' he told her tenderly. 'I'll be back as quickly as I can with a carriage to take you home. Be ready when I get here.'

It took over an hour for Louis to locate a man with a carriage who was prepared to make the journey to the Midlands and back in such appalling weather conditions. Even then, Louis had had to offer him double what he might normally charge, so it was mid-afternoon by the time he returned for Arabella. He found her sitting exactly where he had left her and he quickly ushered her out to the coach.

'We'll not get too far today afore it's dark, sir,' the driver told him. 'I reckon we'll 'ave to stop in Wragby overnight. It'll be too dangerous to try to go further in these conditions. Then 'opefully we'll be able to set off towards Lincoln come the mornin'.'

Louis nodded. 'That will be fine. You lead the way and I'll follow – you know the roads better than me.'

And so, the treacherous journey home began.

Chapter Nine

Late in the afternoon three days later, Hudson stood at her mistress's bedroom window staring out at the snowy landscape. Suddenly she narrowed her eyes and peered towards the leafless trees that bordered the long drive leading to Oakley Manor.

'I reckon there's a carriage comin' down the drive,' she told Lady Bellingham.

The old woman, who had been dozing in the chair at the side of the fire, was instantly awake. 'Can you see who it is?'

'How am I supposed to do that?' Hudson snorted. 'But whoever it is there's someone on 'orseback following them.'

'Perhaps it's guests arriving for dinner?'

Hudson shook her head. 'No, I distinctly 'eard your son tell the housekeeper that there would be no invites until the weather picked up. Who'd want to come out in this?'

'Then go downstairs and find out who it is,' Lady Bellingham ordered.

Knowing better than to argue, Hudson left the room with a martyred sigh.

While she was gone, Lady Bellingham watched the door impatiently and when it finally opened and Arabella came in, closely followed by Louis, she heaved a huge sigh of relief.

'Thank God you've seen sense and left that irresponsible husband of yours,' she said sternly as Louis led his sister to the chair opposite their grandmother. 'Are your parents aware that you are back?'

'No, they aren't.' It was Louis who answered for her. 'And they mustn't know until I tell you everything that's happened and we all get our story straight. But first, do you think you could get a hot drink and something to eat sent up to us, Hudson?'

'Of course.' Hudson had always had a huge soft spot for Master Louis and she bustled away to see to it right away.

Louis proceeded to tell his grandmother about all that had happened and she looked shocked.

'What a bounder! And there you were thinking he was your knight in shining armour,' she told Arabella.

'I don't think she needs to hear that right now,' Louis scolded gently. 'At least she is safely back. Now she just has to decide what she wants to do next.'

'I would have thought that was more than obvious,' Lady Bellingham responded in her supercilious way. 'She is home, she isn't married, the child is taken care of, so now she can proceed with her marriage to Lord Lumley and only we need ever know of this unfortunate affair.'

Louis opened his mouth to protest and say that Arabella needed time to get over everything but his sister shocked him when she nodded in agreement.

'Grandmama is right, Louis.'

'What? You mean that you'd still go ahead with a wedding to a man over twice your age?'

'Why not?' she answered woodenly. 'It doesn't matter who I marry now. I shall never love again so it may as well be Lord Lumley as anybody else. At least it will make our parents and Grandmama happy.'

'Are you sure about this? Why don't you sleep on it?' he suggested but she shook her head.

'I don't need to.'

Hudson arrived at that moment with a tray piled with sandwiches, iced sponge fancies and a large pot of tea, and so for the time being the subject was dropped, although Louis couldn't help but think that Arabella might be making another big mistake. And what about the baby?

Hudson poured them all a cup of tea and placed a plate of sandwiches on Arabella's lap but the young woman just sat staring at them, making no effort to eat or drink anything.

'Just look at the state of you, girl!' Lady Bellingham bellowed as she looked at her granddaughter's crumpled gown. 'Thank goodness your parents haven't seen you like this. You look as if no one owns you!'

Louis scowled at her again but Arabella just stared vacantly towards the window. Her heart was broken and, in that moment, she would gladly have died – anything rather than face the pain of Freddie's terrible betrayal.

After a time, Louis gently helped Arabella to her feet. 'I'm going to take her to her room,' he informed his grandmother. 'I shall instruct her maid to draw her a bath and help her get changed and then I'll tell Mama and Papa that we're back and what's happened.'

'Huh!' Lady Bellingham tossed her head irritably. Had Arabella been younger, she could quite happily have put her across her lap and given her a good sound spanking for all the trouble she'd caused, but instead they would all have to stick to the story that Louis had concocted.

He led his sister along the landing and once they reached her room, he summoned her maid, then slowly made his way down the stairs to go in search of his mother, who would hopefully believe the story he had come up with. Arabella seemed to be in shock, in a world of her own, but that would tie in with their tale about her being involved in an accident.

He had gone no more than a few steps along the hallway when Lily suddenly appeared from the dining room with a crisp white tablecloth folded across her arm.

They both stopped abruptly, then Louis took her elbow and quickly led her back into the room where, after glancing about to ensure they were alone, he told her, 'There have been developments, Moon.' He went on to tell her all that had happened, ending with, 'And so I'm just about to tell my mother that we're back and hopefully she'll believe my story. Arabella has said that she is now prepared to go through with her marriage to Lord Lumley!'

Lily had listened without saying a word but now her eyes widened with shock. '*What?* But she doesn't *want* to marry him.'

'I know.' He shrugged helplessly and spread his hands. 'But what option is open to her now? We can only hope that none of what has happened leaks out or her reputation will be ruined and no one will ever want to marry her, even with a sizeable dowry.'

'The poor girl.' Lily shook her head. 'I can't believe that the captain could have been so cruel and heartless. To use her like that . . .'

He stared at her for a moment, thinking how kind she was. His sister had saddled this girl and her family with an illegitimate baby and yet she could still find it in her heart to have some pity for her. Thoughts of the baby made him ask, 'How is the child?'

'She's very well, sir.' At that moment Lily seemed to remember who she was talking to and straightened her back.

He nodded. 'Good. I shall be visiting very soon, if I may. I'm more than grateful for what you are all doing for her but I'm not at all happy for you and yours to be responsible for her financially. You really should have kept the money.'

'We'll manage,' Lily responded primly and before he could stop her, she sailed from the room without giving him a second glance.

Louis' next stop was to find his mother. He eventually found her sitting in the drawing room next to a roaring fire with an embroidery frame across her lap and a thick rug tucked about her knees.

'Louis, my darling, you're back,' she greeted him, making no attempt to rise as she held out her hand. 'Has Arabella come with you?'

'Yes, Mama, she has, but I'm afraid there was an unfortunate accident on the way home.' Seeing the look of panic that crossed her face he hurried on. 'But there's no need to worry. She's fine, just very shaken and shocked.' Once again, he relayed the story they had decided on.

'Oh, my poor girl.' A lone tear trickled down Lady Clarissa's pale cheek and she dabbed at it with a tiny lace handkerchief. 'Thank goodness she wasn't seriously hurt.'

Clarissa was a petite woman with blonde hair and blue eyes. Once she had been a great beauty but now she was a semi-invalid who rarely ventured outside and she looked fragile. She had taken to her bed after a difficult pregnancy and birth with Arabella. The numerous doctors that her husband had paid to examine her could find nothing physically wrong with her and could only put her condition down to her mental health.

Soon after the birth she had banished her husband to his dressing room and there he had remained, which Louis supposed was why he lost himself in his work and the many businesses he owned. He certainly didn't have a lot to come home for anymore, although to his credit as far as Louis knew he hadn't resorted to taking mistresses as most men in his position would have done.

'You must send her down to me at once,' she ordered, but Louis shook his head.

'I think she will need to rest tonight, Mama. Perhaps you could see her in the morning when she's had a good night's sleep?'

Lady Clarissa sighed dramatically. 'Very well, but soon we really must get these wedding preparations under way. Lord Lumley will be visiting her next week and he'll be staying for Christmas, and if the last letter I received from him is anything to go by, I don't think he's any too happy with her being away for so long. And if we're to have the wedding in the summer there are a million and one things to organise. I shall have to try and get myself well enough to accompany her to London to be measured for her bridal gown for a start. And then there's the bridesmaids' outfits, the caterers, the flowers . . .!'

'Mother, please don't get yourself worked into a frenzy!' Louis was exasperated. It seemed she was more concerned about the wedding preparations than with the fact that her daughter had been in an accident. But that was his mother all over: she had to have the best of everything and would settle for nothing less. Her gowns were designed and made by one of the finest fashion houses in London. His father ordered the expensive perfume she favoured from France, and the house was bulging with the most magnificent antiques, crystal and china money could buy. Priceless works of art by the most renowned artists hung on the walls and expensive Turkish and Chinese rugs covered the floors in most of the rooms, so he wasn't really surprised to hear that she wanted to make Arabella's wedding into the wedding of the century.

Just for a moment he wondered what she would say if he were to tell her that she was a grandmother to an illegitimate baby girl, but he pushed the thought away immediately. His mother was not going to let anything get in the way of having this wedding and should she ever find out about Anastasia's baby she could make things very difficult for the Moon family. As if it wasn't difficult enough already, he thought guiltily. His grandmother's threats had made it impossible for them to refuse to take the baby in. But there was little he could do about it, apart from try to persuade Lily to take the money. It was tucked away in a drawer in his room and that was where it would stay until he could persuade Lily Moon to take it back. At least that might help assuage some of the guilt he felt.

Chapter Ten

Clarissa Bellingham had accepted the story of her daughter's clothes being ruined in the carriage accident without question, and ever since Arabella had returned, she had been subjected to the local dressmaker visiting almost daily to measure her for new gowns. Normally all her gowns were purchased in London but as her mother had pointed out, there was no time for that now, and so she patiently stood while every inch of her was measured as her mother pored over the choice of materials and styles. The dressmaker and her staff were working almost round the clock to get some of the gowns finished as soon as possible – not that Arabella seemed very interested in them. If truth be told, she didn't seem much interested in anything. Her mother put it down to pre-wedding nerves, but Louis knew better and it hurt him to see his sister so low. She was spending most of each day sitting at the window in her room staring vacantly out at the bleak landscape, and that was where he found her on a cold and snowy December morning.

Arabella's maid was just leaving the room to take her mistress's untouched breakfast tray down to the kitchen as he arrived and when he enquired how Arabella was, she rolled her eyes and quickly went on her way.

'Good morning and how are you today?' His voice was bright but his sister merely shrugged and didn't even look towards him. 'Look, Arabella, you've got to try to get over this,' he said gently. 'I know how badly you've been let down and how much you're hurting but Lord Lumley will be arriving later today and he won't be very happy to find you like this, will he?'

60

'I don't much care.' Her voice was so low that he had to strain to hear her.

Louis bit down on his lip and deciding to take a firmer hand with her, he said, 'If that's the case, why have you agreed to go ahead with the wedding? Wouldn't it be kinder to call it off now?'

Another shrug as she returned her gaze to the window. 'This wedding is all Mama talks about; I can't let her down. Anyway, I'm never going to trust another man or love again so I may as well marry him as anyone.'

Louis began to pace up and down the room. 'And what of the baby? The Moon family have called her Anastasia. Lily told them that was what you wanted, but they call her Annie. Wouldn't you like to at least see her?'

'Why should I?' Her voice was clogged with tears now. 'Every time I look at her it will remind me of how Freddie has let me down so it's best that I don't. I'm sure Lily and her family will take good care of her.'

There was a note of anger in his voice when he snapped, 'And what about Lily? Are you aware that it's all around the village that the baby is hers? Her young man has finished with her because of the gossip and I heard that he's now walking out with her sister! Can you even begin to imagine how hard that must be for the poor girl?'

'I didn't ask her to take the baby!'

Louis' eyes stretched wide as he glared at her. '*What?* You mean to tell me that you left that helpless infant with her in Yorkshire when you ran off with Freddie with not a thought of what might become of her? Haven't you *got* a heart?'

'Not anymore,' she said dully. 'Now will you please go and leave me alone, Louis. You're giving me a headache.'

He stared at her for a moment before turning on his heel and slamming out of the room.

61

Later, as Louis was having lunch with his mother, she suddenly said, 'It came to my ears that that girl, Lily Moon – the one who accompanied Arabella to Yorkshire – came back early because she had given birth to an illegitimate child. Do you know anything about this, Louis?'

Louis almost choked on his spoonful of soup. He dabbed at his lips with a snow-white napkin. 'Er . . . yes, I do, as it happens. I was told that a relative of the Moon family who lived close to where Arabella and Moon were staying gave birth to a baby while they were there. The mother is quite ill, apparently, and so Moon agreed to bring the baby back to her family until the mother is well enough to have it home again.'

'Hmm!' Lady Clarissa raised a perfectly plucked eyebrow. 'It sounds a little fishy to me but I suppose it's possible. Better that than knowing one of our maids gave birth to a flyblow – we have our standards to maintain. But seeing as Moon is a good worker, I'm prepared to give her the benefit of the doubt, for the time being at least. Now you'll have to excuse me, darling. I have a million things to do before Lord Lumley arrives. For a start I need to get Arabella to wash her hair and change. She's been so lethargic since she got back, but I suppose it's the shock after the accident.'

'Yes, of course.' Louis watched her leave the room and gave a sigh as he laid his spoon down, his appetite gone. The upcoming wedding seemed to have given his mother a new lease of life. She was up and about almost every day now, organising something or another, which in his opinion just went to show that she wasn't as ill as she made out. He gave a wry smile as he wondered what would happen if she were ever to discover the truth. If she was concerned about one of her servants giving birth to an illegitimate child, how would she react if she was to discover that it was actually her own daughter? No doubt she'd have a relapse.

Late that afternoon, Lord Lumley's splendid coach rattled down the drive and the butler hurried to open the door to him just as Lady Bellingham appeared from the drawing room dressed in all her finery. She was wearing a new silk gown in a delicate shade of lilac, and amethysts glistened at her throat and in her ears. Her hair had been arranged in curls high on her head with loose ringlets falling to her shoulders, and she was wearing her most expensive French perfume, which made Lord Lumley sneeze as she rushed to greet him effusively.

'Gilbert, my *dear* man. How *lovely* it is to see you.' She curtsied as she drew near to him and lifting her hand, he kissed it before sliding his arms out of his greatcoat and handing it to a waiting maid.

'The feeling is mutual, ma'am,' he replied as he took off his hat and glanced around the hallway. 'But I expected Arabella to be here to greet me.'

'Oh, she'll be down shortly, never you fear.' She giggled girlishly, setting her ringlets dancing on her shoulders. 'She's upstairs making herself beautiful for you – you know what these young girls are like. Do come into the drawing room and get warm. George is waiting to see you. Did you have a pleasant journey?'

She took his elbow and swiftly led him into the drawing room where Lord Bellingham was waiting to greet him. Then she turned and hissed to a passing maid, 'Go and tell Miss Arabella to get herself down here *now*!'

'Yes, ma'am.' The young maid scuttled away to do as she was told as Lady Clarissa fixed the smile back on her face and went to join Lord Lumley and her husband.

Arabella joined them ten minutes later and Gilbert Lumley was shocked to see the change in her. Her clothes now seemed to hang off her once shapely figure and her face was pale with none of the glow of youth that he remembered admiring the last time he had seen her.

'Arabella, darling. Have you been unwell?' He couldn't keep the concern from sounding in his voice as he crossed to kiss her hand.

'That shocking carriage accident she was in that I wrote to tell you about has taken its toll on her, poor sweetheart,' Lady Clarissa told him quickly. 'But I'm sure she will be quite herself again in time for the wedding. George, pour Gilbert a glass of brandy while I go to check on the progress of dinner.'

'Yes, dear,' her long-suffering husband answered as he rose to do as he was told.

Out in the hall, Lady Clarissa caught the housekeeper. 'Is everything going to plan for dinner, Mrs Biggles?'

'Oh yes, my lady,' the woman assured her.

Lady Clarissa had ordered five courses to impress their guest and Lily had spent the best part of the afternoon laying out the very best china, the finest silver cutlery and the best crystal glasses in the dining room. A huge bowl of lilies from the hothouse stood in the middle of the table and a log fire was roaring up the chimney. All the staff knew that tonight, and for the duration of Lord Lumley's stay, everything had to be perfect – and it would be to their cost if it wasn't.

Content that everything was in hand, Lady Clarissa returned to the drawing room where Lord Lumley had seated himself next to Arabella and was trying to engage her in conversation. He didn't seem to be having much luck and Arabella was barely answering the many questions he was firing at her, so Lady Clarissa quickly stepped in to tell him, 'I'm planning to take Arabella to London in the New Year to be measured for her wedding gown. Hopefully the weather will have improved by then. It can't keep snowing forever, surely?'

Lord Lumley nodded politely but his eyes kept returning to his betrothed until suddenly remembering something he reached into his pocket and withdrew a small leather box tooled in gold.

'Darling, although our engagement was decided just before you went away, I didn't have time to get you a ring. I do hope you will find this one acceptable. And I thought perhaps we could

hold an official engagement party either here or at my house?'
He sprung the lid on the box open and Lady Clarissa gasped as
she and Arabella looked down at the most beautiful ring – a pear
cut emerald surrounded by diamonds – that they had ever seen.

'Why . . . it's quite breathtaking,' Lady Clarissa gushed to try to
cover for the fact that Arabella was not saying a word. 'Oh, *do* say
something, darling!' Her mother urged excitedly.

'I-it's very nice.' Arabella stared at the ring, her eyes dull.

Lord Lumley took it from the box and slipped it on to her finger.
'This is a family heirloom,' Lord Lumley told them. 'It belonged
to my great-grandmother and has been passed down to the ladies
of the family since she passed away, so I thought it was only fitting
that the next Lady Lumley should wear it.' He decided not to tell
them that it had also been his previous wife's engagement ring.
He knew women could be a little funny about things like that.
His wife had died in childbirth along with their baby some years
before and he was now hoping that Arabella would provide him
with the heir he so desperately wanted.

'Well, say something, Arabella,' her mother said more sharply
than she had intended. 'And don't you think an engagement party
is a wonderful idea? We haven't officially announced it so we could
have a ball and do it then.'

'Er . . . yes, it is. And the ring is lovely. Thank you, Gilbert.'
Arabella stared down at it again. It felt strange on her finger. She
had only just removed the cheap band that Freddie had given her
at their fake wedding and this one meant nothing compared to
that, even though it had been worthless.

An awkward silence followed but thankfully Louis strode in at
that moment to greet their guest and soon after they were called
in to dinner.

The first course consisted of Cook's delicious chicken soup. It
was followed by fish and then the main course of venison in a red

wine sauce with seasoned vegetables and tiny crispy roast potatoes. By that time Arabella was feeling nauseous at the sight and
smell of so much food and suddenly pushing her chair back from
the table she said quickly, 'I'm so sorry, but you'll have to excuse
me. I'm not feeling at all well.' And with that she lifted her skirts
and rushed from the room.

Lord Lumley stared after her, totally bemused. Arabella seemed
to have changed completely since the last time he had seen her,
in both looks and nature. The sparkling flirtatious beauty he had
chosen to be his bride seemed absent. But he supposed it was to be
expected after being involved in the carriage accident. He could
only hope that her sparkle would soon return.

As soon as the meal was over, Lord Lumley and Lord Bellingham
retired to the study to enjoy a cigar and a glass of brandy but Louis
politely declined to join them and instead made his way upstairs to
his sister's bedroom where he quickly dismissed her maid.

'Crikey, Arabella! If you really do intend to go through with
this wedding you could have at least tried to look pleased to see
the chap,' he scolded her. 'You've barely said two words to him
all evening.'

'I can't help it,' she said with a catch in her voice as tears rained
down her pale cheeks. 'I'm just so unhappy.'

Louis could never stay mad at her for long when he saw her cry,
and going to her, he held her close as she sobbed. 'I know,' he
soothed. 'But you've got to put what happened behind you, otherwise you'll never be happy again. Will you at least try? For me?'

She nodded against his chest, but as they stood with their arms
about each other, they were both wondering if things could ever
be right again.

Chapter Eleven

The next night, when Lily returned to the cottage to find her mother sitting in the chair to the side of the fire, there was no welcome smell of a meal cooking and baby Annie was crying lustily. Lily hurried across to the baby and lifted her from the drawer as her mother had a coughing fit and bent double in the chair with a cloth pressed to her mouth.

'Are you all right, Mam?' Lily asked worriedly as she rocked the baby up and down.

'Y-yes, pet. It's just this damn cough. Could you warm Annie's milk and give it to her, please? And when you've done that could you light the oven. The pie only needs warmin' through an' there's some vegetables to cook an' all, if you don't mind. I prepared 'em earlier.'

Lily realised her mother must be feeling very ill indeed. Sara prided herself on always having a meal ready to put on the table when her family came home, and keeping the house as neat and clean as a new pin. But tonight she was ghastly pale and a little finger of fear traced its way up Lily's spine. She had seen far too many women in the village pass away with consumption and the thought of her mother having it terrified her.

'If you're no better tomorrer I'm callin' the doctor in an' I'll take a day off to help with Annie,' Lily told her firmly.

Sara shook her head. 'There'll be no need fer that. Soon as this damn cough eases off I'll be as right as ninepence.'

'That's what you've been saying for weeks.' Lily carefully tipped the warm milk into the bottle and placed a rubber teat on it before settling down to feed Annie. The child sucked on it hungrily but even before she had finished her eyelids were drooping and she didn't even wake when Lily changed her binding and tucked her back into the drawer and set about preparing the meal.

Soon after, her father, Teddy and Richie came home from work and after they'd washed and were settled at the table to eat, Bill looked towards his wife with concern.

'That cough no better, love?'

'It ain't too bad,' Sara replied but Lily scowled at her.

'No, it ain't no better, Dad, an' I've just told her it's time we were callin' the doctor out!'

Sara sighed. 'I'll tell you what,' she said, hoping to reach a compromise. 'You can pop to the pharmacy tomorrer an' get me some medicine, an' if that don't do no good then I will see the doctor. Is that good enough?'

'It's gonna 'ave to be, I suppose. Bridget can go in her dinner hour.' Lily knew that she wouldn't have time to, and it would be shut by the time she finished work.

The boys had left to go out, and with no sign of Bridget yet, Lily was just clearing the table when someone rapped on the door and when she saw who it was, she flushed.

'Oh, er . . . you'd best come in,' she said in a wobbly voice as Louis Bellingham stepped past her. 'What can we do for yer?'

He took off his hat, dropping snow all over the quarry tiles. 'I'm so sorry to disturb you,' he said politely with a nod towards Bill and Sara, 'but I had to come, because I want you to know that I don't agree at all with what's going on.' He looked as uncomfortable as Lily felt, but then his eyes fell on the baby fast asleep in the drawer, and his breath caught. 'May I?'

Lily nodded and watched as he crossed to Annie and gently stroked her hand. After a moment he shook his head and told them, 'I'm so sorry for what's happened. What my grandmama is making you do amounts to blackmail and I don't agree with it.'

'It's not your fault, lad.' Sara had warmed to him immediately, although she had never thought she would see one of the Bellinghams standing in her house. Goodness knows what the neighbours would make of it if they'd seen him arrive.

As if he had read her thoughts, Louis quickly told her, 'Don't worry; I tethered my horse some way away and made sure there was no one about before knocking on the door. I don't want to cause yet more gossip. I understand how difficult this must be for you. In fact, I'm here to ask if you will at least let me reimburse you financially for what you're doing for Anastasia. Goodness knows what would have happened to her if Lily had chosen to leave her in Yorkshire. My sister clearly isn't herself right now or I'm sure she would never have abandoned them like that.'

Bill tapped the contents of his pipe into the fire and rose to stand in front of their visitor. 'I appreciate the offer but there'll be no need for that,' he said proudly. 'You can rest assured the little 'un will be fine wi' us, sir.'

Louis blushed, his eyes dropping to Annie again, and when he saw her staring up at him, they all detected a tear in his eye.

'She's a lovely child, isn't she?' he said softly. 'Could I . . . I mean, would you mind if I held her? Just for a moment. I promise I won't make a nuisance of myself.'

Bill nodded and Louis leant over and very gently lifted the baby from the drawer, a look of wonder on his face. This was his niece and yet she would never know it. He would never be able to play the role of the proud uncle and it almost broke his heart. He stood drinking in every inch of her face as if he were committing it to memory, then suddenly he held her out to Lily and jamming his hat back on, he walked to the door, pausing for just a fraction of a second to glance at the framed sketches on the wall.

Seeing him looking at them, Sara told him proudly, 'Our Lily did them.'

'Really? They're excellent. But I mustn't keep you any longer. Thank you for letting me see the baby. And please remember, if you ever need anything, anything at all, just come to me. Good night.'

After he'd left, they stood looking at each other, before Sara said quietly, 'Seems at least one o' the Bellinghams has a conscience. What a nice young man he is. Handsome too.'

'Hmm.' Lily stared thoughtfully at the door. 'I suppose he is.'

Chapter Twelve

Lily jolted awake as Bridget clambered into bed beside her later that night and put her cold feet on her.

'Ooh! You're freezing.'

Bridget chuckled. 'Sorry, didn't mean to wake you. But Robbie will insist on keeping me out late! It's as if he can't get enough o' me.' She wasted no opportunity to rub her sister's nose in the fact that she had stolen her boyfriend, but could she have known, the only thing that Lily had suffered because of their break-up was hurt pride and the fact that her sister had jumped into her shoes so readily with no thought for her.

'Mm, lovely, now get to sleep an' keep yer cold feet over yer own side o' the bed, some of us 'ave to get up early, yer know. Anyway, I'm too worried about Mam to be bothered what you two get up to.' Lily hotched herself further across the bed but Bridget wasn't done with her yet. She had always had a bit of a spiteful streak when it came to her sister.

'Robbie's a lovely kisser, ain't he?' She sighed dreamily but getting no response from Lily she snuggled down and within minutes her snores were echoing around the cold little bedroom.

The weather had not improved the next morning and after checking on her mum, Lily stepped out of the cottage into the biting cold, her breath hanging like lace in the air in front of her. She had gone no further than the end of the village when she saw a shape standing on the road that led up to the manor. As she drew closer, she was shocked to see that it was Robbie, his hands tucked deep into the pockets of his overcoat.

He turned as he heard her feet crunching through the snow and gave her a half-hearted smile. 'Mornin', Lily.'

'Shouldn't you be at work?' she asked abruptly without slowing down.

He fell into step beside her. 'Aye, I should. I'm on me way there now, as it 'appens, but I needed to talk to you.'

'I don't know why,' she said scathingly. 'I think you've said quite enough.'

'Aye, that's why I'm 'ere.' He suddenly caught her arm and drew her to a halt.

She yanked it away from him and glared. 'Well, go on then! Say what you've got to say an' let me get on. I don't wanna be late fer work, even if you do!'

He looked at her sheepishly for a moment then muttered, 'I'm sorry fer the things I accused yer of. I know you ain't the sort o' lass to play fast an' loose.'

Lily narrowed her eyes. 'So what are yer sayin' exactly?'

'I'm sayin' I want yer to forgive me and let us go back to the way we were afore yer went away.'

Lily could hardly believe what she was hearing. 'Oh yes? And what are yer goin' to tell our Bridget? How do yer think she'd feel about that?'

'I don't want Bridget,' he said quickly. 'I never did. I only took 'er out to hurt you, but she's hearin' weddin' bells aready, an' it ain't 'er I want. It's you!'

Lily frowned. 'Well, I'm sorry, Robbie, but I'm not prepared to hurt 'er even if you are. An' even if she is a little madam. It's over so you'd better get used to the fact.' And with that she went on her way with her nose in the air.

Lord Lumley was just coming down to breakfast when she arrived at the manor so Lily had no time to think on things but went straight into the dining room to set the table before serving the meal. As the staff had soon discovered, Lord Lumley liked everything just so, and they had all been running round like headless chickens and jumping to his demands since his arrival. Worse still, he had no intention of leaving until the new year so things weren't set to get easier any time soon.

'Eeh, I feel dead on me feet aready an' the day's only just begun,' Cook complained when Lily went through to the kitchen to collect the first of the breakfast dishes. 'God 'elp Miss Arabella once she's wed to him. He's a right bloody tyrant,' she muttered.

When Lily got back to the dining room, she found that Lord Bellingham and Louis had joined Lord Lumley, so once all the silver dishes were laid out on the sideboard , Lily bobbed her knee and made to leave the room.

'Er, girl, just one moment.'

Lily stopped to stare at Lord Lumley. 'Yes, my lord?'

He had already helped himself to a portion of almost everything she had carried in and now he stabbed at one of the sausages and curled his lip. 'Get the cook to do me some more sausages. These are rather overdone for my taste.'

They looked perfect to Lily but she nodded. 'Of course, my lord.'

Cook had just sat down to have a rest and a cup of tea when she got back to the kitchen and when Lily told her what Lord Lumley had asked for, she growled. 'Ooh, that bloody man! I swear 'e could find fault in perfection. Yesterday it were the eggs 'e reckoned were undercooked. I tell yer, I shall be grey be the time he clears orf.'

Lily clamped her lips together to stop herself from laughing. Cook was already grey but she could hardly point that out so she stayed silent. In any case, it was hardly surprising that she was feeling sorry for herself. It had been decided that they would announce the engagement at their annual New Year party, so now it would be a much grander affair than usual. This meant that as well as having a very demanding guest, the family to cater to and Christmas almost upon them, Cook also had the party to worry about.

'They needn't think that *I'm* doin' all the food fer the party.' The cook dragged herself out of the chair muttering to herself. 'I've seen the fancy menus Madam Muck 'as come up wi' an' they'll 'ave to get caterers in. I'm only one woman!'

'I'm sure they will, Cook,' Lily soothed, winking at the little kitchen maid.

Everyone was kept so busy that the day seemed to pass in a blur and Lily had no time to think of her meeting with Robbie until she was walking home that evening. She was forced to admit that his declaration of love had gone a long way to mending her hurt pride, but she was also forced to admit that she was actually relieved their relationship had ended. Bridget was welcome to him, although she couldn't help but feel a little sorry for her sister. Bridget's behaviour had hurt her badly but she was clearly besotted with him. Yet if what he had told her was true, he had only walked out with her in the first place to get back at her. Still, she decided, they were old enough to sort it out themselves. As far as she was concerned it was no business of hers, and now she just wanted to get home and see if her mother was any better.

Sara was bustling about the kitchen putting the last-minute touches to the meal when Lily got home and she was pleased to see that she looked slightly better.

'Our Bridget got me some medicine an' I've rubbed some goose fat on me chest,' Sara informed her. 'I can feel it workin' aready. Didn't I tell you I'd be fine?'

Lily smiled as she crossed to the baby who was gurgling away to herself in the drawer. Her father and Richie were already home but glancing around Lily asked, 'Where's our Teddy?'

'Oh, young Jed Watson's 'ome fer a few days to see his mam an' dad so Teddy's gone to see him,' Sara informed her. Jed and

Teddy had been friends since they were old enough to walk and Teddy had been upset when Jed had decided that he wanted to go to sea rather than join his father down the mine.

'And is Bridget not in yet?'

'No, she's probably out with Robbie again,' her mother answered, looking uncomfortable.

'It's all right, Mam,' Lily assured her, deciding to not mention that she'd talked to Robbie that day. The words had barely left her lips when the door opened bringing in a flurry of snow, and Bridget appeared looking disgruntled.

'Looks like it's a night in fer me tonight,' she grumbled. 'I just went round to Robbie's an' he told me he ain't feelin' well.'

No one replied as Lily started to lay the table for dinner and soon the family were seated and tucking into sausage and mash. They were halfway through when Teddy arrived to join them, but Lily noticed that he seemed very quiet.

The meal was followed by one of Sara's delicious jam roly-polys and custard and Sara commented, 'I thought we ought to be makin' some plans fer Christmas soon. It's just over a week away so I thought you might pick us a little tree up in Nuneaton from the market after band practice on Saturday, Teddy?'

Teddy's cheeks reddened and he bowed his head.

Sara frowned. 'Is there a problem wi' that, lad?'

'Aye, there is actually. Yer see, Mam . . . Look, there's no easy way to say this, an' I know you ain't goin' to be none too pleased about it, but I won't be 'ere on Saturday.'

'Oh?' Sara looked confused. 'Where will yer be?'

Teddy licked his lips. 'I'll be on me way to the docks in London wi' Jed.'

'*London*? Whatever for?' Sara's spoon clattered into her bowl.

'Cos Jed just informed me that the ship he's on is lookin' fer crew so I'm goin' back wi' him an' I'm signin' on. He's workin' on

75

a big cargo ship, *The Pride of the Sea*, an' we'll be sailin' to France. And that's just for starters. Can you believe that? Just think – I could go all over the world!'

'I see.' For a moment, Sara could think of nothing to say; she had always known how much Teddy hated working down the pit and that he had a yen to be a sailor, but she had never thought he would actually do it. It was like a knife in her heart. 'B-but ain't it dangerous on a big ship like that?'

'No more than workin' down the pit,' he said defensively.

Unfortunately, she couldn't argue with that. Mining was a dangerous job. Only the month before the men had been forced to make for the surface when the canary they took down with them fell dead off his perch. It warned the miners that there was gas building up and when that happened, they had no option but to get out of there fast in case there was an explosion.

'How long will yer be gone for?' she asked in a wobbly voice.

Teddy shrugged. 'I don't know, Mam, but yer can rest assured I'll come back to see you whenever I can, I promise.' Seeing her distress, he reached across and squeezed her hand. 'I'm so sorry, but yer must know how much I dread goin' down that mine every day. I allus feel like I'm bein' buried alive.'

She nodded as she blinked back tears.

Bill stood and placed his hand on Teddy's shoulder. 'If that's the case, lad, then you go an' live your dream wi' my blessin'.'

Teddy left with Jed to catch the train to London early on Saturday morning looking happy and excited. Sara had packed as many of his warm clothes as she could fit into a rucksack for him as well as filling another smaller one with enough sandwiches and pies to feed both young men for at least two days. She had offered to travel on the cart to Nuneaton with him to see him off at the Trent

Valley Station, but because of her cough Teddy wanted her to stay in the warm, and so his mother's tearful goodbye was said in the warmth of the little cottage.

As she stood at the cottage window watching the two young men swaggering away to catch the cart, Bill kept his arm about her shoulders and gave her a squeeze as tears poured down her cheeks.

'He'll be fine, love,' he assured her. 'Our Teddy's got a good head on 'is shoulders an' it would 'ave been wrong of us to try an' stop him from doin' somethin' he's allus wanted to do.'

'I-I know,' she sniffed. 'But the 'ouse will seem so empty wi'out 'im.'

Bill chuckled. 'I don't know 'ow yer can make that out! Why, you've still got me, Lily, Bridget, Richie and that little 'un there to look after. This is all part of our family growin' up an' allowin' 'em to spread their wings.'

'I know,' she said meekly with a loud sigh. 'But it don't stop it bloody hurtin'.'

Chapter Thirteen

Up at the manor Arabella sat quite still as her lady's maid dressed her hair for dinner. It was Christmas Eve and usually a day she loved but this year she could find no joy in anything. She was still smarting from Freddie's betrayal and felt like she would never be happy again. Admittedly, Lord Lumley seemed to dote on her and she was sure he would have given her the moon had she asked for it, but she would have exchanged the magnificent emerald and diamond ring sparkling on her finger for the cheap gold band that Freddie had given her in a sigh. Sometimes she longed to speak to Lily. They had become close in the time leading up to the baby's birth but as yet she had avoided her like the plague. She suffered all manner of guilty feelings about the way she had abandoned the child, and the fact that Lily's family had been forced to care for her, but she still didn't want to see her. She wouldn't be able to bear it if she resembled the man who had broken her heart.

'There you are, miss.' The maid smiled and stood back to admire her handiwork. 'All done, and even if I do say so meself, it looks lovely. What do you think?'

Arabella glanced into the mirror. The maid had brushed her fair hair until it shone like molten gold then teased it into ringlets that cascaded across her shoulders. It had been pulled up at either side and secured with two ridiculously expensive tortoiseshell combs – just one of the gifts Lord Lumley had presented her with in the lead-up to Christmas.

'That will be fine, Millie. You can go now,' she said dully.

Millie curtsied and left Arabella staring blankly into space. She was dreading the evening ahead, just as she dreaded every minute she had to spend in her fiancé's company, but when she heard the dinner bell sound, she sighed and reluctantly rose to join him and the family.

She had just reached the bottom of the stairs when she almost collided with Lily who was rushing down the hall with a pile of clean napkins for the dining room. They both stopped in their tracks and it would have been hard to say who looked the most uncomfortable. It was Lily who broke the silence when she bobbed her knee and said quietly, 'Good evening, Miss Arabella.'

'Lily . . . how are you?'

'I'm very well, miss, thank you.' She lifted her head and their eyes locked for just a moment. But remembering her place, Lily moved on and the moment was gone.

Lily was still thinking of the misery she had seen in Arabella's face as she set off for home later that evening. With the lights in the tiny cottages shining onto the snow in the valley below her, the village looked like a scene on a chocolate box she had once seen and she was looking forward to getting home. Suddenly she saw a horse and rider coming up the hill towards her, the rider pushing the horse as fast as it could go in the slippery snow.

'Is everything all right?' she shouted as he passed her.

Without slowing he shouted back, 'No, it ain't, miss. There's been a bad fall at the pit. There're men trapped. I need to let Lord Bellingham know.'

Lily's heart skipped a beat as fear traced its way up her spine. Had her father been trapped in the fall? Bundling her long skirts into her fists she almost flew down the slope in a most unladylike manner to find mayhem in Valley Road. The men who worked the night shift should have been relaxing by their fires because they had Christmas Eve night and Christmas Day off, but now they were pouring out of the cottages, pulling their caps and coats on and racing towards the pit to see what they could do to help. One of them brushed past her so quickly that he almost knocked her off her feet but at last she burst into the cottage. 'Is Dad home yet?' she asked her mother breathlessly.

Sara was walking up and down cuddling Annie to her and shook her head. 'N-no. I don't know what to do.'

'You stay here. I'll go and find out what's happening,' Lily told her. 'And try not to worry. It could be that Dad got out and 'as stayed behind to help.'

Outside she found herself amongst a number of women from the village all on the same mission, their faces full of dread. They each had a son or husband who might be one of the trapped miners and the fear they felt was writ clear on their faces.

When they reached the gates of the pit they found a man had been posted there to stop them going any further.

'Let me in, yer bugger!' One of the women shook her fist at him. 'My Jim could be one o' the men trapped down there.'

'Calm down, missus,' he urged. 'We're doin' all we can. They're makin' a list o' the men who got trapped an' soon as we 'ave it you'll be told. Just try to be patient, please.'

And so the vigil began, and as the women stood there feeling afraid and helpless, clutching their shawls about them, Lily began to pray as she had never prayed before. Within the gates it was pandemonium as men prepared to get down to the trapped miners. They scurried about like ants, loading lengths of timber into the cages to be lowered underground so they could try to shore up the roof, lamps were being loaded into another cage and all the time the sound of hobnail boots scraping on the cobbles echoed in the air as men who had heard of the fall rushed from their homes to try and help.

Lily had no idea how long she had been standing there before someone touched her arm and she found Bridget standing beside her.

'I think Robbie might be one of the ones that's trapped; he ain't been 'ome from work yet. I've just been round there,' she said with a tremor in her voice.

Lily didn't know what to say so she simply nodded and squeezed Bridget's hand.

As the evening wore on some of the women returned to their homes to get a warm drink but Lily was determined to stay. At last a man approached the gate with a list in his hand and soberly began to read out the names of the men who were not accounted for.

'Jim Tyler, Will Wright, Mick Carter . . .' As the list went on, sobs were heard amongst the women as they heard the names of their loved ones. And finally, 'Robbie Berry, Sam Preece, Bill Moon . . .'

Both Lily and Bridget gasped as they clung together, their teeth chattering, but they didn't speak. There was nothing they could say that could ease the fear and pain they were both feeling. Very slowly the men assembled disappeared down in the cages and the search began as the waiting went on.

It was Bridget who eventually said, 'I-I think we should go 'ome now.' Her lips were blue with cold and her nose was so red it was almost glowing. 'There's nowt we can do stood 'ere an' someone will get word to us if they find Dad or Robbie.'

Lily patted her arm. 'You go. I'm goin' to wait a bit longer.'

Bridget turned and stumbled away into the fast-falling snow while Lily waited on. Finally, a shout went up from within the gates.

'They've reached the first fall an' they're tryin' to shore the ceilin's up afore they start diggin' to try an' get to 'em.'

Lily could only imagine how exhausted the men working down there must be. Most of them had been at the mine since early that morning but had rushed back to help. One of the women began to chant the Lord's Prayer and soon others joined in, their voices echoing eerily on the cold night air.

'I just pray they'll get to 'em afore the men run out of air,' one of the women said eventually in a hushed voice, and Lily could only imagine how terrifying it must be for the poor men trapped in the pitch darkness, especially if they were injured.

As the evening dragged on, Lily leant against the fence, struggling to keep her eyes open. She had been on her feet since early that morning and now she was so exhausted she was sure she could have slept standing up. The sound of a carriage approaching made her turn and she watched as it came in through the gates and drew to a stop. Lord Bellingham and Louis clambered down from it and began to talk to the man who was organising the search party below ground.

'Huh! I don't know 'ow they dare show their bloody faces,' Sal Robinson from Plough Hill Road growled. 'It's all right fer them toffs, livin' up there in the lap o' luxury while our menfolk slave their guts out to provide 'em with a good livin'.'

'At least they've come,' Lily pointed out and Sal glared at her.

'Oh aye, they've come aright! But do yer reckon they'll be goin' down to 'elp wi' the rescue? Like bleedin' 'ell they will!'

Lily turned away. She could understand the woman's anger but she didn't want to get into an argument so she stayed silent.

After a time, Lord Bellingham strode towards the gates to address the women. 'I understand how worried you must be, but rest assured all that can be done is being done. Now I suggest you go home and get warm, and I promise you that you will be informed as soon as we reach the men and start to bring them up.'

Muttering to themselves, some of the women shuffled away while others stayed where they were. Lily stood her ground until she was so tired that she knew she would fall if she didn't sit down soon, so reluctantly she began to make her way home where she found her mother pacing the floor.

'Any news?' Sara gasped the instant she saw her and when Lily wearily shook her head, tears began to trickle down her cheeks.

Lily staggered towards the fireside chair. Her hands and feet were so cold that she had lost all feeling in them and within seconds of sitting down her damp clothes began to steam in the heat from the fire.

'Keep yer ear out for Annie. I'm goin' to go along there now,' Sara told her as she lifted her shawl from the back of a chair.

'Oh no, you are *not*!' Lily snapped. 'You're barking like a dog already with that cough. If you go out in this, you'll catch your death of cold. We just have to wait it out now. They've promised to let us know as soon as there's any news so you go to bed and I'll wait.'

'I will *not* go to bed,' Sara answered indignantly, although she had sent Bridget to hers. 'We'll wait down 'ere. *Surely* there'll be some news soon!'

For the next couple of hours Lily dozed on and off in the chair as Sara alternated pacing up and down and chewing on her nails. It was still dark when they heard someone hurrying along the street rapping on doors. Lily was wide awake in an instant and flung the door open to see Tim Brace who lived three doors away from them hammering at the doors.

'They've found the first o' the trapped men an' they've got through to 'em,' he told them. 'They're startin' to bring 'em up now.'

'Was my dad amongst 'em?' Lily asked.

He shook his head. 'I couldn't say, love. Not till they've got 'em all out.'

Lily rushed back into the kitchen and snatched up her damp shawl. 'I'm goin' back there. I'll be straight back soon as I 'ave any news.'

Sara snatched the shawl from her and pressed her own into Lily's hand. 'Here, take this one, it's dry an' it's thicker than yours.'

Lily gave her a peck on the cheek and after pulling on her boots she was off again. At the gates of the mine, she was just in time to see the first of the rescued men being brought out of the cage. Some of them were walking, others were having to be carried.

Once again, a man approached the gates to give the names of the men who had been rescued, and some of the women slipped past him to rush to their loved ones. Lily's heart sank when her father's name wasn't amongst them, although Robbie was now safe above ground again.

'Are there many more down there?' she asked in a shaky voice.

The man nodded tiredly. 'It seems there's been two falls,' he told her, 'and they've not yet managed to reach the second one yet cos it seems to be much worse. But the men are workin' on it even as we speak. At least we've got all the men out o' the first one an' all of 'em are alive, though some are injured.'

Hearing her voice, Louis Bellingham looked towards her and frowned with concern. Leaving the entrance to the shaft he approached the gates. 'Are you all right, Lily? Is your father down there?'

She nodded as she blinked back tears, too choked to answer him. It felt strange to hear him address her by her first name but she had far more important things on her mind to give it more than a passing thought.

'I'm so very sorry. I hope he'll be brought out uninjured.'

She nodded and turned her eyes back to the rescued men who were lying in the snow, their wives and mothers hanging over them. She was very conscious of some of the women staring at her, wondering why the likes of Louis Bellingham, the boss's son, would give her the time of day, and she felt slightly embarrassed. Louis seemed to pick up on her feelings so doffing his hat he strode back to stand beside his father who was watching the proceedings with a grim face.

It took the rescuers over two more hours to reach the next fall and as they had feared this one was far worse. They worked like demons, passing the rubble from hand to hand while others tried to prop up the roof. Every few seconds they shouted, hoping for a response from beyond the fall, but only silence greeted them and, as they worked on, they began to fear the worst. Soon it was daylight. A cold grey day, although at least it had temporarily stopped snowing, which was something. After being checked over by the doctor, the men who had been able to walk out of the pit had been allowed to go home – Robbie was one of them.

She didn't recognise him as he walked towards her leaning heavily on his mother's arm, for all that showed of his face were the whites of his eyes.

'I hope your dad is all right, Lily,' he said before a coughing fit had him bent double. The men had swallowed a dangerous amount of dust and soot during the fall but Robbie counted himself lucky to see daylight again. There had been times, while he was trapped in the suffocating darkness, when he had feared his time was up.

'Come on, it's 'ome to bed fer you, me lad,' his mother told him and with a nod towards Lily he allowed himself to be led away.

It was shortly after this when one of the women suddenly said, 'By Jove! It's Christmas Day!'

None of them had given it a thought, but one thing was for sure: although it certainly wasn't merry, it was a day they would remember for as long as they lived.

Chapter Fourteen

Just after midday, the team of rescuers who had been working down in the mine since the early hours of the morning were brought to the surface so they could go home for a few hours' much-needed rest while another team went down to continue their work. The men looked exhausted and their shoulders were slumped as they approached the gates.

'Any closer to 'em, lad?' one of the women asked a young man as he drew level with them.

He shrugged. 'We're all workin' as fast as we can but it's a massive fall an' it's like 'ell down there,' he told her honestly.

'Can you 'ear the men that are trapped?' she asked anxiously.

After a pause he shook his head. There was no point in lying, it would only give them false hope. 'Not as yet. Not a peep.'

Some of the women began to cry again as they fixed their eyes once more on the entrances to the gaping shafts.

It wasn't until the sky was beginning to darken again that a man emerged from the shaft and a cry went up. 'They're through. They should be startin' to bring 'em up very soon now!'

A silence fell on the assembled crowd as they watched and waited with bated breath for the remaining fifteen men to be brought to the surface. At last, the first cage was hauled up and two men on stretchers were carried out.

'Sid Bates and Johnny Felton!' someone shouted and instantly the women who had been waiting for them were through the gates.

A doctor approached and after examining the first man, he stood up and shook his head. The man's wife began to keen as the doctor moved on to the next stretcher. This man was having difficulty in breathing and had a badly broken leg but at least he was alive so they loaded him onto a waiting cart and rushed him away to the cottage hospital in Nuneaton. Very slowly the men were brought up two at a time and by six o'clock, of the ten men who had been rescued, only five were alive.

Lily was shuddering with fear and cold by this time. There were only five men left now and her father was one of them, but would he be alive? She began to pray just as another two men were carried from the cage.

'Abel Langston and Bill Moon!'

At the sound of her father's name, Lily found she couldn't move; her legs seemed to have developed a life of their own and didn't want to work.

'Go on, lass. That's yer dad,' the woman at the side of Lily urged her and she stumbled towards him. The doctor was bending over him by the time she reached him and was holding a stethoscope to his chest. Time seemed to stand still as she stared down at her father's black face. Then the doctor rose and slowly squeezed her hand. 'I'm so sorry . . . he didn't make it.'

For a second the floor seemed to rush up to meet her and some-one caught her and held her upright until the dizziness passed as a man emerged from one of the offices and covered her father with a sheet. She stood for some seconds as if she had been turned to stone as she tried to take in what the doctor had told her. Her kind, lovely father was gone; she would never hear his voice again and it was almost more than she could bear.

'Get yourself home, pet, there's nothing you can do here now,' a gentle voice at her side said. 'You'd best tell your ma an' your family what's happened. I'm so sorry, your dad was a good man.'

Numbly, she turned and staggered towards the gates. As the man had pointed out, there was no point in staying anymore. Her father was dead.

Somehow, she managed to reach the cottage, although afterwards whenever she thought back to that terrible time, she had no idea how she managed it. Outside the door, she paused as she wondered how she was going to break the devastating news, then with a trembling hand she lifted the catch and went inside.

Sara and Bridget were pacing the floor when she stumbled into the kitchen while Richie sat white-faced with little Annie in his arms to one side of the fire.

As it happened she didn't have to say a word, for one look at Lily's stricken face told them all they needed to know and suddenly Sara let out a gut-wrenching scream as she dropped onto one of the chairs. '*Noooooo*! Oh Bill, my love, *noooooooo*!'

Then suddenly they were all in a tight circle with their arms wound about each other as they gave way to their grief and sobbed for the husband and father they would never see again. At some stage as the evening wore on, Lily put the uncooked goose that was to have been their Christmas dinner into the range to cook. None of them were hungry but they had to eat something. As she shut the range door, there came a tap at the door and Lily went to answer it to find Louis Bellingham on the doorstep looking almost as bereft as she felt.

'My father has asked me to visit all the families whose menfolk didn't make it,' he told her solemnly. 'And he asked me to tell you that you have no need to worry about the funerals. My father will be paying for everything.'

'Oh, how bloody *good* o' him,' Bridget said caustically. 'Per'aps if he'd made sure the mine were a safer place to work this would never 'ave 'appened.'

Louis flushed. 'I can quite understand how you feel,' he told her placatingly. 'But believe me, we are going to do all we can to make sure that you are all all right.'

'An' 'ow do you propose to do *that*?' Bridget spat. 'Is your dad gonna carry on payin' the wages my dad earned to pay the rent each week, eh?'

'Bridget, stop it. This isn't helpin',' Lily told her and with a toss of her head Bridget stamped away upstairs to join her mother who was lying in bed staring into the darkness.

'Perhaps now ain't a good time,' Lily told Louis stiffly as he stood there looking uncomfortable.

'Of course. I quite understand, but we just wanted you to know that none of the families affected by loss need worry about burial costs.'

'That's all well an' good,' Lily told him in a shaky voice, feeling much as Bridget had. 'But what'll 'appen to 'em after the funerals, eh? Wi' no men to bring wages in. No one to put food on the table for their children or pay the rent. You know as well as I do that the main of 'em will end up in the work'ouse.'

Louis bowed his head. 'I . . . I'm so sorry,' was all he could say, then, after glancing guiltily towards Annie, he gave a slight nod and left.

The following day the village were told that only eight of the fifteen men who had been trapped in the second fall had made it out of the pit alive, and four of them had horrific injuries, which meant they may never work again. As for the others, they would be haunted by the time they had spent trapped underground in the pitch-black, airless prison for the rest of their lives.

Three days later the first of the funerals took place at the village church when three of the miners were laid to rest in the tiny church-yard. The following day three more, including Bill Moon, joined them.

Early on that cold and frosty morning, Lily and her family set off for the church and stood through the short service that marked the end of their loved one's life. They then followed his coffin into the churchyard and stood with faces as white as the deep snow that lay about them as they watched Bill's coffin being lowered into the yawning hole in the ground.

'Earth to earth, ashes to ashes,' the vicar intoned as he threw a handful of frozen earth onto the cheap pine coffin, but the rest of the words went over Lily's head as she stood dry-eyed remembering the happy times she had spent with her father. At the side of her Sara quietly sobbed, Annie buried in the folds of her shawl and clasped tight to her chest. Richie was crying too, but Bridget was also dry-eyed and keen to go and see how Robbie was now.

At last, it was over and they watched the vicar stride away to begin the next service. Slowly they turned and made their way back to the cottage and once there Richie finally addressed the worry that none of them had yet dared to think about.

'Per'aps Lord Bellingham will let us stay on 'ere, seein' as I work fer 'im up at the stables and Lily works in the house,' he said hopefully as he filled the kettle and swung it over the fire to boil. 'An' if 'e does we'll manage wi' our wages still comin' in.'

As he had promised, Lord Bellingham had covered the cost of the funerals, but it gave no joy to any of the grieving families, as the circumstances they now found themselves in sank in. Not only were they grieving their loved ones but because the cottages they lived in were all tied to the pit, they would no longer be able to stay in them. So where were they to go?

Sara shrugged. She felt numb, as if she were trapped in a nightmare, and couldn't seem to think straight.

Lily supposed that Richie was right: there were still their wages to keep them afloat and Lord Bellingham had fulfilled his promise of paying for the burials so perhaps he would be lenient with the bereaved family's accommodation too. Only time would tell.

Much as she didn't feel like it, Lily went back to work the next day. She was worried about leaving her mother as her cough had worsened significantly in the last few days, and now that she, Bridget and Richie were all working again she would be left to care for Annie alone. But there was nothing she could do about it, so she reported to Mrs Biggles when she arrived at the manor.

'Good to have you back, Moon,' the woman said, looking uncomfortable. 'And I was sorry to hear about your loss. Still, life goes on and it's extremely busy here with the New Year's Eve party tomorrow.'

Lily was shocked to hear that the festivities hadn't been cancelled, all things considered, but she didn't say anything as she joined the other servants in the frantic preparations for the guests who would be arriving the following day.

When she got home that evening, she found Mrs Manning from next door in with her mother telling her that the first of the bereaved families, the Moores, had been forced to admit themselves to the workhouse. 'Poor sods,' she said, shaking her head. Thankfully her husband had been one of the lucky ones who had been brought up from the pit alive. 'Sobbin' 'er 'eart out Margie Moore were, poor bugger.' Mrs Manning sighed as she crossed her arms under her enormous bosoms and heaved them up. 'But what else could she do? Three little 'uns under five, 'ow was she supposed to feed 'em? At least they'll be fed in there.'

Lily shuddered at the thought of it. No one had approached them about whether or not they would be allowed to stay in their cottage as yet but she had no doubt they would and she could barely sleep for worrying about it.

The following day was New Year's Eve but there would be no celebrations in the village this year, although the same couldn't be said up at the manor. Caterers brought in especially for the occasion were annoying Cook in the kitchen and extra maids had also been drafted in to attend to the needs of the many guests who would be coming from as far afield as London. Many of them would be staying overnight, which meant the maids had been rushed off their feet getting the bedrooms prepared as well as helping to get the rest of the house ready for the party.

'I'll be bloody glad when it's all over.' Cook glared at one of the chefs who had taken over her ovens.

Molly the kitchen maid winked at Lily. 'But yer did say there were too much fer you to do all on yer own,' she pointed out to the disgruntled cook.

'Aye, I did, admittedly. But I didn't expect the snobby lot to come in an' take over the whole o' me kitchen,' the older woman grumbled as she sat by the fire with her mob cap askew and a frown on her face.

By mid-afternoon the floor in the ballroom had been polished to a mirror-like shine, and tables and chairs had been arranged around it. The tables in the dining room were almost sagging beneath the weight of all the food. There were game pies, whole pigs, pastries and hams. On another table were freshly baked rolls and a vast selection of cheeses. Another was covered in desserts, some of which Lily had never even seen before. There were cakes and trifles, quivering jellies in all the colours of the rainbow, and dainty tartlets. Lily could hardly believe that all this food could ever be eaten in one single night.

Lord Lumley came down the stairs at six o'clock, looking smart in a black evening suit, and was immediately whisked into Lord Bellingham's study to have a pre-party glass of brandy.

Meanwhile, Arabella was upstairs getting ready but she didn't look happy. As her maid fastened the corseted back of the beautiful pale-green satin ball gown she was to wear, she showed no pleasure at all. Her hair had been piled high onto her head and teased into ringlets, with pearl combs to hold it in place. About her neck was a glittering emerald and diamond necklace, an engagement gift from Lord Lumley, and matching earrings dangled from her ears.

'Eeh, yer look lovely, miss,' her maid commented admiringly as she stood back to look at her.

Arabella managed a weak smile before suddenly asking, 'Is Lily here this evening, Millie? Lily Moon?'

Millie nodded. 'I believe so. Most o' the staff 'ave stayed on late to 'elp get everythin' ready.'

'Could you run down and tell her I wish to see her, please?'

Millie frowned. 'But, miss, shouldn't yer be goin' down now? The guests will be startin' to arrive any minute an' your mother will expect you to be there to greet them.'

'Just do as I say,' Arabella said irritably and Millie turned and hurriedly left the room.

Minutes later there was a tap on the door and Lily appeared, her face solemn.

'You wished to see me, miss.' Her voice was clipped. The atmosphere between them was strained.

'Yes . . . I just wanted to say . . . I'm *so* sorry for leaving you like I did.'

Arabella looked so miserable that Lily couldn't help but feel sorry for her. 'So, you're going ahead with the marriage to Lord Lumley then?'

Arabella stared down at the sparkling ring on her finger. 'I may as well. Freddie didn't want me, so it doesn't really matter who I marry, and at least I'll be making my parents happy. B-but what I really wanted to ask you is, how is the baby?'

'She's very well.'

Arabella bit down on her lip. 'Good. I heard about what happened to your father and I'm so sorry for your loss. I've spoken to my grandmother about it and told her that you and your family must be paid for what you are doing for her.'

'She's already offered me money,' Lily told her. 'But I gave it back to your brother. We'll manage.'

Just then Millie came rushing back in. 'Sorry, miss, but your mother is sayin' you're to come immediately.'

Arabella looked at Lily. 'Perhaps we could continue this conversation another time?'

'There's no need to.' Lily lifted her chin and left without bobbing her knee.

With a sigh Arabella lifted her silk fan and slowly followed her, feeling as if she was going to a funeral rather than her engagement party. Perhaps she was, because this evening would mark the end of all her hopes and dreams of happiness.

Chapter Fifteen

February 1876

In February the last of the snow finally cleared and Lily woke up each morning to leaden skies and lashing, bitterly cold rain. Suddenly the little cottage that had always seemed to be packed with love was a sad place, and without Bill there nothing was the same. Sara was a shadow of the woman she had been as she grieved for him, and Bridget was in a permanently bad mood. The only thing Sara felt she had to be thankful for was the fact that Teddy had left the mine shortly before the fall, otherwise they might have been mourning him too. She had no idea where he might be, but even that was preferable to knowing that he was lying in a cold grave up in the tiny churchyard next to his father.

Richie and Lily continued to work up at the manor, which Lily supposed was why they had been allowed to stay in their cottage, for now anyway, and it was just as well because without Bill's wages theirs were needed more than ever. Everything was changing in the village: the families of the younger men who had been killed in the pit fall had vacated their cottages to return to live with their families, and yet more of the older women had been forced to throw themselves on the mercy of the workhouse, while men from neighbouring villages and the nearby town came in to take their homes and the jobs their men had done.

The only bright spot on the horizon for all of them was little Annie, who was a complete joy. She never cried unless she was tired or hungry and she won the hearts of all who met her. She had a ready smile for everyone and already Sara couldn't envisage her life without her.

Unfortunately, Sara's cough had worsened and the times when Lily returned home to find her sitting exhausted in the chair with no dinner ready were becoming more and more frequent.

'I'm so sorry, love,' her mother would tell her. 'I'm just so tired all the time.'

'It's fine.' Lily would give her a cheery smile and set about doing whatever needed to be done. She didn't have much choice for she knew that Bridget wouldn't do anything.

She was in the process of cleaning some Brussels sprouts for their meal one evening when as usual Bridget stormed in with a face like a dark thundercloud and flung her damp shawl across the fireguard.

'Who's upset you this time?' Sara asked with a sigh; this was getting to be a regular occurrence.

'It's Robbie!' Bridget kicked her boots off and stomped over to hold her cold hands out to the fire. 'I don't know what's got into 'im since the fall. I just went round to sit wi' 'im fer a while an' he told me he 'ad a headache! I thought it were us women who ought to be sayin' that! He's actin' really strange.'

'Go easy on 'im, love,' Sara urged. 'From what I'm hearin' all the men who were trapped down the pit are goin' through much the same. It's bound to 'ave affected 'em. Give 'im a little time an' happen he'll come round.'

'He'd *better*,' Bridget mumbled, crossing her arms and scowling into the flames.

Lily ignored her. She had never told her sister that Robbie had asked her to go back to him and pick up where they had left off. Much as Bridget deserved it, Lily didn't want to hurt her feelings, especially as she had no feelings whatsoever for him anymore. Bridget was welcome to him as far as she was concerned.

Their meal, when it was ready, was eaten almost in silence, then Richie rushed off to get ready for band practice and Bridget again put her boots and shawl back on.

'Where are you off to now, an' on such a filthy night?' her mother asked with a frown.

'I'm goin' back round to Robbie's.' Bridget tidied her hair in the mirror and tried to pinch some colour into her cheeks. 'I shan't be long. Ta-ra for now.' And with that she was off leaving Lily to clear the table and wash the pots.

'I'll help wi' that.' Sara made to rise from the chair but Lily scowled at her.

'No, you will not. I'm perfectly capable. You just sit there and rest an' when I've done, I'll make yer a nice cup o' tea.'

Sara sighed as she settled back in the chair wondering how she had managed to give birth to two such different girls. Bridget had always been demanding, while Lily had always been the helpful one.

'I've got a feelin' young Robbie is tryin' to give our Bridget the elbow,' Sara confided with a shake of her head. 'An' between you an' me, I'm not surprised. I love the bones of 'er but she can be a selfish little bugger. I've got a feelin' he's regretted givin' you the push.'

'I'm sure they'll sort it out,' Lily answered as she dumped the dirty pots into a bowl of hot water to soak.

'Oh, an' by the way,' Sara went on, 'Mrs Manning were fishing the other day about how Annie's mam were, so I told 'er that sadly we'd 'ad news that she'd passed away an' that we'd be keepin' 'er.'

'Aw well, in that case it'll be round the village in no time now. I know some o' the villagers still think she's mine.'

Sara pursed her lips. 'An' all the while that young miss up at the manor is livin' in the lap o' luxury wi' not a care in the world. It don't seem fair.'

'She might be being waited on but she isn't happy,' Lily replied. 'And in fairness, we didn't 'ave to keep Annie, did we? We could 'ave taken 'er to the work'ouse.'

Sara glowered at the thought of it and Lily changed the conversation to safer topics.

Meanwhile, Bridget was storming along Valley Road to Robbie's parents' cottage with a determined look on her face. She was no fool and knew that he'd been trying to avoid her ever since the pit fall, but all that was about to end.

'I've come to see Robbie,' Bridget told his mother boldly when she answered the door.

'Oh, er . . .'old on a minute, love, I'll see if he's up to seein' yer,' Mrs Berry said nervously, but Bridget wasn't about to be put off.

'He will be,' she said, calmly pushing her way past the woman into the tiny kitchen. Robbie was sitting at the table reading the paper while his father sat at the side of the fire smoking his pipe. Robbie glanced up in surprise, but before he could say anything Bridget asked him, 'Could we 'ave a word . . . in private?'

He glanced towards his parents and with a shrug he lifted a candle and led her into the tiny front room. There was no fire in there and it was bitterly cold as the room was only used for high days and holidays and the candle cast flickering shadows about the walls.

Tentatively, he turned to her and said, 'Look, Bridget, it's too cold to be walkin' out tonight. Per'aps when the weather picks up a bit if you still want to, eh?'

'If I didn't know better, I'd think you were tryin' to get rid of me, Robbie Berry,' she told him accusingly, her eyes flashing dangerously in the candlelight.

'Well, er . . .'

'O' course you ain't,' she interrupted him. 'An' it's just as well cos, you see, I'm goin' to 'ave a baby . . . You're goin' to be a daddy.'

'You're *what*?'

Even in the gloom Bridget could see the colour draining out of his face as she went on, 'So, I thought we'd best set a date fer the weddin'. I reckon the baby will be due in about seven an' a half months or so, an' I'd like to get wed afore I'm showin'.'

'*Wed!*' Robbie looked horrified. 'B-but 'ow do I know it's mine?'

Her lips curled back from her teeth as she leant threateningly towards him. 'Don't you *dare* try that wi' me,' she warned. 'You told me you loved me an' yer took me virginity, yer know yer did, so now it's time to stand up to yer responsibilities.' Then softening her voice, she sashayed towards him and began to tenderly stroke his cheek. 'Yer should know 'ow much I love yer,' she whispered. 'An' just think what everyone would say if yer were to leave me wi' an illegitimate baby. Why, you an' yer family would never be able to 'old yer 'eads up in the village again.'

Closing his eyes tightly, Robbie flinched away from her touch. Surely this was just a bad dream? But when he opened his eyes again, Bridget was still there, smiling like the cat that had got the cream.

'So shall we go through an' tell yer mam an' dad that you've asked me to marry yer, eh? We've no need to tell 'em about the baby just yet if yer don't want to. We can go an' tell my lot next an' all.'

'Can I just 'ave tonight to think on it?' His voice held a note of desperation.

'What's the point o' that? There's no time like the present. Come on, will you tell 'em or shall I?'

Half an hour later Bridget was back in her own kitchen, Robbie loitering behind her.

'Ah, 'ere yer both are,' she said cheerily, hauling Robbie forward to stand beside her.

'Where else would we be?' Sara stared at her suspiciously. She could read her daughter like a book and had a feeling that she was up to something.

'Robbie 'ere as got somethin' to tell yer.' Bridget smirked as she dug him in the ribs with her elbow but he kept his head bowed and remained silent so eventually she said, 'I suppose I'd better tell yer then . . . Robbie an' me are goin' to get married.' She looked towards Lily with a smug expression.

Sara's mouth dropped open. 'You're *what*?'

Bridget's smile disappeared and she looked peeved. She'd expected her mother at least to look happy for her but she looked as shocked as Robbie's parents had when she'd told them, and none too pleased about it either. 'You 'eard. We're gettin' wed.'

A terrible silence settled on the room for a few moments and it was Lily who broke it when she said, 'Then I'm very pleased for you both. I hope you'll be very happy. When is the wedding to be?'

'Soon as we can arrange it.' Bridget smirked. 'Ain't that right, Robbie? We can't see any point in waitin' so we'll go an' see the vicar tomorrer an' set the date an' see about gettin' the banns read.'

'Don't you think it's a little soon after . . . Well, the village is still grievin' fer the men that were lost in the fall. I don't think anyone is ready fer a celebration just yet. What's the rush?' Sara said, her lips set in a grim line. As always Bridget was only think-ing about herself.

Bridget shrugged as Robbie seemed to shrink beside her looking shamefaced.

'Your mam could 'ave a point,' he dared to say and she rounded on him.

'Then we'd better tell 'em the truth, 'adn't we?' she snapped, her pretty face flushed. 'The truth of it is we're goin' to 'ave a baby an' I want the weddin' out o' the way before I'm as big as the side of an 'ouse.'

Sara's hand flew to her throat. 'B-but you've only been seein' each other fer a short time!'

'So? These things 'appen, don't they? I won't be the first in the village to walk down the aisle wi' her belly full an' I don't mind bettin' I won't be the last.'

Robbie glanced towards Lily, who was as shocked as her mother, and seeing the misery in his face, she knew instantly that this wasn't what he wanted.

'In that case I dare say we 'ave no choice,' Sara said woodenly. It seemed to be just one thing after another at the minute. 'But you'll 'ave to pay for it yerselves. Now we ain't got your dad's wage comin' in things are tight. An' where are yer goin' to live?'

Bridget frowned at Robbie. 'We . . . we ain't really 'ad time to think about that yet.'

'Well, there ain't room 'ere for you,' Sara pointed out. 'So, you'd better start lookin' fer somewhere, unless Robbie's mam an' dad let yer stay wi' them, that is.'

A fleeting look of panic crossed Robbie's face. His mother had made it more than obvious from the very start that she wasn't fond of Bridget so he couldn't see living with them working. He couldn't see the marriage working, if it came to that, but now he would have to stand by her or he'd look a right cad! It was all such a mess and he just wished he could wave a wand and make things go back to how they had been before Lily had gone away. Too late he had realised that he still loved her, but Bridget had chased him and been so loving and obliging that she'd turned his head and now look!

He wished that he were a million miles away.

Chapter Sixteen

Lily arrived home from work one evening towards the end of February to find her mother in floods of tears and rocking to and fro in the chair by the fire.

'Mam, what's wrong?' She rushed over to place her arms gently about her mother's shoulders.

Sara stared up at her looking as if she had the weight of the world on her shoulders. 'Y-you ain't goin' to believe what's 'appened! The rent man came to collect the rent this mornin' and when I'd paid 'im he told me that we 'ave to be out o' the cottage within a month. The same 'as 'appened to all the rest o' the families who lost their men in the fall now. We've only been allowed to stay as long as we 'ave cos some o' the folks worked for Lord Bellingham in some of 'is other businesses. But he said they're 'aving to give the cottages to the families of the men who are comin' into the village to take the place o' the miners that were lost. Admittedly 'e were right sorry but 'e said Lord Bellingham 'ad given 'im specific instructions to give us all notice. Huh! He then told me that we're all to receive a small pay-out as compensation but 'ow long will that last an' where are we goin' to go?'

Lily plonked down heavily onto the chair opposite her. How could Lord Bellingham make his own granddaughter homeless? But then she remembered that he wasn't even aware of her existence.

She shook her head. 'We'll figure something out,' she said encouragingly, although she felt as fearful as her mother. 'Now you see to Annie while I get the dinner on, eh? Bridget and Richie will be home any time an' they'll want their meal on the table.'

She took the large frying pan down from the nail on the wall and fetched some sausages from the cold shelf in the pantry. Her mother had already peeled a pan of potatoes so this evening she would cook them sausage and mash with onion gravy – it was one of Richie's favourites. While she was preparing it, her mind was working overtime. What were they to do and where were they to go? They couldn't go too far as both she and Richie worked at the manor and needed to be within walking distance. Once Bridget married Robbie, they'd lose her wages as well, so things were going to be tighter still – not that Bridget had ever tipped all of her wages up. She'd always spent a large portion of them on frills and furbelows for herself.

When Richie and Bridget arrived home and were told about the move, Bridget shrugged. She was to be married in just a couple of weeks and was only concerned about herself, but Richie looked worried.

'Empty cottages to rent round 'ere are as rare as rockin' 'orse shit!' he said.

His mother glared at him. 'We'll 'ave none o' that sort o' talk in this 'ouse, if yer please, young man!'

'Sorry, Mam.' He bowed his head.

'Look, we'll find something,' Lily told them, hoping to lighten the mood, but she noticed that even Richie didn't dig into his meal as he normally would – the worry about what was to become of them had affected even his appetite.

Later that evening, as Lily was clearing the table, Bridget suddenly smiled at her mother. 'I, er . . . were wonderin' if yer might like to treat me to a new gown fer me weddin', Mam? Robbie's parents 'ave said they'll put on a small spread an' a cake fer us in the church 'all after the weddin', but I can 'ardly get wed in anythin' I've got, can I? I ain't really got nothin' grand enough an' I could do wi' a new bonnet an' all.'

Sara's head snapped up and she stared at her daughter as if she'd grown another head. 'Didn't you 'ear *a word* I were tellin' yer when yer came in? We've to find somewhere else to live an' be out o' this place within a month. An' now you expect me to find the money fer a new gown? Shall I pop down the garden an' pick some money off the money tree?'

Bridget pouted. 'There's no need to be sarcastic. If you want me to walk down the aisle lookin' like a pauper that's fine!' she spat and with a shake of her head she left the table and flounced away upstairs.

That night, Lily tossed and turned, worrying about what was to become of them all, when she suddenly realised what she needed to do. The thought didn't bring her any comfort, however, and she felt sick with dread at the thought of it. Finally, though, she fell into an uneasy doze just before dawn.

The next morning, as soon as she arrived at work, Lily set about preparing the dining room for breakfast. Louis was usually the first down and while she had been doing her best to avoid him over the last few months, today she hovered in the room, keeping a watchful eye on the door for a sign of him. She had almost given up hope of him appearing and was just about to go back to the kitchen to fetch the hot food when he strolled in with a newspaper tucked under his arm.

'Good morning,' he greeted her pleasantly, expecting her to scuttle away at the sight of him as she usually did, but this morning she surprised him when she crossed to the door and closed it quietly behind him.

'Morning, sir. I, er . . . was hopin' to 'ave a quiet word with you.' What she was about to do went sorely against the grain; Lily was a proud young woman but with things as they were she didn't feel that she had an option – and the family did owe her something, surely, for taking Annie in.

His smile faded as he asked worriedly, 'Is there something wrong with the baby, Moon?' Then with a shake of his head he ended, 'Look, may I call you Lily now?'

Ignoring his last question, she went on, 'The thing is . . . me mam 'ad a visit from your rent collector yesterday an' he's given us notice to quit the cottage.'

'*What?*' Louis looked appalled. His father usually handled the tenancy side of the business and he'd had no idea about this.

'It's true,' she said defensively. 'And not just us, either. All the families who lost their men down the pit who are still in their cottages 'ave been asked to go. The rent man told 'em he needed the cottages for the families of the men who'd be takin' the dead miners' places.'

'But that's *awful*!' Louis sounded genuinely disgusted. 'Where will you go?'

'That's what I needed to talk to you about.' Lily took a deep breath, wishing she were anywhere but in that room. 'Me ma's ill an' me sister is gettin' wed soon, so there'll be just mine an' me brother's wages comin' in. He did tell me mam that we'd be given some compensation.' When she named the sum that had been mentioned he frowned at the pitiful amount. 'But me mam can't work because . . .'

'Because she's busy taking care of my sister's child!' he ended for her. He could see how difficult it was for her to ask for help, and as he looked at her standing there with her chin held proudly in the air and her deep-blue eyes blazing, he was suddenly struck by how attractive she was.

'Please, leave this matter with me,' he said stiffly. He felt thoroughly ashamed. She had gone with Arabella in good faith to try and conceal the fact that his sister was with child and now look what it had cost her. 'We owe you and your family a great deal so rest assured that you will not be made homeless. I'm going to see

105

Grandmama immediately and I shall speak to you very soon. In the meantime, I beg you to try not to worry.'

'Very well, sir.' She inclined her head and bobbed her knee before turning and leaving the room, Louis close behind her. As she made her way down the hall, she could see him racing up the stairs two at a time and if his face was anything to go by, she guessed that he was very angry.

At the top of the stairs, Louis paused to compose himself, then with his face set he went to see his grandmother. She was propped up in bed against lace pillows enjoying her first cup of tea of the day when he entered her room, and without the thick layers of paint and powder on her face, he noticed how old and frail she looked. Even so, he wasn't going to let her off lightly. As far as he was concerned they had treated the Moon family shabbily enough already, and he certainly wasn't going to stand by and watch them be made homeless.

'Are you aware that the Moon family have been given notice to quit their cottage?' he asked abruptly.

She looked mildly surprised at his attitude. Louis was usually so loving but this morning he looked positively angry. 'Why . . . yes. Your father and I discussed the matter and had no choice. But it isn't just them. We are short of men to work the mine and before the new men start, they have to have somewhere to live, don't they? It's doubtful that the ones who lost their menfolk could afford to carry on paying their rent anyway.'

He stared at her as if he could hardly believe what he was hearing. 'So you're telling me that it doesn't concern you at all that whole families are about to be turned on to the street?'

'Your father is making sure they all receive an amount of compensation to help them find somewhere else,' she snapped defensively.

Louis snorted in disgust. 'So I've heard, but the amount he's giving wouldn't even pay their rent for a couple of months. What are they supposed to do after that?'

'That isn't our problem.' She glared at him. 'And you certainly shouldn't be interfering in things that don't concern you!'

'I'm afraid what happens to the Moon family *does* concern me! They are bringing up your first great-granddaughter. Doesn't that trouble you at all? That baby is our own flesh and blood.'

The old lady sniffed as she handed her cup and saucer to Hudson. 'So what do you propose we do? You clearly aren't going to let this rest!'

'I propose that we give them somewhere to live and ensure they have enough money to give the baby everything she needs.'

'I've already given the Moon girl twenty golden guineas,' she snarled. 'Isn't that enough?'

'Actually, Lily Moon gave that back to me almost immediately,' he informed her.

She looked mildly surprised. 'So why didn't you return it to me?'

'I kept it because I feared they might need it one day and now it seems that they do. The trouble is they are very proud.'

'They are mere *servants*,' she told him snootily with a wave of her hand.

Once again Louis felt embarrassed that she could talk of anyone who wasn't of her class that way. 'But if you insist, you may help them to find other accommodation and return the money to them.'

'I fully intended to do just that with or without your consent,' he told her. 'I believe there are a few empty cottages in our grounds and I'm going to see the head groundsman right now to see which one is the most habitable. Both Lily Moon and her brother work here so that should make it easy for them to get to work.'

Lady Bellingham didn't look very happy with that idea at all. 'But won't that mean that the flyblow will be a little too close for comfort? I don't want anything to go wrong this close to Arabella's wedding!'

'Of course not. After all, Arabella is *so* looking forward to being Lord Lumley's wife, isn't she?' Louis couldn't conceal the sarcasm in his voice and the old lady bristled.

'Just remember who you are talking to, young man,' she scolded.

'Actually, I'm not sure just who I'm talking to anymore,' Louis told her in a dangerously quiet voice. 'I always looked up to you and thought you had my and Arabella's best interests at heart, but it appears I was wrong. It seems that the reputation of the Bellingham family is more important to you than our happiness. It's more than obvious that Arabella is deeply unhappy about marrying a man who's almost old enough to be her father but all you care about is the title she'll have. I just hope you'll be able to live with your conscience.' With that he turned on his heel and strode from the room, leaving Hudson to rush to get her mistress her smelling salts.

Lily saw no sign of Louis for the rest of the day and when she set off for home that evening her spirits were low.

Her mother was in her usual seat at the side of the fire and Bridget was trimming her best bonnet with blue ribbons, her face sullen. As usual she had made no effort to start the evening meal and because she had so many other things on her mind, Lily barely glanced at her.

'Look at this.' Bridget waved the bonnet at her with a look of disgust on her face. 'Fancy 'aving to make do wi' sommat I've 'ad fer ages on me weddin' day!'

'If you're marrying the man you say you love, I shouldn't think it will matter what you're wearing,' Lily pointed out as she crossed to her mother to kiss her cheek before checking on Annie. She had outgrown the drawer and Richie had fetched the old crib down from the attic that they had all slept in as babies. As usual she smiled up at Lily and waved her plump little hands in the air and Lily couldn't resist lifting her to give her a swift cuddle before making a start on the evening meal.

'As if this ain't enough,' Bridget went on in a martyred tone, 'Robbie's 'ad no luck at all findin' us somewhere to live so it's lookin' like we're goin' to 'ave to stay wi' his parents for a while. Huh!' She tossed her head. 'Imagine that. Mrs Berry's made no secret o' the fact that she don't want us to get wed, so can yer imagine what it's gonna be like?'

'Per'aps yer should 'ave thought o' that before yer opened yer legs to 'im wi'out a ring on yer finger,' her mother said unsympathetically.

Bridget flung the bonnet onto the table and once again flounced upstairs, slamming the door so loudly behind her that the walls of the cottage seemed to tremble.

'She'll 'ave that bloody door off its hinges one o' these days wi' her bloody temper,' Sara said wryly. Bridget clearly hadn't given a thought to what would happen to them, she only cared for herself, but she had always been that way since she was a tiny girl so Sara supposed she shouldn't have been surprised. 'And how was your day, love? You look tired.'

Lily smiled and settled Annie back in her crib where the baby lay cooing and gurgling happily.

'Oh, you know, much as usual,' she answered as she lifted her mother's apron and tied it about her waist.

Much later that evening when everyone else had retired early to bed, Lily sat at the table finishing a charcoal sketch of Annie by the light of a candle. Outside the wind was howling and rattling the window frames and it was bitterly cold, although it was warm and cosy in the glow of the fire. A tap at the door disturbed her concentration and she frowned, wondering who would visit them at this time of night – unless it was Robbie, perhaps? Although he'd been keeping his distance and it was usually Bridget who visited him.

Lifting the candle, she went to the door and when she opened it her eyes widened. It was Louis Bellingham.

'Er, you'd better come in,' she said, hoping Edie next door hadn't spotted him. It would be all around the village the next day if she had.

Louis paused on the doorstep, taking in the sight of Lily in an old day dress with her hair loose and curling about her shoulders. She looked so different to the girl he had only ever seen in her uniform before that he almost forgot what he'd come for.

'I'm sorry to call so late,' he apologised as he politely took his hat off. 'But I knew how worried you must be so I'm pleased to say I have news for you.'

'Oh?'

He smiled. 'I've been to see our head groundsman today and he informed me that there's an empty cottage on our estate. It's about half a mile from the manor towards Hartshill, so I thought that would make it easier for you and your brother to get to work.'

'I see.' She stared at him suspiciously. 'An' how much rent would yer be askin' for that?'

'I think under the circumstances . . .' He named a ridiculously low price, less than half of what they were paying for the cottage they were in now. He didn't want to charge her anything but he already knew how proud she was and if he didn't at least ask for a peppercorn rent she would probably turn him down flat. 'After all, we are in your debt for what you're doing for Anastasia. I'd also like you to have this back.' He placed the pouch of guineas on the table.

Lily stared at it for a moment. She didn't have much choice but to accept his offer of a cottage to live in, but to take his money was

110

another thing entirely. 'Thank you, but as I've already told yer, we don't want yer money.'

He shrugged. 'I can understand how you feel but I'm afraid I must insist. I have a conscience even if my grandmama doesn't, and I shall be forever in your debt.'

As Lily placed the flickering candle on the table, he glanced down and caught sight of the sketch of Annie and gasped. 'May I?' he asked, gesturing towards it.

At her nod, he picked it up and studied it for a moment.

'Did *you* do this?' he asked incredulously.

She blushed and nodded, surprised to see that there were tears in his eyes. She had captured Annie as she lay sleeping with her long eyelashes curled on her plump little cheeks and her chubby fists bunched under her chin. 'Yes . . . why?'

'It's *superb*,' he said softly. Then he shocked her further when he asked, 'Could I have it? I'll pay you for it, of course.'

Despite the resentment she felt towards him and his family, she couldn't help but feel touched. 'You can have it an' welcome, an' there'll be no charge,' she told him.

He stared at it for what seemed a long time before suddenly remembering what he'd come for. 'The cottage . . . it needs some work doing to it as it's stood empty for some time, but if you decide it will be suitable for you all, I can get my groundsmen to have it ready for you in a couple of weeks. I thought perhaps you might allow me to show it to you after you finish work tomorrow.'

'Does your grandmother know about this?' she asked with a frown. 'An' don't yer think she'd object to you takin' me to see it?'

'She does know as it happens,' he answered. 'I've told her what I intend to do.'

'Hmm, I bet that went down a treat,' Lily said bitterly. But then she remembered that he was trying to help them and her voice softened. 'In that case I'd like to come an' look, but perhaps it would be better if I met you there? If anyone were to see us together the gossips would 'ave a field day. Half the village already believes that Annie is mine an' if they saw me with you, they'd try an' put two an' two together an' come up wi' five, then that would be your reputation shot an' all. I reckon I know the one you're talkin' about. Is it the one standin' next to the copse towards the top o' Plough Hill Road?'

'That's the one.'

She couldn't stop a little smile from forming. She had passed the cottage many times when out walking and had always thought how sad it was to see it standing empty and going to rack and ruin.

'In that case I'm much obliged. I'll meet you there about six o'clock tomorrer. An', er . . . thank you.'

'It really should be *me* thanking you,' he said as he tucked the sketch into his greatcoat pocket and put his hat back on. 'Good night, Lily.'

'Good night, sir.' She saw him to the door and once she had closed it behind him, she leant heavily against it and let out a sigh of relief. Perhaps, just perhaps, things were going to turn out all right after all.

Chapter Seventeen

L ily was a bundle of nerves all next day and by the time she
finished work she felt sick. It had been hard for her to ask
for help and as she set off for the cottage she had to keep reminding herself that it was for the family. It was already dark, wet and
windy and she realised that neither she nor Louis Bellingham had
thought of that when they'd arranged to meet. It was unlikely
she would be able to see much of the cottage at all, but she had
promised him she would be there so she cautiously picked her way
across the wet grass.

At last, the cottage loomed out of the darkness and she saw that
Louis' horse was already tethered to the picket fence that surrounded it. A light was shining from the window and she realised he must have thought to bring some candles along. Slowly
she stepped over the weeds that were growing over the little path
leading to the door and tentatively knocked on it.

Louis opened it with a welcoming smile. 'Miss Moon . . . Lily,
do come in out of the wet. It's an awful night, isn't it?'

The first thing she saw as she stepped inside were two candles
burning brightly on a table that took up the whole centre of the
room. They flickered as Louis hastily closed the door behind her
and she looked around curiously. The kitchen was at least twice as
big as the one back at their cottage and there was a large inglenook
fireplace in the centre of one wall. To one side of it was a deep stone
sink with a wooden draining board beneath a window, which, she
assumed, must look out over the back garden, if there was one. As
well as the table there were mismatched chairs standing around
it and a large dresser against the opposite wall, although it was

113

impossible to see if the furniture would be usable because it was covered with layers of dust. Red quarry tiles covered the floor, but again they were so dirty that it was hard to tell what condition they were in. There was also a large range cooker to the other side of the fireplace and Lily wondered if it was working.

'I know it doesn't look much at the minute,' Louis told her apologetically. 'But just have a look round and see if you think you and your family could live here.'

She nodded as she crossed to a door at the side of the dresser and found herself in a small front parlour. *Mam would love this*, she thought. She had always wanted a parlour, and although it was desperately in need of a good clean Lily could envisage how cosy it could be on a cold winter night with a fire blazing in the fireplace.

'Take this to look upstairs.' Louis handed her a candle and pointed to a second door that she found led to a steep staircase.

Lifting her skirt with one hand she held the candle aloft as she climbed. At the top, she found herself on a small landing with three doors leading off it. The first led to a fairly small room that she thought would be perfect for Annie when she got a little older. The other two rooms were much larger and contained iron bed-steads. There was even a wardrobe in one of them, but as Lily glanced up, she saw the sky through the roof in places.

'Don't worry about the roof.' Louis had come to join her. 'If you think the place will be suitable, I shall have all the repairs done before you move in. I'll also get some men here to cut the gardens down for you – I'm afraid they're rather overgrown. There's also a large garden out the back, an outside toilet and a well so you would have fresh water to hand. So . . . what do you think?'

'I think it could be quite lovely,' Lily told him with a smile, forgetting for the moment that she resented him and his family. The trouble was he was so easy to talk to. Nothing like his grandmother at all.

'Excellent!' He looked genuinely pleased. 'In that case I shall have some of my men start on the repairs tomorrow. I could get some of the maids up from the manor to clean it out for you as well, if you like?'

'Oh no, no, please don't do that,' she said hastily. She could just imagine the gossip it would cause when she and her family were seen to be getting preferential treatment. Things were going to be bad enough as it was. 'I'm quite capable of doing that myself before we move in.'

He shrugged. 'As you wish.' He gallantly stood aside and followed her down the stairs. 'I'll get a new key cut for you tomorrow for the kitchen door then you can come up whenever you like and do whatever you want to do.'

'Thank you.' They were back in the kitchen again and as their eyes momentarily locked, Lily felt colour flood up her neck and into her cheeks before she swiftly looked away.

'Right I, er . . . I'd better be gettin' home.'

'Of course. Would you like me to walk you back to the lane?'

'No . . . thank you, but I shall be fine.' And she was out of the door and walking away as fast as her legs would carry her, wondering why on earth he had suddenly had such a strange effect on her.

Louis stood in the doorway and watched till the night swallowed her up before going back inside to extinguish the candles and make his own way home.

'So, what did she say?' Lady Bellingham asked Louis tartly when he went to report to her in her bedchamber a short time later. She wasn't at all happy about Lily's family being offered one of their cottages to live in, but for once her grandson had stood his ground with her.

'She said that she thinks it will be suitable.'

'*Hmph!*' she snorted in disgust. 'We'll be the talk of the village when this gets out, you just mark my words, my lad,' she said scathingly.

'We'll worry about that when and if it happens,' Louis retorted. 'At the moment I'm just trying to keep my niece from being out on the streets!'

'Don't you *dare* call that flyblow that!' his grandmother stormed, rapping her cane on the floor in her temper.

'Why not, Grandmama? Because whether you accept her or not *that* is exactly who she is, and I for one intend to make sure she is always cared for.'

'You little *fool!*' Lady Bellingham glowered at him. 'You're going to rue this day, believe me!'

'We'll see.' With a short bow Louis turned and left without another word.

'Is there no *way* we can get rid of that girl, Hudson?' the old lady bellowed at her maid when he had gone.

Hudson shrugged. 'Not that I can see. I had a word with Mrs Biggles but she had no reason to call 'er. She says Lily is polite, punctual an' a hard worker.'

'Hmm, we'll see about that!'

The second Lily stepped into the cottage, her mother asked, 'So, how did the visit go, love? Was the cottage any good?' Poor Sara had made herself even more ill fretting about them all being turfed onto the street.

'Well, bear in mind I had to look at it by candlelight,' Lily told her, crossing the room to smile at Annie, who was lying on the rug in front of the fire kicking her heels in the air as she played with a wooden spoon. 'But I 'ave to say I liked what I saw. I've passed it a few times when I've been out walkin' but never took much notice

116

of it before. It's certainly a lot bigger than this place, an' the air feels so much cleaner up there than it does down here in the village – it'll be so much better for your chest. Mr Bellingham is goin' to see to any repairs that need doin' an' I won't lie, it's in a bit of a state at the minute because it's stood empty fer so long. But that ain't nothin' that a bit o' spit an' polish won't put right. I can go up there an' clean each night after I finish work if you can manage 'ere?'

'Of course I can.' Sara smiled for the first time in days. 'Meantime we've got the weddin' comin' up a week on Saturday. Between you an' me, Robbie don't seem too thrilled about it. I reckon he's only weddin' our Bridget cos she's havin' a baby an' I think she knows it.'

Lily shrugged. 'That's their problem, Mam. They're old enough to know what they're doin' so they'll just 'ave to make the best of it.'

Even so, she'd had an idea that might make Bridget slightly happier – not that she deserved it – and so on Saturday afternoon when she had finished work, she set off on the cart into Nuneaton. It was a busy market day and there were people milling about the many stalls, which sold everything from buttons and bows, and buckets and bowls to every sort of food she could imagine. To one end was the cattle market where farmers were shouting about the virtues of the animals they were selling, and as Lily passed the poor creatures enclosed in pens and crates, she couldn't help but feel sorry for them.

An hour later she set off for home again, pleased with her purchase, and when she got home, she was happy to see Bridget sitting at the table, still unsuccessfully trying to sew ribbons on to her best bonnet for her wedding day.

'Oh, *nothin'* I try on this damn thing is workin'!' Bridget flung the bonnet down in frustration and it skidded along the tabletop. 'I'm goin' to be the dullest bride to ever walk down the aisle,' she said resentfully, crossing her arms and pouting.

Lily winked at her mother and grinned. 'Not if I can help it you ain't,' she told her sister, handing her a large hatbox. ''Ere, 'appen this'll cheer you up a bit!'

Bridget's eyes stretched wide as she fell on the box and almost ripped the lid off. She gasped with pleasure when she saw what was inside. 'Oh, Lily . . . this is the bonnet I told yer about that were in the milliner's shop winder in Nuneaton.'

It was a pale blue, the same colour as the gown she would be wearing, with a wide brim lavishly trimmed with silk flowers and feathers, and ribbons that tied beneath the chin.

She quickly put it on and went to look in the mirror to see the effect, turning her head this way and that as she admired it. 'But how?'

Lily shrugged. 'Call it my weddin' present to you. I 'ad a little bit saved up an' wanted to treat yer.'

'Oh, but yer just the *best* sister ever!' Bridget cried, flinging her arms about her in a rare show of affection. Just for a moment, Lily felt a pang of resentment as she thought back to the way Bridget had seduced Robbie without a thought for her, but it was done now and Lily was not one for bearing grudges. Bridget was still her sister, after all.

'Now I shall look forward to the weddin'! I can 'ardly wait to wear it.' Bridget gently placed it back in the box and hurried away upstairs to put it in their room.

Sara smiled at Lily. 'That were a nice thing to do, love,' she said gently. 'Particularly as it were you walkin' out wi' Robbie not so long ago. This can't 'ave been easy for yer.'

'To be honest, I don't think me an' Robbie were ever right for each other, although I admit the way Bridget seduced him without a thought for me did sting,' Lily said, crossing to the pan of stew and dumplings that was bubbling on the range and lifting the lid. 'Mm, this smells delicious. Come on, let's eat, I'm starvin'.'

Over the next few days, Lily visited the cottage that was to be their new home every day and came away feeling pleased with the progress the men Louis had set to work on it were making. Two of them were replacing the broken and missing tiles from the roof and one of the gardeners was scything down the weeds and tidying up the outside. Bridget's wedding was just days away now and once that was over Lily intended to spend every spare minute she had cleaning the inside in readiness for them to move in.

Two nights before the wedding she came home to find Sara looking subdued. 'What's wrong?' she asked.

'Nothin' really.' Her mother sighed. 'It's just that Edie come round earlier on an' asked what we were goin' to do when our notice is up. I 'ad to tell 'er. After all, everyone will know soon enough, but yer should 'ave seen the look she gave me when I told 'er the Bellinghams were lettin' us rent a cottage from 'em. She asked if they were doin' the same fer all the other poor sods who lost their men down the pit and I felt terrible, I don't mind tellin' yer. I could see old Edie's mind doin' overtime an' I've no doubt it'll be all round the village by mornin'.'

'Oh well.' Lily shrugged and started to ladle the stew into bowls. 'As you said, it would 'ave come out sooner or later so try not to worry about it.'

On the night before the wedding, after finishing her day's work, Lily set off for home. Tonight Bridget was going to bathe in the tin bath in front of the fire and Lily had promised to iron her gown for her. For the past two days, Bridget had been taking her things to Robbie's house and it felt strange to think that this evening would be the last night she would spend in her old home.

As she turned out of the drive leading to Oakley Manor, she started when a shadow appeared out of the trees in front of her.

'Robbie! You startled me.' Then she frowned as she took in his appearance. He had clearly just finished his shift down the pit and

119

was still in his filthy work clothes. His face was unshaven and he looked upset as he twisted his sooty cap between his hands.

'Lily . . . I 'ad to see yer!' There was a note of desperation in his voice.

Lily paused before walking on feeling uncomfortable. 'Really? I don't know why. It's the night before yer weddin'.'

He fell into step beside her. 'Look, don't yer think this 'as gone far enough? You know it's you I want an' not Bridget. I've tried to tell yer before but yer won't listen to me. *Please* . . . just say the word an' I'll call the weddin' off. I don't even *like* Bridget. It's *you* I love! I only ever used 'er to get back at you cos she threw 'erself at me!'

Lily stopped abruptly and her eyes flashed in the gloomy night. 'It's a little late to be talkin' like this, don't yer think!' she stormed. 'How do yer think she'd feel if yer jilted 'er now? An' 'ave yer forgotten she's carryin' yer child? Anyway, I realise now that you an' me were *never* right fer each other so yer did me a favour when yer dropped me. I'm sorry, Robbie, but as me mother would say, "You've made yer bed an' now you'll 'ave to lie in it." So if you'll excuse me I 'ave to go an' help the bride get ready an' I don't ever – *ever* – want to 'ear yer talkin' to me like this again, do yer 'ear me?'

'But, Lily—'

She held her hand up as he attempted to get closer and lifting her skirts she raced on as if the devil himself were snapping at her heels. How would Bridget feel if she were ever to learn what he had just said to her? Hopefully she had made it clear to him how she felt and he would buckle down and accept his responsibilities. Even so, the encounter had left her feeling very uneasy.

By the time she reached the cottage she had managed to compose herself and she entered with a smile on her face, determined to make her sister's last night with her family as happy as it could be.

Chapter Eighteen

'Oh love, yer look *beautiful*,' Sara told Bridget the next morning as the girl preened in front of the mirror, wearing her new bonnet. And she did. Her face was glowing and she was smiling from ear to ear. Lily just prayed that Robbie wouldn't do anything silly and that he would turn up at the church. She couldn't begin to imagine how awful it would be for Bridget if he were to jilt her at the altar.

She and Sara were also clad in their Sunday best and little Annie looked adorable in a tiny pink dress that Sara had painstakingly smocked and embroidered for her. Richie, who would be giving the bride away, was uncomfortably tugging at the stiff starched collar of his white shirt. Sara had ordered a small posy of white roses from the florist in Nuneaton, which had cost a ridiculous sum – not that she begrudged it. It was her daughter's wedding day after all, although she was struggling with the fact that her beloved Bill wasn't there to walk his girl down the aisle. She had also ordered a small carriage to take Bridget to the church and now she told Lily, 'Right, we'd best set off. The carriage will be 'ere to collect Bridget soon an' we don't want 'er to get to the church afore us, do we?' She kissed Bridget, then leaning heavily on Lily, who was carrying Annie, the two set off.

Thankfully the church was within walking distance but they hadn't gone very far before the cold air made Sara start coughing and they had to pause.

'Are you all right, Mam?' Lily said with concern.

Sara forced a smile. 'Right as ninepence, love. It's just the cold air makin' me cough. But it could 'ave been worse. It could 'ave been rainin'. Come on, let's get a shufty on, eh?'

The first thing Lily saw when they entered the church was Robbie with his chin on his chest standing next to his best man to one side of the altar. He looked more like a man attending a funeral than one who was about to get wed, but Lily felt little sympathy for him. She led her mother to the front pew and they took their seats. There were only a handful of people there, including Robbie's parents who looked almost as miserable as Robbie. The church was lit by a number of tall pillar candles and the leaden grey sky cast an eerie light through the stained-glass windows.

Soon the organist struck up the wedding march and Bridget appeared at the top of the aisle, her hand resting on the arm of her brother, who solemnly led her to her groom. Her face was alight with happiness and no one could deny that she looked very beautiful as she reached Robbie, who kept his head down and didn't even look at her.

For a fleeting second Lily saw Bridget frown but then the service began and her eyes turned to the vicar.

'Dearly beloved, we are gathered here today in the presence of God and this congregation to join together this man and this woman in holy matrimony,' he began. The service continued until at last it was time for the couple to take their vows and the vicar asked them to turn to each other.

'Do you Robert John Berry take Bridget Joan Moon to be your lawful wife, to have and to hold, for richer for poorer . . .' The vicar's voice droned on until suddenly there was silence as Robbie stood without responding.

'Ahem . . .' The vicar coughed and hot, humiliated colour flamed into Bridget's cheeks.

For a terrible moment Lily thought Robbie wasn't going to go through with the marriage, but finally in a small voice that hardly anyone could hear, he whispered reluctantly, 'I do.'

Lily let out a sigh of relief but the damage was done. Everyone present could see that Robbie wasn't happy – none more so than

Bridget and she would never forgive him. After they'd signed the register, they walked straight-faced down the aisle to be showered in rice as they left the church. But neither of them were smiling, and Lily couldn't help but feel sorry for her sister.

The few guests made their way back to the church hall where Robbie's mother had laid on a small buffet, but the atmosphere was strained and Bridget turned her back on her new husband as people helped themselves to the food. After an acceptable amount of time had passed the first guests made their escape, closely followed by Lily and her family, who hugged Bridget and wished her well before leaving with the Mannings.

'I 'ave to say, Sara,' Edie commented with a wicked grin, 'young Robbie were about the most reluctant bridegroom I've ever set eyes on. There were a time durin' the service when I thought he were gonna walk out!'

Sara flushed. 'It was probably just nerves,' she said lightly, although in truth she couldn't have agreed more. 'But anyway, it's done now an' I've no doubt they'll do well together. Robbie ain't a bad lad.'

'Hmm, funny though, ain't it? I mean, seein' as she couldn't get 'im down the aisle quick enough.' There was a malicious little glint in her eye but Sara chose to ignore it and they walked the rest of the way home in silence.

'Phew, well I'm glad that's over,' Sara said as she dropped into the fireside chair when they got back home. Richie had already shot upstairs to get out of his uncomfortable shirt and suit and Annie had dozed off in Lily's arms on the walk back from the small reception. 'But fair dos to 'er, Martha Berry laid on a good spread. It'll be funny wi'out our Bridget comin' 'ome of an evenin', won't it? An' it felt wrong wi' yer dad and our Teddy not bein' there to see 'er wed,' she ended sadly, wiping a tear from her cheek.

Lily laid Annie gently in her crib and, hoping to lighten the mood, she suggested, 'How about I put the kettle on an' we'll 'ave a nice cup o' tea, eh? Then I'm goin' to get Richie to 'elp me get some o' the cleanin' stuff up to the cottage so I can make a start on gettin' it ready fer us to move into.'

Sara brightened a little at that. She would have loved nothing more than to go up and have a good look at it herself and help, but the walk to the church had worn her out and she doubted she would manage it today.

Half an hour later, in her oldest gown and with her hair tied back with a ribbon, Lily and Richie loaded as much cleaning stuff as they would need into their old wooden hand barrow and set off for the cottage. The sky had darkened and once again the wind was howling as they breathlessly dragged the cart between them up the valley.

When they arrived, there were still men on the roof doing last-minute jobs, but it was mostly finished, and Richie went from room to room with a broad smile on his face. 'Why, this place is over twice as big as the one we live in now,' he said happily, leaning over the deep stone sink and staring out of the grimy window. 'An' just look at this back garden. It's huge. We could 'ave us some chickens an' our own eggs. There's an old pigsty there an all. It only needs a bit o' work to make it sound again. An' there's fruit trees an' a vegetable plot.'

'You approve?' There was a twinkle in Lily's eyes as she saw him looking so happy.

'Approve? I bloody *love* it. An' Mam's goin' to love it an' all. Just think 'ow nice it'll be fer Annie to 'ave a garden to play in when she's a bit bigger. I could run a pipe from the well to the sink so as yer could pump the water instead o' havin' to fetch it in in buckets an all, if yer like?'

'That sounds like a wonderful idea,' she told him indulgently. The wedding might not have gone as well as she had hoped but at least Richie was happy.

They unloaded the cart and Richie fetched water so they could get cracking on the cleaning.

'Don't get tryin' to light the fire though,' he warned after staring up the chimney. 'It looks like there could be a bird's nest in there so it'll need sweepin' afore we move in. I could borrow some brushes an' do it meself,' he offered.

Lily nodded. She wasn't going to turn down an offer of any help and was just pleased that her brother liked the place as much as she did.

An hour later, Lily was down on her hands and knees scrubbing away at the tiled floor in the kitchen when the man who had been repairing the roof tapped on the door. 'The roof's all finished now, miss. Yer shouldn't 'ave any leaks from it now.'

She thanked him and carried on, but the light was fast fading. Richie had had to leave to go for band practice and she was enjoying the peace of the place when a large shadow blocked the doorway and whirling about with her heart in her mouth, she saw Louis Bellingham standing there.

'Sorry, Lily. Did I startle you? I just dropped by to see how you were getting on.' His eyes swept the room taking in the clean floor and the shining windows, and he was impressed at how much she had already achieved. 'It looks different already,' he praised. 'Do you think you and your family will be happy here?'

'I'm sure we shall be, sir.' She bobbed her knee.

He frowned. 'Look . . . couldn't you just call me Louis? There's no need for all this sir and Mr Bellingham!'

'I'm not so sure your grandmother would agree with that,' she said wryly.

He sighed. She was quite right, of course. His grandmother was an awful snob but he liked Lily and had hoped that she would learn to trust him. 'What she doesn't know won't hurt her,' he commented, admiring the dresser. It had been under layers of dust

125

the last time he had seen it but now it had been polished until it shone, as had the table and chairs.

'Is there anything I can do to help?'

Lily almost laughed aloud as she looked at his expensive jodhpurs and riding jacket. 'Thank you, but no. I shall have to be leaving soon myself; it's getting dark.'

'Right.' He suddenly thought of the evening ahead and his spirits dipped. His parents had invited some friends of theirs for dinner with their daughter who Louis knew his parents saw as a possible wife for him. He had met the girl in question, Samantha Thompson, at a number of social events and while she had the face of an angel, she was so incredibly spoilt and pampered that he wasn't looking forward to being forced to spend any time in her company. Suddenly remembering something he fished in his pocket and handed her two keys. 'I had these cut for you so you can lock the place up when you come and go if you wish. And of course, you're welcome to move in whenever you're ready.'

'Thank you.' She slipped the keys into the pocket of her apron and after insisting that she mustn't hesitate to ask if there was anything more he could do for her, Louis left.

Lily watched him ride away before finishing the job she'd been doing and setting off for home. As she entered the village, she passed the Berrys' cottage and glancing through the window, she saw Robbie and Bridget sitting stiffly side by side on the horsehair sofa looking as miserable as sin.

If that's what being married is I don't think I'll bother, she thought ruefully.

Three days later, after finishing work and going straight to the cottage to clean another bedroom by candlelight, Lily arrived home to find Bridget sitting by the fire staring glumly into the flames with a mug of tea in her hands. Although she was exhausted, she raised a smile for her sister and said cheerfully, 'Hello, Bridget. And how is married life suiting you?'

Bridget stuck her chin in the air. 'It's fine! Why wouldn't it be?'

'All right, I was only asking. There's no need to snap me 'ead off,' Lily answered irritably as she crossed to the table to pour herself a cup of tea. Bridget certainly didn't look too happy but she decided it was best not to comment.

Her mother glanced at her and raised her eyebrow. 'And 'ow are things coming along at the cottage?' she asked anxiously. She felt guilty because she wasn't well enough to go and help and Bridget certainly hadn't offered.

'If you 'ave the curtains ready, I can start 'anging them tomorrow,' Lily told her as she kicked her boots off and held her cold feet out to the cheery flames. She was so tired that she was sure she could have slept for a month but she was also proud of what she had achieved so far. The cottage was almost unrecognisable from the way it had been when she first went to see it. Richie had swept the chimney as promised and had also chopped a load of wood ready for them to light the fire when they moved in.

'I can't wait to see it,' Sara said.

Bridget sniffed. 'It must be nice to get preferential treatment from the gaffer's son,' she quipped sarcastically. 'I wonder what you've done to deserve it?'

'I haven't done anything. Louis is just trying to help because we lost Dad down his father's pit, and on top of that me and Richie still work up at the manor for the family,' Lily snapped back.

'Hmm, or perhaps he's keen to make sure that Annie 'as a home.'

'That's *quite* enough.' Sara stepped in to prevent what she could see developing into a full-scale row. 'And I'm shocked that you begrudge us 'aving a home to go to, our Bridget.'

Bridget shrugged and slammed her mug onto the table. 'It just don't seem fair that me an' Robbie can't even find a 'ome of our own,' she complained. 'It could be ages afore another pit cottage comes up for rent. You don't know what it's like 'aving to live wi' that witch of a mother of 'is. It's "Bridget do this, Bridget do that" all day long!'

'Perhaps you shouldn't 'ave given yer job up so soon then,' her mother suggested.

'Why should I go to work when I 'ave a 'usband to keep me? Anyway, I'm off.' She snatched up her shawl and slammed out of the room with a face like thunder.

'Oh dear, I 'ave a feeling things aren't going so well fer 'er,' Sara said worriedly. 'Although I 'ave to say she only has 'erself to blame fer the mess she's in.'

'They'll settle down,' Lily told her kindly – she hated to see her mother upset. 'It's probably just that everything is new to them.'

'Let's 'ope so.' But if the way Robbie had acted in church was anything to go by, Sara wasn't so sure.

Chapter Nineteen

It was the night before they were to move, and in the small cottage everything was hustle and bustle as Lily tried to get the last of their things packed. Richie had hired a horse and cart from Eddie Brewster the baker to transport Sara, Annie and their possessions up the hill to their new home. With Sara's cough getting no better it was too far for her to walk.

'Phew, I never realised we had so much stuff between us,' Richie huffed as he dumped a large pillowcase full of bed linen down at the side of the front door. 'Are you sure you'll be able to help lift the furniture onto the cart, Lily?'

'Of course I will,' she assured him.

As it happened, though, she soon found out she wouldn't need to, for as they were sitting down to enjoy a much needed cup of tea, the door suddenly opened and Sara cried out with delight as she sprang out of her seat and raced towards it.

'Oh, *Teddy* . . . we didn't know when to expect yer! What a lovely surprise this is. How long are yer home for?'

She almost knocked him over as she threw herself into his arms and Teddy chuckled as he lifted her from her feet and swung her round as if she weighed no more than a feather.

'I 'ad no way o' lettin' yer know I were comin,' he explained as he stood her back down and threw his kitbag to one side. 'I'll be able to stay fer about five days. Me ship sails again in a week so I 'ave to allow enough time to get back to the docks.' He looked about the bare room and the curtainless windows and frowned. 'But what's goin' on 'ere? An' where's me dad an' Bridget?'

129

Sara gulped to swallow the tears that had sprung to her eyes as she led him to the chair to the side of the fire and pressed him down onto it.

'I'm afraid shortly after yer left there were a fall down the mine an' . . . yer dad didn't get out alive. I'm so sorry yer 'ad to find out like this, lad, but we 'ad no way o' lettin' yer know. As fer Bridget, she's married to Robbie now an' they're goin' to 'ave a baby.'

Teddy looked stunned and the ruddy colour drained out of his cheeks. He could hardly believe that so much had happened since he had been gone and was heartbroken to think that he would never see his father again. With an effort he managed to compose himself and asked, 'An' what's all this?' He waved towards the many bags and boxes piled by the door.

Slowly Sara explained about them being given notice to quit and about the way Louis Bellingham had stepped in and offered them another cottage to live in.

He shook his head. 'Huh! I bet that went down well wi' the neighbours!'

Sara nodded. 'Mm, 'alf of them 'ave always thought that Annie were our Lily's baby, but they're convinced of it now an' they think Louis Bellingham is her dad! Still, like I said to our Lily, sticks an' stones can break our bones but words can never 'urt us!'

'An' what about our Bridget, eh? I mean, I knew they were walkin' out, but I didn't expect them to wed, let alone 'ave a baby. How do yer feel about that, Lily?'

Lily shrugged and poured him a cup of tea. 'To be honest, I don't think Robbie were ever the one fer me. An' anyway, we've been so busy gettin' the new cottage ready that I ain't 'ad much chance to think about it for a while. I'll just be glad when we've gone from 'ere. It ain't the same wi'out dad an' I reckon the cleaner air up at the new place will be better for Mam.'

'When is the move?'

She grinned. 'Tomorrow as it 'appens. You couldn't 'ave timed your leave better. Richie were just askin' me if I'd manage to 'elp 'im get all the heavy stuff onto the cart in the mornin'.'

'Well, there yer go. Yer won't 'ave to worry about that now, will yer? Where are we goin'?' He was thinking it was a good job he had turned up when he did, otherwise he might have come back to find someone else living there and panicked.

Lily told him and he nodded. 'I reckon I know the place. But ain't it a bit run down? If it's the one I'm thinkin' of it's stood empty fer years.'

'It had,' she agreed. 'But Louis . . . Lord Bellingham got some of his men in to fix it up for us and I've been going up there cleanin' every night for the last two weeks so all we need to do is put the furniture in an' put everythin' away now.' She grinned ruefully as she showed him her work-reddened hands.

He tutted. 'Didn't our Bridget come an' help yer?'

'Did she 'ell as like,' Sara said with a shake of her head. 'Yer know what our Bridget is like – she likes to be waited on. Goodness knows 'ow she'll go on when she 'as a cryin' baby to look after. But that's enough about us; tell us where you've been an' what you've been doin'.'

For the next half an hour they sat enthralled listening to the places in France Teddy had been to. It sounded like another world to them, for none of them, apart from Lily, had ever ventured further than Nuneaton. Eventually everyone retired to bed and there was only Lily and Teddy left downstairs in the dim glow from the dying fire.

'It seems strange to think that this is our last night in this place,' Lily said sadly. 'It might not be much but it's always been 'ome to us, ain't it?'

Teddy nodded. And after lifting the candle he lit the way up the steep narrow staircase. Tomorrow looked set to be a long day.

Thankfully they awoke early the next morning to a dry day and Lily sighed with relief as she set about frying some bacon and eggs while Richie went to fetch the horse and cart from Eddie Brewster.

An hour later they started to pile everything on the back of it until the house stood empty.

'That's it then, Mam.' Teddy gave Sara a smile as he handed her old shawl to her. 'Let me take Annie out to the cart while yer say yer goodbyes to the place.' Gently he took Annie from her arms and left Sara alone.

She stood in the centre of the room staring around as memories flooded back. She could remember Bill carrying her over the threshold as a bride on the day they were wed. They had been so happy then, with their lives stretching ahead of them. All of her children had been born in the upstairs bedroom while her beloved Bill nervously paced this very floor waiting for news. They had faced good and bad times, but always together and now she realised that although she would be leaving this cottage forever, she would be taking her memories with her and that made it a little easier. And so with a sigh she had one last glance around before closing the door behind her.

Edie Manning was standing by the cart with her arms crossed beneath her large chest.

'This is it then, eh, Sara.' She sighed with a loud sniff. 'I shall miss yer, gel.'

'You can come an' see us whenever yer want,' Sara assured her. 'You'll always be welcome, Edie.'

'Aye, 'appen I'll do that when you've 'ad time to settle in. Good luck – not that you'll need it.'

Ignoring the hint of sarcasm in her old neighbour's voice, Sara let Teddy help her up onto the bench seat of the cart, then he passed Annie up to her, and at last they set off, with Richie driving and Lily and Teddy walking alongside.

As the old horse toiled up the valley, they looked back. This wide-open space was so different to the cramped rows of tiny terraced houses they were used to and they knew it was going to take some getting used to.

At last the cottage appeared in front of them and Lily frowned as she saw a plume of smoke rising from the chimney. She had laid a fire in the inglenook the night before ready for them to put a light to and she had no idea who might already have lit it. Richie drove the old horse up to the little picket fence and secured the reins and they all trooped inside. The freshly washed diamond-leaded windows were gleaming in the dull sunshine and now that all the weeds had been scythed down and removed it looked neat and tidy.

'Oh, it's lovely!' Sara gasped in delight at the first glimpse of her new home. She had been trying to picture what it might be like in her mind's eye but it was so much better than she'd hoped for. As they entered the kitchen the warmth from the fire met them and Lily's eyes immediately fell on a large wicker hamper that had been placed on the table with an envelope with her name on it propped against it. As her mother and Teddy set off to explore the rooms, she tore it open and quickly read the short message inside.

Dear Lily,

I hope you will excuse me for taking the liberty of getting one of the maids to come up and light the fire for you this morning. I thought you might be tired and cold by the time you arrived. I have also got Cook to put together this hamper for you to save you having to cook today. I'm sure you will be busy settling in. I do hope you will all be very happy in your new home. If there is anything else that I can do for you, please don't hesitate to ask.

With kind regards,

Louis

Lily flushed as she opened the lid of the hamper and gazed at the contents. There was a large roast chicken, still warm from the oven, and two freshly baked loaves. There was a slab of butter and another of cheese and a dozen eggs, as well as a large jar of pickled onions and what looked like an enormous meat pie. There was also a large fruit cake and an assortment of biscuits along with several jars of jam.

'What's this then, love?' Sara came to stand beside her and gazed at the gifts in amazement.

'It's, er . . . from Louis.' She pushed the note into her mother's hand and blushed furiously as Sara read it.

'Why, bless 'is soul.' Sara beamed. 'I don't know about not 'aving to cook today – this lot'll keep us goin' for a good couple o' days at least. What a kind soul 'e is, eh?'

'Either that or it's his guilty conscience,' Lily answered as she dropped the lid on the hamper. 'Now, let's get the sofa in an' then you can sit wi' Annie while we bring the rest o' the stuff in.'

By mid-afternoon the place was beginning to look like home. Everything had been carried in and Richie had left to return the horse and cart to Eddie Brewster while Teddy did a tour of the outside.

With the chairs set out and the rugs on the floor the downstairs looked warm and cosy and now Lily was upstairs putting the clean linen on the beds.

'We'll 'ave to keep us eye out fer some second-'and furniture fer the parlour,' Sara commented happily. 'The other place were so much smaller than this that there ain't nowt to put in there as yet. Still, I can wait. I've allus wanted a separate little parlour.' She was also very impressed with having her very own bedroom and was thrilled with the furniture Lily had managed to salvage. Unfortunately, after a good clean some of the pieces had been found to be full of woodworm so Lily and Richie had carried them outside and stacked them in readiness for a bonfire.

Now Sara was sitting to the side of the inglenook giving Annie her milk with a contented smile on her face.

'Just hark at that!'

'At what?' Richie paused but couldn't hear a thing apart from the birds singing. 'All I can 'ear is the birds.'

'Quite. Down in the village we could 'ear the pit an' the sound o' the men's boots on the cobblestones as they went to work. It's so peaceful 'ere, ain't it? I reckon we're goin' to like it.'

'How could we not?' Richie grinned. 'Soon as I can, I'm gonna get some wood to mend the sty so we can 'ave a pig an' I reckon some o' the hen coops in the garden can be repaired, so we can get us some birds an' all. I could go into Nuneaton an' get some from the cattle market when we're ready. Imagine 'aving our own eggs, eh? An' that garden . . .' He sighed with pleasure as he pictured how it would be when he'd done some work on it. 'I'm gonna do a grassy area fer Annie to play in when she's a bit bigger an' fix 'er a swing up in the old oak tree. I shall be plantin' some veg soon an' all when the weather improves a bit.'

His mother smiled. He was clearly very happy with the move and in truth she was too, although it still felt very strange. If it hadn't been for having her own familiar things about her, she would have thought she was sitting in someone else's home.

At teatime they tucked into some of the food Louis had sent and then the two young men decided to go for a drink.

'We're off up the Plough,' they told their mother.

Sara smiled indulgently. 'Good, you've certainly earned it today. Go on the pair of you an' enjoy yerselves, but don't go gettin' plastered, mind! I don't reckon our Lily would 'ave the strength left to put yer both to bed tonight.'

An hour later, Sara retired early to spend her first night in her new bedroom, with Annie in her crib at the side of her, and Lily settled down at the table to do some sketching. Tonight, she did a sketch of the inglenook with the flames roaring up the chimney and the brass pans she had hung on the beam above it glistening. Then, tired but happy, she turned down the oil lamp on the table so that her brothers wouldn't come home to darkness and went off to her own room where she fell into an exhausted sleep almost the instant her head hit the pillow.

Chapter Twenty

Lily reported for work bright and early on Monday morning to be greeted caustically by the cook.

'Oh, you're back, are you? Nice when you can get time off just when yer want it, eh?'

'I was allowed time off to move into our new home,' Lily retaliated. Just then her eyes settled on Ginny Davis, a young neighbour from further along Valley Road.

'Hello, Ginny.' Lily gave her a friendly smile, for the poor girl looked petrified.

'Ginny's goin' to be the new kitchen maid, if I can ever get the stupid girl to understand what she's supposed to be doin'.' The cook glared at the girl. 'The young master took her on – the rest o' the family's had to go into the workhouse, the poor sods. Her dad died in the pit fall same as yours but no one else got offered a cottage.'

Ignoring the sarcastic remark, Lily began to prepare old Lady Bellingham's tray – it had been some time since she had come down to dine with the family now – and once that was done, she was kept busy until lunchtime, when she finally had a chance to have a word with Ginny.

'How are you?' she asked gently as they sat together snatching a hasty cup of tea before it was time to get back to work. The rest of the staff had ignored Lily in the main and had made it more than clear that they didn't approve of her family getting preferential treatment from the young master.

Ginny glanced fearfully at the cook before answering in a small voice, 'I'm all right . . . but I miss me mam an' me family. I can only go to see 'em on Sunday on me afternoon off.'

Lily's heart went out to her. Ginny was just fourteen years old and young for her age and she wouldn't say boo to a goose, so Lily could only imagine how fearsome the cook must appear to her. She was the oldest of the Davis brood and Lily guessed how hard it must be for them all to be parted.

At that moment there was a scratching on the back door and when one of the maids went to answer it a small bundle of fluff with its tail wagging furiously barged past her and rushed straight to Ginny who bent to fondle the little dog's silky ears.

'That *damned* dog again,' Cook roared, waving her wooden spoon at it. 'I swear I'll get one o' the men to shoot the bloody flea-ridden thing if it keeps pushin' its way into my clean kitchen!'

Ginny's eyes brimmed with tears as she caught the piece of rope tied about the dog's neck. 'S-sorry, Cook.' She looked petrified as she tried to drag the animal back to the door. It was a funny little thing, black and tan with a long furry coat, which looked in need of brushing, and huge soft brown eyes. 'It's only cos she don't know where to go now. She followed me 'ere when me mam an' the kids went to the work'ouse an' I can't make 'er understand that I can't keep 'er anymore.'

'What's her name?' Lily asked gently.

'Sassy! We've 'ad her since she were a pup an' now she's homeless.'

'As if we need yet another stray wanderin' about the place!' Cook huffed. 'If she goes anywhere near the stables an' upsets any o' the horses one o' the grooms *will* shoot the bloody cur. And the sooner the better, I say!'

'There'll be no need for that,' Lily said quickly. 'Let her stay in the boot room until I finish me shift an' then I'll take her home wi' me.'

'*What?* You mean you'll keep the damned thing?' Cook was incredulous. 'Then you're even dafter than I took you for. An' what's yer mam goin' to say when you turn up wi' another mouth to feed?'

'She'll be fine.' Lily scooped the little bundle of fur into her arms. She could feel the poor thing's ribs and guessed she must have been surviving by scavenging for some days.

'Well, on your head be it!' Cook said with a sneer, and turning about she continued to beat the batter she was making for the Yorkshire puddings.

When her shift finished that evening, Lily went to the boot room to collect the dog and after tying another length of rope to the one about her neck she led her out into the chilly night. Despite what she'd said she had no idea how her mother was going to react when she met Sassy but she needn't have worried. As soon as Sara set eyes on her and Lily told her what had happened, her mother's eyes filled with tears.

'That poor family,' she whispered as Sassy slunk up to her on her belly and licked her hand. 'Give her some stew out of the pan on the range, Lily. The poor thing isn't as far through as a line prop. She must be starving. And then you can take her outside and give her a good wash in the tin bath. She can stay but I don't want her bringing fleas into the cottage.'

And so after dinner Lily found herself outside up to her arms in water rubbing carbolic soap into Sassy's matted fur. The little dog looked three shades lighter after her bath, and once she had been brushed, she settled down on the rug in front of the fire as if she had always been there.

'Poor little thing,' Sara said. 'I just wish we could help the whole family.'

At that moment there was a tap on the door and when Lily hurried to answer it, she was shocked to see Louis Bellingham.

'Good evening, Lily. I thought I'd just pop by and make sure that you all have everything you need.'

Lily stood aside and he stepped past her, stopping abruptly to look around in amazement.

'Why, you've done wonders with the place,' he praised. He nodded towards Sara who smiled proudly as she followed his eyes around her new home.

'We're very comfortable, sir. It's so much bigger than I expected. We ain't even got enough furniture to fill the parlour yet, but it'll come in time. And thank you kindly for the lovely hamper you left for us. It was much appreciated.'

'You are most welcome. And I heard on the grapevine that you gained a new member of the family today.'

'We did indeed. Our Lily couldn't think o' the poor little thing bein' left to fend for herself,' Sara answered as she glanced down at Sassy who was snoring softly, her damp coat steaming in the heat from the fire.

'Quite right too. But is there anything else you need?' As always, his eyes were searching the room for a sight of Annie, and when they settled on her crib where she lay blowing bubbles, his face softened.

'She's so beautiful, isn't she?' he said quietly as he crossed to her, and she gave him a toothless grin. Annie always had a ready smile for anyone.

'Yes, she is.' Lily had gone to stand beside him. 'But I thought your mother had invited Miss Thompson and her parents to dinner again? Shouldn't you be joining them?'

He grinned ruefully. 'Yes, I should, and I will be shortly, although I suppose the talk will all be about Arabella's forthcoming wedding as usual! I just wanted to make sure you had everything you needed.'

'We do, thank you,' Lily answered primly and he nodded.

'In that case I shall leave you all to enjoy your evening. Good night.' Louis gave a gallant little bow to Sara and with a smile at

140

Lily he turned to leave before pausing at the door and looking towards Sara again.

'I was wondering . . .' he began hesitantly. 'You mentioned that you're needing some furniture for the parlour, and it just so happens that we have an outbuilding rammed with stuff my mother has replaced over time. She's notorious for changing her mind about things, I'm afraid. Would you be offended if I had some sent over to you? I wouldn't mind at all if it wasn't suitable and you chose not to use it.'

'Well, I, er . . .' Sara blushed prettily and Louis smiled.

'I'll get what I think may be of use to you and one of the men will bring it across. But now I must be off. Good night again.'

'I wonder what he really came for?' Sara mused when he had gone. 'I could almost believe he had a fancy for you, our Lily!'

'Don't be so silly,' Lily snapped. 'What would someone of his standin' be botherin' wi' someone like me for? Why, he's one o' the most eligible bachelors in the county.'

'He might well be, but stranger things have happened.' Then seeing that Lily wasn't amused Sara quickly changed the subject and Lily went to help Richie hang the sketches their father had painstakingly framed for her about the walls. The place really did feel like home once that was done.

When Lily got into work the next morning, the first thing she spotted was a huge black eye on Ginny.

'Whatever happened to you? You look like you've done ten rounds wi' a pugilist,' she said worriedly as she lifted Ginny's chin and examined the bruise.

'It were her own fault,' Cook said smartly. 'The silly little devil dropped yet another plate an' when I went to clip 'er ear she turned 'er head.'

Ginny quickly stepped away from Lily and with her head bowed began to clear the table. Most of the staff had finished their breakfasts but Lily noticed that none of them attempted to speak to her and the reason why soon became clear.

'We heard you 'ad a visitor last night?'

Lily stared at the cook. 'Oh, did you?' It was more than clear that someone had spotted Louis coming or going to the cottage and so the gossips were at it again. She supposed under the circumstances that she should have expected it.

'Aye, Master Louis. Fancy . . . I've never 'eard of him visitin' any of the other servants before.' Cook's voice held a wealth of meaning and Lily felt herself flush. She really was a nosy old bat!

'He just popped by to check that all was well,' she responded defensively. 'He wasn't there more than a few minutes.'

'Oh yes? I thought perhaps he'd called to see the baby.'

Lily's heart sank as she fetched Lady Bellingham's tray to start the daily routine. Now she understood! She was perfectly aware that some people suspected Annie was hers, and that when they were given the cottage some had started to assume that Louis was the father, but this was the first time she'd been confronted by it so bluntly. Clamping her lips together, Lily gave Ginny a sympathetic smile and left the room, reminding herself that she would need to warn Louis of what was being said the next time she saw him. Should word of his visits to the cottage ever get back to his parents it could cause untold trouble for him and he didn't deserve it. He was the only one of the Bellinghams who had ever shown an ounce of concern for Annie and she appreciated that.

Her worst fears were realised when Richie arrived home shortly after her that evening. 'Everyone in the stables 'as been sayin' they think Master Bellingham is Annie's dad an' you're her mam!'

Lily's stomach sank. 'I know; Cook were droppin' hints this morning.' She started to chew nervously on her lip.

'Oh, let 'em gossip.' Sara was angry. 'That's the trouble wi' folks round 'ere! They're always too keen to jump to conclusions!'

'But if you look at it from their point of view it must look fishy,' Lily pointed out.

Sara shook her head. 'Just let it go over your head an' forget about it,' she urged and although Lily nodded, she thought it might prove to be easier said than done.

It was mid-morning the following day when Mrs Biggles approached Lily to tell her, 'Miss Arabella wants to see you, Moon. *Now!*'

'*Me?*' Lily looked surprised. She had avoided Arabella as much as possible since last time they'd spoken but now with a sigh, she laid down the beeswax polish and duster she'd been using on the dining-room table and, straightening her apron and cap, she made her way upstairs.

'Oh, Lily . . . here you are.' Arabella had been pacing up and down her room but as Lily entered, she immediately crossed to close the door behind her.

'Is something wrong, miss?' Lily was respectful but cold and Arabella sensed it.

'Oh, *please* don't hate me for what I did, Lily.' Arabella's eyes welled with tears. 'You know how besotted I was with Freddie and you are the only one I can talk to about it. But it isn't that I needed to speak to you about. You might have heard that my lady's maid has been called away indefinitely due to an illness in her family. It's most inconvenient with the wedding fast approaching but it seems her mother is very ill so she's had to go to her – goodness knows how long for! Anyway, Mama informed me last evening that I must go to London to have the final fitting for my wedding dress and seeing as Brookes isn't here to accompany me, I wondered if you would? Mama says she doesn't feel well enough to go at present.'

Lily frowned. 'I don't know about that,' she said cautiously. The trouble Arabella had caused her and her family after the last time she had gone away with her was still very fresh in her mind, and she was still trying to live down the gossip, while Arabella appeared to have walked away without a single blemish on her character or a single thought for the baby she had so callously abandoned. 'The thing is, my own mother isn't well and now that she has a baby to care for while I'm at work . . .'

'I do understand.' Arabella placed her hand on her arm and stared at her beseechingly. 'Oh, *please* say you'll come, Lily. We needn't be gone for more than two or three days at the most. We will travel by train and stay at my parents' London house in Kensington. You might actually enjoy seeing a little of London. I presume you've never been there before?'

'Well . . . no, I haven't,' Lily admitted; it was a place she had always wanted to see. 'But before I give you an answer, I'll have to check with my mother that she could manage with Annie on her own while I was gone.'

'Oh, thank you. Will you let me know in the morning? You'll never know how grateful I would be.'

Lily nodded and after bobbing her knee she quietly left the room. As she reached the hallway, she could vaguely hear Cook screeching at poor Ginny through the green baize door that led to the kitchen and she felt sorry for the girl, but she had enough things of her own to worry about for now so she decided to ignore it. Poor Ginny would just have to learn to stand up to Cook, otherwise the sharp-tongued woman would make the girl's life hell.

When she arrived home, she found her mother bossily telling Richie where she wanted their new furniture to be placed in the parlour. One of the groundsmen from the manor had brought it on the back of a cart earlier in the morning and Sara could hardly believe her luck.

'Look at this sideboard,' she said excitedly. 'I never thought I'd own anythin' like this in me whole life!'

Lily had to admit it was a beautiful piece, although it took up almost the whole of one wall in the small parlour. It was coated with thick layers of dust but she could imagine how lovely it would look after a good clean and polish.

'An' there's this lovely sofa an' all! Ain't it grand? An' a leather wing chair to go with it. An' look at this dainty little side table, an' this plant stand. Did you ever see anythin' so posh?'

Lily sighed. As beautiful as the pieces were, she wasn't entirely happy about her mother accepting them. She really didn't want to be any more beholden to Louis Bellingham than they already were. But seeing the pleasure on her mother's face how could she begrudge her?

'They're very nice,' she murmured, before going back into the kitchen to get herself a well-earned cup of tea.

Chapter Twenty-One

A week later Lily kissed her mother and Annie goodbye and, dressed in her Sunday best linsey-woolsey skirt and a plain white linen blouse beneath her drab grey cloak, set off for the manor clutching a small valise. Her mother had insisted that she would be fine on her own for a few days while Lily went to London, after all, she had pointed out, Richie would still be there so she had encouraged her to go.

Arabella had been ecstatic when Lily had told her that she would accompany her, although Lily still had grave misgivings. But, she had asked herself, what could go wrong this time? They would only be gone for three nights if all went to plan, although if there were any more alterations to be made to Arabella's gown it could possibly be for a little longer, but hopefully all would be well.

The carriage was already at the entrance when she came to the end of the drive and seconds later Arabella appeared dressed in a beautiful two-piece travelling costume in a soft green velvet, trimmed with black braid, and a frilled white blouse. Over it she wore a warm cloak, and a matching hat was perched at a jaunty angle on her hair. And yet despite her fine clothes her face looked gaunt and the clothes seemed to hang off her – she certainly didn't look like a young woman who was looking forward to her wedding day.

'Ah, Lily, here you are.' She rushed forward to meet her across the carriage sweep. 'I was afraid you were going to be late.'

'You said nine o'clock and I'm a few minutes early,' Lily responded in a clipped voice. She was already regretting her decision.

Arabella took her valise from her and gave it to the coachman to stow on top of the carriage with her own luggage, which looked to Lily like enough clothes to last her for a month rather than a few days. But then, as she had discovered since working there, the gentry always took too many clothes when they went away. There were morning gowns, day gowns and evening gowns as well as the many petticoats and nightwear the women always insisted they would need.

Arabella ushered her into the carriage and as it pulled away, she flashed Lily a grateful smile. 'Thank you so much for agreeing to come with me.'

Things were still a little strained between them but even so Lily was quite looking forward to catching her first glimpse of London, although she doubted there would be much time for sightseeing.

At the train station the coachman hailed a porter to stow the luggage in the hold at the back of the train while Lily and Arabella made their way to the platform. The train arrived a short time later in a puff of steam and smoke that floated amongst the rafters of the station and Arabella urged her inside. They were fortunate to find a carriage to themselves and Lily settled down for the journey ahead feeling rather apprehensive. It was the first time she had ever been on a train, but as it pulled out and began to rattle along the track, she found she was enjoying it.

Arabella was very quiet and withdrawn so Lily turned her attention to the window. It was very relaxing watching the fields flash by and eventually she fell into a doze. Sometime later a hand gently shaking her arm brought her springing awake.

'Wake up, sleepy head. We're almost in London.' Arabella pointed to the window and knuckling the sleep from her eyes Lily saw that they were passing more buildings than she had ever seen all in one place in her entire life. 'We should be pulling into Euston soon.'

Lily could hardly believe she had slept so long, but sure enough, the train began to slow and then ground to a halt with a hiss of steam.

As they stepped out onto the platform, Arabella looked around for a porter to fetch their luggage from the hold, while Lily stayed nervously close to her side. There were so many people from all walks of life buzzing about the place. Men in top hats and warm greatcoats, women in beautiful gowns and striking bonnets, and then others who were dressed much as she herself was, and others who looked even more down at heel.

At last, Arabella beckoned to a passing porter and while he went to fetch their luggage, she squeezed Lily's arm reassuringly. 'Don't look so afraid. It's always like this in London. And if you think this is busy just wait until we get out into the streets.'

Soon after the porter reappeared with Arabella's many bags and Lily's small valise piled on a trolley and they followed him out to where a line of cabs stood waiting for fares, the horses impatiently pawing at the ground and seemingly oblivious to everything that was going on around them.

The driver of one of them hopped down and began to stow the luggage aboard while Arabella ushered Lily up into the cab.

'Kensington Place, if you please,' Arabella told the man before climbing in behind her.

The carriage jerked away from the station and Lily felt as if she had been transported into another world. Smart carriages, dray horses pulling huge carts, and horse-drawn cabs seemed to be coming at them from every direction, and Lily saw now why the horses wore blinkers, poor things. She was disappointed to note that her first glimpse of the capital was nowhere near as glamorous as she had thought it would be. Everywhere looked dirty and sooty and most of the buildings were so high that the roads were gloomy, although it was only early afternoon. There were people of all nationalities milling around and Lily's eyes were wide as she tried to take everything in.

Eventually the cab turned into a smarter area and Arabella informed her, 'We're almost there. This is Kensington – Kensington Palace isn't far from here.'

The carriage finally stopped in front of a large terrace of townhouses whose roofs were so high they seemed to disappear into the sky. There were steps leading up to a smart red door adorned with brass furniture and to one side of it, another set of steps led down to the servants' entrance and the kitchen.

The cabbie lifted their luggage down and almost instantly a man appeared from the house to greet them. 'Good day, Miss Arabella, we've been expecting you. If you'd like to go in, I'll follow with your luggage and get the maid to put everything away for you.'

'Thank you, Benson.' Arabella swept up the steps with Lily close behind her and once inside the large black-and-white tiled hallway a young maid in a frilled apron and a matching mob cap, who Lily judged to be about the same age as herself, hurried forward to take their cloaks from them.

'Mrs Morton says to go frough into the drawing room, miss.' The maid bobbed her knee. 'I'll bring your refreshments presently.' She spoke with a curious accent and as Lily followed Arabella to double doors on the right, she gave Lily a shy smile.

'Thank you, Elsie.'

Lily found herself in a room just as grand as the one at the manor, although slightly smaller. Silk wallpaper covered the walls and dainty gilt-legged sofas covered in a rich green velvet stood to either side of a marble fireplace.

'This is nice,' Lily commented as Arabella tidied her hair in the large gold-framed mirror above the fireplace.

'Do sit down, Lily. You must be tired after the journey, and thank you, again, for agreeing to accompany me. I don't know

149

what I would have done if you hadn't. Mama would never have agreed to me coming unchaperoned.'

Minutes later Elsie reappeared bearing a large tray on which stood a delicate china teapot, matching cups and saucers and a sugar bowl and milk jug. There were also dainty cucumber sandwiches and some tiny tartlets.

'Cook said to tell you she hoped this'd keep you goin' till dinner,' Elsie told her. 'Is there anyfin' else I can get for you, miss?'

'No, thank you, Elsie. But perhaps when we've had this you could take Lily upstairs and show her which room she'll be in. I'd like her in the one next to mine. Oh, and, er . . . is there any mail waiting for me, by any chance?'

'Not that I know of, miss. I'll go and check.' Elsie disappeared the way she had come and was soon back shaking her head.

'Thank you, Elsie.' Clearly disappointed Arabella turned to Lily to ask, 'Would you like to pour?'

They ate the sandwiches and tarts between them and after two cups of tea Lily felt ready for anything. Arabella pulled on the rope to one side of the fireplace and Elsie soon returned to take Lily to her room.

'How long 'ave you been Miss Arabella's maid?' she asked as they mounted the ornate staircase.

Lily chuckled. 'I'm not her maid. I'm a parlour maid back at the manor but Miss Arabella asked me if I would come with her while she has the final fittings for her wedding gown.'

'Oh, live in there, do you?'

'No, I go home each night. Where are you from, Elsie?'

'Souf of the river.' Elsie grinned. 'Me family live by the docks down Poplar. Crammed in like sardines. I've got twelve bruvvers an' sisters back home so I dropped on me feet when I got this position. I'd never had a bed to meself till I came here an' seein' as the family ain't here for most o' the time the job is a doddle, although the housekeeper, Mrs Morton, can be a bit of a tyrant.' She glanced at Lily from the corner of her eye and lowering her voice, she asked, 'Is it true that Miss Arabella is marryin' a lord whose almost old enough to be her da?'

'I'm not quite sure 'ow old Lord Lumley is, but yes I would say he is a lot older than her,' Lily answered cautiously. She had a feeling that she and Elsie were going to get on really well. She was a pretty girl with dark brown hair tucked under her cap and deep tawny-coloured eyes that reminded Lily of warm treacle.

They stopped at a door and, throwing it open, Elsie told her, 'This'll be your room. Miss Arabella's is that one right next door. But I'd best get off now an' get her unpackin' done, else Mrs Morton will have me guts for garters.'

Lily grinned as she watched Elsie leave, and once the door had closed behind her, she turned back to look at her room. It was certainly the biggest and prettiest room she had ever slept in. The walls were a soft shade of lilac and deep purple velvet swags and tails trimmed with gold tassels hung at the long window. There was a wall-to-wall carpet on the floor and a huge four-poster bed stood against one wall draped in a purple satin bedspread. On either side of it stood dainty bedside tables and a little further along was a marble washstand on which stood a pretty jug and bowl. An ornately carved mahogany armoire next to a matching chest of drawers stood opposite the bed and the look was completed by a small dressing table on which stood triple mirrors with a matching stool.

Lily unpacked the few clothes she'd brought with her and sat at the dressing table to brush her hair before venturing next door to see if there was anything Arabella needed. Suddenly she was very glad that she had agreed to come.

Elsie was there busily lifting Arabella's clothes from the large trunk she had brought with her while Arabella sat with a forlorn expression on her face staring out at the sea of roofs visible from her window.

'I'll do that now, Elsie,' Lily offered. She had nothing else to do.

'Are you sure, miss?' Elsie looked uncertain but Lily smiled at her.

'Quite.'

After she'd left, Lily asked, 'When is the first fitting for your gown?'

Arabella sighed and waved her hand dismissively. 'Oh, tomorrow will be soon enough.'

Lily couldn't help but think that most young women would have been excited to get a glimpse of their wedding gown, but Arabella seemed totally disinterested. She continued to unpack the trunk, hanging the beautiful gowns carefully away in the armoire until a tap came on the door and Elsie appeared again.

'Sorry to disturb you, miss.' She bobbed a little curtsey to Arabella. 'But Mrs Morton asked me to bring this up to you.'

She handed an envelope to Arabella and it was as if someone had waved a magic wand over her because suddenly she was beaming from ear to ear.

'Thank you, Elsie.' When the maid had left the room, she turned to Lily. 'Would you mind giving me a few moments alone to read this, Lily, please?'

'Of course.' Lily followed Elsie and once back in her own room she frowned. There was only one person she could think of who might get that reaction from Arabella. *Captain Frederick James*. But surely after the abominable way he had treated her he wouldn't have the gall to get in touch with her . . . would he? And even if he did, surely Arabella wouldn't be stupid enough to fall for his sweet talking again! Or would she?

A cold finger of dread traced itself up Lily's spine and she waited impatiently for a few moments before going back to Arabella's room where she found her mistress smiling from ear to ear. For the first time in months her face was glowing once more. Lily continued with the unpacking before asking innocently, 'Was there good news in your letter, miss?'

'What? Oh, er . . .' Arabella blushed before saying rapidly, 'Yes, it was as a matter of fact. It was from an old school friend and she suggested we should meet up, so I shan't be in for dinner this evening. Could you run downstairs and tell Mrs Morton for me? And then perhaps you could help me pick out a gown to wear?'

Lily nodded and quietly left the room, but the bad feeling continued.

Chapter Twenty-Two

'Hmm, this one or this one, which do you think, Lily?'
Lily looked at the two gowns spread across the bed. 'Perhaps this one?' she suggested, stroking the soft material of a cream satin silk one. 'But then it will depend on where you're going. It might be a bit too much if you're only visitin' a friend?'

Arabella stood beside her pensively staring down at it. 'Oh, I'm sure we shall probably be going out for a meal.'

Arabella was totally transformed from the sad girl she had been just hours before. 'And now I thought you might help me put my hair up into a more becoming style?' For months she had simply scraped her hair back into an unflattering bun on the back of her head, but tonight she obviously wanted to look her best.

She sat down on the stool in front of her dressing table as Lily began to brush her long silky curls. Ten minutes and many pins later, she stood back and asked, 'Will that do?'

'Oh yes, thank you.' Arabella turned her head from side to side, smiling broadly. Lily had piled her hair into loose curls, allowing a few ringlets to hang over her shoulders and it was very becoming. 'And now can you help me get into my gown?'

'Will, er . . . you be wantin' me to come with you?' Lily asked cautiously. 'Your mother did say that she wanted me to chaperone you at all times.'

'Oh, don't worry about that.' Arabella giggled as she stepped out of her dressing robe and turned so that Lily could start to lace her corset. 'I won't be on my own, will I? I shall be meeting my friend so I shall be quite safe. Oh, and do the laces up as tightly as you like.'

She had lost so much weight that it was hardly necessary but Lily did as she was told before slipping the silken gown over her head and tackling the long row of tiny pearl buttons that ran all up the back.

Arabella slipped her feet into a pair of dainty satin shoes that exactly matched her gown before twirling this way and that in front of the cheval mirror. 'Lovely. I think perhaps my blue cape with this outfit.'

Lily hurried to fetch it from the wardrobe. 'An' where will you be meetin' yer friend, miss?' she asked worriedly as she draped the cloak about Arabella's shoulders. She had promised Lady Bellingham that she would accompany Arabella everywhere she went and already she had a grave suspicion that this friend Arabella spoke of might not be the truth.

Once again Arabella waved aside her concerns. 'Oh, do stop fretting, Lily. I'm not a child, you know? We shall be meeting in Oxford Street, if you must know, and I shall be going in a cab, so I shall be quite safe. Now I really must get off. I don't want to be late.'

'Very well . . . what time will you be back? Shall I wait up for you to help you undress?' Lily couldn't keep the note of concern from her voice.

Arabella snatched up her bag and sighed. 'No, Lily, you needn't wait up. Get yourself an early night and I'll see you in the morning. And don't look so worried. I'm quite capable of taking care of myself.'

With that she breezed from the room as if she hadn't a care in the world and all Lily could do was watch her go. Once alone she began to tidy the room and it was then that she spotted the charcoal sketch of Annie she had given to Louis lying on the chest of drawers. He must have given it to Arabella and for the first time Lily wondered if perhaps Arabella did have regrets about abandoning her baby. She shrugged. Even if she did it was too late to do anything about it. Annie was settled and it would break her mother's heart to part with her now. She finished tidying and turned the bed down then set off to her own room just in time to see Elsie climbing the stairs.

'Cook says would you like to 'ave your dinner in your room on a tray or would you like to join us in the kitchen, miss?'

'I think I'll come and join you if you're sure Cook won't mind, Elsie.' She didn't have anything else to do now that Arabella had gone out and she supposed it would be better than sitting on her own all night.

'Right y'are.' Elsie gave her a cheeky wink. 'See you downstairs in half an hour. An' be sure not to be late. Cook is a stickler for us bein' on time for our meals.' Elsie shot off back the way she had come so Lily went to get washed and tidied before she presented herself for dinner.

'Evenin',' the red-faced cook greeted her when she went downstairs shortly after. She was a small woman who was almost as far round as she was high, with greying hair tucked beneath a mob cap, but her smile was friendly enough.

Lily took a seat at the table with a man who introduced himself as Ned, the gardener, and another girl called Polly who was the parlour maid. There were nowhere near as many staff here as there were back at Oakley Manor but then again, seeing as the Bellingham family weren't there for much of the year, Lily supposed any more wouldn't be necessary.

'So, where's her ladyship gone?' the cook asked as she bustled around the kitchen with Elsie helping.

'She's gone to meet a school friend.'

'Hmm, 'as she indeed,' the woman said caustically. 'Always get done up like a dog's dinner to meet a girlfriend, does she?'

Lily wasn't sure how to answer so she remained silent as the cook placed a tray of perfectly cooked lamb chops in the middle of the table along with a bowl of mashed potato. There was also a selection of vegetables and a jug of thick gravy, and Lily suddenly realised how hungry she was.

At last, the cook joined them and as they all helped themselves to the food she commented, 'You ain't as stuck up as Lady Bellingham's lady's maid, I 'ave to say. She always takes 'er meals in the housekeeper's room with 'er when she stays 'ere.'

'Oh, I'm not a lady's maid,' Lily explained. 'Least I am, but only till we get back. Miss Arabella's maid couldn't come so I agreed to 'elp.'

'I thought you were young to 'ave such a post.' The cook eyed her as she helped herself to a sizzling lamb chop. 'An' how are you likin' the job?'

'It's fine,' Lily said cautiously. Thankfully, after that the conversation turned to other things.

The chops were followed by a large apple pie and custard, one of Lily's favourites, and by the time she had finished she felt as if she was going to burst.

'That was delicious,' she told the cook. 'Thank you, now may I 'elp you clear up an' wash the pots?'

'Not at all, that's what I've got Elsie 'ere for. Come an' sit by the fire an' tell me all about yourself.'

And so for the next half an hour Lily told her all about her family, but she was careful not to mention baby Annie or the time she had spent in Yorkshire with Arabella. Eventually she retired to her room and tried to read a book, but she was restless and found herself continually going to the window to check the street below for any sign of Arabella returning. Taking the pad and charcoal she had brought with her from her bag, she sketched the rooftops of London from her window. Normally once she was sketching she could lose herself in the drawings but tonight even that couldn't hold her attention so finally, as the night drew on, she changed into her nightclothes, deciding she may as well lie in bed and wait for Arabella to come home, but she hadn't realised how tired she was and soon she was fast asleep.

The sound of horse's hooves and traffic on the cobbles outside woke her the next morning and for a moment she lay there disorientated, wondering where she was. Then with a start she realised and swinging her legs out of bed she pulled her robe on and hurried next door, cursing herself for falling asleep before she knew that Arabella was safely home.

After a quick tap at the door, she entered Arabella's room. 'I'm so sorry I wasn't here when you—' She stared in consternation at the empty bed. It was turned back just as she had left it but Arabella clearly hadn't returned and Lily's stomach started to churn. What was she to do now? If anything had happened to her, Lily knew that she would be to blame, for hadn't she promised Arabella's mother that she wouldn't allow her to leave the house unchaperoned! But how could she have stopped her?

She turned and flew back to her own room where she began to pull her clothes on. She had no idea where to start looking for her young mistress. Admittedly she had told her that she was meeting a friend on Oxford Street but she wondered if that might have been a lie. Even if it wasn't, London was such a vast place that she could be anywhere by now. Her stomach sank with apprehension as she realised it would be like looking for a needle in a haystack, especially if Arabella had no intention of being found.

However, her panic abated somewhat when she reached the top of the stairs just as Elsie was admitting Arabella at the front door.

'Where 'ave you been?' she said shortly as Arabella started up the stairs. 'I just found out you didn't come back last night an' I was sick with worry.'

Arabella, she noted, looked somewhat dishevelled, but her face was glowing.

'I'm quite old enough to look after myself, Lily,' Arabella retorted. 'Now come along, we have some packing to do.'

'*Packing?* But why? I thought you 'ad a dress-fittin' today?'

'Oh, don't worry about that,' Arabella said dismissively as she barged past her. 'Just hurry up, we don't have a moment to lose.'

Really worried now, Lily followed her back to the bedroom and the second they were inside Arabella dragged a trunk into the middle of the floor and began to haphazardly sling her clothes into it.

'B-but what are you doin'? An' where are you goin'?' Lily was seriously frightened now.

'Look, just go and pack your things; I'll explain everything on the way. But first, run downstairs and ask one of the servants to have a cab waiting at the door for us as soon as possible.'

Lily quietly went to her room where she stood for a moment chewing nervously on her lip. There had been no mention of them going anywhere else when she had agreed to come, so what was Arabella up to?

Making a hasty decision, she rushed over to her drawers and after snatching up a sheet of paper, some ink and a quill pen she quickly wrote a note to her mother telling her what had happened and that she and Arabella would be away for a little longer, then she popped it into an envelope with the cottage's address on it. Next, she packed her own things into her small valise and grabbing her coat and bonnet she went back to Arabella's room.

Arabella had summoned the gardener who was now in the process of lugging her heavy trunk downstairs and Arabella pushed her after it.

'But where—'

'Oh, *do* shush, Lily. I told you I'd explain everything later,' Arabella said impatiently.

Seconds later they were in the hallway where Lily passed her letter to Elsie, who looked almost as confused as she herself felt.

'Can you make sure this is posted for me?'

'Course I will, but where are you goin'?' Elsie asked.

Lily gave Elsie a quick hug. 'I've no idea, I just hope this isn't the start of trouble.'

The gardener was now heaving the trunk down the outside steps to the waiting cab and Arabella urged her through the door so Lily could do nothing but go along with her, although she now had a sick feeling in the pit of her stomach.

The trunk was placed on the top of the carriage and as Arabella pushed Lily inside it, she told the driver, 'London Euston, if you please.'

'We're going back to Euston?' Lily frowned. 'Does that mean we're catching the train home?'

Arabella shook her head. 'No. We'll be catching a train to Maidstone. And when we get there, we'll be changing for another one to Dover.'

'*Dover!*' Lily stared at her, her eyes bulging. 'But isn't that where the ferries that go to France leave from?'

Arabella nodded and crossing her arms she remained mutinously silent as the carriage rattled on over the cobblestones towards Euston Station.

Chapter Twenty-Three

Once the luggage had been hauled into the baggage hold, Arabella shoved Lily ahead of her onto the train at Euston. All Lily knew was that they were going to Dover but she was still none the wiser as to where they were going to end up from there, and she was starting to panic.

Arabella found them a carriage with only one elderly gentleman inside it. 'Here, this will have to do.' She entered it and took a seat, looking expectantly at Lily.

Lily followed hesitantly. She didn't really feel as if she had much choice. She had promised Lady Bellingham she would take good care of Arabella and was being paid handsomely for doing just that, so she could hardly allow her to go careering off on her own, although she would have dearly loved to.

'So *now* will you please tell me what's going on?' she hissed in exasperation, keeping a wary eye on the gentleman sitting opposite them who was seemingly engrossed in reading a newspaper.

Arabella crossed her arms and glared at her. 'Now isn't the time,' she answered with a nod at the gentleman and with that, for then at least, Lily had to be content.

The journey to Maidstone passed very quietly and by the time they had arrived Lily was imagining all sorts. However, once they'd alighted it was a mad dash to cross to another platform to catch the train that would soon be departing for Dover, so once more there was no time for explanations, and in no time at all they were off again. The station at Maidstone was much quieter than Euston and this time they managed to get a carriage to themselves so before they had even settled in their seats Lily asked again, 'Will you please give me a hint as to where we're going?'

'We'll be catching the ferry to Calais when we get to Dover.'

'*What?*' Lily was shocked. 'But why? And how can *I* go? I don't even have a passport and surely you need one to travel to other countries.'

'Don't worry about that.' Arabella looked smug. 'I already have one for you. I got it some time ago because I knew that if I ever travelled abroad, I would want to take you with me.'

Lily was even more shocked. It seemed that Arabella had thought of everything. 'But I thought I was just coming to London with you to attend your fitting for your wedding gown. Why do we need to go to France?'

Once again Arabella stubbornly clammed up. 'You'll find out soon enough. But for now, just try and relax and look on this as an adventure. Don't worry, you'll be safe with me and I shall make quite sure that you get back home safely.'

'But *when*? I would never have agreed to come with you if I'd known you had this planned,' Lily pointed out. 'Do your parents know where we're going? Or Lord Lumley, if it comes to that? I thought we were only going to be away for a few days at most.'

'You'll be back before you know it,' Arabella assured her.

'And will you be?'

Arabella shrugged and no matter how many more questions Lily asked, Arabella remained stubbornly tight-lipped.

They finally arrived in Dover late that afternoon and once they had hailed a cab Arabella instructed the driver, 'Take us to a hotel as close to the docks as you can, please.'

The driver tipped his cap and hoisted the luggage aboard, then once more, they set off. It was then that Lily's stomach began to growl and she realised that neither of them had eaten that day.

'Don't worry we'll dine at the hotel,' Arabella told her as the docks came into sight.

Suddenly her hunger was forgotten as Lily peered from the window at the enormous ships anchored there. 'Will we be meeting anyone 'ere?' Lily asked as the carriage drew up outside a hotel. When Arabella shook her head, she sighed with relief. Lily had had a horrible feeling that Captain James might be waiting for them but it seemed she had been wrong, which was one relief at least.

As they swept into the hotel, the man behind the desk in the foyer took one glance at Arabella's splendid costume and gave her the best room in the place with the one next door for Lily. They were delighted to find that there was a lovely view of the docks from their windows but they were tired and hungry so they hurriedly washed and changed and went down to the dining room for their evening meal.

Arabella chose a steak for her main course while Lily had fish, but despite being hungry she was so concerned that she merely pushed it about her plate.

'Should we go out and explore the docks?' Lily suggested after coffee, but Arabella stifled a yawn and shook her head.

'I'm too tired,' she admitted. 'But you can if you wish, although I wouldn't advise it – there will be lots of sailors about. We have to be up very early, too, as I've booked us on the first ferry to Calais tomorrow morning. If we want to have breakfast before we leave, we shall have to be down here for seven o'clock at the latest.'

Seeing the sense in what she said, Lily followed Arabella back upstairs and after helping her get ready for bed she retired to her own room where she slept like a log despite her concerns.

The next morning at breakfast, Lily asked cautiously, 'So how long will we be staying in Calais?' It sounded like the other side of the world to her, and she still had very grave reservations about Arabella's reasons for going.

'Oh, no more than a few days I shouldn't think.' Arabella patted her lips on a white napkin and they set off back to their rooms to prepare for leaving.

Two hours later they boarded the ferry and Lily couldn't help but feel a little excited, although she was desperately worried about her mother and Annie. She wondered if this was how Teddy felt each time he set off on a voyage. Once the ferry left the dock, Lily's anxiety returned full force as she watched her homeland fading into the distance and wondered how long it would be before she saw it again. But she didn't have time to think of it for long, for suddenly Arabella leant over the rail and was violently sick. She had gone an alarming shade of pale green but all Lily could do for her was rub her back.

'Oh dear, I do hope you're not going to be like this all the way,' Lily fretted. 'How long will the crossing take anyway?'

'We should do it in four hours if the weather is right,' Arabella said weakly as she clung to the rail. 'But I don't think I'll make it! I think I'm dying.'

Lily chuckled. 'I don't think anyone ever died from sea sickness,' she assured her as the wind tugged at her hair and brought colour to her cheeks.

It was just after one o'clock in the afternoon when the ferry arrived and by then poor Arabella could barely stand and she clung to Lily's arm as she guided her down the gangplank onto solid ground.

'Thank goodness.' She mopped ineffectively at her forehead with a scrap of lace handkerchief. Holding on to Arabella with one hand, Lily hailed a porter with the other and once he had their luggage on a trolley, he directed them to a waiting cab.

The docks were teeming with people of all nationalities and they had to pick their way past barrels and all manner of goods that were being unloaded from the cargo ships.

'Where are we going now?' Lily asked.

'Hotel Chez Vous,' Arabella croaked weakly as Lily helped her into the cab.

As they set off, Lily was relieved to see that Arabella was looking better by the minute.

The hotel wasn't far from the docks and looked very grand. Arabella swept up to the desk in the foyer as if she owned the place and shocked Lily when she asked for two rooms in perfect French.

A porter hurried forward to take their luggage into a nearby lift and they followed him upstairs in another. 'The beach is not far from here,' Arabella informed Lily and it was obvious then that she had been there before. 'We could perhaps have a stroll along it when we've had a rest.'

They arrived at their rooms to find their luggage waiting for them and Lily instantly went to the window to stare at the view. Below them, the street was bustling, with cafés dotted along the length of it and tables set outside where people sat enjoying carafes of wine. Men in brightly coloured neckerchiefs and berets were strolling along as if they had all the time in the world and Lily suddenly felt a moment of panic. She was in a foreign country where she couldn't speak a word of the language; what would become of her if she were to get separated from Arabella? She didn't even have enough money to book a passage back to Dover.

As if Arabella had read her mind, she told her, 'Don't worry, you're quite safe here with me. My parents often used to bring me and Louis on holiday to France when we were children.'

'But what if we were to go out and I lost you?' Lily questioned. 'I wouldn't even be able to ask my way back to the hotel.'

Arabella smiled. 'I shall make sure that doesn't happen so why don't you try to relax and enjoy yourself,' she said, opening her trunk. After the way she had tossed all her clothes into it most of her gowns were terribly creased.

'But how long will we be here?' Lily persisted.

Arabella sighed. 'No more than two or three days at the most. Now go and unpack in your room, it's next door on the left.'

Lily could see that she wasn't going to tell her any more, so with a sigh she went to inspect her own room, which appeared to be very clean and comfortable.

Later they ate in the hotel dining room and Arabella had to translate the menu for her because she couldn't understand a word of it.

'*Merci*, mademoiselle.' The waiter bowed and left after taking their order and once again Lily felt totally out of her depth.

After dinner they strolled along the busy street before heading for the beach where they discreetly removed their shoes and stockings and strolled along the sand. Under any other circumstances, Lily would have enjoyed it, but as things were she was still desperately worried.

On the way back to the hotel, they sat down at one of the small tables outside one of the cafés where Arabella ordered a carafe of wine, which they shared between them. Gradually Lily started to feel better about things. She had rarely drunk alcohol before and felt a little tipsy, but it wasn't an unpleasant feeling and she even began to enjoy herself a little.

For the next two days they wandered about exploring the area and gazing into the shops, but Lily noticed that as time went on Arabella seemed to become more and more tense.

When Lily woke on the third morning, she heard the faint sound of voices coming from Arabella's room next door. Hastily slipping into her dressing robe she peeped out of the bedroom door and up and down the corridor to make sure no one was about before going to Arabella's room and tapping at the door. Not waiting for an answer, she shot inside and stopped dead in her tracks as shock coursed through her. Freddie was standing there, but even more

166

shockingly, he was holding Annie, who beamed when she caught sight of Lily and held her chubby little arms out to her.

Freddie had the good grace to blush and look away as Lily rushed forward to snatch Annie from his arms.

'Just *wh-what* the *hell* is going on?' Lily growled as she gazed from Arabella to Freddie. 'And what is Annie doing here? Does my mother know you 'ave her?'

'Yes, don't worry, she does,' Arabella said placatingly. 'And now I think it's time we gave her an explanation, don't you, Freddie?'

Chapter Twenty-Four

'Go on then, I'm waiting!' Lily ground out. 'And, Arabella, how could you even *think* of speaking to *this* . . . this *person* after the appalling way he treated you!'

Arabella crossed to Freddie and slipped her arm through his. 'Freddie has changed,' she said defensively. 'I know you might not believe it but he realised how wrong he was to treat me and our daughter the way he did and now we're going to make a fresh start . . . as a family. We are going to be married – *legally* this time – in Paris next week.'

Freddie nodded in agreement. 'It's true. I've been a complete ass but I intend to make everything right now. I have left the army and have a job and a home for us to go to in Paris. I'm just grateful that Arabella found it in her heart to give me a second chance and I assure you I won't let her down this time.'

He sounded genuine enough but Lily was appalled and it showed in her face as she stared at her young mistress. 'B-but what about your *parents*? And Lord Lumley? What are they going to say? The wedding is just weeks away and I'm the one who'll get the blame for this if I go 'ome without you!'

'No, you won't.' Arabella shook her head. 'I shall write to Mama and Papa and explain that I can't go through with the marriage to Lord Lumley and hopefully they'll forgive me in time, especially when they discover they have a granddaughter.'

Lily hugged Annie to her. She could only imagine how heartbroken her mother must be back at home. She and her mother had cared for the baby since the day she was born.

'And how did you get my mother to part with Annie?' she asked Freddie, her eyes flashing fire. 'She loves this baby like she were one of our own. You never showed an interest in her, nor did you, if it comes to that,' she snapped at Arabella. 'So why the sudden decision to want 'er now! My mother must be devastated!'

Shamefaced Freddie shrugged. 'She was pretty upset,' he admitted reluctantly. 'And for a while I thought she was going to refuse to let me take her, but I pointed out that if she didn't Arabella and I would take her to court if need be to get custody of our daughter.'

Lily shook her head in disgust. 'It's a shame neither of you felt that way after her birth!' she ground out.

'I wouldn't allow myself to grow attached to her when she was first born.' A tear trickled down Arabella's cheek. 'But when Louis gave me the sketch you had drawn of her, I realised just how much I was giving up. Try to forgive us, Lily. We really are grateful for what you and your family have done.'

Lily's shoulders sagged as Arabella gently took Annie from her arms. In that moment, she realised, sickeningly, that there was nothing she could do to change the couple's minds. 'And what about me?' she asked dully. 'It's all right fer you two ridin' off into the sunset to live 'appily ever after, but I'm stuck 'ere in a foreign country wi' no way of gettin' 'ome.'

'Oh, don't worry about that. We intend to give you enough money to ensure that you get back safely,' Arabella assured her.

'Well, fer what my opinion is worth, I think yer makin' a grave mistake trustin' him! But if you've made up yer mind there's nowt I can do to change it so if you don't mind I'm goin' to go an' do me packin'. I don't want your family thinkin' that I had any part in this.' And with that Lily stormed from the room.

An hour later she stood staring from the window wondering when she might be allowed to leave. Her small valise stood packed and she just wanted to get back to England and put this whole sorry mess behind her. She wanted to believe Freddie when he said he had changed but she had a horrible feeling this might all end in tears.

Arabella came to her an hour later to ask tentatively, 'When would you like to go home, Lily?'

'As soon as possible,' Lily said crossly.

Arabella nodded. 'Very well, I shall get Freddie to go and find when the next ferry back to Dover leaves. Will you be all right travelling alone?'

'I shall 'ave to be, shan't I?' Lily turned her back on her; in truth the thought of it filled her with dread. Once Arabella had left the room, she sank down onto the bed. All she could do now was wait.

A tray of food was delivered to her later that day, ordered by Arabella, and soon after she appeared to tell her, 'The next ferry doesn't leave until the morning, Lily. Freddie and I are leaving for Paris now. Will you be all right? I've paid for you to stay here again this evening and here is some money for the rest of the journey when you get to Dover.' She paused before ending, 'And I'm so sorry to involve you in all this.'

'You should be,' Lily said sulkily, and yet deep down she could understand why Arabella didn't want to marry Lord Lumley. Even so, she still felt that she was making a grave mistake in trusting Freddie again but there was nothing she could say to change her mind now. 'Had I known what you were getting' me into I would never 'ave agreed to come with you. It's me that's got to go 'ome an' face the wrath o' yer parents an' yer grandmother.'

Arabella bowed her head and placed an envelope containing Lily's money on top of the drawers.

'Try to be happy for me,' she said softly. 'And thanks again for all you've done for me, Lily. Try to think kindly of me and rest assured that Annie will be loved and well taken care of.'

'May I . . . may I see Annie just one more time to say goodbye?' Lily asked throatily and with a nod Arabella left the room.

As soon as she returned with Annie in her arms, Lily took the child from her and held her close. She felt as if her heart was going to break – Annie had become such a big part of their lives and had gone some way to helping them come to terms with the loss of her father, but now she and her family were going to lose her forever too, and she dreaded to think what the baby's loss would do to her mother.

'Have a good life, sweet girl,' she whispered, then she handed her back to Arabella.

At the door, Arabella turned. 'Goodbye, Lily,' she said softly, and then she was gone.

Tears welled in Lily's eyes as she crossed to stare down into the bustling street below. A cab drew up and she watched as Freddie and Arabella, with Annie in her arms, appeared. Lily's tears flowed faster then as she realised this might be the last time she would ever see the little soul. She could only pray that Arabella would keep her promise and take good care of her.

As Freddie handed Arabella and the baby into the carriage a porter appeared and loaded Arabella's trunk onto the back, and soon they were gone. It was only then that Lily realised that she hadn't asked Arabella for her new address in Paris, but perhaps it was just as well. If she and Freddie really did mean to make a go of things, the last thing they needed was an avenging family chasing after them. At least this way she could honestly say that all she knew was that they had been heading for Paris. Like London, she imagined it would be a big place and they would be hard to find.

Rising from the seat in the window she turned, wondering what she should do with herself for the rest of the day, and that was when she spotted the sketch she had done of Annie lying on the floor. Arabella must have pushed it under the door on her way out.

Lily stared at it for a moment before tucking it away in her bag. It was all she had left of the child now.

Collecting her cloak and bonnet, she left the hotel. She supposed it wouldn't hurt to do a little exploring to take her mind off things, as long as she didn't venture too far away and get lost.

Once again, Lily found herself staring into shop windows and watching the many people sitting outside at the tables on the pavements. Soon she came to a small art gallery and she stood admiring the framed oil paintings in the window. She could only imagine how wonderful it must be for the artists to see their work displayed there. She had always daydreamed of becoming a real artist one day, but was sensible enough to know that things like that didn't happen to ordinary working-class people like herself. The paintings were quite beautiful and as she stood there a small portly man with a handlebar moustache and oiled hair came to the door and started to speak to her in French.

Lily spread her hands, trying to explain that she couldn't understand him. He smiled and nodded. 'Ah, you no understand the language, mademoiselle?'

When Lily nodded, he began to talk to her in broken English. 'You like the paintings, *oui*?'

'Oh yes, very much.' She nodded enthusiastically and he beckoned her inside.

'But I'm afraid I can't afford to buy anything,' she told him worriedly.

'Ah . . . do not worry. We are quiet and I like to meet people who appreciate the arts. Do you paint yourself?'

Lily shook her head. 'I'm afraid not.' She was too embarrassed to tell him that she had never been able to afford the canvases and paints. 'But I do like to sketch.'

Suddenly remembering the one of Annie in her bag she withdrew it and handed it to him.

He became quiet as he stroked his little goatee beard and studied it intensely. Suddenly he broke into a radiant smile. 'This is quite exquis— How you Engleesh say? Exquisite!'

Lily blushed with pleasure at the compliment.

'You wish to sell it. *Oui?*'

'Oh no.' Lily held her hand out for it. She knew her mother would treasure it now that Annie had gone and she couldn't part with it.

'Ah, this ees a shame.' He shook his head. 'Charcoal sketches sell very well. Do you 'ave any more?'

'Lots, but they're back at home in England,' Lily told him.

'Ah.' He held his hand out to shake hers. 'I am Monsieur Levigne. I have also galleries in London and Paris. Per'aps I could see some more of your sketches the next time I am there?'

'I, er . . . don't often get to London,' Lily explained. 'I live some way away in the Midlands.'

'Ah, that is a shame . . . but then you could always post some to my gallery? If they were satisfactory, I would pay a fair price for them.'

Lily was almost beside herself with excitement. 'I suppose I could,' she said breathlessly.

'Good, good, then I shall write down the address in London for you and you could perhaps kindly give me yours?'

He took up a quill pen and after dipping it in the inkwell he wrote the address and handed it to her. Lily then wrote hers for him and he tucked it into his pocket.

'There, and now that is done per'aps you would like to wander round and look at some of my other paintings?'

'Oh, *yes* please.' Lily enthusiastically wandered from one painting to another, staring at them in awe and wishing that one day she could be as good as the artists who had painted them.

Almost before she knew it an hour had passed and Monsieur Levigne told her kindly, 'I am sorry, but it is ees time for me to close now.'

At the door she thanked him profusely and with a twinkle in his eye he told her, 'Do not forget to post me some of your work. You 'ave talent, mademoiselle.'

'Thank you, goodbye for now.' Lily could hardly believe what had just happened, and for a while it took her mind off her anxiety about the journey home. But once back at the hotel, she began to panic a little. She took a deep breath and decided that she was being silly. Even so sleep eluded her that night and by the time she rose to find her way to the ferry the next morning, she didn't feel as if she had been to bed.

There was one thing for sure, she thought as she packed her valise, it had certainly been an eventful trip one way and another.

Chapter Twenty-Five

Two days later, late in the evening, the train bringing Lily home from Euston finally chugged into Trent Valley Station and Lily sighed with relief. It had been a long, arduous journey, wrought with tension, and now she just longed to be home. She had decided to return to the cottage straightaway – she would break the news about what had happened to old Lady Bellingham in the morning when she went to work the next day. She just hoped the old lady wouldn't try to blame her, but that remained to be seen.

After alighting the train, she walked out of the station and seeing a cab waiting there, she decided to spend the rest of the money Arabella had given her to get home. Normally she would have been happy to walk but tonight she was just too tired. It was already dark and as Lily sank back again the leather squabs it was all she could do to keep her eyes open.

After arriving in Dover she had found that she had missed the last train to Maidstone and so she had spent the night on a hard bench in the waiting room at the station and barely had a wink of sleep. The same thing had happened when it came to changing trains at Euston, so she had been forced to spend a second night in a waiting room and now she was exhausted.

As the cab rattled up Tuttle Hill she smiled to be back in familiar surroundings and when it turned out of Chapel End into Galley Common, she glimpsed the cottage and almost cried with relief. The cab dropped her at the end of Valley Road and she began the uphill walk to the cottage with her valise seeming to get heavier by the minute. The lights were shining from the windows in the small kitchen-cum-sitting room as she reached the brow of the hill and

Lily was sure she had never seen a more welcome sight in her life. As she opened the small gate in the picket fence, Sassy came barking and bounding towards her with her tail wagging furiously and Lily bent to stroke her.

'Hello, girl, missed me, 'ave you?'

The door opened and Richie, who had heard the dog, appeared holding an oil lamp aloft. As his eyes settled on his sister he beamed. 'Lily, thank God yer back safe. We've been worried 'alf to death. Come on in.'

As Lily stepped past him into the kitchen, her mother came dashing over to give her a hug. 'Eeh pet, what a carry on, eh? Come an' sit down an' have a cup o' tea then yer can tell us what's goin' on. Did you get to see Annie?'

Sara bustled away to push the kettle onto the hob while Lily dropped into the fireside chair.

'Oh, Mam, it's been so *awful*,' she told her in a choked voice, and she went on to tell her mother and brother all that had happened. 'And yes, I did get to see Annie and she's fine. But goodness knows what's goin' to happen when old Lady Bellingham finds out what's happened,' she finished weakly.

'I shouldn't worry too much about that. They already know that somethin's amiss.' Sara mopped at her eyes as she began to tell her side of the story. 'See – the day after you left fer London, this young man turned up sayin' he was Annie's dad and that he'd come to claim her. I argued but by the description of him you'd given us I knew it were 'im. He said he'd arranged to meet Arabella and that they were goin' to make a go o' things so there weren't much I could do to stop 'im takin' 'er, although I'll admit I did me best.' Tears trickled down her cheeks as she thought of the baby who she had come to love as her own. 'I told 'im that you an' Arabella were in London but he already knew, so after a while he left takin' the baby with him.' She swiped a tear from the end of her nose before

176

going on. 'I were in a right old state, I don't mind tellin' you, an' then not long after he'd left Master Louis turned up wi' them that he left for you.' She pointed to a far corner and Lily's mouth gaped as she stared at a pile of canvases stacked against the wall along with a beautiful pallet of oil paints and an easel.

'B-but why would he bring them for me?' she asked shakily.

Sara shrugged. 'I've no idea, but more importantly I told 'im what 'ad happened wi' Annie an' he were off like a shot from a gun. Apparently, Richie 'eard he'd caught the first train to London but you an' Arabella 'ad already disappeared by then an' no one 'ad any idea where you'd gone. Then your letter arrived this mornin' but that didn't 'elp much because you didn't say where you were goin'.'

'I didn't know when we first left.' Lily dragged her eyes away from the canvases. 'Do her family know she's run off again or just the old lady?'

'That I couldn't tell you but there'll be blood on the moon no doubt when they do know.'

Lily agreed with her but she was just too tired to think of it any-more that night so after another quick cup of tea she climbed the stairs and fell into bed, grateful to be home.

The next morning, she was up with the lark and dreading the day ahead. She had decided that it might be best to go and see old Lady Bellingham as soon as she got there, for she had no idea whether or not Arabella's parents had any idea what had happened yet, and she didn't want to make an already very bad situation worse.

'There's goin' to be ructions after what happened last time Arabella cleared off,' Lily told her mother as they sat together having a cup of tea.

'Well, it's better they find out now rather than later,' Sara answered sensibly. 'I just hope that baby is bein' properly cared for.' She was clearly fretting for Annie if the dark circles beneath her eyes were anything to go by.

'Ah well, I'd best go an' face the music. There's no point in puttin' it off.' Lily drained her cup and was just rising from the table when the sound of a horse's hooves thudding on the grass outside reached them, followed by a loud rap on the door.

'I wonder if it's our Richie come back from work cos he's forgotten somethin'?' Sara mused as she hurried to answer it.

Lily thought that was highly unlikely, and even if it was him, why would he knock on the door? And why would he be riding one of the master's horses?

Sara inched the door open and without invitation Louis Bellingham entered the kitchen saying, 'I'm so sorry to disturb you so early, Mrs Moon, but Richie told me Lily was home and I . . .' His voice trailed away as he caught sight of her and she gave him a tentative smile.

'Lily!' She could hear the relief in his voice. 'I'm so glad to see you back. But where is Arabella and the baby?' His eyes searched the room, but not finding them he looked back at Lily expectantly.

Lily's heart gave a little flutter and she flushed. 'I'm afraid I have some very bad news fer you. Why don't yer sit down an' I'll tell you everythin',' she suggested. As her mother hurried away to fetch another cup and saucer for their visitor Lily hesitantly told him everything that had happened.

As the story went on, he lowered his head into his hands and she watched the colour drain from his face like water from a dam.

'I'm so sorry,' she ended in a small voice. 'I did try to stop 'er, honest I did, but Arabella 'ad made her mind up.'

'It's not your fault, Lily.' He ran his hand through his hair making it stand on end. 'I know how stubborn my sister can be when she's made her mind up to something. There would have been nothing you could have done to stop her. I just hope she takes good care of Annie! But goodness knows what will happen when my parents and grandmother find out what she's done. Somehow, we managed to keep her last disastrous escapade from my parents, but there'll be no hiding it this time. And poor Lord Lumley. Although, saying that, Arabella has probably done him a favour by jilting him. She never did want to marry him.'

Lily chewed on her lip as she saw his agitation. He clearly loved his sister and she knew this would have hurt him.

'I don't suppose you'd care to come wi' me to tell your gran'mother what's 'appened, would you?' she asked hopefully and he nodded.

'Of course. She's not going to be best pleased and I don't want her taking her anger out on you. Are you ready to go?'

She nodded and after pecking her mother's cheek she followed him outside and they made the journey to the manor together with Louis' horse walking placidly beside them. Once they entered the stableyard, Louis handed the reins to one of the grooms and asked, 'Are you ready?'

Lily took a deep breath. 'As I'll ever be.' And so they entered the manor and climbed the stairs to old Lady Bellingham's suite of rooms.

Louis entered first with Lily close behind him, and the old woman scowled. 'Oh, so you're back! But where is Arabella? Did the gown-fitting go well?'

Lily glanced at Louis for support before tentatively beginning the story, and as it unfolded, she watched the different emotions flicker across the old woman's face.

'*What!* So you're telling me that that *stupid* granddaughter of mine has run off with that scoundrel for a second time and this time they've taken their flyblow with them?'

When Lily nodded, keeping her eyes downcast, Lady Bellingham flew into a rage. 'But *why* didn't you stop her, you *stupid* girl! And you say they're going to live in Paris? What are they going to live on I ask . . . *fresh air?*'

'That's enough, Grandmama,' Louis scolded. 'None of this is Lily's fault. How could she have known what Arabella was planning? And even if she had how could she have stopped her?'

'The family's reputation will be *ruined*.' The old woman fanned herself with her handkerchief. 'And what will your parents say? And Lord Lumley! Goodness me, what a mess!'

'I'll go down and speak to them,' Louis told her. 'But I shall have to tell them everything. I think Mama has had an idea that all wasn't well ever since Arabella came back the last time.'

His grandmother waved her hand at him dismissively. 'Go and get it over with then. Goodness knows I can do no more to help the little fool. I wonder how long it will be this time before she comes back with her tail between her legs. And, Hudson, bring me my smelling salts, I feel quite faint after such a shock.'

Louis ushered Lily out onto the landing. 'Leave this to me,' he told her. 'You've been through quite enough. I'll break the news to my parents, though God knows how my mother will take it. She's going to be mortified to discover that my sister had a child out of wedlock and that she is now a grandmother.'

'Good luck.' Lily turned to leave but suddenly remembering something she turned back. 'Louis, why did you leave those canvases and paints back at the cottage?'

He shrugged, delighted that she had chosen to call him by his first name. 'I suppose I thought with a talent like yours for sketching you should try your hand at painting too. I hope I haven't offended you?'

'No, not at all. It was very kind of you. As it happens, I have something else to tell you about my time in France but it can wait until another day.' The thought of Monsieur Levigne caused a little ripple of excitement to run through her as she hurried off to report for duty to the housekeeper.

Chapter Twenty-Six

When Lily entered the kitchen a short time later, she found Ginny crying.

'What's wrong?' she asked.

The cook glared at her. 'She's dense an' I've boxed her ear, that's what's wrong,' she answered for her. 'We'll 'ave no pots left the way she breaks them!'

Lily bit back the hasty retort that sprang to her lips. The staff resented her enough already for what they considered the preferential treatment she and her family had received from the Bellinghams, and she didn't want to make things worse. Even so, she didn't think the cook should be allowed to bully Ginny as she did and she felt sorry for her.

She gave Ginny a sympathetic smile as she collected the duster and polish before setting off to the dining room. It was as she was polishing the long mahogany table that a terrible thought occurred to her and she paused. She had an inkling that she and her family had been allowed to live in the cottage because they were caring for Annie, but what would happen now that Annie was gone? Should they be told to leave they would be homeless and houses and cottages to rent were hard to find, which was why so many families had had to go into the workhouse following the fall at the pit. Glancing towards the window, she saw Louis walking past and she decided that she would question him as soon as she had the chance.

That chance came much quicker than she expected when he strolled into the room a short time later, quietly closing the door behind him.

'I'm sorry that my grandmother was so rude to you, Lily.' He looked stressed. 'I'm afraid she and my parents are so upset they are just looking for someone to blame for what Arabella has done. As you can imagine, my parents have taken the news very badly. It's come as a complete shock to them and now they face having to tell Lord Lumley. I've no doubt we'll be the talk of the town when word gets out, which I'm sure it will in no time. Mother is so upset she's taken to her bed and my father is so angry he looks as if he's about to have a heart attack. Still, what's done is done – there can be no turning the clock back. They're very angry with me too for covering up for Arabella when we sent you off to Yorkshire with her to have the baby. As things have turned out, it was all a waste of time trying to keep everything quiet, wasn't it?'

He plonked down onto a chair and Lily felt sorry for him. How could he be blamed for trying to help his sister? She would have done exactly the same had it been one of her siblings. But now there were more pressing things on her mind and so plucking up her courage she said, 'I'm sorry that things didn't work out as you planned. But, er . . . I know this might not be the right time but there's somethin' else I need to 'ave a word with you about.'

'Oh? What is it?' She instantly had his full attention.

'The thing is . . .' She gulped and forced herself to go on, dreading what she might hear. 'The thing is . . . I believe you let us rent the cottage from you cos we were carin' for little Annie. But she's with her mam now, so does that mean you'll be askin' us to move out? I 'ave to know cos if you are I'll 'ave to start lookin' round fer somewhere else to rent for us.'

Louis scowled. 'I wouldn't dream of asking you to move out,' he said decisively. 'The cottage was standing there going to rack and ruin and you're all welcome to stay there for as long as you like as far as I'm concerned.'

'That's very good o' you, but will your parents think the same? I know some o' the staff didn't like us gettin' the place an' now . . .'

'It's no business of the staff who my family rents their properties to, and just leave my parents to me. And wasn't there something else you wanted to tell me you mentioned this morning?'

'Oh yes.' Her face lit up and Louis thought again how pretty she was. 'It's just that while I was in France with Arabella, I went out for a walk one day an' came across this little art gallery. Ooh, yer should 'ave seen the lovely paintin's an' sketches they 'ad in there. Anyway, Monsieur Levigne, the owner, invited me in an' I showed 'im the sketch of Annie I did that you gave to Arabella. The long an' the short of it is, he wants me to send 'im some more to 'is London gallery. I mean, I'm sure nothin' will come of it, but I was so thrilled that he liked it.'

'And why wouldn't he?' Louis was happy for her. Just for a short time she had dropped her guard with him and spoken without watching what she was saying as she usually seemed to do, and with her expression unguarded and a flush of excitement on her face, she took his breath away. 'You have a great talent, Lily. Why don't I come up to the cottage and help you choose which ones to send him one evening? I'll post them for you as well.'

Lily blushed. He was so kind, was Master Louis. 'Well . . . so long as you're sure it would be no bother.'

'It would be a great pleasure.' He stood up and made for the door where he stopped to tell her, 'And don't worry about the cottage anymore. It's yours and your family's to live in for as long as you like, you have my word on it.' And with that he left and Lily returned to her work with a smile back on her face.

When Lily got home from work that evening, she found Bridget sitting at the table drinking tea with a sullen expression on her face.

'I 'ear there's trouble up at the manor,' she greeted her sister.

Lily frowned. 'What do you mean?'

'It's all round the village that Miss Arabella 'as run off wi' her captain an' that Annie were 'er baby! Still, I suppose it'll stop people sayin' she were yours.'

'Crikey that didn't take long.' Lily hung her shawl up and crossed to see if there was any tea left in the teapot. 'Mind you, I didn't think it would. But how are you?' Bridget's pregnancy wasn't obvious yet, but she looked pale.

'Fed up, if yer must know.' She scowled at her mother, and sensing that all was not well Lily wisely said no more until Bridget had left.

'Someone got out of bed the wrong side this morning,' Lily commented.

Sara sighed as she took a steak and kidney pie from the oven. 'She's been up an' down 'ere more times than I can count while you've been away an' she wants to come 'ome an' live here wi' Robbie. Apparently, her and Robbie's mam don't get on at all. They're at each other's throats all the time an' from what I could glean things ain't goin' too well between 'er an' Robbie either. She says he's changed since he were caught in the fall down the pit an' he keeps actin' strangely. It's no surprise really. It's bound to 'ave affected 'im. But like I told 'er, "you've made yer bed an' now you'll 'ave to lie in it, me girl". She were keen enough to snatch Robbie from under yer nose, but it seems married life an' havin' a baby ain't all she'd expected it to be.'

'Oh dear.' Lily couldn't help but feel a little sorry for Bridget. She really did look miserable.

Just then Richie appeared. 'Blimey, there's ructions goin' on back there,' he told them as he shrugged his jacket off. 'The master an' the mistress are goin' at it 'ammer an' tongs, and the word is well and truly out that Miss Arabella 'as cleared off wi' that captain again.'

'I figured it must be,' Lily said wearily. It was astonishing how quickly news sneaked out.

'An' I passed our Bridget on the way 'ome an' it took her all her time to talk to me. She had a face on her like a wet weekend, what's up wi' her?'

'Oh, I think she's just finding it hard to settle into married life,' Lily said sensitively.

'Huh, I'm not surprised. Will back at the manor likes a pint an' he reckons Robbie is almost livin' at the pub when he ain't at work. He told Will he goes there to get out o' Bridget's way.'

'Aw well, there's nowt we can do about it, lad,' his mother said stoically. 'So go an' get yourself cleaned up an' we'll eat while the meal's still hot.'

Lily was secretly relieved to see that while her mother was clearly upset about losing Annie, and was, despite what she said, concerned about Bridget, her cough did seem a little better now that the weather was improving, and as she sat down to eat, she prayed it would continue. Lily had a feeling that having Sassy for company might have helped a little. Her mother did seem very fond of the little dog.

That night she sat outside with a warm shawl about her shoulders and sketched the view down the valley from the cottage until it got too dark to see. Already she was looking forward to her Sunday afternoon off when she might find time to try painting on canvas, and she could hardly wait.

Louis waylaid her the next morning after breakfast to tell her, 'My grandmother is hiring a private detective to try and trace Arabella, though goodness knows what she thinks it can achieve, even if he manages it.'

'How are your parents?'

'Mother's taken to her bed and refuses to get up, saying we are all ruined, and Father is going about with a permanent frown on his face. I certainly wouldn't like to be in Freddie's shoes if ever he catches up with him. But enough about that. I was wondering if I may visit the cottage this evening to go through your sketches so that we can decide which ones to send to Monsieur Levigne.'

'Er . . . of course, if yer sure you can spare the time,' Lily answered, blushing prettily.

The rest of the day dragged for Lily, and she could hardly wait to get home and get her sketches out. Finally, though, she was back at the cottage, and as soon as dinner was over she shot away up the stairs to put on her prettiest gown before brushing her hair until it shone. She could no longer deny to herself that she felt drawn to Louis, although she knew nothing could ever happen between them – they were from different classes. Even if he had returned her feelings it would have been hopeless because his family would never allow him to marry someone like her, nor would she have wanted to. People would probably think she'd only married him for his money, and Lily was too proud to ever allow that to happen.

With a sigh she went downstairs and laid the sketches across the table, then sat down and patiently waited for Louis to arrive. Her mother had decided to take a gentle stroll down into the village to see her old neighbour, taking Sassy with her, and Richie had gone to band practice so there was nothing to be heard but the birdsong in the trees outside. Lily waited and waited, and as dusk approached she realised that Louis wasn't coming, so she packed her sketches safely away and headed off upstairs for an early night feeling strangely disappointed.

The reason for his non-appearance became apparent when the next morning Ginny told her in a whisper, 'Eeh, we 'ad a right old panic on after you left last night. The Thompsons arrived unexpectedly wi' their daughter an' the master invited 'em to stay for dinner.

186

Cook were in a right old flummox an' took it out on me as usual. Anyway, we managed the meal for 'em an' then the master invited 'em to stay fer a few days so there'll be extra cleanin' for you to do an' more places to lay in the dinin' room.'

'That's all right, Ginny, I'm sure we'll manage.' Lily pictured Samantha Thompson's pretty face and felt an unexpected pang of jealousy. It was more than obvious that Louis' parents wanted him to wed Samantha and although Louis hadn't seemed very interested, she wondered if he might change his mind.

At that moment the housekeeper appeared to ask her, 'We have unexpected guests, Moon. Could you work a little later each evening until they are gone so that you can clear the dining room after their evening meal and lay the table for breakfast?'

'Of course, Mrs Biggles.'

'Oh, and unfortunately there will be two extra bedrooms to clean too. Could you make sure they are done?'

When Lily nodded, the housekeeper strode away, the keys on her chatelaine jingling. Like the cook, the woman was clearly harassed.

Lily hurried into the dining room and began to set the table. The family and their guests would be down for breakfast shortly and it was her job to ensure that everything was prepared for them. She rushed back to the kitchen and found that some of the dishes were ready, so after placing silver lids over them she began to carry them through to the long sideboard in the dining room so they could help themselves to what they wanted.

Once that was done, she carried a large pot of coffee and one of tea through, and she had just placed them on the table when Miss Thompson appeared looking beautiful in a pale-green shot silk gown and her lovely dark hair curled about her shoulders.

'Pour me some tea, girl,' she said curtly as she sat down.

Lily disliked her immediately, but she bobbed her knee and began to do as she was asked. The cup was almost full when

Miss Thompson suddenly lifted her napkin and shook it, catching Lily's hand, and causing her to spill some tea on her gown.

'You *stupid* girl! Just *look* what you've done!' she screeched as she leapt out of her seat and began to dab ineffectively at the stain just as Louis entered the room.

'Whatever is going on in here?' he asked, taking in Miss Thompson's furious face.

'This . . . this *idiot girl* just ruined my gown. Just *look* what she's done! You really should make sure your staff are properly trained, Louis.'

'Excuse me, miss,' Lily said before she could stop herself. 'I *didn't* spill it; you knocked my hand when I was pouring your tea.'

'How *dare* you answer me back, girl. Louis, are you going to just stand there and let a mere *servant* speak to me like that?' Miss Thompson bellowed indignantly.

'I'm sure it was an accident,' Louis told her, desperately trying to keep the peace. 'Why don't you go and change. I'm sure the laundry maid will be able to get the stain out if it isn't allowed to dry.'

Miss Thompson growled and after throwing a murderous glance at Lily she threw her napkin down and stormed out of the room, her silk skirts swishing.

'I, er . . . apologise for Samantha's behaviour, Lily. I'm afraid she can be a little hot-tempered. And I am so sorry for not turning up to go through the sketches with you last night. The Thompsons turned up rather unexpectedly. I did go to the stables to send word with Richie but he had already left.'

'It really doesn't matter.' Lily plonked the teapot down and strode past him with her head held high.

Louis sighed. What a start to the day it had turned out to be.

Soon after breakfast as Lily crossed the yard, she saw Miss Thompson and Louis heading for the stables. Miss Thompson was now dressed in a very becoming dark green velvet riding habit with a little matching hat perched on her head, and Louis looked very handsome in tight-fitting jodhpurs and knee-high leather boots. She couldn't help but notice what a smart couple they made and again she felt the little pang of jealousy, although she knew it was stupid. Louis had never shown her anything more than kindness, so why shouldn't he enjoy the company of the beautiful Miss Thompson?

She entered the kitchen to hear the staff gossiping over their morning cup of tea, and there was certainly enough for them to gossip about at the moment, what with Miss Arabella disappearing off into the blue and the Thompsons turning up so unexpectedly.

'I'm tellin' you, Miss Thompson an' Master Louis will be announcin' their engagement afore the year is ended, you just see if I ain't right,' the cook said confidently as she spooned another two sugar lumps into her tea. 'I reckon the master an' the mistress are just grateful the Thompsons still want owt to do wi' 'em after the way Miss Arabella 'as let 'em down. The silly girl; she could 'ave had it all wi' Lord Lumley, as it is, she'll probably end up livin' hand to mouth. An' poor Lord Lumley, eh? Apparently, Lord Bellingham is goin' to see him today to tell him what's happened afore somebody else does. Still, at least the Thompsons turnin' up has got the mistress out o' bed. She'll be keener than ever to make sure as Master Louis makes a good marriage now after what Miss Arabella 'as done. If Louis marries the young madam the two families between 'em will own half the businesses in the county.'

Feeling strangely deflated, Lily went about her work and tried not to think of it. *I'm being silly*, she scolded herself. But try as she might, she couldn't get the picture of Louis and Miss Thompson out of her mind.

Chapter Twenty-Seven

The next week passed in a blur, as Lily worked longer hours every day, not getting home at night until nine o'clock sometimes. By then, Samantha Thompson had made her dislike for Lily more than obvious and so she avoided her as much as she could, but it was impossible at meal times when she served their meals.

Louis continued to be friendly towards her whenever he saw her, which Lily suspected was the cause of the problem, although she had no idea why it should be. She and Louis Bellingham were as far apart in class as it was possible to be so she wondered why Miss Thompson would see her as any sort of a threat.

She found out why one morning when she went to Miss Thompson's room to clean it and found the young woman still there. Lily had thought she had gone out riding but she realised she'd been mistaken and went to leave.

Samantha was sitting at her dressing table while her lady's maid dressed her hair and her lip curled as she caught sight of Lily in the mirror.

'Sorry, miss, I thought you'd gone out and I came to tidy your room but I'll come back later.' Lily bobbed her knee politely and began to back out of the room but Samantha's words stayed her.

'Wait a minute, girl. I'd like a word.'

Lily said nothing as Samantha swivelled on her stool to stare at her coldly. 'I think it's time you learnt your place,' Samantha snapped. 'I don't like the way you address Louis.'

When Lily raised an eyebrow, she went on, 'He should be *sir* to you. I think you are both far too familiar with each other. In my household the servants are addressed by their surnames, so make sure you do that in future.'

'Yes, miss.' Lily ground her teeth. Who did this jumped-up little madam think she was anyway? Anyone would think she was royalty the way she went on. Even so, she was aware that she needed her job so she said nothing as she hastily left the room, closing the door firmly behind her.

And then who should she almost bump into but Louis himself, and seeing the colour in her cheeks, he asked, 'Is everything all right, Lily? You look rather flushed.'

'Everything is fine, *sir*,' she said. 'But Miss Thompson has just informed me that you and I are far too familiar with each other so I'd prefer it in future if you would address me as Moon.'

'I see.' Louis did not look pleased. 'Then I can only apologise to you. Samantha had no right to speak to you, or any other member of staff like that. I shall speak to her immediately.'

'I'd rather you didn't, *sir*,' Lily replied, looking at him coldly. 'I believe it would make matters worse, so now if you'll excuse me, I'll get on wi' me work. It's what I'm paid for after all.' And with that she stormed away leaving him with a bewildered expression on his face.

Her mood slightly improved, however, when just before lunch the housekeeper entered the kitchen to tell them all, 'The Thompsons will be leaving tomorrow shortly after breakfast, so hopefully things may return to some sort of normality.'

'Phew, I'm pleased to hear it,' the cook said. 'They're a 'ard family to please right enough. I've been all but chained to the cooker ever since they arrived.' Then turning to Ginny she barked, 'An' 'urry up wi' them vegetables, can't you, girl? If you went any slower, I'm sure you'd stop! Neither use nor ornament, you ain't.'

Poor Ginny went into a fluster and seconds later she yelped as the knife she was using to peel the veg sliced into her thumb and blood began to trickle everywhere.

'*Now* look what you've gone an' done,' the cook screeched, giving her a sound clout round the ear that nearly knocked her flying.

'Steady on, Cook. She didn't do it on purpose,' Lily said as she rushed to the sobbing Ginny and snatched up a cloth to wrap around her finger.

Cook groaned. 'Fer two pins I'd get Mrs Biggles to sack 'er,' she threatened.

At that Ginny began to sob even louder. 'No, *please* don't, Cook. I ain't got nowhere to go,' she pleaded. The only thing she had to look forward to now was visiting what was left of her family in the workhouse on her Sunday afternoons off and she was terrified of having to join them there.

'So pull yer socks up then.' The cook unfeelingly went on with what she had been doing as Ginny went back to work, and with a sigh Lily went back to hers.

Once again it was late when Lily finished that evening and as she came out of the gates from the manor, she was shocked to see Robbie standing there.

'What are you doing here?' Lily said in surprise. 'Why aren't you at home with your wife?'

'I've come to apologise,' he said, twisting his cap between his hands. 'I know now that Annie weren't yours. It's all round the village that she were Miss Arabella's child, an' I want yer to know that I'm sorry I ever doubted yer.'

'Well, what's done is done.'

'I know,' he said regretfully. 'An' it were the biggest mistake o' me life. But the truth is, I still love you, Lily. I allus 'ave.'

'Why are you telling me this now?' Lily was annoyed. 'You're married to my sister with a child on the way so I suggest you get home to her. I appreciate you admittin' you made a mistake but like I said, it's too late.'

He fell into step beside her, making Lily feel uncomfortable. 'But we could 'ave been so good together.'

'No, we couldn't.' She stopped abruptly to stare up at him. It was time for him to learn the truth. 'I realised after you left me that I wasn't sure about marryin' you, so even if you 'adn't finished wi' me the chances are we'd never 'ave been wed anyway. I ain't ready for marriage.'

The colour rose in Robbie's cheeks and his expression changed. 'Is that right? But I bet you'd marry Louis, his lordship, who gives out so many favours to yer, in an 'eartbeat, eh?'

'Don't be so stupid!' Lily was furious. 'Why would a man like 'im look at me? I'm a pit wench an' one day he'll be lord o' the manor. Now go 'ome to your wife, Robbie.'

He caught her arm roughly. 'I'm tellin' yer now. If I can't 'ave yer, *nobody* else will,' he spat.

She shook him off and glared at him. 'Don't talk so bloody daft. Threats like that could get yer danglin' from the end of a rope. What do yer think our Bridget would say if she knew about this conversation, eh? Now clear off, we've nothin' else to say to each other unless it involves me sister.' And with that she picked up her skirts and shot away leaving him to stare after her with a grim expression on his face.

'You all right, love?' her mother asked when Lily entered the cottage shortly after.

'Yes, fine.' Lily hung her shawl on the nail on the door and sighed. What with one thing and another she wouldn't be sorry to see the back of this day. But she wouldn't tell her mother of anything that had gone on. She seemed a little better physically but Annie's leaving had affected her badly. Although she had Sassy to keep her company, her days seemed so empty and lonely now, with Lily and Richie at work and without Annie to care for, and she was still grieving for her husband, so Lily had resolved not to say anything that might upset her further.

'The Thompsons are leavin' in the mornin',' she said instead. 'So I might be able to get home a little earlier each night again.'

'Good. Oh an' there's a letter come fer you this mornin'. It's on the mantelshelf an' the envelope looks very posh.'

'Oh!' Lily was curious as she hurried to lift it down. 'I wonder who this is from?'

'Well, if you open it you'll find out, won't yer?' Sara chuckled.

Settling into the chair, Lily slit the envelope and took out the single sheet of paper it contained.

Dear Miss Moon,

I hope this finds you well and safely back in England. It was a great pleasure to meet you at my gallery in France and I now very much look forward to seeing any sketches you have done that you might care to send to me.

With kind regards,
Monsieur Andre Levigne

'It's from that French gentleman I told you about that I met in the art gallery in Calais,' Lily told her mother, smiling properly for the first time that day. 'He's still keen to see some more of me sketches. Do you think it's worth sendin' any?'

'I'm sure he wouldn't 'ave wasted 'is time askin' for 'em if he wasn't interested,' Sara pointed out sensibly.

'Hmm, in that case I'll per'aps sort some out tomorrow.' Lily stifled a yawn. 'I'm just too tired tonight, I'm off for an early night.'

Despite her exhaustion, though, a little bubble of excitement in her stomach kept her awake for some time.

As Lily was trying to sleep, back at the manor Louis and Samantha had been left alone to retire to the drawing room following the evening meal.

'That girl . . . Lily Moon, don't you find her rather overfamiliar for a servant, Louis?'

He frowned. 'In what way? I've always found Lily to be very pleasant. And she's certainly been a great help to the family over the last months – although of course things with my sister didn't work out at all as my parents had hoped.'

'Hmm, quite.' She looked at him slyly as she suggested sweetly, 'Do you think perhaps the Moon girl had a hand in that? What I mean is, do you think she may have encouraged Arabella to follow her heart rather than her head? Think of it – half these servants come from hovels, they don't know what it's like to live in a decent home so the Moon girl wouldn't have given a second thought to what Arabella would be giving up if she didn't make a good marriage.'

'I have visited both of the Moons' family homes, as it happens,' Louis answered in a clipped tone. 'And I can assure you that while they didn't have a lot of fancy furniture, what they did have was spotlessly clean and far from being a hovel. They might be servants through circumstance but they are still people with feelings, just the same as yours and mine, and so I think they deserve to be treated with courtesy and respect. And may I add, knowing my sister as I do, I'm quite sure Lily would not have been able to sway her decision to leave with Captain James whatever she said. Arabella has a mind of her own. She was only going through with the marriage to Lord Lumley because it was what was expected of her.'

'But surely your parents were only trying to ensure that she lived a life of comfort and plenty?'

'My parents clearly didn't take her feelings into account,' he answered. 'And furthermore, I don't believe anyone should be forced into a marriage for gain. If and when I marry it will be to a woman of my choosing.'

Samantha pouted prettily, sensing that he was annoyed. 'Of course,' she purred, batting her long eyelashes at him. 'But let's just hope that when you do choose your life partner it will be someone who will be worthy of you. But now, come and sit beside me.' She patted the seat at the side of her and spread her silken skirt becomingly about her. 'After spending this last week with you I've come to realise just how much we have in common, including our love of horses.'

'Thank you, but if you'll excuse me, I think I'm ready to retire now.' He gave a gallant little bow and turned towards the door.

Samantha scowled. 'When will I see you again?'

He paused. 'I'm sure our parents will arrange something and I will of course be here to see you off in the morning after breakfast. Good night, Samantha.'

As the door closed behind him, she clenched her teeth and thumped the seat with her small fist. That *dratted* servant girl. She had noticed how easily Louis spoke to her and the way his eyes would light up when he saw her, and it wasn't right. She had been so sure when she arrived that this would be the week Louis asked for her hand in marriage, but apart from being friendly and allowing her to go riding with him, he had shown no interest in her at all. Somehow, she must devise a way to get the Moon girl dismissed, she decided, searching her mind for ways she might go about it.

Chapter Twenty-Eight

Lily arrived at the manor the next morning to find the kitchen in chaos.

'Ah, you're 'ere!' Cook said the second she set eyes on her. 'You'll 'ave to 'elp me get the breakfast ready.'

'Of course, but where's Ginny?' Lily glanced around but there wasn't a sign of her.

'She's cleared off, an' bloody good riddance, that's what I say! She were about as much use as a chocolate teapot,' the disgruntled cook snorted.

'What do you mean, she's cleared off? When did she go?' Lily hurried over to the stove where the cook had got a number of different breakfast dishes cooking all at once, and after rolling up her sleeves, she quickly turned the sausages frying in the pan before they burned.

'She must 'ave gone sometime in the night. She weren't 'ere when I come down this mornin'. There were no fire lit – *nothin'*.'

'Had you had a row? I can't believe she'd just go for nothing. Ginny was terrified of ending up in the workhouse.'

'Well . . .' The cook sniffed. 'I did give 'er a bit of a clout as it 'appened, just before I went to bed.'

'What for?' Lily was persistent, although she could see the cook was getting agitated.

'She broke another cup last night while she were washin' up.'

Lily's face said it all and the cook's chest puffed with indignation. 'Well, what were I supposed to do? We'd 'ave had no pots left the way she were breakin' 'em.'

'Have you ever stopped to think that she was clumsy because she was afraid o' you?' Lily asked.

Colour flooded into the older woman's cheeks. 'That's enough about it fer now,' she snapped. 'She's gone an' as far as I'm concerned, she can stay gone. Now, are you gonna 'elp me get this breakfast on the table or not? I shall be bloody glad to see the back o' them Thompsons an' all.'

Lily secretly agreed with her on that score, although she didn't voice her opinion, and eventually all the dishes were ready. When Lily carried them through to the dining room, she found Lord and Lady Bellingham, Louis and the Thompsons already seated at the table and as usual Samantha glared at her.

After putting the dishes on the sideboard, Lily stood discreetly to one side until she was sure there was nothing else they required. Samantha was the first to approach and lift the lids of the dishes one at a time.

'Where are the devilled kidneys, girl?'

'I don't believe Cook did any this morning, miss. She did bacon and sausages instead,' Lily answered politely.

'But I don't *want* bacon and sausages. I *want* devilled kidneys. Go and tell her to do some immediately. And make it quick. We don't have all day!'

Lily gritted her teeth and bobbed her knee before making her way back to the kitchen where she told Cook what Samantha wanted.

'The cantankerous little devil,' the cook ground out. 'I've cooked devilled kidneys every day for 'em since they've been 'ere an' every day they've come back untouched. Then the one day I *don't* do 'em they're what she wants. Well, she'll 'ave to wait, it'll be at least half an hour afore they're ready so you'd best go an' tell 'er that, the bloody awkward little madam!'

Lily went off to do as she was told, but once the message was passed on Samantha pouted. 'Our servants back at home make

198

sure that we have everything we want every morning,' she said plaintively. 'You really should have a stern word to your staff, Lady Bellingham. I fear they are letting you down badly. And you, girl' – she turned her attention back to Lily – 'go and tell the cook not to bother. We shall be leaving in an hour and I don't have time to wait. I shall just have to make do with what's there.'

'Yes, miss.' Lily backed out of the room with a last glance at the vast array of dishes spread out on the sideboard; there was enough food there to feed an army. It wasn't her place to say anything, but she knew Samantha was just being contrary, and she could tell that Louis was none too happy with her. She could just imagine what sort of a life he would lead once they were married, but she supposed that was his choice.

The atmosphere in the house eased immediately later that morning when the Thompsons finally departed, and all the servants breathed a sigh of relief. They had been very demanding visitors and they were all glad to see the back of them, although the bedrooms they had used now all needed a clean.

It was as Lily was stripping the sheets in Miss Thompson's room that she noticed something catch the light just beneath the bed. Bending down, she found a fine gold chain on which a diamond pendant was suspended. Lily guessed that it must be worth a small fortune and she took it downstairs to Mrs Biggles immediately.

'I think Miss Thompson must have dropped this,' she told the housekeeper. 'I just found it on the floor in her room, would you see that it's returned to her?'

'Of course, thank you, Moon.'

Lily went back to her cleaning and didn't give it another thought as the day continued and she counted the hours until she could go home.

When she finally left for the day, it was still light, so she decided to take a short cut through a copse of trees; it was wonderful to see the leaves unfurling and the wild flowers bursting into life. There were violets, yellow cowslips, deep purple deadly nightshade and cow parsley growing in profusion and amongst them her favourite foxgloves. It was the end of March and she was looking forward to April when the bluebells came out and the forest floor would resemble a sea of blue.

She was so intent looking at the early blooms that it was some minutes before she became aware of a noise and she stopped to listen. It sounded like someone crying and she frowned as she stared through the trunks of the trees. Suddenly she saw it: a small figure in a drab grey dress crouching down and sobbing bitterly.

'Ginny? Ginny, is that you?' She had been worrying about the girl all day and it was a relief to find her.

Clearly terrified, the girl stood up and stared about her and as her eyes found Lily she began to sob even louder.

Lily hurried over to her and wrapped her arms around her. 'Oh sweet'eart, are you all right?'

Ginny had a large bruise on the side of her face and another even larger one on her arm.

'Y-yes but I ain't got nowhere to go,' she whimpered piteously. 'Cook give me a right pastin' last night cos I dropped another pot an' I just couldn't take it no more, so when she went to bed, I run away.' She sniffed as she stared up at Lily from tear-filled eyes. 'I'm goin' to 'ave to go an' admit meself to the work'ouse wi' me mam an' the rest o' the kids now, ain't I?'

'No, you're not.' Lily tenderly wiped a damp lock of hair from the girl's battered little face. 'You're goin' to come home wi' me, for tonight at least, an' then we'll decide what's to be done.'

'*Really?*' Ginny blinked and swiped the back of her hand beneath her runny nose. 'But won't yer mam mind?'

'Of course she won't. Now come on. I bet you ain't eaten since yesterday, 'ave you?'

They walked on hand in hand and when they emerged from the copse and the cottage came into view, Ginny gazed at it in awe. With pretty flowers sprouting in the front garden and the windows gleaming in the early evening sunshine, it looked a million miles away from the little terraced cottage in the shadow of the pit that she had been brought up in.

'Cor, it's posh, ain't it?' Her eyes were as round as saucers and Lily smiled as she led her up the little front path. Suddenly, to Ginny's delight a little figure dashed round the side of the house, barking madly as she flew to her old mistress. Ginny bent down and gathered the little dog to her, the tears streaking down her face as Sassy licked them away enthusiastically.

Lily smiled, knowing that if anything could cheer Ginny up, it was her little dog. Sassy had been a godsend since Annie had gone – without her, her mother would have been alone all day.

'Who's this?' Sara asked pleasantly when they entered the kitchen, Sassy leaping happily around Ginny's legs. She had just taken a batch of jam tarts from the oven and the smell of them made Ginny's stomach rumble as she realised how hungry she was.

'This is Ginny, Mam, the kitchen maid I told you about. She's Mrs Davis's daughter from Valley Road. I'm afraid she's had a bit of a falling-out with Cook again and she has nowhere to go. I wondered if she might stay here tonight?'

'Of course she can, so long as yer don't mind her sharin' your room.' Sara frowned as she noted the girl's bruised face and nodded towards the table.

'Sit yourself down, luvvie. I bet a drink o' milk an' a few jam tarts wouldn't go amiss, eh?'

Ginny nodded and perched on the very edge of the chair like a little bird about to take flight and Sara's maternal instincts kicked in. Poor little mite, she wasn't as far through as a line prop and all those bruises! Why, she'd have liked to give that cook a taste of her own medicine, the bully.

And so, with Sassy on her lap, Ginny tucked into a large glass of frothy milk and at least five tarts, until Sara advised her, 'Don't 'ave any more just yet, pet. Save some room for yer dinner, eh? An' then you're welcome to 'ave some more after that.'

Ginny nodded, but she looked frightened, and her eyes followed Sara about the room. When Sara leant over to take the empty plate from in front of her, she flinched away.

'Poor little sod!' Sara said angrily as she slammed the plate into a bowl of hot water in the sink. 'The kid is afraid of 'er own shadow. I'd like to give that damned cook a piece o' my mind.'

'I found 'er in the copse on me way 'ome,' Lily whispered. 'An' I could 'ardly leave her there. She's got nowhere to go.'

'Then she can stay 'ere fer a while,' her mother said decisively as she glanced at Ginny. 'To tell the truth I get fed up 'ere on me own all day while you an' Richie are at work an' since little Annie went. I love Sassy, but she ain't no good for a natter, so Ginny'll be good company for me.'

For dinner there was a large dish of creamy mashed potatoes, some sizzling lamb chops and cabbage, and Ginny tucked into the meal as if she hadn't eaten for a month. As soon as they'd finished the girl rose and began to clear the table without being asked and Sara smiled. 'I've got a funny feelin' that girl is goin' to be a good little 'elp to me,' she commented. 'She doesn't seem afraid o' work.'

'She isn't,' Lily agreed. 'I think she was just so afraid and nervous of Cook that it made her clumsy.'

'Then let's let 'er stay fer a while an' see how it goes.' Sara took the opportunity to sit with her feet up while Ginny washed up the dinner pots in the large enamel sink without breaking a single one.

Lily, meanwhile, decided to try her hand at painting before the light faded and so after carrying the paints and a blank canvas outside, she stared at the view for a while before beginning to mix some paints. In a surprisingly short time, she was totally engrossed in what she was doing and it was only when her mother came outside to tell her that it was getting dark that she sat back to study what she'd done. She had started to paint a view of the valley with the pit in the distance and the copse on the hill, and she was surprised to see that it wasn't at all bad for a first attempt.

'Bring it in an' let it dry in the kitchen,' her mother advised after admiring it. 'Then you can do a bit more on it tomorrow.'

Lily did as she was told and after a nice cup of cocoa she and Ginny retired to her room. Her mother had placed a straw mattress and some pillows and blankets down on the floor next to Lily's bed and Lily was tickled to see that the girl was gently snoring within minutes of her head hitting the pillow. She obviously felt safe, and Lily went to sleep with a smile on her face. If things worked out as she hoped, Ginny might be just the thing to take her mother's mind off the loss of Annie.

Chapter Twenty-Nine

The next morning when Lily got to work, she found Mrs Biggles waiting for her. 'Old Lady Bellingham wishes to see you immediately,' she told her and Lily frowned wondering what she had done wrong now.

She set off for the old lady's quarters with her heart in her mouth. Hudson answered her knock and nodded towards her mistress who was already dressed in her frills and furbelows. Her cheeks were heavily rouged and the gemstones she wore flashed in the sunshine pouring through the window.

'Ah, Moon, come here where I can see you properly,' she ordered. When Lily had done as she was told she went on, 'Thanks to a person I hired to track her down I now have news about my granddaughter. I also have the address in Paris where she is living, which is why I wanted to see you . . .' She paused as if she was choosing her words carefully. 'The thing is . . .' The old lady looked decidedly uncomfortable. 'As you are aware, Arabella heaped shame on the family when she disappeared as she did, and it has affected her mother badly. My first reaction was to say that I never wanted to set eyes on the wretched child again. We have all had to accept that there can be no question of her marrying Lord Lumley now. But even so . . . Well, I suppose this is a sign of weakness, but I have always had a soft spot for both her and Louis, not that she deserves it, of course! Anyway, I have decided that if I can persuade her to come home, we may be able to salvage something from this whole sorry mess, so what I want is for you to go and persuade her to come back.'

Lily's eyes popped and she shook her head as she backed away from her as if to ward her off. 'Oh no . . . no, I'm sorry. I went away wi' Arabella twice before an' look what 'appened! I don't want to get involved again.'

'Oh, don't be so dramatic, girl!' Lady Bellingham scolded. 'For some reason Arabella is fond of you so if anyone can persuade her to come home it's you.'

'She won't leave Freddie or the baby,' Lily insisted.

The old woman nodded. 'I understand that, but if we can just get them all back here, we can perhaps concoct a story that people will believe. We can say she secretly married him some time ago before the brat came along and my son might be able to find Freddie a position and make him respectable. At least she'd be back in the family fold again. So what do you say?'

Lily's head wagged from side to side. She was adamant that she wouldn't go. 'No, ma'am, I'm sorry but there's no way I'd want to go to Paris all on me own! It were bad enough havin' to make me way back from France.'

The old woman sighed. 'What if Louis were to come with you? Would you consider it then?'

'Wouldn't that just give people somethin' else to gossip about? After all, from what I 'ear he's all but engaged to Miss Thompson. What would she 'ave to say about that? An' it's hardly right for a single woman to be harin' off wi' a young man.'

'Pah!' Lady Bellingham waved her hand dismissively. 'Just leave Samantha Thompson to me. And as regards the other . . . Well, everyone knows that Louis would never bother with a servant girl. They needn't even know he's come with you. We can spread the word that he's away on business for his father.'

Seeing Lily waver slightly she hurried on, 'So shall I ask him how he feels about the idea? I'm sure he'd want his sister safely back home where we could at least keep our eye on her.'

Lily felt as if she'd been backed into a corner. Both she and her brother relied on the Bellinghams for their living, and now they lived in one of their better properties, she couldn't afford to upset her.

'I suppose so,' she said uncertainly, although she really wasn't happy with the idea.

'Good. Go about your work now and I'll speak to you later when I've spoken to Louis. And, girl . . . not a word to anyone, do you understand?'

'Yes, ma'am.' Lily dipped her knee and left; it was going to be hard to concentrate on anything until she knew what Louis had said. She half hoped he would refuse to go and then at least she wouldn't have to either.

Once back downstairs she found the cook still in a filthy mood and barking orders at anyone and everyone.

'That *damned* Ginny,' she swore as she slammed some dirty pots into the bowl. 'Clearin' off an' leavin' me in the lurch like that. If I could get me hands on her I'd wring her scrawny little neck. I shall be glad when Mrs Biggles 'as got me a new kitchen maid. I can't go on doin' everythin' meself.'

Lily found it hard not to smile. While Ginny had been there, Cook had always been saying how little she did, but it seemed that now she was gone she was finally realising just how much Ginny had done. She decided that it might not be a good time to tell her that Ginny was staying with her and so she stayed silent and went to collect some clean sheets from the laundry.

It was as Lily was laying the table for the family's lunch later that morning that Louis appeared.

'So what do you think about my grandmama's idea of us going to Paris to try and persuade Arabella to come home, Lily?' he asked.

She frowned. 'I ain't too keen on it, to be honest,' she admitted. 'I mean – what if we go all that way an' she refuses to come back?'

He shrugged. 'Then I suppose at least we'll have tried.' He looked sad. 'I know she's been a fool but I do miss her, and I have to admit I'd love to get to know my little niece.'

Lily couldn't help but feel sorry for him. After all he was the only one of the family who had ever shown the slightest interest in Annie.

'In that case . . . I suppose we could try.'

His face lit up and her heart gave an unexpected little lurch. Hastily she averted her eyes and continued to lay the silver cutlery out. It was then that she remembered something and reaching into her pocket she told him, 'I appreciate what you said about us being allowed to stay in the cottage but I'd like you to return this to your grandmother now. It's the money you gave us fer lookin' after Annie, but seein' as she ain't wi' us anymore I'd like yer to 'ave it back.'

He scowled and backed away from the pouch she was holding out to him. 'No, really, I'd rather you keep it, for all the inconvenience we've put you through.'

Lily shook her head and placed it down on the table beside him, her chin in the air. 'That's very good of yer, but like I say, we'd rather you 'ave it back now. We've never spent a penny of it an' don't feel right about keepin' it any longer.'

Louis sighed. She really was a proud young woman and he guessed that there would be no changing her mind.

'Very well, if you're quite sure. Thank you, Lily. I shall see that it's returned to Grandmama straightaway. Oh, and did you know that a messenger came from the Thompsons early this morning to say that Samantha was missing a diamond pendant? Thanks to you finding it and handing it in to Mrs Biggles I was able to return it to her with the messenger.' He didn't tell her that the messenger had actually come with a message from Samantha saying that she thought Lily had stolen it from her room. He hadn't believed it for a moment but it had made him realise how jealous she was of Lily. It appeared that she'd stop at nothing to discredit her.

He smiled at her. 'Thank you again for agreeing to come to Paris, Lily. Just leave everything to me and I'll let you know when we're going.'

After he left, Lily chewed on her lip nervously, wondering if she'd made the right decision.

When she told her mother about the proposed trip that evening, Sara was no happier with the idea than she was, although a little part of her hoped that Lily and Louis could persuade Arabella to come home. At least if they came back, she'd get to see Annie again. She still missed her dreadfully.

'How 'as Ginny been?' Lily asked next.

Sara smiled. 'Oh, good as gold. She's out plantin' in the veg patch at the minute. Nothin' is too much trouble fer that girl an' she an' Richie are gettin' on like a house on fire. She suggested we should get a goat fer milkin' and Richie thinks it's a great idea. He's goin' down into the cattle market later this week to see if he can get one, an' he's bringin' some more chickens back an' all. Just think, the way things are goin' we won't 'ave to buy 'ardly anything anymore, what wi' our own eggs, milk an' vegetables on tap. Richie's on about gettin' the pigsty shipshape next an' gettin' a pig an' all, although I ain't so sure about that. I mean, imagine havin' to kill it when you'd fattened it up an' got to know it.'

Lily chuckled. The warmer the weather got, the better her mother appeared to be and she just hoped it would stay that way.

'I was thinkin,' Sara went on, 'that per'aps we could let Ginny stay on fer a while longer? What I mean is, she's such a good 'elp. But if she does, she'll 'ave to go to the rag stall in the market an' get 'erself some clothes. The poor kid's only got what she's stood up in.'

'I'm sure we could afford that,' Lily agreed. 'And when the hens do get laying and all the veg comes through, we'll 'ave far more than we could eat. She could per'aps get the carrier cart into the market each week an' sell what we don't need to bring a bit of extra cash in.'

'What a clever idea. I'll ask her if she wants to stay on in that case, shall I?'

'It's fine by me,' Lily agreed. 'Although I'd better just 'ave a word wi' Louis an' make sure he doesn't mind before we say anythin' to her. This is his cottage after all, ain't it?'

'You're right,' Sara agreed and she hurried away to put the finishing touches to their evening meal.

As it turned out, Lily got the chance to speak to Louis much sooner than she had expected because later that evening as she sat outside working on her painting, she saw him riding up the valley on his stallion. He drew the horse to a halt and tied his reins to the small picket fence before striding towards Lily with a broad smile on his face. 'So, you decided to try the oils?'

'Yes, and I 'ave to say I'm really enjoyin' it. Thanks again.'

He went to stand beside her and studied the canvas for a while before saying, 'Is this really your first attempt?'

When she nodded, he shook his head and rubbed his chin. 'You're a natural,' he said quietly and she flushed with pleasure. It was then that an idea came to him and he suggested, 'Didn't you say Monsieur Levigne had a gallery in Paris?'

'Yes, why?'

'Why don't I write to him and ask if we could drop some of your sketches off there instead of posting them? They have more chance of not getting lost if we do that.'

'But what if he isn't there?'

'I'm sure he would have someone running the gallery in his absence, so as long as he lets them know to expect you it wouldn't matter,' he pointed out.

'Hmm, I suppose you're right.' Lily still felt a little apprehensive about Monsieur Levigne seeing any more of her sketches. After all, he might just have been being polite when he said that he liked the one she had shown him. But then, she had nothing to lose, and he had written to ask for more of the same.

'All right,' she agreed. 'Do you want to help me choose the sketches?'

He nodded enthusiastically and they entered the cottage together to sort out which ones they wanted to take.

Louis seemed to particularly like the ones Lily had drawn of wildlife and he chose one of a squirrel holding an acorn between its tiny paws and another of a family of rabbits playing in a field. Next he selected some of flowers, and another one he liked of the pit head that she had sketched just as dusk was falling. By the time they'd gone through them he had at least fourteen sketches in a pile.

'Let's see what he thinks of these first,' he suggested.

She nodded, although deep down she didn't really expect too much. She was only an amateur, after all, and Monsieur Levigne's art galleries sold some very expensive works of art.

Ginny appeared just as they were making their final choices, and the moment she set eyes on Louis she looked terrified.

'If you've come to take me back to the manor, I ain't goin',' she said mutinously, crossing her arms and scowling at him.

'Aren't you the kitchen maid that's gone missing?' he questioned gently, noting her bruised face, and she nodded.

'I was going to talk to you about her,' Lily said quickly and she went on to tell him why Ginny had run away and why they had offered her shelter.

'If that's the case I don't blame you for going,' he told Ginny with a kindly smile. 'And if Mrs Moon doesn't mind you being here, you're welcome to stay for as long as you like as far as I'm concerned. You can rest assured I shall be speaking to the cook about this too!'

Ginny's face lit up like a ray of sunshine and she hurried away to make a cup of tea for their guest.

But when she was gone, Lily frowned. 'I'd rather you didn't – speak to Cook, I mean. I'm afraid she would take 'er frustrations out on me if she got wind that Ginny were 'ere,' she explained.

'Ah, of course. I hadn't thought of that.'

Louis stayed chatting easily to Sara and Lily while he drank his tea, then after collecting the sketches together, he said, 'Right, I'll let you know when the arrangements for Paris have been made. Good night, all.'

'Eeh, he's such a lovely young man,' Sara said when he'd left, glancing at Lily from the corner of her eye. 'An' I get a sneaky feelin' he's got a soft spot for you, our Lily, an' if I ain't much mistaken, I reckon you've got one fer him an' all.'

Lily flushed. 'Don't talk so daft, Mam. He's nearly engaged to be married to Samantha Thompson.'

'Is he?' Sara responded innocently. Then with a sly grin, she said, 'Well, we'll just 'ave to wait and see about that, won't we?'

Chapter Thirty

'Are you quite sure you've got everythin'?' Sara fretted.

It was a beautiful morning in April and Lily had just finished packing her bags.

'Mam, that's the tenth time you've asked me in as many minutes!' Lily smiled at her. 'And yes, I'm quite sure. Here's me passport, look – Arabella gave it to me when she left me in Calais. Right, I'd best be off. We don't want to miss the train.'

'I still ain't sure this is such a good idea,' Sara said as she straightened the ribbons on Lily's bonnet beneath her chin. 'You just make sure you stay close to Master Louis; we don't want yer gettin' lost in a foreign country.'

'I'll be fine.' Lily gave her and Ginny a kiss, then set off for the manor where the coach would be waiting to take her and Louis to the train station. The air was alive with the sound of birdsong and as she walked through the copse she saw the first bluebells pushing their way through the earth beneath the canopy of trees.

She and Louis had agreed to meet outside the gates of the manor on the lane to try and prevent unnecessary gossip, although she had no doubt news would soon get out that they had gone away together. Old Lady Bellingham had told her that Samantha Thompson wasn't at all happy with the arrangement and had offered to go in Lily's place, but she'd soon put paid to that idea.

'My granddaughter knows Lily well,' the old woman had informed her imperiously. 'And if anyone can persuade Arabella to come home it will be her, so we'll leave the arrangements as they are, thank you very much, miss!'

And so, Samantha had stamped her daintily shod foot and stormed away. She wasn't used to not getting her own way. Lily half wished she had got her own way, because she was still apprehensive about going and couldn't believe she'd allowed herself to be talked into it in the first place.

Louis was waiting in the coach exactly where he had said he would be and he hopped down as soon as she approached to lift her luggage inside before helping her in and clambering back in behind her.

'All ready?'

Lily nodded and they lapsed into silence as the horses broke into a trot. The train was exactly on time when they reached Trent Valley Station and soon it was steaming through countryside passing fields full of frolicking lambs and cattle. The carriage they were in was fairly full, so there was little conversation between them, but every now and again Louis would smile at her and she would return it.

Euston Station was just as busy as she remembered and there was a mad dash to get the train to Maidstone where they would have to change yet again for the train to Dover. Louis had told her that he had booked them into a hotel for the night when they reached the ferry port and as the day wore on, Lily found herself looking forward to it.

It was early evening by the time they arrived at the hotel and Lily was tired and hungry.

'Would you join me in the dining room for an evening meal?' Louis asked.

Lily looked uncertain. 'Actually I, er . . . was going to say that per'aps I could have some sandwiches sent up to me room,' she said hesitantly.

He shook his head. 'No, you've been travelling all day and you need to get a good meal. Please join me, Lily. I hate dining alone, especially as I don't know anyone here to chat to.'

'All right, but can I go to me room an' get washed an' changed first?'

'Of course.' He collected their keys from the desk and they went upstairs in the lift.

Their rooms were on the same landing and once alone, Lily frowned as she glanced through the clothes she'd brought with her. Knowing how the gentry dressed for dinner she was painfully aware that none of her clothes were particularly suitable, but even so, she unpacked her best dress and had a hasty wash. It was one her mother had made her for her birthday. It was cotton with a full skirt and was dotted with tiny blue forget-me-nots, and once Lily had released her long blonde curls from the pins and brushed her hair till it shone, a glance in the mirror told her that she didn't look too bad at all.

She met Louis in the foyer and at sight of her he smiled appreciatively. 'You look charming,' he told her and gallantly held out his arm to lead her into dinner.

The restaurant was quite full and could she have known it, Lily got more than a few admiring glances as the waiter led them to their table.

Louis ordered a steak while Lily chose a salad and while they were waiting for it to be served, they had a glass of wine, which went straight to Lily's head and made her feel quite tiddly.

The meal was delicious and when they'd finished Louis asked tentatively, 'Would you like a stroll around the docks before we retire?'

Lily hesitated. The wine had helped her to relax in his company over dinner but she was still afraid of crossing the class divide. Anyone seeing them together would immediately guess that he was gentry and she was working class just from looking at the way they were dressed.

'Are you sure we should?' She stared up at him apprehensively. 'What I mean is, I don't think Miss Thompson would approve.'

'She isn't here,' he answered with a scowl and so Lily nodded and they set off.

It was pleasant with the breeze in her hair and she smiled at the seagulls wheeling and diving in the sky. Once again there were ships of all shapes and sizes in the dock and burly seamen were rushing up and down the gangplanks busily loading them in readiness for sailing on the tide the next morning. Far away, the sun was sinking into the sea and Lily sighed contentedly. It was like being on holiday and Louis was very good company.

'I wonder how we'll find Arabella when we get to Paris,' she mused.

Louis sighed. 'Hmm, I'm hoping that cad will have done the right thing by her and married her legally this time, otherwise I'm likely to knock his block off.'

Lily giggled. She couldn't imagine Louis getting violent, but then, she didn't really know him that well.

'It's strange to think that until a few months ago I had never been further than the market place in Nuneaton, and now I've been to Yorkshire, Calais, London, and tomorrow we're off to Paris. I'm getting' to be what me mam would call "a bit of a gadabout".'

He laughed as he tucked her arm into his. That was one of the things he liked about Lily: there were no airs and graces to her. She was kind and pretty, and he couldn't help but think that if she had been born a lady of class, she would have had every eligible bachelor in the county after her.

'I suppose we ought to think of getting back to the hotel. We've got a very early start in the morning,' he suggested after a time as he stifled a yawn. It had been a very long day.

He walked her to the door of her room where he gave her a little bow. 'Good night, Lily. I'll see you in the morning.'

'Night, sir.' When he frowned at her, she grinned. 'Sorry . . . Louis.'

'That's better,' he said, before walking down the corridor to his own room.

As she got into bed, Lily hoped for his sake that they would find Arabella and Annie well; he clearly cared about them. But then the combination of the travelling and fresh sea air caught up with her and she fell asleep immediately, waking rested and refreshed the next day.

She met Louis in the dining room and they enjoyed a good breakfast before setting off for the ferry, which would sail with the tide. Thankfully the crossing was fine and Lily couldn't help but remember the last time she had sailed with Arabella who had been ill all the way.

When they reached Calais, Louis took her for a meal in a small café and they sat at a table outside enjoying their meal beneath a parasol. Then they started the journey to Paris, finally arriving in the early evening.

'I think we'll find a hotel for the night. It's a bit late to be visiting Arabella,' Louis told her as he hailed them a cab. 'We'll go and see her first thing in the morning and then we'll go and find Monsieur Levigne's gallery and deliver your sketches.'

'I wonder what sort of reception we'll get?' Lily said thoughtfully, gazing around her with interest.

Louis grinned. 'Who from – Arabella or Monsieur Levigne?'

'Both, I suppose,' Lily admitted. She was beginning to wonder if they had done right in bringing the sketches and was nervous about what Monsieur Levigne would think of them.

'Well, I'm fairly confident the sketches will go down well,' he assured her. 'As for Arabella . . . that remains to be seen, doesn't it? She might send us away with a flea in our ear, but at least I'll be able to tell Mama that I've seen her and hopefully that she is well.'

The cab came a stop shortly after and as they alighted, Lily gasped in wonder at the sight of the majestic domes of Montmartre towering in the distance. It was quite magnificent and seeing the look of awe on her face Louis smiled.

'It's quite something, isn't it? Hopefully we'll have time to visit it before we leave to go back home, and you might enjoy a boat trip on the River Seine too?'

'Oh, I would!' Lily's eyes were glowing with excitement and she had to keep pinching herself to make herself believe that she was really there in Paris.

They had no sooner set foot on the ground when a man in uniform rushed down the steps of the hotel to greet them and instruct a porter to carry their luggage inside.

'*Bienvenu*, mademoiselle, monsieur,' he said, tipping his hat respectfully.

And as Louis took Lily's elbow and guided her up the marble steps, Lily felt like visiting royalty. Inside she gazed around her in awe. It was the most magnificent foyer she had ever seen with enormous gilt mirrors dotted on the silk wallpapered walls, and her feet sank into a thick-pile carpet in a lovely shade of forest green stretched from wall to wall.

Louis approached the desk and spoke rapidly in perfect French to the gentleman behind it before shaking his head and looking back at her with a grin.

'He thought we were married and offered us a double room,' he said and she flushed, staring down at the floor in embarrassment.

When Lily got to her room, she was shocked to find a maid in a pretty uniform already unpacking her small valise. She flushed again as she wondered what the maid must think of her unfashionable clothes, but when the maid spoke to her in French, she could only spread her hands to show her that she couldn't understand what she was saying.

The maid gave her a kindly smile and leading her to a door in one wall she flung it open.

'*Voilà, votre salle de bain.*'

Lily was shocked to see her very own bathroom complete with a toilet, washbasin and an elegant roll-top bath with running water.

'Er, thank you . . . thank you,' Lily said and with a smile and a nod the maid left.

Louis tapped on her door shortly after she'd had a wash and tidied her hair, and in her excitement, she forgot herself and almost dragged him into the room to show him her bathroom.

'I have one almost identical,' he told her, pleased to see how happy she looked. That was yet another thing he liked about her: it took so little to please her, whereas with Samantha everything had to be perfect or she threw a tantrum. But then, she and Lily were very different girls. Both beautiful but from very different classes. Lily's smile faded almost as quickly as it had come and turning to him, she muttered, 'I'm afraid all this must be costing a terrible amount o' money. I would 'ave been quite 'appy with a room a little less luxurious.'

'Nonsense.' He could see that she was embarrassed. 'You deserve a nice room. Don't forget, you're doing me a favour by coming with me. Now, let's go down to dinner, shall we? I'm famished. Or better still, why don't we go for a stroll and find a restaurant somewhere?'

'Oh, I'd like that,' Lily said enthusiastically. It wasn't every day she visited Paris after all.

Once out on the street they strolled along admiring the goods in the shop windows, until eventually Louis paused outside a small restaurant. 'Should we try this one?'

When she nodded, he led her inside and soon they were sitting at the window where they could dine and watch the world go by. It was a small but intimate restaurant, with candles in wine bottles in the centre of each table. Lily was enchanted – it was like something out of a storybook; in fact, everything felt unreal to her – as though she was living someone else's life.

'What would you like?' Louis asked. The menu was written in French and Lily couldn't understand a word of it. 'Would you like to try something a little different? Frog's legs or snails perhaps?'

'Oh *no*, thank you.' Lilly looked horrified and he laughed.

'Then perhaps some soup followed by chicken or maybe fish?'

They each tried the French onion soup and Lily settled on a chicken dish while Louis had pork chops, which he declared were cooked to perfection. For dessert they had tiny tartlets full of pears served with whipped cream and although Lily was full by that time, it was so delicious that she forced herself to eat every mouthful.

'That were lovely, thank you,' she told him as she dabbed at her lips with a snow-white linen napkin. 'But I've eaten so much I think I'll burst!'

'I feel the same,' he admitted. 'But I've got room for a coffee.'

After they'd finished their drinks, Louis said, 'How about I take you for a stroll along the River Seine before we go back to the hotel – that's if you're not too tired, of course?'

She nodded eagerly, so he helped her up from the table and they set off, her small hand tucked into the crook of his arm. It was a beautiful, balmy evening and when they came to the river she stared at it with childlike delight. It looked so pretty with the late sun glinting on the water.

'Oh, it's just . . . just wonderful,' she breathed.

He smiled. Lily was like a breath of fresh air, so gentle and undemanding.

'There are so many couples strolling about,' she observed as she glanced around and he laughed.

'Well, they do say Paris is the city of lovers.'

Just for a moment as she looked up at him, their eyes locked and something magical passed between them like a bolt of lightning. Then Louis' head leant towards hers and she was sure he was going to kiss her. And despite all her promises to herself that they could never be more than friends, she knew that she would be powerless to stop him.

Suddenly an open-topped carriage with a young couple clopped along behind them so close that they could have reached out and touched it and the magical moment was broken. As they sprang apart it would have been hard to say who looked the most embarrassed.

'We, er . . . we'd better be gettin' back to the hotel now. We've 'ad a long day,' Lily said in a shaky voice.

'You're right. And we have a long day ahead of us tomorrow. I wonder how we'll find Arabella?' he mused.

Lily shrugged. 'Well, we 'aven't got long to wait now before we find out, 'ave we?'

He nodded in agreement and soon after, they arrived back at the hotel and went to their rooms, each wondering what the next day would bring.

Chapter Thirty-One

Lily was woken by a gentle tap on the door the next morning and a maid appeared carrying a tray of hot croissants and a pot of coffee.

'*Bonjour*, mademoiselle.' The maid placed the tray down on a small table at the side of the bed and went to swish the curtains aside, letting in shafts of early morning sunshine. Lily sat up in bed and the maid placed the tray on her lap, telling her, '*Bon appétit.*'

After she left, Lily sank back against her pillows and poured herself a cup of coffee. I could get used to this, she thought happily. Soon after she rose, washed and hurriedly dressed and she'd just finished when Louis tapped at the door.

'Are you ready?'

'I am,' she told him, and snatching up her bonnet, she followed him out onto the landing. She had worn her cotton dress again and with her hair lying loose about her shoulders she looked young and pretty.

Outside the hotel, Louis hailed a cab and after talking rapidly to the driver in French he ushered Lily inside and settled on the squabs opposite her.

His face was grim now as he wondered what the day would bring. The address he had for Arabella was in a very poor part of the city and despite Arabella's assurances that Freddie had changed, he still didn't trust him. Still, he consoled himself, hopefully they would know very soon now.

Lily sat quietly, drinking in the sights of the city from the cab window. She sensed that Louis was nervous and worried, so she remained silent as the cab rattled across the cobblestones. In the city centre they passed shops that almost made her eyes pop. Expensive jewellery was displayed in some of the windows, the sunlight making the jewels sparkle, and life-sized mannequins wearing fabulous gowns were displayed in others. Dotted between them were chic eateries with tables and chairs beneath gaily coloured parasols out on the pavements where people sat drinking wine, talking and laughing in the sun. The way of life seemed so much easier here than back at home, but Lily supposed that the people who could afford to shop and eat in such a place wouldn't need to think about work.

At one point they crossed a bridge across the River Seine, sparkling in the sunshine, but soon the cab turned to the left and the streets became narrow with shabby terraced houses on either side. Skinny mongrel dogs were scavenging in the gutters for any scraps of food they could find and barefooted, emaciated children sat lethargically with their backs against the walls of the houses as if they didn't even have the energy to play. Women in grubby aprons stood in little groups gossiping and as the cab passed them, they stared at it curiously.

After a time, the cab stopped and the driver came to speak to Louis through the window, gesticulating wildly.

'The driver says he won't go any further,' Louis told Lily with a grim expression. 'But don't worry, he assures me the address we need isn't too far away now.'

He paid the man and helped Lily down from the cab and she shrieked as a large rat suddenly scurried across her foot. The street was covered in litter and in places raw sewage was running along the gutters, the smell of it making Lily want to retch.

'I can't believe Arabella and Annie are living in a place like this. What the *hell* was Freddie thinking, bringing them here?'

Lily could see how angry Louis was so she said nothing as he took her elbow and started to march her along. The women were openly staring at them now and Lily felt embarrassed. Back at the hotel she had been self-conscious about her clothes being too poor, but here she suddenly felt very overdressed, for most of the women were clad in rags.

Louis kept his eyes straight ahead, trying to ignore the children who chattered to him in French as they begged for coins.

'Poor little things,' Lily whispered. 'They look 'alf starved.'

'Yes, I know, but the trouble is if we give to one we're likely to be mobbed,' he told her through clenched teeth. 'Come on, just keep going and try to ignore them.'

After a short time, he took the piece of paper with Arabella's address on it out of his pocket again and studied it. 'I think that's it over there.'

Lily looked with dismay at the crumbling terrace he was pointing at. The houses were so close together here that hardly any sunlight could filter past them and the smell was worse than ever. The front door of the house was swinging open and as they approached a young woman with an old face came through it clutching an emaciated baby to her chest.

Louis spoke to her rapidly in French and she nodded and waved her hand to the top of the building.

After thanking her Louis pressed a coin into her hand and her thin face lit up.

'*Merci*, monsieur.' She hurried away clutching the coin as if it was the crown jewels as Louis and Lily tentatively entered the house.

Lily's heart sank. The night before she had dared to believe just for a little while that Louis might have feelings for her, but seeing these conditions, she saw how out of place he looked and it brought back to her just how far apart their worlds were.

Here the smell was even worse, if that was possible – a mixture of stale cooking, the stench of unwashed bodies and overriding that the stink of stale urine and faeces. Lily put her hand over her mouth as they looked around in dismay. It seemed there were whole families living in each room and the sound of babies crying and people arguing was echoing about the filthy hallway.

'The woman told me Arabella is on the top floor,' Louis said, his face set, and quietly Lily followed him up the stairs. The distemper was peeling off the walls and the bare wooden stair treads were rotten in places making Lily wonder if they were safe. The further they climbed, the darker it grew, and Lily began to feel as if she was walking into hell. But at last they reached the top floor and Louis pointed to a door. 'That's it, number twenty-two.'

As they approached it, they heard a baby crying and Lily instantly recognised it as Annie's cry.

Louis rapped on the door, and when there was no reply, he rapped again, louder this time.

'Arabella . . . it's me, Louis. Open the door this minute!'

As he and Lily stood there anxiously waiting, they faintly heard footsteps shuffling towards it and when it opened, there was Arabella, but she looked nothing like the woman Lily had left in Calais just a few short weeks ago. Her hair hung in rats' tails about her shoulders and she had lost so much weight that her crumpled gown, which looked as if it hadn't been changed in days, hung off her. There were dark circles beneath her red-rimmed eyes and they had a hopeless look in them.

'Good God! What's happened to you?' Louis took a step towards her but she stepped back from him.

'If you've come to gloat and tell me what a fool I've been, you might as well leave now,' she said sullenly.

'Of course I haven't come to gloat.'

Uninvited, Lily pushed her way past them both and hurried into a room at the end of a short passage where she found Annie crying piteously.

'Oh Annie, sweet'eart. Look at you!'

The child was lying on a crumpled bed and at sight of Lily she held her arms up. Lily scooped her up immediately as a solitary tear slid down her cheek. Annie looked even worse than Arabella, if that was possible. Her small face was gaunt and pale making her eyes look huge, and her arms and legs were stick thin. She looked nothing like the chubby, happy baby she and her mother had cared for back in Galley Common. She stank too, and Lily could see at a glance that her binding was sodden.

Arabella and Louis joined her and Louis looked just as horrified at the first sight of his niece and the room she had been living in. Damp was running down the walls in places and bits of rags serving as curtains hung at the windows, blocking out the draughts from the broken panes. Apart from the metal-framed bed, the only furniture was an old table, which leant drunkenly to one side, and two mismatched hard-backed chairs. There were holes in the skirting boards and Louis shuddered as he imagined the mice and rats that lived inside them.

'She's crying because she's hungry. We both are. The last of the moncy Freddie left me is gone now,' Arabella told him dully.

'Where is he?' Louis asked angrily.

Arabella shrugged. 'Who knows? When I met him in London, he told me that he'd left the army and had a home for us and a job to go to in Paris. He said he would fetch Annie and we would be a family and get married, and, fool that I am, I believed him . . . *again*! Everything was wonderful for a few days, but then he began to complain about Anastasia constantly crying and he started to stay out at night and not come home. The so-called job turned out to be gambling, and in no time at all we had to leave the house he'd rented to come here. It's like living in hell and that one there doesn't stop crying!' She nodded towards Annie who was gripping on to Lily as if she was a lifeline. 'Then about four days ago there was a knock on the door and two army men arrested him and took him away. Apparently, he hadn't left the army at all – he had gone absent without leave. The small amount of money he left me ran out yesterday and we haven't eaten since. So go on, tell me *I told you so.*'

Louis shook his head. 'Pack up all your and the baby's things. I'm getting you out of here *right* now.'

She shrugged. 'I have nothing but what I stand up in. I pawned my gowns to get money to buy food.'

Louis gritted his teeth as he took a last look around the damp, dark room before taking her elbow and leading her out of it with Lily carrying Annie closely behind him. They had almost reached the foot of the stairs when a plump middle-aged woman appeared in the hall and began to shake her fist and rant at Arabella in French.

Louis quickly answered her and after feeling in his pocket he took some money from it and pressed it into the woman's hands.

'It appears that Freddie didn't bother to pay any rent,' he told them angrily, but the woman was seemingly happy now and let them pass with a smile on her face.

The walk back to the main street took them longer because Arabella was weak, but at last they reached it and after Louis had put them all into a cab, they set off back to the hotel.

'What's going to happen to me?' Arabella asked worriedly as the horse clip-clopped along. 'I can't come home now that Mama and Papa know about Anastasia!'

'Let's just get you and the baby clean and fed and then we'll decide what's best to do,' her brother told her. 'There's no way you could have stayed there. It's a good job we turned up when we did because the landlady was going to throw you out anyway.'

When they reached the hotel, Louis booked another room for Arabella and ordered some food for her and the baby to be sent up immediately.

Annie was still clinging to Lily for dear life, and it broke Lily's heart to see such a drastic change in her. She had always been such a happy, sweet-natured baby but now she seemed to be a mere shadow of her former self.

While Arabella and Annie ate, Louis gave one of the porters a healthy tip to go out and buy all the basics the child would need, and an hour later, with a full belly and a clean bottom, Annie fell fast asleep on the bed.

At that point, Louis pressed some money into Lily's hand asking her, 'Could you take Arabella to get what she needs? She can hardly travel in the clothes she's wearing. Perhaps a new gown and a cloak and, er . . . whatever it is you women wear beneath your gowns.'

Lily grinned to see his embarrassment, but Arabella yawned and shook her head. She looked totally exhausted.

'Could we perhaps do it tomorrow, Lily? I'm so tired.'

When Lily glanced at Louis, he nodded. 'Very well, you get some rest. Lily and I have some business to attend to, so we'll see you later.'

Outside the room, hc told her, 'We may as well go and find Monsieur Levigne's art gallery and make some good use of our time.'

Lily suddenly looked nervous. 'All right . . . if you're sure the sketches are good enough.'

'We'll let the monsieur be the judge of that,' he responded.

So soon after, with the sketches tucked safely in a folder, they were off and once again Lily was grateful that she had Louis there with her, for she had no idea of where they were going.

The cab dropped them outside a very smart art gallery and as Lily saw some of the priceless works of art displayed within, her stomach sank. It was hard to believe that after being used to handling such brilliant works by well-known artists Monsieur Levigne would be interested in her efforts. She licked her lips nervously, and sensing her hesitation, Louis said, 'Come along, nothing ventured nothing gained! We've come this far, it would be silly to turn back now.'

As they entered the gallery, a middle-aged woman in a very chic gown came forward to greet them in French. She spoke to Louis for a few moments before smiling and beckoning them to follow her to a small office where they found Monsieur Levigne sitting at a desk.

'Ah, Miss Lily.' He rose to greet them with his hand outstretched and Lily hastily introduced Louis. 'Eet is so nice to see you . . . but come, I am keen to see more of your beautiful sketches.'

Lily took them from the folder and the monsieur spread them across his desk and began to study them avidly.

'They are quite excellent,' he said eventually, tapping his finger on the one Lily had done of the pit from the top of the valley. 'But theese one is outstanding. You 'ave managed to combine the beauty of the surroundings with the harsh reality of the pit!'

Lily blinked in surprise and Louis beamed. 'So would you be interested in buying any of them?'

'I think the best thing to do, if you would entrust them to me, would be to allow me to show them in the gallery and see what sort of interest they receive. Depending on that I would price them accordingly and then forward to you for each one that is sold, shall we say, fifty per cent? I will of course first 'ave to 'ave them framed to show them to their best advantage and deduct the cost of that. Does that sound fair?'

'Yes, sir, it does,' Lily assured him. Anything she could get for them would be better than nothing, she supposed, otherwise they would just remain in their folder.

'In that case, we shall shake on it and 'ave a leetle drink to celebrate, *oui*?' He summoned the woman who had greeted them and spoke rapidly to her in French. She disappeared, only to return minutes later with a silver tray on which stood a bottle of champagne and three cut-glass goblets.

Monsieur Levigne popped the cork and poured it. 'Here's to a prosperous partnership for both of us, *ma chérie. À votre santé!*' They clinked glasses and Lily giggled as she sipped and the bubbles went up her nose.

Half an hour later, she walked out of the gallery on Louis' arm with a broad smile on her face. Hopefully this would be the start of a mutually advantageous partnership with the charming little Frenchman.

Chapter Thirty-Two

To allow Arabella to rest, Annie slept in Lily's room that night, and following breakfast the next day, she and Arabella went shopping for basic necessities, while Louis entertained Annie.

Arabella chose a plain gown and cloak and some underwear without showing much interest, but after what she had been through Lily supposed that fashion would be the last thing on her mind. Louis had booked them on a ferry that would leave the next morning, so when the young women returned, he asked them, 'How would you like a boat trip on the River Seine?'

Arabella shook her head. 'I won't, if you don't mind. I'm not really in the mood, but why don't you two go and take Annie? I'm sure she'd enjoy it.'

Louis looked at Lily questioningly and she nodded. 'I'd like that very much. Thank you.'

And so after lunch, she dressed Annie in one of the new outfits and they set off. It was an afternoon that Lily would never forget, and as the boat sailed along the river with the sunshine sparkling on the water she wished it could go on forever. People who saw them smiled, thinking what a charming little family they made and the looks were not lost on Lily, and she wished with all her heart that it could be true. As they pandered to Annie, she felt the closeness that had come briefly between them two nights before return with full force. Louis obviously adored his little niece and would make a wonderful father one day, but she would not be the mother and it put a dampener on her mood.

On the way back to the hotel Louis became sombre again. 'Arabella is very upset, isn't she?'

'I think she's more angry an' humiliated than upset,' Lily answered. 'Angry that she gave 'im a second chance and 'e betrayed 'er again. But what do you think will 'appen when we get 'ome? How do you think your parents are goin' to treat 'er an' Annie?'

Louis sighed. It had been troubling him too. 'I'm not going to pretend they're going to be happy about it,' he admitted. 'Mama is a frightful snob, as you know, and she'll be mortified when word gets out, but I have had a thought.'

'Oh? An' what's that?'

'I thought perhaps we could put the word around that Arabella had been widowed. People seem to have more sympathy for widows than unmarried mothers. What do you think?'

'I suppose it's worth a try. There ain't no one can prove any different, is there?'

'I'll put it to Arabella the minute we get back to the hotel and see what she thinks of it.'

At first Arabella wasn't keen on the idea but when her brother asked if she could come up with a better one, she shrugged. 'I suppose it's worth trying. But people aren't stupid,' she said miserably.

At that point, Lily left them to have some private time, and as she sat in her room watching the busy streets below, she felt sad. Arabella had clearly loved the young captain with all her heart and he had betrayed her in the worst possible way – not once but twice. *If that's what love is I reckon I'll avoid it*, she thought, trying to banish the picture of Louis' kind face that flashed before her eyes. *Don't go thinkin' daft things that can never be*, she scolded herself. But no matter how hard she tried to stop them, thoughts of Louis never strayed far from her mind.

They were on the last leg of the journey to Trent Valley Station two days later when the last vestiges of hope that Louis could ever return her feelings were dashed.

231

'How are things going with you and Miss Samantha Thompson?' Arabella asked.

Louis blushed and stared out of the window. 'I think Mama is hoping we'll announce our engagement when we get back,' he muttered.

'Oh!' Arabella sounded mildly surprised. 'I wasn't aware that you had feelings for her?'

He sighed. 'To be honest, I'm doing what's expected of me. You know Father has always wanted a union between the two families. He and Mr Thompson will be the biggest landowners in the county if Samantha and I get married.'

'And you feel that's enough to get married for, do you?' Arabella scowled at him. 'Where does love come into it, Louis?'

He was annoyed now and scowled back at her. 'We certainly couldn't do any worse than you and your captain, could we? And that *was* supposed to be a love match!'

Arabella looked as if he had struck her and tears stung at the back of her eyes. But she couldn't argue with him because he was right, and so she shrugged and fell silent.

Hearing this, Lily felt utterly bereft, even though she knew it was stupid. Closing her eyes, she silently urged the train to go faster. The sooner she was back home and away from Louis the better!

Finally they arrived at Trent Valley Station, where Louis hailed a cab to take them to Oakley Manor.

'Do you think perhaps it would be best if you went and saw Mama and Papa alone to tell them what's happened?' Arabella said fearfully once the cab had set off.

'You could come back to the cottage with me,' Lily volunteered. 'Just till Louis 'as paved the way, so to speak. I know my mam will be thrilled to see Annie again.'

Louis smiled at her gratefully. 'I think that's an excellent idea, Lily. Thank you.'

She stared out of the window, cursing herself for a fool. Over the last few months, she had felt closer to him, but now she realised that he could never have had anything other than friendly feelings for her. Louis was simply a very nice, kind young man and anything else had been in her imagination.

Sara was ecstatic when Lily entered the cottage with Arabella and Annie, and the baby instantly held her arms out to her. Sassy was so excited, her tail was turning circles and Ginny was beaming from ear to ear. Arabella, however, could only stand there looking embarrassed. Richie was at band practice, her mother informed her, but he would be happy to see her home when he returned.

'You see, the thing is, miss,' Sara said cautiously to Arabella. 'We only 'ave three bedrooms so if yer plannin' on stayin' overnight—'

'She isn't, Mrs Moon,' Louis assured her hurriedly. 'I'd just like to go and pave the way home for her with my parents, if you know what I mean?'

'Aye, I do, sir.' Sara had no idea why Arabella and Annie had returned but she had no doubt she would find out in due course. Meanwhile she told Ginny, 'Go an' put the kettle on an' make a brew, would yer, luvvie? I bet they're all dyin' fer a cuppa after the long journey.'

Lily watched Ginny almost skip across the kitchen, and could hardly believe the change in her. Her once lank, dull hair was now clean and shining in waves across her shoulders and she had some colour in her cheeks. But the biggest change was in her face. Her eyes were no longer fearful and she seemed to be wearing a permanent smile. Life at the cottage away from the cook's bullying was obviously suiting her and Lily was glad.

She walked back outside to the cab with Louis. 'Thank you once again, Lily,' he said sincerely.

'I didn't do that much.' She kept her eyes averted from his. Now that she knew his intention to wed Samantha Thompson, she felt she needed to put some distance between them before her feelings for him went any further.

Could she have known it, Louis was feeling much the same as he gazed pensively from the carriage window on the journey back to Oakley Manor. There was something about Lily that drew him to her like a magnet. Admittedly, she was working class but she was kind and loyal with not a selfish bone in her body from what he had seen of her, whereas Samantha was pampered and spoilt. Even so, he knew that he owed it to his parents to make a good marriage, especially after the way Arabella had behaved. They were depending on him to pull the family's reputation back, but the thought of spending the rest of his life with a woman he didn't love filled him with dread.

He was aware that many men in his position would have offered to put Lily in a small house and keep her as his mistress but he would never dream of insulting her in such a way. He doubted very much she would agree, anyway, so the best thing from now on was to try to put her out of his mind.

His thoughts moved on to what his grandmama and parents were going to say about Arabella's latest predicament. Would they accept her and her illegitimate child back into the family fold? He shuddered as he realised that he wouldn't have long before he found out. Best to get home and just get it over with.

The first thing he saw when the carriage drew into the passing circle in front of the manor house was the doctor's carriage and he frowned as he paid the cabbie and strode up the steps.

The butler hurried to answer the door and as Louis passed him his hat and coat he asked, 'Are my parents both in, Pennyworth?'

The butler looked slightly harassed. 'Indeed they are, sir, but, er . . . I'm afraid the doctor is with your father at present. He took ill this morning.'

Louis frowned. 'What do you mean, *took ill*?'

'The manager from the pit arrived just before lunchtime to tell us that your father had collapsed and they were bringing him home. It appears he has had some sort of seizure.'

'I see. Is my mother with him? And are they in their bedroom?'

'Yes, I believe so, sir.'

Louis took the stairs two at a time and barged into his parents' room to find his mother standing at the side of the bed dabbing at her eyes with a little lace-trimmed handkerchief while the doctor leant over his father's inert figure.

'Oh darling, you're back. Thank goodness.' Lady Clarissa started to cry in earnest.

'What's happened?' he asked urgently.

As the doctor straightened from his patient, Louis caught his first glimpse of his father's face and was horrified. His eyes were rolling and one side of his face had dropped significantly making him look as if he were grimacing. Drool trickled from one corner of his mouth and it was clear that he was oblivious to everyone and everything around him.

'I'm afraid it appears that your father has suffered a severe seizure,' the doctor told him, his face grave.

'I see . . . and will he survive it?'

'Hmm . . .' The doctor tapped his chin as he stared down at Lord Bellingham. 'I can't answer that, in all truth. What I can say is, if he survives the first twenty-four hours, there is a chance he'll come through it, but even then, I'm afraid he might never be the same man again. This is a warning and he'll have to learn to take things much easier.'

Louis wiped his hand across his eyes. This would mean he would have to take over the running of the pit and the many other businesses much sooner than he'd anticipated. Immediately he felt guilty for thinking of himself and crossed to place his arm across his mother's shoulders.

'What can we do for him?'

'Well, he will have to have someone with him at all times. Try and get as much fluid into him as you can. There's some laudanum there to be administered in small doses should he appear to be in pain. Other than that, I'm afraid there's very little we can do but keep him as comfortable as we can and pray.' The doctor snapped his bag shut. 'But now I must be on my way. Of course, should you need me during the night you must fetch me, and I shall come immediately. If not, I shall be back first thing in the morning. Good evening.'

After the doctor left, Louis and his mother stood looking down at George Bellingham. He had been such a virile, energetic man but now suddenly he looked old and frail, as if all the life and energy had been sucked out of him.

'What can we do now?' his mother asked in a trembling voice.

Louis gently squeezed her hand. 'We wait, Mama, and as the doctor said, we pray.'

He bit his lip. He had come home to inform his parents of Arabella's return and she was now waiting at the Moons' cottage for him to come back and fetch her. He'd never considered that he'd be walking back into a crisis. But there was no way he could leave Arabella where she was for the night. The Moons' cottage was full as it was and so cautiously, he said, 'Could I have a quick word with you, out on the landing, Mama?'

'Can't you say whatever it is in here?' She glanced anxiously at her husband.

Louis shook his head. There was no way of knowing if his father could hear them, and the last thing he wanted was to put yet more stress on him, so he gently guided her from the room and once they had the door closed behind them, he hurriedly told her of the state they had found Arabella and the baby in.

'The long and the short of it is, she's at the Moons' cottage right now waiting for me to go back for her. There's no way she can stay there. They're packed to the rafters as it is, so I shall have to bring her home.'

'Oh dear!' Lady Clarissa began to gnaw at her knuckle, something she always did when she was upset.

'But what will your father say? And what will people say when word gets out that she's back! And with a *baby*!'

Louis sighed and wiped his hand wearily across his eyes. Even now his mother could worry more about their reputations than her own daughter and grandchild.

'It will be fine,' he said testily. 'For a start, Father needn't know that she's back, at least until he's over the worst. As for the rest, I'll tell you about my idea later.'

His mother wrung her hands together and Louis sighed again. It had been a hectic few days and he was exhausted, but it was obvious that he was going to have to take control now. His mother was certainly in no state to.

'You go back in to Father and leave everything else to me,' he ordered and with a nod she went back into the bedroom.

Chapter Thirty-Three

When Louis arrived back at the cottage in the carriage a short time later, he found the atmosphere inside tense. Lily's younger sister was there and she glowered at him as he entered, although he had no idea what he might have done to offend her.

Arabella rose from her seat immediately, looking anxious to leave.

'I'm afraid I have some bad news,' he told her quietly. 'Father has had a seizure.'

'Will he be all right?' This was Lily.

He spread his hands. 'From what the doctor said it could go either way, so we'd best get back as soon as we can. But thank you for all you've done again, Lily.'

Arabella lifted a dozing Annie and added her thanks to her brother's before they both left, keen to get home.

'Eeh, if it ain't one thing it's another,' Sara said sadly. 'Poor Lord George, eh? It just goes to show that when your time is up it's up, be you a beggar or a king.'

'Let's just hope it doesn't come to that,' Lily replied, then turning her attention to Bridget she asked, 'And how are you?'

'Getting' fat,' Bridget spat churlishly, although in truth her pregnancy was barely visible.

'Well, you were the one who wanted to get wed,' her mother pointed out. 'An' babies are usually what follow after a weddin', especially in your case.'

Bridget pouted and crossed her arms. 'Happen I didn't realise how borin' bein' married is.' She glared at Lily. 'An' look at you, all done up like a dog's dinner. Ma tells me you've been jauntin' off again wi' Master Louis. It's all right fer some, ain't it?'

'That's quite enough o' that sort o' talk, our Bridget,' her mother scolded, wagging her finger at her.

'It's fine, Mam.' Lily stared at her sister. 'I only went jauntin' off, as you put it, to 'elp bring Miss Arabella an' Annie home. But don't worry, I ain't gettin' ideas above me station. I shall be back to bein' a parlour maid tomorrow.'

'So you don't have any feelin's for 'im then?' Bridget said snidely.

'Don't be stupid. What chance would I stand? I'm a pit wench an' he'll be the lord of the manor when owt happens to his father, which might be sooner than we thought, goin' on what he just said. Why would 'e look at someone like me? I reckon you'll be hearin' of his engagement to Miss Thompson any time now.'

Bridget sniffed, but thankfully she let the subject drop and soon after she set off for home, albeit reluctantly.

'She really ain't happy, is she?' Lily said quietly as she stood at the window watching Bridget walk off down the valley. Even from the back she looked as if she had the weight of the world on her shoulders. Perhaps being wed and having children wasn't all it was cracked up to be, she thought. It certainly hadn't done much for Miss Arabella or their Bridget.

'She were keen enough to split you from Robbie,' her mother answered. 'An' now she's payin' the price. Robbie don't seem any happier either, but there you are . . . they both knew what they were doin'.'

Lily went on to tell her mother of all that had happened in Paris and when she had finished, Sara sighed. 'Goodness knows what sort of a greetin' she's goin' to get up at the manor. I can't see either her mam or her dad welcomin' 'er back wi' open arms after the way she's performed.'

'She only did what she did because she loved the captain,' Lily pointed out.

Her mother shook her head dismissively. 'Happen she did, but after the way 'e treated 'er the first time, you'd 'ave thought she'd 'ave more sense than to lay 'erself open to bein' 'urt a second time. Still, what's done is done an' no doubt they'll sort it out one way or another. But now you should get yerself off to bed, miss. You must be tired after all that travellin'.'

'I am.' Lily stifled a yawn and after giving her mother and Ginny a peck on their cheeks, she stroked Sassy and set off to the bedroom.

For a few moments, she stood staring from the window, thinking back to the boat trip on the River Seine. Her cheeks grew warm as she remembered the way it had felt to sit so close to Louis; it would be very easy to let her feelings develop into love but, as if what he'd told Arabella on the train wasn't enough, the conversation with Bridget had reminded her again how foolish that would be. She'd come close to forgetting her station but now she would keep her distance. If she didn't, she could well end up with a broken heart. On that sad note she hopped into bed and tried to sleep.

As time wore on, she heard the rest of the family retire to their rooms and Ginny joined her in theirs. Lily didn't feel like talking so she pretended to be asleep and soon Ginny's gentle snores echoed around the room.

Shortly after, Lily heard what sounded like a tap on the bedroom window and she started. It's probably a bat or a bird flown into the glass, she thought. But seconds later it came again, so creeping out of bed she peered out to see a dark shape standing on the path.

'Psst . . . Lily . . . come down 'ere. I need a word.'

Recognising Robbie's voice, she frowned. She would have ignored him, but it occurred to her that something might have happened to Bridget, so, flinging a shawl around her shoulders, she crept down the stairs. Stepping through the door, she peered into the darkness. 'Is that you, Robbie? Is Bridget all right?'

'Aye, it's me,' he told her. 'And yes, Bridget is fine far as I know.'

'So what do you think you're doin' comin' 'ere at this time of night disturbin' me?' she said shortly.

He was standing in front of her now and as she looked up at him, she could see that he was unsteady on his feet and he stank of ale.

'Word went round the inn that you'd been seen comin' back in a carriage with the boss's son. Had a good time, did yer?' She could hear the jealousy in his voice and her blood ran cold. She wished now that she hadn't come down but she'd just have to handle the situation as best she could.

'We didn't go on a joyride,' she informed him with her nose in the air. The last thing she wanted to do was let him see he was intimidating her. 'We went to see Miss Arabella and the baby and once we had, she decided to come back with us for a visit to her parents. It's just as well she did too, what wi' Lord Belling'am bein' so ill. But anyway, it's none of your business what I do, Robbie. When are yer goin' to get that into yer 'ead? Now get yourself back to yer wife where you belong!'

'Ah, but that's the trouble,' he said pathetically. 'I *don't* belong with 'er. It's you I love an' allus will.'

Inch by inch, Lily was backing towards the door hoping she could get inside and shut him out, but as if he could read her thoughts, he lunged at her and grasping her arms in a vice-like grip, he pulled her towards him. 'Come on, Lily. Give us a little kiss. Yer know yer want to.'

Realising her strength stood no chance against his, Lily became compliant in his arms. She could feel his breath on her cheek now and biding her time she waited until she was pressed close before suddenly raising her knee into his most private parts with all the strength she could muster.

Robbie instantly let go of her and doubled over groaning. 'Ah Lily . . . what did yer 'ave to do that for? You've crippled me so yer 'ave!'

Lily didn't wait to hear any more but turned and ran for the door and once it was shut behind her, she slammed the bolt home and stood with her back against it, allowing her pounding heart to slow to a steadier rhythm. Outside she could hear Robbie wittering and groaning, but eventually he began to curse her, threatening that she would be his no matter what. She ignored him until, after what seemed like a lifetime, he finally staggered away.

Only then did she climb the stairs once more, promising herself that she wouldn't fall for that trick again, not even if he threw a brick straight through the window.

After leaving the cottage, Louis and Arabella pulled up in front of the manor, and once he had taken Annie from her and helped her down from the carriage, he asked, 'Are you ready?'

Arabella took a deep breath. 'Ready as I'll ever be. Come on, let's go and get this over with before I go in to see Papa.' Side by side they climbed the steps to the door.

The maid was just taking Arabella's cloak from her when her mother appeared on the stairs. She paused for a moment to stare at the child in Louis' arms then said tersely, 'We'd best go into the drawing room.'

Louis and his sister glanced at each other before quietly following their mother and once they were safely in the room with the door firmly closed behind them, Lady Clarissa turned in a swirl of satin skirts to glare at her daughter. '*Really*, Arabella, do you have *any* idea at all what you have done turning up here with that . . . that child? Once word gets around our reputation will be ruined for sure this time.'

'No, it won't,' Louis said defensively. 'People already think that Arabella is married to the captain so all we need to say is that she came home for a visit.'

'Oh yes, and what happens when she doesn't go back to him?' Clarissa's eyes were flashing.

'Then we put the word about that Freddie met with an accident and has been killed. Everyone will believe that she is a widow.'

Clarissa began to march up and down. What with George taking ill and Arabella showing up again out of the blue, it hadn't turned out to be the best of days. She stopped abruptly and tapped her foot as she considered what Louis had said before admitting reluctantly, 'Hmm, I suppose that *could* work.'

'Who is to know any different?' Louis asked.

Annie was squirming in his arms and his mother turned her attention to her. She had to admit she was a beautiful child. She reminded her very much of Arabella at that age. Tentatively she held her hand out and the child gripped her finger and gave her a gummy smile. 'And you say her name is Anastasia?'

Arabella nodded. 'Yes, Mama, but we tend to shorten it to Annie.'

'Well, you won't from now on. Annie sounds like a servant's name. From now on she will be called by her proper name as befits her rank. I'm going to call one of the maids to look after her while I go back to sit with your father. I dare say you will want to see him too, Arabella. Tomorrow I shall have the nursery prepared for her and we shall have to think about employing a nanny.' She pulled the silken rope to one side of the fireplace and a maid soon appeared and dipped her knee.

'Yes, ma'am?'

'Bradley, take the child and get her fed and bathed then have someone carry the crib from the nursery down into Miss . . . Mrs James's room.'

'Yes, ma'am.' The maid took Annie, pausing at the door to ask, 'What's the baby's name, ma'am?'

'She is Miss Anastasia.'

Louis suppressed a sigh of relief. It sounded like his mother was softening so there was just a chance that his sister would be accepted back into the fold after all.

Next, they all trooped back upstairs to see Lord George, and after checking on him, Louis left Arabella and their mother to sit with him while he went to visit old Lady Bellingham in the west wing.

'Ah, here you are. I heard you were back. Now tell me – what's gone on?'

So once again Louis explained what had happened to Arabella in Paris, and when he had finished the old woman clucked her tongue disapprovingly.

'Put the word out that she's come back to visit her sick father and that her husband is still in Paris,' she demanded bossily after thinking for a few minutes.

'That's our intention,' Louis assured her with a weary glance at Hudson who was hovering nearby. His grandmother was clearly very angry and he pitied Arabella when she came to see her – the old lady's tongue could be as sharp as a knife. The only saving grace was that she loved the girl so would hopefully forgive her eventually, especially when she met Annie. Who could resist her?

'The Moon girl,' she said starchily. 'Can we trust her to keep her mouth shut about what's gone on?'

'I'm sure of it. Lily isn't a gossip.'

At his quick response, she frowned and her arched eyebrows rose. '*Lily* . . . I hope you're not getting too friendly with her,' she warned. 'Just remember you are almost betrothed to Samantha Thompson, my boy. We've had enough stress with Arabella going off the rails without you following her with a common servant girl. Now make yourself useful and help me get along to your father's room. I want to check how he is.'

'Yes, Grandmama.' He offered the old lady his arm and they made their way along the seemingly never-ending landing, the old lady leaning heavily on him, until they came to the main part of the house.

When he finally made it back to his own room, he dropped onto his bed and sighed sadly, as visions of Lily filled his mind. He threw an arm over his eyes, trying unsuccessfully to block out the picture of her beautiful face laughing across the table at him in France. He needed to stop this, he groaned. It was hopeless and nothing good could ever come of his feelings for her.

Chapter Thirty-Four

Lily was sitting with her mother the next morning drinking a cup of tea before she set off for work, when Sara said, 'Listen, luvvie, promise me yer won't get goin' off on any more jaunts for them at the manor. It's put folk against us. Even though everyone knows the baby ain't yours, they're still sayin' there's somethin' goin' on between you an' the young master, cos why else would he let us stay in the cottage now Annie's back where she belongs?'

'I assure you there ain't!' Lily answered bluntly, but she knew all too well what her mother was talking about and dreaded to think how the rest of the staff would treat her when she got to work that morning – things had been bad enough before the trip to Paris.

Once again, she'd decided not to mention what had happened with Robbie the night before. It could only cause yet more trouble and she didn't want to make things even more miserable for Bridget.

She set off for work feeling nervous, glancing over her shoulder to make sure Robbie wasn't following her, but all was quiet and as soon as she reached the manor, she went into the boot room, which led off the manor's kitchen, to hang her shawl up. It was then that Cook's voice reached her from the kitchen.

'Hmm, there's more goin' on here than meets the eye, you just see if I ain't right,' the woman said. 'Huh! It's a bit of a coincidence, ain't it, that Miss Arabella, or Mrs James as we've now been told to call her, turns up sayin' she's come to see her dad! Think of it, he didn't take ill till yesterday so how could she have known it? She'd have been well on the way home afore he took bad. An' if

246

she's married all legal an' above board, why did Lily Moon's family spend the first few months o' the baby's life lookin' after her?'

Lily sighed with dismay – this wasn't going to be easy. Taking a deep breath, she sailed into the room where the cook was talking to the new kitchen maid. Biddy had taken the place of Ginny and thankfully Cook seemed to be a little more kindly disposed towards this one.

'Good morning,' Lily said brightly.

Cook sniffed. 'I were just sayin' to young Biddy here that it's strange Miss Arabella . . . er, Mrs James, has turned up just as her dad's had a turn. And where's her husband?'

'Captain James had to stay in Paris to work and so Arabella took the opportunity to come back with us for a visit.' Lily stuck to the story Louis had come up with. 'As it turns out, it's just as well she did, ain't it? Wi' the master takin' ill, I mean.'

The cook sniffed again, clearly not believing a word she said.

'Anyway, how is the master this mornin'?'

She'd already noticed that the house seemed unnaturally quiet.

'Not good by all accounts. The family an' the doctor are all wi' him right now. Still, we'd best serve the breakfast same as usual in case any of 'em decide to come down.' She was flipping bacon in a large frying pan, so with a nod Lily hurried away to set the table in the dining room.

Louis appeared just as she was finishing and she looked at him enquiringly.

He shook his head. 'I'm afraid father is still very unwell.'

'I'm sorry to 'ear that, sir.'

He was very aware that she had returned to calling him sir, but still, he supposed it wouldn't do for the rest of the staff to think they were overfamiliar with each other. He was painfully aware that Lily had been the subject of enough gossip as it was.

'Would you know 'ow many might be down for breakfast?'

He shrugged and ran his hand through his dark tousled hair. He clearly hadn't had much sleep, if any, and he was still dressed in the clothes he'd travelled home in.

'I'm not sure. Perhaps you could just put everything on the sideboard as usual and if they want to come down, they can help themselves.'

At that second the door burst open and a maid appeared all of a fluster. 'Lady Bellingham says you're to come straightaway, sir.'

Without another word, Louis turned and rushed from the room and Lily's heart went out to him.

She finished what she was doing and had just stepped into the hallway when a sob echoed down the stairs and a cold hand closed around her heart. It sounded like Arabella and had come from the direction of Lord and Lady Bellingham's room, so she feared the worst.

A few minutes later, back in the kitchen, Mrs Biggles appeared, her face solemn. 'I'm afraid the master passed away a few moments ago. I shouldn't bother preparing any more food, Cook. I doubt any of the family will want it.'

As she went back into the hallway Lily heard another sound and her ears pricked up.

'Is that Anni—Miss Anastasia crying?' she asked the housekeeper.

The woman nodded. 'Yes, one of the maids is with her but she's cried on and off all night,' she said wearily.

'May I go up to her? She knows me,' Lily pointed out.

'I suppose you could,' the housekeeper agreed uncertainly. The last thing the family needed at the moment was to have to listen to a squalling baby.

Annie's little eyes were swollen from crying when Lily entered the room shortly after, but the minute she saw Lily she stopped as if someone had turned a switch off, and held her arms out to her.

'You can go now, Mary, I'll take over,' Lily told the harassed maid and with a grateful nod the girl shot away.

During the course of the morning the undertaker and the local vicar arrived and Lily had never known the house to be so quiet, as the servants crept about their business. When Annie finally went down for a nap, Lily went to the kitchen to find the staff in a sombre mood.

'I wonder what'll 'appen to us all now?' Cook fretted. 'Do yer reckon the young master will keep us on, seein' as he's the lord now. It's a lot o' responsibility fer such young shoulders.'

'I hope things will go on much as they are now,' Mrs Biggles answered. 'After all, I assume his mother and grandmother will continue to live here.'

As they were speaking, they heard the undertakers carrying the coffin containing Lord Bellingham's body down the stairs and the cook mopped at her eyes with the hem of her apron.

'God bless him, may he rest in peace,' she blubbed. 'He weren't a bad master.'

They all nodded in agreement just as Mary appeared in the doorway to tell Lily, 'Miss . . . I mean, Mrs James would like a word wi' yer, Lily, up in her room.'

Ignoring the cook's sneer, Lily hastily placed her cup of tea down and followed Mary back up the stairs where she checked on Annie before continuing to Arabella's room.

Once inside she told her softly, 'I'm so sorry fer yer loss, miss.'

Arabella sniffed away a tear. 'Thank you, Lily. I'm just grateful that I managed to get home to see him before he passed. But that wasn't what I wanted to see you for. You see – I was wondering if you'd consider taking on the role of Anastasia's nanny, just until we can find a full-time one?'

'But wouldn't that mean me livin' in?' Lily looked uncertain. She couldn't see her mother being too happy with that arrangement.

'Yes, it would, but as I said, it would only be until we could find someone suitable. And we would, of course, be willing to raise your wages.'

'I, er . . . I'd have to 'ave a word wi' me mam,' Lily told her.

Arabella nodded in understanding. 'Of course you would, I quite understand, but as I said it would probably only be for a few weeks. Once we've had Father's funeral, I shall advertise for someone more permanent.'

'Does that mean that yer mam has allowed yer back into the fold?'

Arabella shrugged. 'To be honest, I think she's so in shock over losing Papa that she can't think of much else at present, but I'm hoping so. Otherwise I don't know what will become of me and Anastasia.'

'I'm sure she will,' Lily said kindly. 'And I believe she's told the staff to get the nursery ready for 'er today, so that's a good sign, ain't it? They're up there workin' on it even as we speak an' I can't see 'er goin' to all that trouble if she wasn't plannin' on yer both stayin'. But now, why don't yer come along an' spend a few minutes wi' her, she'll be awake any minute. It might cheer you up a bit.'

'I think I will.' Arabella slowly followed Lily from the room. She was still reeling from Freddie's second betrayal and now with the grief of losing her father she was as low as she could get.

It was mid-afternoon, when Mrs Biggles informed Lily that the nursery was ready for Annie to move into.

Lily had never been up there before and she was touched to see that the toys Louis and Arabella had once played with were still there. The window was open to allow the spring sunshine to flood into the room and everywhere was gleaming like a new pin. The crib was now made up with fresh sheets and blankets and there was a comfy chair to the side of the fireplace where the nanny could sit and watch her small charge.

'It's just lovely!' Lily told Mrs Biggles as she balanced Annie on her hip.

The older woman nodded in agreement. 'It will be nice to have a child about the place again,' she said. She could still remember

Louis and Arabella occupying the room as children. 'It's just a shame that she had to come when the house is in mourning for his lordship. Still, I dare say everything will come right so I'll leave you to it, Lily.'

'Er . . . there's just one thing.' Lily stopped her in her tracks.

'Yes?'

'Well, the thing is, I need to go an' see how me mam feels about me livin' in as a nanny till a more permanent one can be found. I can't just not go 'ome! She'd be worried sick.'

'Hmm, you're quite right,' Mrs Biggles agreed reasonably. 'Why don't I send Mary back up to watch the child while you get off and see her now?'

Lily gave her a grateful smile as she lay Annie in the crib and placed a colourful rattle in her hand.

Once Mary had turned up, Lily set off back to the cottage. As she approached the back way, she saw Ginny taking the dried washing off the line that Richie had strung up across the yard for them, and once again she was shocked at the change in her. She was humming away to herself with a smile on her face and whereas before Lily had always thought what a plain little thing she was, she suddenly realised that the girl was actually quite pretty. If the way Richie's eyes followed her about was anything to go by, he certainly thought so too!

'Why, Lily, what are you doin' back at this time o' day?' Ginny asked worriedly when Lily came into the kitchen. 'You ain't got the sack, 'ave yer?' Her mother was rolling pastry on the kitchen table and looked surprised to see her.

'No, nothing like that,' she said. 'But I'm afraid I've got bad news.' Lily plonked herself down on one of the hard-backed wooden chairs. 'Sadly, Lord Belling'am passed away this mornin'.'

'Oh dear, bless 'is soul.' Sara listened carefully as Lily told her about the offer of being a temporary nanny to Annie, and when

251

she'd done her mother tapped her lip thoughtfully. 'Hmm, I suppose it'd be in Annie's interest if you did,' she admitted. 'She knows you, don't she? But 'ow do you feel about it?'

Lily shrugged. 'I suppose it'll be all right, just till they find somebody more permanent.'

In truth, Sara wasn't altogether happy with the idea of Lily living in at the manor for a number of reasons. The first was she knew she would miss her, although now she had Ginny to keep her company, she supposed it wouldn't be so bad. But her main concern was that Lily would be in direct contact with Louis again, and that did trouble her. She'd seen the way Lily's eyes would light up when she caught sight of him, and the way his would soften when he saw her. They were clearly attracted to each other, even if they hadn't admitted it to themselves yet. The trouble was, should any relationship between them blossom, it could only end in heartache. They were from two different worlds. Particularly now Louis would be taking his father's place as lord of the manor. Still, she consoled herself, as Lily had said, it was only for a short time so she agreed to it.

'I'll pop back to see yer on Sunday afternoon an' bring Annie wi' me,' Lily promised her mother after she had packed a bag with a few essentials. And with that she set off back to what was to become her temporary home.

Chapter Thirty-Five

Two days later Lord Bellingham's body was returned to the manor in an open coffin to lie in state in the drawing room. There was an endless stream of visitors who came to pay their respects and the atmosphere in the house was subdued. In the kitchen the cook was rushed off her feet preparing the food for the wake that would follow the funeral that Friday, and tempers were frayed. Apart from up in the nursery, that was, where Annie was happily settling into her new home. In no time at all she had many of the staff who met her eating out of the palm of her little hand, but as yet she had spent little time with her grandmother, who had been busy with Louis organising the funeral and grieving for her husband.

Annie spent quite a few hours every day with her mother, who would take her out into the gardens for some fresh air, and every evening, just before her bath, Louis would visit her in the nursery.

It was funny, Lily thought, that she had hoped to see less of him when they got back from Paris, and now here they were living in the same house. But one evening he didn't come at the usual time and when Mary brought up Lily's supper, she found out why.

'The Thompson family 'ave just arrived,' she informed Lily. 'An' Mrs Biggles says they'll be stayin' till after the funeral, so Cook ain't pleased. It'll mean even more work for 'er havin' to feed them as well as get everythin' ready for after the funeral.'

Lily felt a little pang of jealousy but didn't comment.

'I saw Master Lou— Ooh, I should say Lord Bellingham now, shouldn't I?' Mary giggled. 'Anyway, I saw him an' that Samantha strollin' round the rose gardens afore I brought this up. She didn't look none too 'appy, I don't mind tellin' yer. In fact, she 'ad a face on her like a slapped arse! Spoilt bitch. None o' the staff like 'er, you know.'

Again, Lily didn't comment, and soon after Mary left her in peace to give Annie her supper. It was only when Annie was fed, bathed and settled in her crib that Lily crossed to the window to stare down into the grounds but the only people she saw there were the gardeners who were still busily hoeing the flower borders. She'd heard them complain that it seemed to be a never-ending job, for the weeds seemed to grow even faster than the flowers.

Once Annie was asleep, Lily settled down to read her book. It was one she had borrowed with Louis' permission from the manor's library, *The Adventures of Tom Sawyer* by Mark Twain, but she was restless for some reason, and couldn't seem to concentrate so she began to tidy the nursery yet again, although it didn't really need it.

She had almost finished when there was a tap on the door and Louis entered. 'Sorry I'm late this evening. Is she asleep?' he whispered as he crossed to the crib.

'I'm afraid so.' Lily continued to fold the small pile of Annie's clothes she was sorting. She expected him to leave but instead he took a seat and leaning back he sighed.

'I'm exhausted,' he admitted. 'I didn't realise just how much my father had to do. And now the Thompsons have arrived so Mother and I will have to entertain them until after the funeral. I'm afraid Samantha isn't any too pleased with me.'

'Oh, an' why is that?' The words were out before Lily could stop them.

'Well, I think she was hoping to hold a ball to announce our engagement sometime soon. But of course, that will be out of the question now, at least until my family have observed the twelve months' mourning period for my father.'

'Oh!' Lily felt guilty for being pleased about this but said nothing and soon after Louis left.

On a showery day in the middle of April, Lord George Bellingham was laid to rest. The curtains at the manor were tightly drawn until after his coffin left for the church in a hearse pulled by four magnificent matching black stallions wearing plumed headdresses, and all the servants wore black armbands on their uniforms. The women of the family were soberly dressed in black from head to foot and would be for the next twelve months.

As soon as the funeral cortege had departed, the maids rushed about the house starting up all the clocks that had been stopped within seconds of Lord George's passing, and following the service the house seemed to be bursting at the seams with mourners. Lily stayed out of the way upstairs in the nursery with Annie, but at last, in the late afternoon when they had all eaten and drunk their fill, the mourners, including the Thompsons – much to the servants' relief – began to leave. Now it only remained for the solicitor to read out the will to the family and they all joined him, solemn-faced, in the drawing room.

There were no surprises: the title, the manor, the London town-house and the many businesses all passed to Lord Bellingham's son. His mother, wife and daughter would be allowed to reside in the manor for the duration of their days and would receive a more than generous monthly allowance to be paid from the profits of the businesses.

Once he had finished reading it, the solicitor, a small, red-faced man with a balding head who was almost as far round as he was high, peered at Louis over the top of his pince-nez spectacles. 'Do you have any questions you wish to ask, my lord?'

'Er . . . no sir, thank you.' It felt strange to be addressed as 'my lord' and Louis wondered if he would ever get used to it, or the many duties that being a lord entailed.

'In that case my duty is done.' The man stood up and offered Louis his hand. 'Please get in touch should I be able to be of any further assistance to you.' Turning to Lady Clarissa and Arabella, he bowed. 'And once again, please accept my sincere condolences. Lord George was a good man but I have no doubt your son will fill his shoes admirably. Good day to you, ladies.'

When he'd gone, Louis sagged in his seat while Arabella and his mother sat dry-eyed and shaking. It had been an exceptionally hard day for all of them and he was glad it was almost over.

'I suppose I should go up and tell Grandmama about the contents of the will,' Louis said eventually. 'Not that there was anything that we weren't expecting. But I think I should tell you I intend to make a few changes. Nothing awful,' he assured his mother when she raised startled eyes to his. 'It's just that I feel the mine and Father's other businesses will run just as well with trustworthy managers in place. I shall keep a close eye on them, of course, but I don't wish to be as involved with them as Father was. I'd like to start breeding more horses and eventually have a stud farm that's known across the country.'

Lady Clarissa wasn't at all surprised. Horses had always been her son's first love and she had no doubt he would achieve his ambition now he'd set his mind to it.

'I'm more than happy to leave everything in your capable hands,' she confessed. The businesses had never really been of interest to her. 'But there is something I would like to talk to you about.'

'Oh?'

She shook her head and raised her hand wearily. 'Not tonight, darling. I'm exhausted, but it's nothing to worry about, I assure you. And now if you'll excuse me, I think I shall go and lie down for a little while.'

'Yes, and I should come up with you to check on Anastasia,' Arabella said as she too rose from her seat and they quietly left the room.

'How is she, Lily?' Arabella asked when she entered the nursery a few moments later. Lily was giving the baby her tea and at sight of her mother Annie smiled. They were growing much closer now, which Lily was happy about.

'She's been as good as gold as always,' Lily assured her, thinking how tired Arabella looked. 'How did the funeral go?'

Arabella sighed. 'As well as could be expected, I suppose.' She spent some time with the baby before she too went to have a rest and Lily started to get Annie ready for bed. She was almost done when Louis appeared, and he too looked drained.

Lily flushed when she saw him. 'Good evenin' . . . er, what do I call you, now you're a lord?'

'You call me Louis,' he said shortly as he crossed to Annie and lifted her. She instantly giggled with delight; she adored her uncle and it was obvious that he adored her too.

'Right.' Lily felt uncomfortable so while he spent time with Annie, she busied herself about the nursery until eventually she asked, 'An' how are you feelin'?'

'I'm glad the funeral's over,' he admitted. 'Although I'm still struggling to accept that my father has really gone. I keep expecting him to walk in the door.'

'I felt like that when I lost my dad too.'

'Oh Lily, I'm so sorry, I didn't think when I said it.'

'It's all right.' She smiled at him sympathetically. 'You'll find it gets a bit easier as time passes.'

'I hope so.' He passed Annie back to her and after saying good night he left the room.

It just went to show, she thought, whether you were rich or poor, the loss of a loved one hurt just the same.

Over the next week, Louis visited the managers at the mine and it was obvious that he had changes in mind, all of which Lily approved of. For a start, he told her during one of his visits to Annie, that he intended to reduce the hours the miners worked each week and to give them all a slight pay rise, which Lily felt was long overdue. He also intended to raise the age that children were allowed down the mine, and he ordered repairs to be done to the houses that his father let out. But for all that, it soon became clear that he would be spending more time in the stables. He also intended to buy more horses, which thrilled Richie, who loved the animals as much as Louis did.

All these changes, however, did not meet with old Lady Bellingham's approval. 'You'll rue the day you spoilt the workers!' she warned him. 'They'll start to take advantage of you, you mark my words, my boy.'

'But I'm *not* a boy, Grandmama,' Louis pointed out shortly, standing up to his grandmother. 'And surely contented workers who feel they are being fairly treated will be more compliant than those who are worn out and feel they are being underpaid?'

'We'll see!' She sniffed disapprovingly but Louis would not be swayed and stuck to his decisions.

As for Lily, her promotion to being Annie's nanny hadn't gone down well with the rest of the staff, and things had got so uncomfortable for her that she only ventured into the kitchen when she had to and all her meals were served in the nursery. On the odd occasion she did have to go down, she was met with scathing remarks from the cook.

'Must be nice to be favoured by the young master,' she said cuttingly one day when Lily was taking Annie's dirty clothes to the laundry. 'Every one o' the maids 'ere would 'ave jumped at the chance o' that job, but o' course with you about they didn't get a look-in. Makes us all wonder what you've done to get such preferential treatment. An' then there's the cottage an' all. I hear yer mam loves it there. It's no surprise, really. I mean it beats the little pit house she came from, don't it?'

Lily had learnt to bite her tongue and try to ignore the sarcasm. Anything she said could only add fuel to the fire, so she tried to say nothing. Even so, she was getting concerned. She had been told quite clearly at the outset that the post of Annie's nanny was only going to be temporary, but what would happen to her when she was no longer needed? Somehow, she doubted if she would be able to return to her job as parlour maid, and if she couldn't, what would happen then?

She said as much to her mother on her next afternoon off and Sara looked concerned. 'Try not to worry, pet,' she said gently. 'Something'll turn up. Ginny got our Bridget's old job in the shop this week so there's a bit more comin' in. Our Bridget ain't none too pleased about it, though. I think she's bitterly regrettin' goin' after Robbie now. She's as good as asked again if she can come here to live wi' us but I've said no. She made her choice when she married 'im an' she's got to stick by it. Oh, an' by the way, there's a letter come for you yesterday, it's behind the clock on the mantelpiece an' it looks very posh.

Lily went to fetch it, wondering who it could be from. When as she saw the London stamps her heart began to beat faster. She slit the envelope hurriedly and as she drew out the paper inside, two crisp five-pound notes dropped into her lap.

'It's from Monsieur Levigne,' she gasped. She began to read aloud.

Dear Lily,

It gives me great pleasure to enclose the money for the first of your sketches. I had some of them framed and placed in my London gallery and the first one sold within two days. They are getting much interest so I ask that you forward me some more as soon as you are able.

Kind regards,

Your friend, Andre Levigne

'Good grief!' Sara clapped her hands with delight and started to do a little jig as Lily stared down at the money in her lap in amazement. 'Didn't I allus tell yer how good yer were!' she crowed. 'An' wait till Louis . . . I mean, Lord Belling'am hears about this. He'll be tickled pink.'

Lily flushed with pleasure as she passed the money to her mother. 'And here was me worryin' about how we were goin' to manage if I lost me job, eh? Put that away in case we need it.'

'Per'aps yer could become a full-time artist. Your dad allus said you were good enough,' Sara said excitedly.

Lily chuckled. 'Now don't get carried away, Mam,' she warned. 'Monsieur Levigne has only sold one sketch up to now. It might just 'ave been beginners' luck an' he'll never sell another. Admittedly it's what I've always dreamed of, but that's what it's always been – a pipe dream.'

'Hmm, well we'll see, won't we?' Sara chirped. 'It could be that this is the first step towards your dream comin' true. You just make sure as yer work on some more up at the manor when the little 'un's asleep.'

'I will,' Lily promised. Suddenly the day had got better and she could hardly wait to tell Louis the good news.

When he visited Annie in the nursery that evening and Lily told him what had happened, he was almost as thrilled for her as her mother had been.

'Didn't I tell you you had talent,' he laughed. Then on a more serious note he asked, 'Have you got plenty of paper and charcoal to be going on with? It would be a good idea to keep them going to Monsieur Levigne.'

She nodded and he suggested, 'You could perhaps do some more of the pit from the top of the valley. That one you did was so descriptive. In fact, I wouldn't be surprised if that was the one that sold. And perhaps another one of Annie now she's a little bigger? You're very good at portraits too. Although I'd also like you to continue with the oil painting. That first one you did was incredible for a first attempt.'

'Thank you.' She blushed prettily and Louis' heart did a little flutter.

He rose abruptly. 'Right, I, er . . . I'd better be off. Good night, Lily.'

'Good night.' She frowned as she watched him leave, wondering what had caused his sudden change of mood, then after checking Annie was fast asleep in her crib she went to sit in the chair by the open window and was soon absorbed in sketching a family of rabbits that were playing on the lawn. It had been a good day.

Chapter Thirty-Six

It was late in May on a beautiful clear day when Louis was summoned to his grandmother's room. He had just taken delivery of his latest purchase – a stunning thoroughbred Arabian stallion – and didn't want to leave him even for a moment. The horse was coal black and Louis had decided to call him Midnight. He hoped to breed from him when he was a little older but now, he reluctantly left him in Richie's capable hands as he set off to see what his grandmother wanted.

She was clad in all her finery when he appeared in her room and she had so much rouge on her cheeks that she reminded him of a china doll.

'You wished to see me, Grandmama?'

'Well, of course I did otherwise I wouldn't have sent for you, would I?' she said stiffly, leaning on the handle of her cane with both hands.

Hudson was tidying some drawers and she grinned and raised an eyebrow at Louis.

'So, what's so important that it couldn't wait until later?' Louis was still a little annoyed at being dragged away from the stallion and he tapped his foot impatiently.

'I wanted to see you for two things, the first being that your mother has just informed me that she and Arabella intend to take the baby to the house in London to spend the rest of the mourning period there. They will leave within the next few days.'

'I see.' Louis was surprised that his mother hadn't mentioned it to him at breakfast – not that he had a problem with it. In fact, he supposed it might make things a little easier for her. 'And the second reason?'

'Ah.' She looked vaguely uncomfortable now. 'I, er . . . I was thinking . . . I know you can't officially announce your engagement to Miss Thompson during the mourning period, but perhaps we could arrange a ball for the week after the period ends and you could announce it then? Samantha called to see me last week and it's obvious she isn't happy about the delay, although of course she understands it couldn't be avoided.'

He frowned and began to pace up and down, then shook his head. 'I'm not so sure that would be a good idea.' His voice was cold. 'I think even after the official period is over, we should show some respect.'

'Hmph.' She looked annoyed. 'Are you quite sure that's the only reason?'

He scowled at her. 'What else would it be?'

'You tell me,' she snapped back. 'There's still a lot of talk flying around amongst the servants that you spend a lot of time up in the nursery with that . . . that *servant* girl who has ideas above her station!'

'I go to the nursery to see my niece.' Louis was keen to be gone now. He could see this fast developing into a row and he wanted to avoid it if he could. 'And if you're referring to Lily Moon, she's doing a grand job of looking after Annie.'

'Huh! And no doubt she's enjoying it. It's a lot easier than being a parlour maid, don't you think? I should warn you, Louis, that the servants are gossiping about you two. Hudson has heard them. What's more, Samantha has mentioned her too. She doesn't like her and thinks the girl has designs on you.'

'Then they think wrong and so does Samantha!' It was getting harder to control his anger now, so with a nod Louis turned and barged from the room before he said something he would regret. His grandmother could be an annoying old bat, but for all that, he loved her and didn't want to upset her.

For no reason that he could explain, his next stop was the nursery. He supposed he just wanted to check that none of this gossip had got back to Lily. She was playing on the floor with Annie when he arrived and when the little girl saw her uncle she squealed with delight and held her arms up to him to be lifted.

'I saw your new horse being delivered when me and Annie were lookin' out of the window,' Lily said conversationally as he slowly started to calm down. 'He's beautiful, ain't he?'

'He certainly is.'

There was a tap on the door and a maid appeared to tell Louis, 'Miss Thompson is downstairs waiting to see you, m'lord.'

He frowned. 'Tell her I'll be right down, Bridges, please.'

He patted Annie's springy curls and nodded politely towards Lily looking none too pleased. 'I'll see you both later. I dare say Samantha has come to see the new horse.'

Lily swallowed down her disappointment that the visit had been cut short. No matter how hard she tried, she looked forward to every minute they spent together. In some ways, she thought ruefully, life would be much easier if she could just go back to being a parlour maid.

Two days later Richie brought another letter from home for Lily and when she opened it yet another two five-pound notes dropped into her lap. In his letter Monsieur Levigne begged her to forward as many sketches as she could and when Louis came for his morning visit to Annie, she showed him the letter.

He beamed his approval. 'And do you have any more ready?'

She nodded and fetched them from her room, spreading them out on the table. Luckily, she had much more time now than she had when she was working as a maid. Whenever Annie had a nap or spent time with Arabella and her grandmother, Lily would busy herself sketching and so she had a sizeable amount ready to be posted.

'Which do you think I should send?' she asked as she studied them critically.

'All of them. They're excellent, and I shall post them for you,' he answered firmly.

She glanced up at him anxiously, still unable to believe that anyone would like her sketches enough to actually buy them. 'Thank you, but you must let me pay for the postage.'

'Actually, I could hand deliver them if I went to London with Mama and Arabella.'

Lily had been informed of the plans to take Annie to stay in London so she was already aware that her time as a nanny was almost at an end.

'Better still, why don't you come with us and then you can see some of them hanging in the gallery for yourself?'

'Oh, I, er . . .' Lily was flustered. 'But as soon as Annie goes I shall 'ave to get back to bein' a parlour maid else I'll 'ave Mrs Biggles after me. That's if I still have a job to come back to!'

'Oh, don't worry about the housekeeper. Leave her to me.' Louis looked embarrassed. 'I know the rest of the staff are giving you a hard time,' he admitted. 'And I did think of having a stern word with them but I didn't know if that might make things worse for you.'

'I think it would.' Lily met his gaze with her head held high. 'But don't worry about me, I can 'old me own.'

'So how about considering coming to London with us?'

She thought about it for a moment before nodding. 'All right. Arabella has hinted that she'd like me to go till they employ a new nanny for Annie but I felt bad about leavin' me mam. Still, I'm sure she'll understand. But I'd rather no one knew about my drawin's. That would just give 'em somethin' else to gossip about.'

265

He nodded in agreement.

'And when is your mother thinkin' o' goin'?'

'Early next week, I believe.' He ran his hand through his hair, something she'd noticed he did whenever he was nervous. 'Can you be ready to come with us by then?'

'Of course, I don't need to take much,' Lily assured him. 'Once I've seen Mr Levigne an' the new nanny 'as started I can come back.'

On her next Sunday off Lily told her mother of her plans and Sara looked a little worried. 'Won't this just give everybody sommat else to gossip about?' she asked with concern.

Lily chuckled. 'They're already gossipin', Mam, so what's the point o' worryin' about it.'

She went upstairs to pack her best clothes, and came down with a carpet bag full of everything she would need. She was pleased to see that her mother seemed fully recovered now. In fact, she looked better than she had for some long time, although Lily knew she still sorely missed her father. Even so, she and young Ginny had grown close and even Richie doted on the girl. Between them they had transformed the little cottage and the land surrounding it. There were now two pigs in the sty, chickens roaming the yard that supplied them with more eggs than they could eat, and the vegetables Richie had planted in the garden were thriving, as were the fruit trees in the orchard. They had a goat for their milk and Sara was teaching Ginny to cook, although without much success.

'I reckon she could burn water,' Richie confided to her one evening after tackling one of her culinary disasters. Ginny had taken the teasing in good stead and was slowly improving.

Now that Ginny was working at the shop during the day and contributing towards the expenses, they were managing more than comfortably, although Ginny had stated that she would like to save enough to rent a house so that she could get her mother and siblings out of the workhouse. Lily knew that her mother would miss her when she eventually moved out but already Sara had been able to put some money away for the winter and all in all they seemed content.

'So when yer get home from London will yer be comin' back 'ome again of a night?' Sara asked hopefully. She had missed her, and when Lily nodded, she beamed.

'Good, that's sommat to look forward to. But now come on, try some o' this blackberry an' apple pie afore yer go. It's delicious even if I do say so meself.'

Lily was only too happy to oblige and soon after she set off for the manor again to find Arabella waiting for her in the nursery. She had agreed to watch Annie while Lily went home.

'Lily . . .' she began when Lily appeared. 'I don't want to offend you but Mother and I are planning on some clothes shopping trips when we get to London. Most of the clothes I have from before I went to London and Paris are far too big for me now that I've lost so much weight, so I was wondering if you might like some of them? I've laid some out on my bed for you to look at if you're happy with the idea?'

When Lily hesitated, she rushed on, 'I shall only be getting rid of them. And if you don't want them perhaps your mother might like them to cut down?'

'In that case I'll 'ave a look, if yer sure.' Lily lifted Annie and they all trooped along to Arabella's bedroom where the bed was covered in clothes, the like of which Lily had never dreamed of owning.

'I thought this might be nice for you to wear to travel in.' Arabella held up the two-piece green velvet travelling costume that Lily had always admired. 'You might need to take the jacket in a little at the waist but I know you're good with the needle. And this is the blouse

I used to wear beneath it. And what about these two day gowns? You can have the petticoats to go beneath them too. Come on, why don't you try some of them on and then you can choose what you like.'

For the next hour, Lily almost forgot they were mistress and maid as Arabella helped her into one outfit after another. Eventually they had whittled the pile down to some clothes that her mother could make into skirts and blouses for herself and Ginny, and another pile for Lily to wear.

'Eeh, I'm goin' to feel very posh in this.' Lily grinned as she preened in front of the mirror in the travelling costume.

'You may as well have the bonnet to match. I don't have anything else it will go with,' Arabella told her kindly, and once she had placed it on her head, Lily could only stare at herself in amazement.

'You look every bit a lady,' Arabella assured her and Lily blushed wondering what Louis would think when he saw the transformation. But then she silently scolded herself. What did it matter what Louis thought of her? She was forgetting herself again and must remember that he was her master.

She thanked Arabella profusely and once she was dressed in her plain uniform again, she scuttled off back to the nursery. Suddenly she was looking forward to the trip; it would be nice to get away from the gossip and the jealousy of the staff for a few days.

One person who wasn't at all pleased to hear that Lily would be accompanying them to London was old Lady Bellingham, and she told her grandson so in no uncertain terms the first time she saw him.

'Are you going out of your way to upset Miss Thompson?' she snorted in disgust. 'She's going to be none too pleased when she hears that *that girl* is going with you again! An' what do you think the rest of the staff will think of it, eh? You're doing yourself no favours at all mixing with that pit wench,' she said spitefully.

'Surely you're aware that the family is relying on you to make a good marriage? Even more so after Arabella's escapade! I can't see anyone wanting to take her and the baby on if word gets out that the child is illegitimate.'

'Illegitimate or not she's still a part of our family and anyone can make a mistake,' Louis pointed out.

'Or several in Arabella's case,' Lady Bellingham said sarcastically. 'And why is Moon going with you anyway? Is she going to continue to be the child's nanny in London?'

'Temporarily, yes . Mother and Arabella will be interviewing for a new nanny once they've settled in,' Louis informed her. 'Lily was offered the position but she didn't want to live so far away from her family, which is quite understandable, don't you think?'

'Hmm, I would have thought beggars can't be choosers. If you ask me that young woman has ideas above her station.'

Once again, Louis felt they were teetering on the verge of an argument so he smiled down at her, saying, 'I must be off now, Grandmama. I have a new Andalusian mare being delivered today and I want to be in the stables when she arrives.'

'Oh, you and those dratted horses.' She scowled at him. 'Why can't you be like your father and just be happy to run the estate and the businesses? You shouldn't be down in the stables getting your hands dirty. We have grooms to do that! You're a lord now, although no one would know it from the way you behave.'

'The businesses are doing perfectly well,' he assured her. 'And why shouldn't I do what makes me happy?'

When she started to mutter, he grinned and made a sharp exit knowing that her bark was far worse than her bite.

Chapter Thirty-Seven

On the night before their departure to London, Lily was given a couple of hours off to return home and say goodbye to her family. It was a beautiful June evening with a gentle breeze blowing up the valley, and as she set off, there was a spring in her step. As she often did, she took the short cut through the copse, smiling as the late sunshine shone through the canopy of leaves overhead, dappling the ground with molten gold.

But her happiness was short-lived when about halfway through, she heard a twig snap behind her and whirling about she saw Robbie striding towards her, his face grim.

'Is it true what they're sayin? That you're off to London wi' yer toff again?' he ground out as he drew level with her.

Lily started to walk on, hoping that he'd take the hint and see that she didn't wish to speak to him, but he doggedly stayed at her side.

'I'm going with Miss Arabella and Lady Bellingham as well as Lord Bellingham,' she pointed out. 'I shall be looking after Annie for a time and I also have a little business to do there. As soon as it's done, I shall be coming back.'

'Oh aye, an' what business would that be?'

Lily suddenly stopped in her tracks and with her hands on her hips and her eyes blazing she turned to face him. 'Actually, Robbie Berry, as I've told yer before – what I do or where I go ain't no business o' yours anymore,' she snapped. 'If you'd care to cast yer mind back it were *you* as believed the worst o' me an' finished wi' me when I got back from Yorkshire wi' Miss Arabella's baby.

An' then, as if that weren't enough, yer set yer cap at me sister and had her pregnant wi' your baby wi'in weeks!'

Robbie scowled and dropped his eyes, looking ashamed. 'Happen I were wrong not to believe yer,' he admitted. 'But it were your Bridget as set her cap at *me*!'

'Whatever,' she growled, not giving him an inch. 'But the end result is, you're now a married man wi' a baby on the way, so just leave me alone!' She flounced away, leaving him in no doubt whatsoever that she had well and truly washed her hands of him.

Things got even worse when she entered the cottage shortly after to find Bridget sitting at the table with a face like a wet weekend.

She had been ranting to her mother about Robbie again but stopped when Lily came in.

'Hello, pet. I didn't expect to see yer again before yer left,' her mother commented, pleased to see her. She couldn't say the same about Bridget. All she ever seemed to do when she visited was whinge, and Sara was fed up with it.

'Oh, Miss Arabella has taken the little 'un visitin' so she gave me a couple o' hours off an' I thought I'd pop back to check everythin' was all right.'

'Why wouldn't it be?' Sara said cheerfully as she put the kettle on the hob to boil for a fresh cup of tea. Then turning to Bridget, she asked pointedly, 'Hadn't you better be gettin' off to see to yer husband's tea?'

'Huh!' Bridget tossed her head. 'His mam'll 'ave that ready. She still waits on 'im 'and an' foot. I might as well not be there; she does everythin' for 'im apart from wipe 'is arse!' she grumbled and behind her back Sara raised an eyebrow at Lily.

An awkward silence settled until Lily broke it when she asked, 'So when are yer getting' yer own place? I'm sure things will be much better when yer do.'

'Chance'd be a fine thing.' Bridget pouted as she crossed her arms above her swollen stomach. 'All the money we should be savin' fer us own 'ouse is goin' over the bar every night. Robbie is never in, an' even when he is he don't seem to notice I'm even there.'

Ginny appeared at that moment after working her shift at the shop and Bridget glared at her. She didn't like the closeness that had developed between the girl and her mother, nor the fact that Ginny was now doing the job that had been hers.

Lily on the other hand was happy to see her and they chatted amiably for a while until Bridget rose from her seat and started towards the door. 'I'll be off,' she said over her shoulder and the next second she was gone.

'Phew, I ain't sad to see the back of her today,' Sara admitted. 'She comes most days now an' all she does is moan.'

They sat together for a while chatting and enjoying a cup of tea but eventually Lily too rose saying, 'I'd best be off. I've still got the rest of Annie's clothes to pack afore I go to bed tonight. We're off early in the mornin' so I'll see you both when I get back.'

She chose to go the longer route back to the manor, just in case Robbie was lying in wait for her again, but thankfully there was no sign of him, although she frequently glanced over her shoulder just to make sure.

The following morning, Louis was standing in the hall with his mother and Arabella with Annie in his arms, when Lily appeared on the staircase in the travelling gown Arabella had given her, and at first sight of her his mouth dropped open.

Lily had dressed her hair into a neat chignon and with the pretty bonnet sitting atop it she looked every inch a lady, and a very pretty one at that.

'Why, Lily, you look . . .' He was almost lost for words. He had always thought Lily was a pretty girl but now she looked positively beautiful. 'Lovely,' he finished lamely.

'So, are we all ready?' Lady Bellingham was keen to get going. 'Come along, we don't want to miss the train.'

They were just about to get into the carriage when another came speeding down the drive. When it drew up alongside them, Samantha Thompson appeared with a wide smile on her face.

'Hello, darling, I thought I'd surprise you,' she addressed Louis.

He looked embarrassed. 'Oh, well it's very nice to see you but unfortunately we're just on the way to London.'

She giggled and batted her long eyelashes at him. 'I *know* that, silly, that's why I'm here. Mama and Papa have given me permission to come with you. I thought it would be nice for us to spend a little time together after all that's happened recently.'

'Oh . . . I see.' Louis looked shocked.

Lady Bellingham stepped in then. 'But of course you are welcome to join us, dear. You and Louis spend far too little time together. But what about your luggage?'

'It's already waiting for us at the station,' she assured her. It seemed she had thought of everything.

'In that case, hop in and we'll be on our way,' Lady Bellingham said cheerfully.

Louis helped his mother into the carriage first, closely followed by Arabella and the baby, Samantha, and finally Lily, who looked very colourful against the dark mourning clothes that Lady Bellingham and Arabella were wearing.

As Samantha settled gracefully in her seat, she stared at Lily as if she had a bad smell under her nose. 'Do you usually allow the servants to travel in the same carriage as yourself, Lady Bellingham?'

'On this occasion, yes I do,' Lady Bellingham answered graciously. 'Miss Moon has been a great help to us over the last few months and has kindly agreed to look after Annie until we can appoint a new nanny. She is also going to London on business of her own.'

'Oh really, and what would that be?' Samantha was intrigued.

'Lily is a very talented artist and is going to see a gentleman in London who is selling some of her sketches for her,' Louis answered.

'Really?' Samantha sniffed before turning her attention back to Louis with a dazzling smile. 'In that case it won't stop you and me from spending some time together, will it? I'm sure Moon is more than capable of conducting her business on her own.'

Louis remained tight-lipped and Lily had the distinct impression that he wasn't at all pleased with the latest development.

Once they had boarded the train, Miss Thompson made sure that Louis took the seat next to her own while Lily spent most of the journey keeping Annie entertained, not that she minded. She knew that he intended to follow through with his family's plans for him to marry Miss Thompson when the time was right, and she had accepted it, although she had to admit Louis didn't seem too happy to have his future fiancée joining them.

By the time they finally arrived at the house in Kensington much later that day, Annie was fast asleep on Lily's shoulder and once they had entered, the maid showed Lily up to the nursery while the others were shown to their rooms.

'Cor, you don't 'alf look smart,' Elsie told her as Lily lay the baby in the crib they had ready for her. 'An' it ain't 'alf nice to see you again, Lily.'

'It's nice to see you too, Elsie.' Lily gave the girl a warm smile. 'Do yer happen to know if anyone has applied for the post of nanny to Miss Annie 'ere yet?

'Not as I'm aware of. Don't think the 'ousekeeper 'as posted the notice yet.'

'Hmm!' Lily frowned as she took off her bonnet. 'Looks like I might be stayin' on fer longer than I thought then.'

Shortly after, Lily went to seek out Louis to ask him about her sleeping arrangements. 'It seems it might be a while till you find a nanny, so if I 'ave to stay longer, I will.'

He looked vastly relieved and grateful. 'Oh, yes please, if you would. I'm so sorry, Lily. I thought the position would have been advertised by now, but it seems nothing's been done.'

'I don't mind,' Lily assured him. 'Just so long as yer let me mam know when yer go back. I told 'er I shouldn't be gone for long an' I don't want her worryin'.'

'Of course, I'd be glad to. And thanks for saving the day yet again, Lily.'

A rustle of skirts sounded behind him and Samantha Thompson bore down on them like an avenging angel.

'Oh, here you are, darling,' she simpered. 'I was wondering where you had got to.' She pushed her arm through his possessively and glared at Lily. 'And what are *you* doing in this part of the house, girl? Don't the servants have their own accommodation away from the main house here?'

Before Lily could answer, Louis snapped, 'Actually, as I explained, Miss Moon here has just saved the day yet again by offering to stay on longer than expected to look after Annie.'

'Oh, how very *noble* of her!'

Lily gritted her teeth at the woman's sarcasm. Already Miss Thompson was dragging Louis in the opposite direction, so she turned and made her way back to Annie but not before she heard her say, '*Whatever* is that girl wearing, darling? I'm sure she couldn't have afforded an outfit like that on a servant's wage. She hasn't been stealing clothes from Arabella, has she?'

They were too far away for her to hear Louis' reply and she went on her way seething. Miss Thompson had made it blindingly obvious that she couldn't stand her and as far as Lily was concerned the feeling was mutual.

The following morning, Arabella came to relieve Lily of her duties while Lily began to gather her sketches together, placing them carefully in the leather folder Louis had bought for her.

The art gallery was on Oxford Street, but she was not sure where, but she was sure she could find it eventually, even if it meant traipsing up and down until she did. In the end, she didn't have to because as she was leaving the house Louis appeared from the drawing room, Miss Thompson trailing behind, hands clasped at the waist and her lips set in a grim line

'Ah, here you are,' he greeted her. . 'I realised you might be going to the gallery this morning so I thought I'd come with you.'

'I'm sure she can find her way perfectly well by herself, darling.' Miss Thompson's words came out in a hiss.

Lily raised her chin and looked steadily back at her. 'You're quite right, I'm sure I shall, Miss Thompson,' she said.

'No, I insist,' Louis told her. 'It was me that set you on this path and I just want to make sure that you're fairly treated. Elsie, fetch me my hat would you, please?'

The maid nodded and shot away to do as she was asked and seconds later, Louis followed her to the door. 'We shouldn't be too long, Samantha. Why don't you go shopping with my mother? I'm sure she would welcome the company. Goodbye.'

They stepped outside and he closed the door firmly behind them with a wide grin at Lily.

'I'm not so sure you should be doin' this,' she told him worriedly. 'Miss Thompson clearly ain't none too 'appy about it.'

Louis shrugged as he took the folder from her and tucked it under his arm. 'She'll get over it. Come on, let's go and sell some sketches, eh?'

Half an hour later they paused outside the art gallery in Oxford Street, which looked every bit as impressive as the ones in Calais and Paris. Displayed in the window on a gilt easel was an ornately framed still-life painting of fruit and flowers by Thomas Webster. It was so lifelike that Lily could scarcely take her eyes off it. It was no wonder he was such a popular artist.

'It's quite beautiful, isn't it?' Louis remarked.

'It ain't 'alf,' Lily responded in awe.

Louis smiled. Dressed in Arabella's cast-offs Lily looked every inch the lady. It was only when she spoke that you realised she was thoroughly working class, but that was just one of the things he liked about her: there were no airs and graces to Lily.

'Let's go in and see what they think to this lot, shall we?' he suggested.

So, licking her lips nervously, Lily followed him inside.

Chapter Thirty-Eight

As the bell above the door tinkled with their entrance, a young man appeared. He was tall and dark with a moustache and twinkling blue eyes. Lily thought he was probably the most handsome man she had ever seen and was temporarily rendered speechless.

'Good morning,' he greeted them in English, although he had a strong French accent, which only added to his charm.

'Good morning,' Louis answered. 'Is Monsieur Levigne here by any chance?'

'Certainly. He ees my father. Please wait and I will fetch him for you, sir.'

He disappeared through a door and soon reappeared with Monsieur Levigne, who beamed when he saw who they were.

'Ah, Lord Bellingham, Miss Moon, 'ow delightful it ees to see you both again. 'Ave you brought me some more sketches? They are selling like . . . what do you Engleesh say – 'otcakes?'

He had managed to put Lily instantly at ease and she giggled as he came forward to give them both a firm handshake. He led them to another room where they were able to spread the sketches out on a large table and as he examined them, he smiled his approval. 'They are *magnifique*,' he declared. 'I shall take them all and get them framed, if I may? But first you must come and see the others I 'ave already 'ad done that 'ave not sold yet, although I am confident they will in the next few days.'

He led them to another part of the gallery where Lily saw her sketches displayed on the wall and a little thrill went through her.

'I 'ave some more money for you,' Monsieur Levigne told her happily. 'I sold two more yesterday – they are proving to be remarkably popular so please keep them coming, as many as you can.'

His son appeared with four glasses of champagne on a silver tray and after handing them out, Monsieur Levigne proposed a toast, 'To Miss Lily, may she go from strength to strength!'

'Hear, hear,' Louis said, raising his glass to her.

Lily blushed, hardly able to believe this was happening to her.

'But now, forgive my manners. I 'ave not introduced you properly to my son. This is Jean-Paul.'

The young man took Lily's hand and gently kissed the back of it with a little bow. 'It ees a pleasure to meet you, mademoiselle.'

'Er . . . and you too, Jean-Paul,' she stammered nervously. He really was extremely handsome!

They were given a tour of the art gallery next and as they were walking around it the Monsieur Levigne asked, 'So, 'ow long are you in London for, Miss Lily?'

'Well, it was supposed to be just for a couple of days but I shall be staying for a little longer now.'

'Then you must visit us often,' he urged her. 'My son runs this gallery and I divide my time between the three of them, but it would be nice for you to get to know 'im a leettle better an' see 'ow the gallery is run.'

'I'd like that.' Lily smiled.

Soon after she and Louis left with yet another ten pounds tucked in Lily's purse. He hailed a cab for them and for a while they spoke of the lovely works of art they'd seen, but then suddenly becoming serious he turned to her and said soberly, 'I apologise for the way Samantha spoke to you before we left the house, Lily.'

She shrugged. 'It doesn't matter. It's obvious she don't like me.'

'Mm, and I know why. You see, she senses that I have feelings for you.' Lily looked shocked but he rushed on. 'I'd be a liar to

279

say I didn't, but being a lord comes with certain responsibilities and unfortunately one of them is making a good marriage. You do understand, don't you? Even so I'll tell you now . . . if things had been different . . .'

'Don't say any more,' she pleaded all of a fluster. 'I understand what's expected o' you an' o' course I wouldn't fit anybody's idea o' what your wife should be. I'm a pit wench an' you're a lord, that's an end to it.'

He nodded, his eyes sad. 'You're right, but I wish things could have been different. You're a very beautiful girl, Lily, inside and out.' Before she could stop him, he leant forward and as his lips gently brushed hers a delicious shock ran through her.

'Per'aps in another life, eh?' she said thickly as they broke apart. 'But as things stand I could never have married you anyway. I wouldn't have wanted it said that I had only married you for your position. I'm more than capable o' makin' me own livin'. But let's not talk o' this again, please.'

He nodded, his expression bleak. 'You're a very proud young woman, Lily.' And the rest of the journey passed in silence as they both thought of what might have been.

Samantha was hovering at the window in Kensington Place and the moment they set foot through the door she came from the drawing room and ignoring Lily completely took Louis' arm possessively and led him away, leaving Lily to make her way up to the nursery, her heart heavy with the thought of what she could never have.

That afternoon, while Annie spent time with her mother and grandmother, Lily finally finished the first oil painting she had attempted and wondered if it was good enough to show to Monsieur Levigne and his son.

'It certainly is,' Louis assured her when he came to see Annie before she went to bed that evening. 'The paint will be properly dry by tomorrow so we could drop it in to them and see what they think.'

Lily sadly shook her head and as their eyes met an unspoken message passed between them. 'It might be better if I go on me own.'

'Oh . . . yes, you're probably right.' Once the period of mourning for his father was over there would be no more excuses not to become engaged to Samantha. He would have to get on with his life and he knew that it was only fair to allow Lily to do the same.

And so, the next morning, Lily carefully wrapped the painting and hailed a cab to take her to Oxford Street.

Monsieur Levigne was delighted with her first attempt and assured her he would send it to be framed straightaway. 'Thees one must go in a more elaborate gilt frame,' he told her. 'Come back in a few days to see what you think of it and then we shall 'ang it.'

He left her with Jean-Paul as he went off to attend to a customer and the young man asked her tentatively, 'Do you get much free time, mademoiselle?'

'Well, I, er . . . yes, I do get quite a bit of time to myself.' Lily wondered why he was asking. 'But the family will be starting to interview next week fer a new nanny an' when they've found one I'll be goin' back 'ome.'

'I see, then perhaps before you go you might allow me to take you out one evening for a meal?'

'Oh!' Lily was really flustered now. 'I'm not sure,' she croaked as her hand rose to her mouth.

'Aw, come, Miss Lily, eet would give me great pleasure and what could be the harm in eet?' He was very persuasive.

'I suppose I could,' she said uncertainly and his handsome face lit up.

'*Très bien*. 'Ow does tomorrow evening suit? I know a very good eating 'ouse.'

'All right.' Lily just hoped that she was doing the right thing and that Arabella would allow it.

'I shall pick you up at seven o'clock,' he told her.

She nodded, shocked that she had agreed to it.

Monsieur Levigne joined them again at that moment and with her business done Lily took her leave. On the way back to the house she wondered what Louis would think of the arrangement but she put it from her mind. They had agreed that there could never be anything between them, so it shouldn't matter to him who she saw or what she did.

Arabella was tickled pink when Lily told her later. 'Oh, we *must* find you something suitable to wear,' she told her.

Lily grinned. 'I could wear one of the gowns you gave me,' she pointed out. A couple of them were so pretty that she had thought she would never have an occasion to wear them.

'Yes,' Arabella said thoughtfully. 'The blue shot silk one, I think. And you could wear my dark blue cloak over it. And I'll do your hair for you too.'

'There's no need to fuss, really,' Lily assured her, embarrassed. 'Jean-Paul is only takin' me out fer a meal.'

'That's how it starts,' Arabella told her. 'If he didn't really like you, he wouldn't have asked you out, would he?'

Lily couldn't help but wish it was Louis she'd be dining with, but she firmly pushed the thought aside.

'There's just one other thing . . .' Arabella looked at her apprehensively. They had grown closer and she didn't want to hurt her feelings but she felt that this was something she needed to say. 'The thing is, your dialect.'

'What's wrong wi' me dialect?' Lily said defensively.

Arabella giggled. 'Just that. It should be "with my" not "wi' me". You have to remember, Jean-Paul is probably used to mixing

282

with the upper classes. He might not understand half that you say, so how about I give you a few elocution lessons? It's mostly just thinking about what you're going to say before you speak really, and now that you'll be moving in upper-class circles it could stand you in good stead. What do you think, Lily?'

Lily wasn't all that keen, but she supposed Arabella had a point, and so the first lesson began.

'We'll begin with "How now brown cow".'

By the end of the first hour Lily's head was spinning and she knew she had a long way to go before she would be able to speak as the toffs did without thinking. Still, Jean-Paul was very handsome so she supposed it was worth giving it a try.

The next evening Arabella was almost as excited as Lily as she put the finishing touches to her hair. Lily grinned wryly as she realised that it appeared they had swapped places.

'You look stunning,' Arabella told her as she patted the last curl into place. 'Now, tell me again, how do you reply if Jean-Paul tells you you look nice?'

'I say, "Thank you very much, sir," and bow my head.'

'Perfect!' Arabella clapped her hands, and Annie, who was watching from her cot, followed suit. 'And just remember, take a second or two to think before you speak. That way you won't slip back into your old slang.'

'I'll try,' Lily promised.

Arabella fetched her cloak and placed it about her shoulders. 'Now, get off downstairs and wait in the hall. You want to be ready when he arrives. And don't worry about Anastasia and me, we'll be just fine, so go and enjoy yourself.'

Lily was already wondering if she'd done right by agreeing to go but it was too late to back out now so she slowly made her way downstairs, careful not to trip over her many petticoats and silken skirts.

Louis was just leaving the dining room as she reached the foot of the stairs and his eyes almost popped out of his head as he caught sight of her.

'Why, Lily. You look . . . *stunning*!'

She smiled, remembering what Arabella had told her. 'Why, thank you, sir.'

He looked astounded. Not only did she look different, she sounded different too.

At that moment the doorbell rang.

'That'll be Jean-Paul Levigne,' she told Louis as the maid hurried to open it. 'He's taking me out to dinner this evening.'

'Oh . . . I see,' he said, a pang of jealousy shooting through him. 'In that case, I hope you'll have a pleasant time.' And with that he strode away straight-faced as Jean-Paul entered and came to take her hands.

'Your carriage awaits, mademoiselle.' His deep-blue eyes were twinkling like stars. 'And may I say you look *magnifique*.'

'Thank you, sir.' Lily felt as if she was acting a part as he tucked her hand into the crook of his arm and led her outside.

He took her to a beautiful restaurant where bowls of sweet-smelling flowers, glittering candelabra and silver cutlery was laid on crisp white cloths on every table.

Lily felt a little overawed but remembering what Arabella had told her she behaved impeccably and anyone seeing her would have thought she was used to this way of life. She certainly looked the part and Jean-Paul could hardly keep his eyes off her.

He was easy to talk to and as the night progressed and the champagne flowed like water, Lily began to relax and enjoy herself.

'Your painting should be framed and back in the gallery tomorrow,' he informed her. '*Mon père* has spared no expense with the frame and has 'igh 'opes of it selling for a good price. We actually 'ad someone come in today who 'ad seen one of your sketches that

284

a client had bought from us, and they too wanted one. Already you are becoming known and this is only the beginning.'

Lily felt a little thrill of excitement.

'Eet is only sad that you cannot commit to painting and sketching full-time,' he said.

Lily shook her head. Her sketches were selling far better than she had ever expected them to, but what if it was just a flash in the pan and people stopped buying them?

'It is very kind of you to say so,' she told him. 'But you must understand I am a working girl. My mother relies on me and my brother to pay the rent on our cottage, which is owned by Lord Bellingham.'

'Eet was just a thought,' he answered pleasantly. 'I just 'ate to see such talent not being used to the full.'

He went on to tell her something of his childhood and she listened entranced. As well as the art galleries, his father owned a chateau in France where grapes were grown before being made into wine, which Lily supposed must be why Jean-Paul was such a connoisseur. He had a sister slightly younger than himself called Fleur, who he spoke of with great affection, and they had both been educated by private tutors at the chateau. The more she learnt of him the more she realised that they were just as far apart in class as she and Louis were, and yet it didn't seem to bother Jean-Paul a jot, whereas Louis was very conscious of what was expected of him.

She was sorry when the evening came to an end and he escorted her out to the waiting carriage.

'Eet 'as been the most pleasant evening.' He raised her hand to his lips and gently kissed it, and a little shiver ran up her spine. 'Do you think you might be prepared to come out with me again? I thought per'aps we could go to the theatre?'

'I'd like that.' Lily's voice came out as a squeak, excited at the prospect of going out with him again.

Once they arrived back at the house, he escorted her to the front door and waited with her until the maid opened it. Then lifting his top hat, he bowed, kissed her hand again. She entered the house and made for the nursery feeling as if she were floating on air.

Chapter Thirty-Nine

The following afternoon when Arabella and Lady Bellingham took Annie to visit friends for a couple of hours, Lily couldn't resist visiting the art gallery to see her oil painting framed. It had already been hung on the wall and she felt a glow of pride. The frame Monsieur Levigne had chosen complemented it, although she was sure the painting itself was nowhere near as good as the rest that were displayed there.

'Practice makes perfect, ma chérie,' Monsieur Levigne replied when she said as much and she blushed with pleasure as she glanced around for a sight of Jean-Paul.

'My son tells me you 'ad the most pleasant evening,' Monsieur Levigne said, almost as if he had been able to read her mind and she blushed even more. 'He is out on business at the moment and tomorrow I shall be returning to France, but I am sure 'e will keep you informed of sales and so forth. I know the sketches are selling well and I 'ave 'igh 'opes that the painting will also. I was thinking, now that we know your work is selling, we should come to a better arrangement. How would it be if I gave you sixty per cent of what each piece of your artwork sells for?'

'Thank you.' Lily was delighted and she shook his hand and gave him a warm smile. 'You've been so good to me.'

'No, no, no.' He chuckled. 'Eet 'as been my pleasure and I will be sure to tell Jean-Paul you called in. *Au revoir* for now, *ma chérie.*'

Lily left, slightly disappointed not to have seen Jean-Paul but delighted to see her picture hanging in the gallery. When she arrived back at the house in Kensington Place she was just in time to see Samantha and Louis stepping into a cab.

Samantha didn't acknowledge her, although Louis did incline his head. Wherever they were going, he didn't look too happy about it, but it was none of her business anymore, so she tried to shut him from her mind.

It was only when she got to the nursery and started to take her bonnet off that she suddenly had a thought and she sat down on the nearest chair with a resounding thud. Wasn't she about to make exactly the same mistake with Jean-Paul as she had with Louis? Admittedly, Monsieur Levigne seemed happy to see them become friends but how would he feel if he thought they might become romantically involved? No doubt Jean-Paul's parents would expect him to make a good marriage and she needed no one to tell her that she didn't fit the bill. Perhaps it would be wise to step back if he asked her out again, she decided.

Annie arrived home then and for the rest of the afternoon Lily was kept busy looking after her young charge. The interviews for the new nanny were due to begin the next day and Lily wondered how long it would be before she could return home. Deep down she knew it would be no bad thing. At least back in her role as parlour maid she wouldn't be tempted to have ideas above her station.

Arabella and Lady Bellingham interviewed two women the following morning and declared both totally unsuitable.

'The first one looked like she had been dragged through a hedge backwards, and she didn't smell very nice either,' Arabella confided when she popped up to see Annie before lunch. 'And the second one was like a sergeant major. She even scared me.' She sighed. 'Let's hope the two that we're interviewing tomorrow fare a little better, eh?'

The next two were just as unsuitable. One was so old she almost dozed off during the interview and the other wore so much rouge and powder that to coin Lady Bellingham's phrase, 'She looked like a lady of the night.' Arabella also told Lily that Louis and Samantha Thompson would be returning to Oakley Manor the following day and Lily wasn't sorry to hear it. She was tired of trying to avoid him, which was no mean feat when he was visiting Annie in the nursery all the time.

It was almost tea time that day when Elsie appeared to tell her, 'There's a gentleman downstairs an' he asked me to give yer this, miss.'

Lily stared down at the small card; it was from Jean-Paul and he was asking if she would like to go to a music hall that evening.

Arabella was playing with Annie and she grinned as she peeped at the card. 'Tell the gentleman Miss Lily would love to,' she told the maid.

Lily stared at her aghast. 'No, Elsie, wait . . . Arabella, what are you doing?'

'I'm trying to make sure you have some fun,' Arabella told her. 'Annie will be perfectly all right with me, and if and when we do find a suitable nanny, you'll be going back home, so enjoy London while you can.'

Lily sighed and nodded at the maid, so the girl rushed off to do as she had been told, returning a few minutes later to breathlessly tell Lily, 'The gentleman says 'e'll pick you up 'ere at seven o'clock, miss.'

'Oh . . . what shall I wear?'

Arabella giggled. 'I'm sure we shall find you something suitable. Now run along and let me have Annie to myself for a while. You can look through your wardrobe and find which gown you'd like to wear this evening. I thought perhaps that pale-green shot silk gown I gave you might be suitable.'

Lily went off to do just that and was ready in plenty of time that evening. As she came downstairs in all her finery to wait for Jean-Paul, she again bumped into Louis in the hallway.

He gave her an appreciative look before asking rather unnecessarily, 'Off out again, are you?'

Lily eyed him steadily and nodded just as Samantha, who was never far behind Louis, took his arm, saying spitefully, 'Goodness me, darling, your servants really do have an easy life. I promise you they won't have so much freedom when I become lady of the manor. I'm a firm believer in the staff knowing their place.'

Lily opened her mouth to reply but was stopped from doing so when there was a rap on the front door. It was Jean-Paul looking very handsome in a dark evening suit with a silk waistcoat and a matching cravat, and he smiled as he saw Lily.

'Why, you look *très belle*,' he declared, moving forward to offer her his arm. Then he gave a polite little bow to Louis and Samantha. 'Good evening, monsieur, mademoiselle. Fear not, I shall not have her 'ome too late.'

The evening that followed was magical for Lily, one she knew she would never forget and Jean-Paul was an entertaining companion. She enjoyed every second of the various artists at the music hall and when the show was over and Jean-Paul led her outside to hail a cab there were stars in her eyes.

'Oh, it was wonderful,' she told him as she settled in her seat.

He smiled. 'I am glad you enjoyed it, *ma chérie*. And now I 'ave yet more good news for you; this afternoon we sold your first painting.' He began to fumble in his pocket and when he placed some money in her hand, she stared at it in disbelief.

'B-but there's twenty-five pounds here!'

He laughed and nodded. 'That is correct. *Mon père* informed me that you are to be paid sixty per cent of the buying price from now on, and so that is your share.'

Lily could hardly believe it. She had never held so much money all in one go in her whole life and was beyond delighted.

'And now we shall eagerly await some more of your paintings,' Jean-Paul went on. 'Are there any more ready yet?'

'One is, almost,' Lily told him. 'I've been working on it up in the nursery when Annie has her naps and it should be finished in the next couple of days.'

'Excellent.' He patted her hand. 'The lady who bought the other one is keen to see any more you do, so let me 'ave it as soon as possible and I will get it framed.'

As the horse drawing the cab clip-clopped through the cobbled streets Lily felt as if she was in a fairyland. London had been a grave disappointment to her during the day with its grimy streets and sooty roofs, but at night in the lamplight it took on a magical quality. Even the dirty Thames River shone serenely as the stars reflected in the dark waters.

When the cab pulled up outside the house, Jean-Paul helped her down from the carriage and insisted on seeing her safely to the front door where he gallantly rang the bell.

'Until we meet again, ma chérie.' He raised her hand to his lips and kissed it. With a smile Lily slipped inside, wondering if it had all been a dream – surely things like this never happened to people like her.

Three days, and many interviews later, Arabella finally appointed a new nanny for Annie, who would be moving in the following Monday. Louis and Samantha had returned to Oakley Manor some days before and soon there would be nothing to stop Lily doing the same.

The day before, she had delivered her latest painting along with some more sketches to Jean-Paul and he had taken her out to lunch. As always, she had enjoyed his company and knew she was going to miss him when she went home.

On Sunday afternoon, he took her for a drive around Regent's Park and when they returned to the house, she said her goodbyes.

'But it will not be for long,' he assured her as he tenderly kissed the back of her hand. 'I shall come personally to collect your work from Nuneaton when it is ready. I shall also bring any monies you 'ave made. They are selling, as my père says, like 'otcakes!'

'Long may it continue,' Lily giggled, still hardly able to believe her luck. She would be taking a substantial amount of money home for her mother and couldn't wait to see her face when she gave it to her.

They said their goodbyes somewhat sadly and Lily went in to begin her packing. She would be returning with considerably more clothes than she had arrived with, as Arabella had given her yet more gowns, although she doubted she would wear the majority of them once she was home.

The following morning, she said a tearful goodbye to Annie and Lady Bellingham. Lily had met the new nanny and approved of their choice, and now Arabella insisted on going to the station with her to see her off.

'I shall miss you,' Arabella said sadly as the cab drew up outside Euston Station. 'Promise you won't leave it for too long before you come and see us again.'

'That will all depend on 'ow . . . I mean *how* much time Mrs Biggles allows me to have off.' Lily smiled. She was still desperately trying to remember Arabella's elocution lessons.

'If you have any trouble with her, just contact me or Mother,' Arabella said indignantly. She and Lily had grown even closer and she was missing her already.

When Lily entered the cottage later that evening, she was given a rapturous welcome. Ginny was clearly thrilled to see her as was

Richie, and Sassy's tail wagged so hard that she almost fell over. But it was her mother who rushed to give her a hug, commenting, 'My, don't you look grand! You're quite the young lady now. We weren't sure when to expect you but it's luvvly to 'ave yer back, pet.'

'It's lovely to be back,' Lily answered.

Her mother grinned. 'Why, you even sound different!'

Lily giggled as she took off her bonnet and laid it on the table. 'Arabella has been giving me elocution lessons.'

'Ellywhat?'

'She's been trying to teach me how to speak properly and I'm doing quite well, so she says, although I do forget sometimes and go back to the village slang.'

'But why would yer want to change the way yer speak?' Sara looked none too pleased with that idea.

'Because when I'm in the art gallery speaking to customers it's expected of me. Jean-Paul says—'

'Ooh . . . an' who is this *Jean-Paul*?' Sara teased with a twinkle in her eye.

'He's Monsieur Levigne's son and he sold my first painting and look . . .' Lily emptied her purse onto the table and Sara's eyes almost bulged out of her head.

'You got all *that* fer just one paintin'?'

'Well, no, that was for some of my sketches as well,' Lily admitted. 'They seem to be selling as fast as I can do them at the minute.'

'In that case you'd better get yer 'ead down an' get some more done. Strike while the iron's 'ot, that's what I say.'

Lily frowned. 'I agree but it might prove to be easier said than done after I go back to work tomorrow. I shall have to do my sketches and painting of an evening when I get home. But now, tell me what's been going on here while I've been away.'

'Well . . .' Sara glanced towards Richie and Ginny who were both grinning like Cheshire cats. 'We all got to thinkin' that if we were to put another room or two on the end o' the cottage we could get Ginny's mam an' the little 'uns out o' the work'ouse. Richie says he could do most of it an' there'd be more than enough comin' in now to keep us all. But do yer think Lord Bellingham would allow us to?'

'I'm not sure.' Lily bit her lip as she pondered. 'But I suppose I could ask him the next time I see him.' She wouldn't look forward to it because she felt he had already done more than enough for them. But she could also see how much it would mean to her mother and Ginny.

Sara's face lit up like a ray of sunshine. 'Luvvly, but now let me go an' get yer a nice cuppa an' somethin' to eat. Yer must be starvin' after yer long journey.'

As Sara bustled away to put the kettle on to boil Ginny and Richie disappeared off saying they were going to feed the pigs and Lily smiled. 'They seem to be getting on well.'

Sara nodded. 'They do that. In fact, I've a feelin' they've taken a right shine to each other.'

'Oh!' Lily was surprised but not displeased. They were both very young as yet, but Ginny was a genuinely nice, kind girl and she knew her brother could do far worse. Still, she supposed, time would tell and she laid her head back against the chair and sighed contentedly. Be it ever so humble, it was good to be home.

Chapter Forty

As Lily entered the kitchen at Oakley Manor the following morning ready to begin her shift, Mrs Biggles looked mildly surprised to see her and not a little uncomfortable.

She had been sitting at the table enjoying a cup of tea with the cook before the breakfast rush but now she rose and clasping her hands she pressed them into her waist.

'I, er . . . I'm afraid we had no idea when to expect you or even if you would be coming back,' she began tentatively.

'I thought you knew Lady Bellingham only asked me to stay on until she appointed a new nanny for Miss Anastasia,' Lily replied, noting the smirk on the cook's face.

'I see. Unfortunately . . . the thing is, the elder Lady Bellingham summoned me last week and told me to appoint a new parlour maid to take your place, and so I'm afraid the position you had here is filled.'

'You *what*!' Lily forgot all about the elocution lessons Arabella had given her as she stared back at the housekeeper appalled. 'Yer mean I've got the sack?'

'I simply followed the old mistress's instructions.' Mrs Biggles drew herself up to her full height.

'Then that's fine be me!' Blinking back tears of humiliation and anger, Lily gathered what dignity she had left and sailed out of the room with her head held high. She still had her pride even if she'd lost her job and she'd be damned if she'd give the staff the satisfaction of seeing her upset.

It wasn't until she had turned out of the drive and into the lane leading down to the village that Lily's footsteps slowed and the tears came hot and fast. Most of the staff had never made a secret of the fact they were jealous of her; she had grown used to that. But now she felt disgusted at the way the old woman had treated her. It was she who had asked Lily to go with Arabella to Yorkshire in the first place, and yet now it felt as if she was being punished for doing as she had been asked.

When she entered the cottage shortly after her mother looked up from the pots she was washing in the sink in surprise. Richie and Ginny had already left for work and seeing the expression on her daughter's face she asked, 'Is everythin' all right, pet? Yer look like you've lost a shillin' an' found a sixpence!'

'Actually no, it ain't all right,' Lily fumed as she dragged her lace mob cap from her head and flung it on the table. 'I've just got the sack!'

'*Eh?*' Sara could hardly believe what she was hearing. 'What do yer mean, you've got the sack? What for?'

Lily shrugged as she picked at the fringe on the chenille table-cloth. 'Exactly what I say. It seems the old mistress set somebody else on in me place while I was in London!'

'Why the *rotten* old *cow*, an' after all you've done for 'em an' all!' Sara said heatedly as she dried her hands on her apron and joined her at the table. 'But what shall yer do now?'

Lily chewed on her lip for a moment and then in a happier tone she answered, 'I shall paint and sketch. I'll have more time to do it now, so sod the lot of 'em! I know Jean-Paul will be able to sell 'em, so we certainly won't be no worse off. In fact, we'll probably be better off.'

'There is that in it,' Sara admitted, although she could see how upset Lily was. 'But per'aps if yer were to 'ave a word in the young lord's ear he could get yer job back for yer? I wouldn't mind bettin' he won't even know you've been fired an' he is supposed to be in charge up at the manor now.'

'I most certainly will *not* ask him for anything!' Lily declared in a determined voice. 'We ain't at the point that I've got to beg anyone fer anything yet!'

'I never said we were,' Sara pointed out, feeling as if she was walking on eggshells. 'Now 'ow about I make yer a nice brew, eh? Everythin' allus looks better after a nice cuppa.' And with that she bustled away leaving Lily to come to terms with what had happened.

In actual fact, Lily quite enjoyed the next few days. The weather was kind, the sky was blue and the sun shone, so each morning she would carry her easel outside and paint to her heart's content. Her next painting was almost finished when she heard the sound of a horse trotting up the hill towards her and glancing up, she saw Louis astride it, his dark hair glinting in the sunshine and a broad smile on his face. Her heart gave a little leap but she kept her face straight as he drew level with her and hopped effortlessly down from the saddle.

'Good morning, and what a fine morning it is,' he greeted her as he tied the horse's reins to the picket fence. 'I thought I'd pop by and see how you are, seeing as you haven't reported back to work yet. I had a letter from Mother telling me she had appointed a new nanny for Anastasia so I guessed you must be home.'

Lily frowned. He clearly didn't know she had been fired. 'I did turn up for work the day after I arrived home,' she told him primly. 'But when I arrived, Mrs Biggles informed me that your grandmother had instructed her to give my job to someone else and that I was no longer required.'

Louis' mouth fell open and he looked so shocked that she knew he'd had no idea.

'B-but *why* would she do that?'

Lily shrugged. 'I have absolutely no idea but I imagine it's because she thought . . .' She had been about to say that it might

be because his grandmother feared that she and Louis were growing too close but thought better of it and clamped her mouth shut.

He stood stamping his foot on the earth for a moment then turning back to Lily he gave a little bow before heading back to his
horse, saying over his shoulder, 'Don't worry. I'm going to go and
sort this out with my grandmama right now.'

'Louis . . . no!'

When he paused to stare back at her she blushed. 'I wouldn't go
back now even if your grandmother herself begged me to,' she told
him. 'I shall make a living perfectly well by painting and sketching,
thank you very much, and of course if you want us to leave the cottage now that I no longer work for your family, I will quite understand. I can comfortably afford to rent us somewhere else now.'

'Leave the cottage!' He looked appalled at the very idea of it.
'But your family are settled here.'

He looked so upset that Lily almost felt guilty. He couldn't be
held responsible for his grandmother's actions, after all.

'Oh, and before you go, I have the rent for you,' she said.

He flushed. 'There's no need really!'

'While we rent from you, we shall pay our way,' she told him
firmly, disappearing into the cottage.

While she was gone, he studied the painting she had nearly completed and it almost took his breath away. She had brought the valley to life on canvas: the wild flowers looked so real that he felt he
could almost reach down and pluck them from the grass, and she
had caught a squirrel hopping amongst the branches of the trees
bordering the coppice. He was still admiring it when she reappeared.

'This is just breathtaking,' he muttered, in awe of her talent.

She shrugged as she held some coins out to him. He wanted to
argue again but seeing the proud look on her face he took them
and dropped them into his pocket and after nodding, he mounted
his horse and rode away.

He was in a terrible mood when he rode into the stableyard a short time later, and after dismounting, he threw the reins towards Richie, asking him shortly, 'Give him a good rub down, would you?' Then he strode away, his lips set in a straight line.

Richie frowned. 'I wonder who's upset 'im?' he commented to the head groom who had come out of the stables to have a smoke on his pipe.

Inside, Louis took the stairs two at a time and once he reached the west wing, he barged into his grandmother's room without even knocking, causing her to glance up from her chair in surprise.

'Ah, Louis. Hudson, go and fetch another cup for my grandson, would you?' she told her long-suffering maid. She assumed Louis had come to have morning tea with her.

'I haven't come for tea, Grandmama,' he told her icily. 'I've come to see just what the hell you think you're doing dismissing Lily Moon!'

Lady Bellingham's smile disappeared and she stared at him defensively, 'She was no longer needed and I had every right to do so.'

'No, you damned well did *not*!' Louis fumed. She was so shocked that her mouth fell open. He had never spoken to her like this before. 'In case you'd forgotten, *I* am the lord here now, so I decide who stays or goes.'

'Now, come along, Louis,' she said cajolingly, patting the seat at the side of her. 'It should be up to the lady of the house to see to staff matters.'

He shook his head, his eyes flashing with anger. 'No, it isn't. And furthermore, you seem to forget that you are no longer the lady of the house. That title passed to my mother when Grandfather died. Then when Father died the title passed to me, so it's up to *me* who I have working here.'

Her chin jutted obstinately and she leant forward, her hands clutching the ebony-topped walking stick she favoured. 'I was just trying to stop the gossip that is circulating about you and that . . . that *pit wench*,' she answered in a low growl. 'Do you *really* want to make a laughing stock of yourself, Louis? I mean, she was getting ideas far above her station and I couldn't allow it to go any further. Samantha doesn't like her either. Surely you will take your fiancée's feelings into account if not mine?'

'Samantha isn't my fiancée yet, nor will she be until we have observed the correct period of mourning for my father. And furthermore, I don't much care if Samantha likes Lily or not!' Louis was almost spitting the words out in his anger. 'I'm only marrying her because it's expected of me, but let me tell you something – Lily is more of a lady than Samantha will *ever be* and she doesn't deserve to be treated this way.'

'Pah!' Lady Bellingham waved her hand at him. 'Talk sense, my boy. You have better things to occupy your time than to worry about the hiring and firing of staff.'

'If you're talking about the pit and the businesses, I can assure you they are all running like clockwork under the guidance of the very competent managers I've appointed,' he informed her. 'And as you're very well aware I am concentrating on building up the stock for my stud farm. But none of that has anything to do with Lily Moon.'

The old lady sniffed disparagingly. 'I think it's time you got rid of the whole family,' she said meanly. 'Turf them out of our cottage and let them go somewhere else to live.'

At this, Louis' chest seemed to swell to double its size and it was a moment before he could bring himself to reply. When he did, he almost spat the words at her. 'Actually, I've decided to gift the cottage to them,' he told her. 'I feel it's the least I can do after all Lily has done for Arabella and the way you've treated her. At least then, even if she doesn't get another job, she'll have a roof over her head.'

'*What!*' The old lady banged her stick on the floor in a fury. 'Have you taken leave of your senses? Imagine what people would say! And how can you even *think* of giving away a part of our estate? Your father would turn in his grave if he could hear you.'

Hands clenched, Louis eyed her steadily. 'My father was actually a fair man and I rather think he'd agree with my decision. What's more, as I've just pointed out, it isn't *our* estate, Grandmama. It's *mine* now to do with as I please, so I'll thank you to keep your nose out of things that no longer concern you!' And with that he turned on his heel and slammed out of the room.

A week later on a balmy afternoon in late June, Louis once again rode to the cottage to find Lily outside busily painting at her easel again.

She watched him approach and when he dismounted, she raised a questioning eyebrow. 'Good afternoon, Lord Bellingham, to what do we owe the pleasure of this visit? Our rent isn't due again yet, is it?'

Ignoring the hint of sarcasm in her tone he shook his head. 'Not at all. In fact, it won't be again. Here, this is for you.'

Sara had seen him arrive from the window and now she came out to greet him with a welcoming smile. 'Lord Bellingham, how nice it is to see yer. Would yer like a cold drink?'

'No, thank you, Mrs Moon. I just brought this for Lily.'

'Oh . . .' Sara watched her daughter open a large formal-looking envelope and then saw Lily frown as she stared up at him.

'I don't understand . . . What's this?' she asked.

'It's the deeds to this cottage and the land surrounding it,' he told her. 'I've had my solicitor place it in your name. It's yours now to do with as you like.'

'*What!*' Lily looked shocked and flustered and then angry as she tried to hand it back to him. 'It's very kind of you but we don't want or need your charity!'

'It isn't charity,' he answered calmly. 'Call it payment for all you've done for my sister and the baby. You've more than earned it. And I'd also like to offer my sincere apologies for how my grandmother has treated you. I hope this will go some way to making it up to you.'

'You mean yer *givin'* us the cottage?' Sara looked as if she couldn't believe what she was hearing and when he nodded solemnly, she did a little jig on the spot. 'Eeh, lad, I can 'ardly believe it. Just think, our Lily, we *own* our own home!'

Lily still looked none too happy about it and yet she knew this would mean security for her mother for the rest of her life.

'So . . . does this mean you will accept it in the spirit in which it has been given?' Louis questioned hopefully, and when she still hesitated, he rushed on, 'It would really go some way to salving my conscience if you would.'

'In that case I will,' Lily forced herself to say, for the words seemed to be sticking in her throat. 'And . . . thank you.'

Their eyes met and locked for a brief second but she quickly looked away. There was no point in thinking of what might have been. She was a lowly miner's daughter and Louis was now the lord of the manor, and his future with Miss Samantha Thompson was mapped out for him. Now there would be no need to see him again, which could only be for the best as far as she was concerned.

Even so, as she watched him ride away, a lump formed in her throat and she had to blink away the tears that were burning at the back of her eyes.

Chapter Forty-One

It was the end of July, and since Lily had been home, Bridget had become a constant visitor. Bridget was now as big as a house and moaned constantly. Sometimes Robbie came with her, so whenever they arrived together, Lily would grab her canvas and easel and take herself off to paint somewhere out of the way. Anything was better than having to endure the way Robbie stared at her mournfully.

The month before she had set her easel up beside the small pool in the middle of the nearby copse and let her imagination run wild. The beautiful dragonflies that hovered above the still water became tiny fairies with iridescent wings dancing on the water lilies on the canvas, and once it was finished and sent to London, Jean-Paul wrote to her within days to tell her that it had sold immediately for a very substantial sum of money and asked for more of the same. Lily was only too happy to oblige and she was busily painting one day when she heard footsteps in the trees and after glancing up, she gasped with shock.

'Jean-Paul! What are you doing here?'

He grinned as he grasped her hand and kissed it. 'I was missing you, *ma chérie*, and so I came. Your *mère* told me where I might find you and 'ere I am. Are you not pleased to see me?'

'Why, of course I am,' she assured him. 'It's just that I wasn't expecting you.' Her hand rose self-consciously to her hair, which hung loose across her shoulders, and she was suddenly painfully aware of the old gown she was wearing. It was covered in splatters of paint and she knew she must look a sight.

'You look beautiful,' he assured her, bending to study the painting. 'It is magnifique,' he told her eventually as he pulled a bundle of notes from his pocket. 'And I bring you this. It is your share of the money for the last one.'

'B-but there's forty pounds here!' Lily gasped disbelievingly.

He laughed. 'There is, and I 'ave no doubt this one will sell for the same. But one of the reasons I 'ave come is to put a proposition to you.'

He sat down on the grass beside her and leaning on his elbow he told her, 'I wish to do an exhibition of your work. But if I were to do it, it would be better if you could be there at least for the opening night. Better still if you could move to London where your work would be easier to hand. I could rent you somewhere to stay. What do you think?'

Lily was astonished. It was something she had never even considered. 'You mean live there?'

He nodded. 'Yes, there are apartments not too far from the gallery where you could easily afford to live while your work is fetching such a good price. Will you give it some thought?'

Lily's teeth nipped down on her lower lip as she gazed at the canvas thoughtfully. Richie had already started work on extending the cottage and once Ginny's family moved in it was going to be very cramped even with an extra room. Now they no longer had to pay rent the family could comfortably manage on what Ginny and Richie earned and of course she could always send money back to them.

'Will you *pleese* at least give it some thought?' he asked.

She nodded and smiled. 'Well, I shall have to speak to my mother about it, but yes I will.' Deep down the thought of moving to the capital was quite attractive. At least there she wouldn't have to worry about seeing Louis Bellingham coming and going. 'But come back to the cottage, won't you? You must be hungry and thirsty after your journey. When do you have to go home? I have some more sketches and another painting ready if you'd like to take them back with you.'

'I would like that very much indeed,' he answered with a grin as he helped her to pack up her paints. 'But unfortunately, I 'ave to return to London this evening. My *père* is returning to France tomorrow so I must get back to the gallery.'

The rest of the afternoon was spent pleasantly as Sara plied Jean-Paul with food and drink and he discussed ideas for paintings with Lily. All too soon it was time for him to leave and Lily walked down to the village with him where he would be able to get a lift on the carrier cart to the train station. On the way along Valley Road they passed Robbie, who had just finished his shift at the pit, and he glared at them as he passed.

'Who is that man?' Jean-Paul asked with a frown.

Lily giggled. 'He's my brother-in-law actually.'

'Oh!' Jean-Paul sounded surprised. 'You are not on, what is it you say – the good terms?'

'Not really,' she admitted. 'But that's another story. I'll tell you all about it another time. Meanwhile I can see the cart ahead so we'd best rush or you'll have a long walk ahead of you.'

There was no time for lengthy goodbyes and once Lily had waved him off, she set off back up the valley only to find Robbie waiting for her. He was lying on the grass in his sooty clothes chewing on a blade of grass and the moment he saw her he leapt to his feet with a grim expression on his face.

'So, who were that I saw yer wi' then? Another of yer fancy men, were it?' he said caustically.

'That was Jean-Paul Levigne,' she told him with a sigh. 'He and his father own the art galleries that are selling my paintings and sketches.'

'Ooh, fancy yerself as an *artist* now, do yer?' He leered. 'Ain't the lord o' the manor enough fer yer, eh?'

Lily glared at him. 'Why don't you grow up and go home to your wife,' she said cuttingly. 'Jean-Paul is a friend but even if he was more than that it's time you got it into your head that it's none of your damned business who I see or what I do. You're a married man with a baby due very soon, Robbie, so why don't you start acting like one? Now go away and leave me alone.' And with that she lifted her skirts and raced away leaving him glaring after her.

Perhaps it is time I moved away, she thought as the cottage came into sight, life was becoming uncomfortable here, what with Robbie harassing her and trying to avoid Louis.

Once home, she told her mother about Jean-Paul's suggestion.

Sara chewed her lip and looked worried. 'But wouldn't it be dangerous for a young girl like you to be in London alone?'

Lily grinned. 'But I wouldn't be alone, would I, Mam? I'd have Jean-Paul and his father to keep an eye on me and I would of course be coming home regularly to see you. And Arabella and Lady Bellingham won't be far away. Once Ginny's family move in you won't have time to miss me and I'd send you money back.'

Sara scowled. 'There'd be no need for that, my girl,' she said sternly. 'We're managing very well as we are.' She looked at her daughter thoughtfully. Lily had grown into a very beautiful young woman, although she seemed to be completely unaware of the fact. It had been obvious that Jean-Paul was more than a little fond of her and perhaps if Lily lived closer to him their relationship might blossom. He was such a nice young man and Sara quite liked the idea of having Jean-Paul for a son-in-law. Then there was her artwork to think about. Would she be denying Lily the right to make the best of herself if she told her that she didn't want her to go? And so, after taking a deep breath, she agreed, 'All right, I suppose you could go and see how you like it. Just so long as you promise to come back and write regular. Just don't forget, this is your 'ome.'

'As if I could ever forget.' Lily plonked a kiss on her mother's cheek before rushing away to write a letter to Jean-Paul before she changed her mind.

By the end of the following week, Jean-Paul wrote back to tell her that he had found somewhere for her to rent that might be just right for her. It was the top floor of a large townhouse not too far away from the gallery, and he had paid a deposit to reserve it until she could come to see if it would be suitable, although, he urged, she should make it as soon as possible.

Bridget scowled and pouted when told. 'It's all right fer some!' she moaned plaintively. 'Here's you goin' off to live the 'igh life while I'll be stuck 'ere wi' a screamin' brat 'anging round me bloody neck an' a husband I barely see. Robbie spends more of 'is free time at the pub than he does at 'ome!' She could have added that he only ever came to visit with her so he could see Lily but her pride wouldn't allow her to.

'That were the way o' life yer chose,' Sara pointed out unsympathetically. 'If I remember rightly yer couldn't wait to get 'is ring on yer finger, my girl.'

'Well, Robbie were different then!'

'Was he?' Sara raised her eyebrows. 'Then per'aps it's cos you ain't makin' 'im 'appy? Nobody ever said marriage was a bed o' roses. A good marriage 'as to be worked at.'

'An' 'ow am I supposed to do that when we're stuck livin' wi' 'is mam an' dad?' Bridget moaned. 'Now if yer'd let us move in 'ere wi' you . . .'

'I've told yer before that ain't goin' to 'appen,' her mother told her firmly. 'Richie is workin' 'is socks off to get that extension finished an' when it is, Ginny's family will be movin' in. There wouldn't be room fer you anyway.'

'Huh! An' you'd rather put them afore yer own daughter!' Bridget griped.

Sara rounded on her, hands on hips. 'How *could* I 'ave you 'ere? Just cos Lily is goin' to London don't mean she'll never be comin' 'ome an' imagine 'ow uncomfortable that'd be fer everyone – Robbie an' her under the same roof! No, my girl, I've told you, that ain't goin' to 'appen so make yer mind up to it!'

Not long after, Bridget left in a huff and although she loved her sister, Lily wasn't sorry to see her go.

'I can't help but feel sorry for her,' she commented to her mother.

Sara shook her head. 'She asked fer all she got the way she snatched Robbie away from under yer nose, an' now she's got what she wanted, so as far as I'm concerned, she's got to make the best of it. Don't fret about her; you just go off an' make the best o' this opportunity that's been offered to you. Yer deserve it.'

Two days later Lily's bags were packed and she was feeling nervous. It was such a huge step to take and already she was wondering if she was doing the right thing. She had written to Arabella and told her what she was going to do, and Arabella wrote back saying that she could hardly wait to see her. Both she and little Annie had missed her, although she said the new nanny was working out well.

'What time does yer train leave tomorrow?' Sara asked for at least the tenth time. She was feeling as nervous about her going as Lily was.

'Ten thirty, Mam,' Lily told her with a patient smile. She was going to miss her family but at least they wouldn't be a million miles away so she could come back to see them often. If things didn't work out, she might well be back for good.

Later that afternoon, she was at the kitchen table putting the finishing touches to some sketches she would be taking with her when Sara appeared. 'You've got a visitor, pet.'

When Louis appeared over her shoulder, Lily gulped. It was the first time she had seen him since the day he had gifted the cottage to her and she realised with a little shock that she had missed him. Even so, her face betrayed nothing of her feelings as she smiled politely and said, 'Good afternoon, Lord Bellingham. What can I do for you?'

'Right, I'll leave you two to it while I go an' finish in the garden,' Sara said tactfully and she bustled away.

Louis looked uncomfortable. 'Do we really have to be so formal, Lily?' he said sadly. 'It was always Louis before. And I just called in to wish you good luck in London. Arabella told me in her last letter that you were going. She also said that Monsieur Levigne will be putting on an exhibition of your work. How exciting for you. I really hope it goes well, although I'm sure it will. You have a rare talent.'

'Thank you.' She was suddenly aware that it was actually Louis who she had to thank for all that was happening to her. It was he that had first recognised that her sketches could be of worth and he that had supported her. 'I, er . . . doubt any of this would ever have come about if it weren't for you.'

He shrugged and they stared at each other long and hard before he suddenly said, 'I believe you are going tomorrow? May I ask how you're getting to the station?'

'I'm going on the carrier cart,' she informed him.

He shook his head as he stared at the small mountain of luggage packed at the side of the door. 'Perhaps you would allow me to take you in the carriage? I can see you have quite a lot of baggage and it would be a nightmare trying to get all of that down into the village.'

'Well . . . I . . .' She hesitated but seeing the look in his eye, she nodded. 'That would be very helpful, thank you.' She told him what time her train would be leaving and he left promising to be back the next morning.

As promised Louis appeared with the carriage bright and early the next morning and tactfully began to load her luggage, leaving Lily to say her goodbyes to Sara.

'I've hardly slept a wink all night worryin' about yer goin',' Sara confessed tearfully. 'You 'ear such terrible stories about what can 'appen to young women alone in London.'

Lily smiled. 'I'm a big girl now, Mam, and I won't be alone. I'll have Jean-Paul and Monsieur Levigne to keep their eye on me. And don't forget Arabella is there too if I need help. I'll be fine, honestly. You just take good care of yourself and I'll be back to see you before you know it.' She kissed her mother soundly and after bending to tickle Sassy under the chin, she climbed into the carriage with Louis and the driver urged the horses on.

They were quiet on the way to the station, neither of them quite knowing what to say to each other. When they arrived, Louis hailed a porter to take the luggage to the train. Then it was time to say goodbye and they stood on the platform together as the train hissed into the station.

'This is it then,' he said softly. 'The start of a new life for you. I hope it will be a good one. I just wish . . .'

As his voice trailed away, she smiled at him sadly. 'I know.' There was no need for words. They both knew what the other was thinking. 'Perhaps in another time and another place.' She leant forward impulsively and pecked him on the cheek before turning quickly so that he wouldn't see the tears in her eyes. She climbed aboard the train and started along the corridor until she saw a carriage that had an empty window seat. Seconds later, she heard the guard slamming the doors and the train rumbled into life again and she leant out of the window waving at Louis until he was lost to sight. There could be no going back now. A whole new life lay ahead of her and she prayed that she had made the right decision.

Chapter Forty-Two

As promised, Jean-Paul was waiting for her on the platform at Euston when the train arrived and his face lit up as he spotted her.

'Ma chérie!' He rushed forward to embrace her, thinking how pretty she looked in her blue gown and matching bonnet. 'I 'ave been so looking forward to you arriving. But come, we must find a porter and get your luggage. We will take a cab to the apartment. I only hope you like it.'

'I'm sure I shall,' she assured him with a warm smile. Jean-Paul was such a kind man that it was impossible not to like him and she enjoyed his company, although she didn't feel romantically inclined towards him, not like she felt with— She stopped her thoughts from going any further. She had left Louis and her old life behind and now she had to look to the future.

Soon they were rattling through the streets of London and once again Lily was shocked at the number of people and vehicles milling about the busy streets. It was a world away from the little village she had been brought up in but from now on it would be home. They passed the gallery on Oxford Street then turned off into one of the side streets.

'I shall never find my way about,' she fretted, realising she had no idea where she was.

Jean-Paul chuckled. 'Ah, but you will,' he promised.

She could only hope he was right.

Soon after he stopped the cab in front of a long row of four-storey terraced houses. 'This is the place I 'ave reserved for you. Are you ready to look?'

'Oh yes.'

He instructed the cab driver to wait for her to inspect her new home before unloading the luggage then led her inside.

'I am afraid it is rather a climb to the top floor but once we get there you will see why I thought this would be the most suitable one for you,' he told her as they began to climb the steep staircase. It seemed to go on forever but at last they emerged onto the landing and taking a key from his pocket he unlocked the door and ushered her inside. She found herself in another small hallway with three doors leading off it. The first led into a decent-sized bedroom complete with a brass bed, drawers and a wardrobe. It was a little shabby but spotlessly clean and Lily smiled her approval. The second led into the tiniest kitchen she had ever seen, but even so there was a sink, a small oven and some shelves stocked with pots and pans.

Jean-Paul then opened the final door with a flourish. 'This is the room that decided it for me. It would be perfect for painting in.'

Lily was delighted to see that he was right. It was quite a large room, sparsely furnished but with a huge window which allowed the light to flood in. 'Unfortunately, you will 'ave to share a bathroom and toilet with the tenants down on the next floor,' he apologised, but that didn't trouble Lily. It would be nice not to have to go outside to it in the winter.

'You're right,' she said enthusiastically. 'It's perfect, but can I afford it?'

He mentioned a sum that sounded more than reasonable so with a grin she told him, 'Would you go down and ask the driver to bring my luggage up, please? I'd like to get settled in and set my easel up.'

Within a month, Lily felt as if she had lived there forever. She spent each day painting and sketching and Jean-Paul informed her that he now had nearly enough of her work to set up an exhibition.

'We could 'ave done it sooner, but the problem is as soon as I get them framed and 'ung they sell,' he told her with a happy grin.

Lily was delighted. Her little apartment was perfect for painting in, as Jean-Paul had told her, and the light that flooded through the window ensured she could paint and sketch from morning until night. She'd also taken her easel and a canvas and painted some of London's famous landmarks. Nelson's Column, Trafalgar Square and Buckingham Palace were all brought to life on canvas and proved to be very popular in the art gallery. And then she started to venture into the poorer parts of the city, painting barefoot urchins with hollow eyes playing in the gutters, and starving dogs scavenging amongst piles of rubbish.

It was there that one child in particular caught her eye: a little girl who only looked to be seven or eight years old. She was painfully thin, her hair was tangled and matted, and Lily had no doubt it was probably alive with lice. Her eyes seemed to have sunk into her face and they had a haunted look that touched Lily's heart. She felt so sorry for her that as she passed her, she slipped two shiny pennies into her hand and the child shot away clutching them as if they were the crown jewels. Lily had thought she had seen poverty back in her home village but that was nothing compared to this and she wondered how people could survive in such awful conditions.

The day after that she went to the docks and painted the ships with their towering masts, and burly sailors heaving huge barrels up and down the gangplanks. Just for a moment, while she was there, she thought she spotted the child again but she couldn't be sure.

'I don't know where you get your ideas from,' Jean-Paul praised her as she presented each finished one and she smiled. She had painted an old flower seller on the steps of St Paul's Cathedral selling little bunches of heather, and another day she sketched an organ grinder with his monkey. She sketched an old man selling tiny bags of bird seed for the pigeons to the many tourists that flocked to the city, and when she presented it to Monsieur Levigne, who was on one of his frequent visits to the city, he shook his head in amazement.

'You 'ave the gift of bringing everything you paint or sketch to life,' he told her reverently. 'I think you are going to become a very famous artist, *ma chérie*, and I am honoured to be part of your journey.'

'But it's all thanks to you that this is happening,' Lily pointed out.

He shook his head. '*Non*. It is thanks to you for bringing your work to me in the first place,' he insisted as he studied the sketch he was holding. 'And very soon now your exhibition will begin and you will get to meet some of the public who love your work so much.'

'I might treat myself to a new gown especially for the occasion,' Lily told him happily. She could easily afford it and she thought it might be nice to buy something brand new for herself. All her decent clothes had been Arabella's but now she was in a position to spoil herself a little and she decided she would ask Arabella if she would like to come with her – they still saw each other regularly and had become even closer.

Deciding there was no time like the present, she set off for Lady Bellingham's townhouse and as always Arabella and Annie were delighted to see her.

'I can't believe how much she's growing,' Lily chuckled as Annie crawled across the floor. It was clear to see that she was the apple of both her mother's and grandmother's eyes and although they were still soberly dressed in black, it was obvious they were much happier now.

'Have you heard from your mother lately?' Arabella asked as they sat drinking coffee together.

'Oh yes. I send a little money home every month, although they don't seem to need it anymore,' Lily told her happily. 'Ginny's family have moved into the cottage now and my mother and hers have become close friends and are good company for each other. Oh, and Bridget has had her baby. A little girl called Emily. Let's hope the baby can cheer her up, but I won't hold my breath. What about you, have you heard any news from the manor?'

'Louis wrote to me last week to tell me that Grandmama is very unwell,' Arabella answered before leaping up to stop Annie sucking a piece of coal she had grabbed from the coal scuttle. She seemed to be into all sorts of mischief now and Arabella jokingly said that she needed eyes in the back of her head.

'I'm sorry to hear that.' Despite the way the old lady had treated her, Lily bore her no grudge.

Arabella looked sad. 'She hasn't been well for a long time so it's not totally unexpected. Mother has suggested we should go home at the weekend and stay for a while till we see how she is.'

'Oh, I shall miss you.' Lily and Arabella met up most weeks to have lunch or do some shopping and it would feel strange being in London without her.

'Don't worry, I shan't stay longer than I have to,' Arabella promised her.

It was then that Lily suggested they might go shopping together for a dress for her exhibition which was due to take place in the middle of October and Arabella was keen on the idea.

'Oh yes, you must have something really nice to wear,' she agreed. 'Didn't you tell me that Jean-Paul was going to advertise it in the newspapers?'

Lily nodded and blushed. It was still hard to believe that all this was really happening. Already she had earned more than enough money to move to a better apartment if she wished to but she liked where she was because it was close to the art gallery and the shops.

She was getting to know her way about now and it was beginning to feel like home.

After agreeing to meet for their shopping trip in two days' time outside the gallery, Lily set off for home, eager to get back to her rooms and spend a quiet afternoon painting.

Late afternoon she was doing just that when there was a tap on her door and laying her paint brush aside, she went to open it to find Jean-Paul standing there with an enormous bunch of flowers in his hand. They were beginning to droop already and she laughed as she ushered him inside.

'Thank you,' she said accepting the gift and moving into the kitchen to stand them in water. 'And what brings you here today?'

'I was rather 'oping that you might accompany me to the music hall this evening,' he said hopefully.

'Oh, I see.' Lily wasn't sure what to do. She had spent quite some time in his company since moving to London and she had enjoyed it but she didn't want to look as if she was encouraging his affection, for she now realised that as much as she liked him, she considered him only as a friend. Her heart lay back in the village with a man who she could never be with. 'I, er . . . was planning on having a bath and an early night, to be honest,' she said gently, and his face fell.

'Oh, I see . . .'

Realising she needed to be honest with him before things went any further, she took a deep breath and said, 'The thing is Jean-Paul, I worry that your parents would have concerns if they thought we were forming an attachment to each other.'

His eyebrows rose. 'But why would they, *ma chérie*?'

'Because we are far apart in class. You must remember that I was brought up in a pit miner's cottage while you were brought up in a beautiful chateau. I'm sure your parents will want you to marry someone of your own class, and I certainly don't fit the bill.'

To her surprise he threw back his head and laughed. 'Non, you 'ave the wrong idea of my family. You see my mother met my father when 'e was very young and 'e was grape-picking on my grandfather's estate. He 'ardly 'ad a franc to 'is name but they fell in love and the rest is 'istory. They 'ave always told me that the secret to a good marriage is love, and that I must follow my 'eart and you must know that I am more than a little fond of you?'

'Oh, I'm very fond of you too, Jean-Paul,' she assured him for she didn't want to hurt his feelings. 'But could we just carry on as friends for now and see if anything comes of it? I don't feel ready to commit myself to anyone just yet.'

'Very well, I understand,' he said quietly, although he looked sad. 'But be warned' – the twinkle was back in his eye as he headed for the door – 'I do not give up easily. *Bon après-midi*, mademoiselle.' And with a cheeky wink he was gone, leaving her to smile and shake her head as she turned her attention back to her painting.

Two days later she met Arabella as planned outside the art gallery and asked, 'Do you mind if I just pop in for a moment? I have these sketches I need to give to Jean-Paul.'

Arabella followed Lily inside and wandered around slowly, admiring the beautiful pieces of art displayed on the walls. Just then Jean-Paul appeared and spotting Lily and her companion he hurried over to them.

'Ah Lily, you 'ave brought the sketches, *oui*? And who is your charming friend?'

And then right before Lily's eyes something strange happened, for as Arabella turned to Jean-Paul colour swamped her cheeks.

'Jean-Paul, this is Arabella,' Lily introduced them.

Jean-Paul kissed Arabella's hand and, though it seemed impossible, her cheeks went even redder.

'How do you do,' Arabella said formally.

He smiled. 'Very well, mademoiselle.'

The two hardly seemed able to tear their eyes away from one another and Lily wondered if she was witnessing the start of something special. They certainly seemed to be very taken with one another.

'Well, er . . . should we be going now?' Lily asked, hoping to break the spell.

Reluctantly taking her hand from Jean-Paul's Arabella nodded. 'Oh . . . of course. Goodbye, Jean-Paul, it was nice to meet you. I've heard so much about you from Lily.'

'*Enchantée*, mademoiselle,' Jean-Paul said as the two young women took their leave.

'Goodness, did I detect a bit of a spark between you two back there?' Lily teased as they wandered along to the lady's emporium. She had never known Arabella to so much as look at another man since Freddie had betrayed her so badly, yet here she was now with stars in her eyes and a bloom in her cheeks.

'Of course not,' Arabella denied a little too quickly. 'Didn't you say that you thought Jean-Paul was fond of you?'

'Fond yes, but we're not in love.'

Arabella sighed. 'It doesn't really matter anyway, does it? What I mean is, once he discovers that I am a fallen woman with an illegitimate child he'll probably run in the opposite direction.'

'None of that was your fault,' Lily scolded. 'Freddie lied to you, so stop whipping yourself about it and just look at the beautiful little girl you gained. You have to put him far behind you now and go on with your life.'

Once inside the emporium they began to look at the gowns on display. They were dotted about on mannequins for people to decide what styles they liked and Arabella sighed as she stared down at her own dull black attire. 'I can't wait to be able to wear colours again,' she confided. Then she stopped suddenly as she spotted a satin gown in a soft champagne colour. 'Oh Lily,' she urged excitedly. 'This would be just perfect for the exhibition.'

It was cut very simply with only a ruffle of lace about the sweet-heart neckline but Lily had to admit it looked elegant. She glanced at the price and gasped: it was more than she had ever spent on a dress in her whole life but, as Arabella pointed out, she could easily afford it now so she called one of the shop ladies to ask if one could be made in time for her exhibition. When the woman assured her that it could, Arabella clapped her hands with delight.

'That's the one,' she said. 'It's just perfect!'

And so, feeling more than a little guilty at spending so much on herself, Lily allowed the woman to take her measurements and left the shop with a wide smile on her face. She could hardly wait for the exhibition to open now so that she could wear it.

Chapter Forty-Three

Once outside they had gone only a few steps when Lily got the sensation that someone was following her and turning quickly, she was just in time to see the little girl she had given the money to duck out of sight into a shop doorway.

'Is something wrong?' Arabella stared along the street behind them.

'Not wrong exactly, but I think I just saw a child I gave a little money to the other day,' Lily explained.

'Oh Lily, you should *never* do that,' Arabella scolded. 'These street urchins will fasten on to you like limpets if you give them money.'

'But the poor little soul looked like she was starving!'

'They all do,' Arabella said patiently. 'But the trouble is you can't help all of them.'

Lily sighed and they continued on their way. There was no further sighting of the child and she began to think that she must have been mistaken so she put the incident from her mind.

It was the next evening as she went to visit the local shop to buy some bread and milk that the child appeared again and this time there could be no mistake. It was the same little girl she had taken pity on. She was standing outside the house when Lily emerged from the front door staring up at the top floor and Lily realised with a little shock that the child knew where she lived. She must have followed her home. As soon as she saw her, the child began to back away from her.

'Hello again,' Lily said kindly.

The child paused and stared at her suspiciously as Lily took some pennies from her purse and held them out to her. 'Here you are,' she urged. 'Are you hungry? Go and buy yourself some food.'

She knew that Arabella would scold her again if she were to find out what she was doing but there was something about this little girl that tugged at her heartstrings.

Very, very cautiously the barefooted child approached and when Lily's hand was within reach, she snatched the money and shot off, leaving Lily to shake her head in dismay.

Poor little tyke, she thought as she moved on to the shop.

The same thing happened the next day and the day after that until Lily finally asked her, 'What's your name?'

The child's mouth opened and closed.

'Come on,' Lily said cajolingly. 'You must have a name. Mine is Lily.'

'I-it's Merry,' the child muttered, so quietly that Lily could scarcely hear her.

'Merry? That's an unusual name. Are you sure you don't mean Mary?'

The child shrugged as she scratched at a scab on her skinny leg. 'I fink that's what me ma used ter call me.'

'And where is your ma now?'

Another shrug. 'Don't know. She went orf wi' a sailor an' I ain't seen her since.'

'When was that?'

'Don't rightly know . . . a long time ago I fink,' the child answered eyeing the coins in Lily's hands.

'So where do you live now, with your dad?'

Merry shook her head. 'Ner, I ain't gorra dad that I know of. An' I sleep 'ere an' there.'

Lily felt tears sting at the back of her eyes. The poor kid was homeless. No wonder she was so thin and filthy. Despite Arabella's warning she made a hasty decision. 'If you wait here for me while I go to fetch some food, I'll take you up to my rooms and cook a meal for you,' she promised.

Merry stared at her suspiciously. 'An' why would yer do that?'

'Because I want to,' Lily said cheerfully. It was obvious the child was about to take flight at any second and she sensed she was going to have to go carefully if she didn't want to frighten her away. 'But it's up to you, of course. You don't have to,' she went on nonchalantly and set off again.

Merry was still there when she got back, hovering uncertainly like a little bird about to take flight, so with a smile Lily opened the door and left it wide. It would be up to the child if she followed her inside. As she climbed the first set of stairs, she heard the patter of footsteps on the bare wooden treads behind her, but she continued on without looking back. She didn't want to frighten her away.

Sure enough, as she inserted the key in her door, the child appeared on the little landing behind her so once again Lily left the door open and entered her small apartment.

Lily went to the kitchen and began to unpack the basket of food she had bought and seconds later Merry appeared in the doorway her eyes wide with awe.

'Cor, is this where yer live?' She was staring around at the place as if she was in a luxury hotel.

'Yes, it is, and do you like bacon?'

'I's only ever tried it once, I reckon,' Merry told her as Lily threw some into a large frying pan.

'Right, well while I cook this you can lay the table for us,' Lily told her. 'You'll find the cloth and the knives and forks in that drawer there. I'll do you a fried egg as well, shall I?'

Ten minutes later she placed a large plateful of food in front of Merry. There was a sausage, bacon, an egg and a big slice of fried bread and the little girl stared down at it with a look on her face that said 'have I died and gone to heaven?'

'Is this all fer me?' she asked incredulously and when Lily nodded, she began to cram it into her mouth so quickly that Lily feared she would choke. She completely ignored the knife and fork and Lily wondered if anyone had ever taught her to use them. She certainly had no table manners. Within seconds her plate was clean and Lily pushed her own meal towards her.

'Here, can you manage mine as well? I'm not really hungry.'

'Nor 'alf!' The child proceeded to clear that plate too, which told Lily she probably hadn't had a proper meal for some time. It was hard to believe that a child so small could eat so much all in one go but she didn't comment as she took the plates away. Merry then swallowed three cups of hot sweet tea one after the other before sitting back and patting her belly contentedly. 'Fanks, missus, that were luvvly!'

'You're welcome.' Lily eyed her cautiously before asking, 'How old are you, Merry?'

'I fink I'm nine or ten,' the child answered.

Lily was surprised; she'd thought she was a lot younger. But then, without proper food, she supposed she wouldn't have been able to grow. The little girl was scratching furiously at her dirty brown hair and Lily wondered how long it might have been since it had been washed. The garment she was wearing was no better. It hung to mid-calf and was so filthy and full of holes that its original colour was indistinguishable.

'Right . . . I'd berrer be off now,' Merry said as she rose and edged towards the door.

'But where will you sleep?'

Merry shrugged. 'Anywhere I can find that's under cover 'opefully,' the child responded. 'It ain't so bad in the summer when it's warm. But winters are the worst.'

'Surely there's somewhere for children in your position to go instead of having to sleep rough?'

Merry frowned. 'Oh ar, there is, the work'ouse, but I'd ravver die than end up in there. They reckon that once you go into that place you'll never come out again so I'd ravver take me chances on the street. I get by, I beg an' pick a few pockets an' that buys me some grub.'

Lily was horrified and hesitated for a moment. She knew Arabella wouldn't approve of what she was about to do but she couldn't help herself.

'Why don't you stay here with me?'

'*What?*' Merry looked astounded. 'Yer mean to like live 'ere an' sleep 'ere?'

'Yes, I suppose that's exactly what I mean,' Lily answered and when the child looked suspicious, she hurried on. 'I could do with someone to help to keep the place clean. I'm working full-time on my artwork and you could do the shopping and run my errands for me.'

'An' that's all?' Merry was suspicious of everyone.

'That's all,' Lily assured her. 'But there would have to be a few rules put in place. For a start, you'd need to have a good bath and let me buy you some decent clothes. Those you're wearing are almost dropping off you.'

'*A barff!*' Merry didn't much like the sound of that.

'Yes, it would mean we have to boil the kettle and fill the bath down on the next floor but I think you'll feel so much better for it.'

'Hmm.' Merry narrowed her eyes and thought about it before saying, 'All right . . . bur it'd just be fer a trial, right, to see 'ow we gor on?'

'Deal.' Lily grinned. 'So shall we start to boil some water? I shall have to make you a bed up on the floor in here for tonight but if you decide you want to stay, I can buy another bed to go into my bedroom.'

It took almost an hour to heat enough water to fill the bath but surprisingly Merry climbed into it with no fuss whatsoever and when Lily handed her a bar of carbolic soap she began to rub at herself, tickled pink to see her skin changing from grubby brown to pink.

Lily had to blink back tears at the first sight of the child's emaciated little body. Her ribs stood out and she was covered in bruises and sores but she was a plucky little thing and Lily instinctively knew that she wouldn't thank Lily for commenting.

'How about if I help you with your hair?' Lily offered and when Merry nodded she set to scrubbing the tangled mess until she could rub her fingers through it. Next she took a fine-toothed comb and removed as many of the nits as she could until finally Merry was ready to get dry.

'Here, you can borrow this for tonight.' Lily handed her one of her plain white blouses. It hung down to the little girl's knees and she had to roll the sleeves up but at least it was clean and would serve as a nightshirt for now.

Once they had emptied the bath, a painstaking exercise that involved them lugging the buckets of water all the way down to the yard, they returned to Lily's rooms and she fetched a blanket and pillow, telling Merry, 'I'm afraid you'll have to manage on the floor in front of the fire for tonight.'

'It's berrer than bein' out in the cold,' Merry said cheerfully. Already as her hair dried Lily could see that it was a soft strawberry-blonde colour and inclined to curl, and that she would be quite pretty when she had a little meat on her bones.

'In that case I'll leave you to it.' Already Lily was wondering if she'd done the right thing. She could well wake up in the morning to find the place stripped of anything of any worth, as Arabella had warned her, but she was prepared to take a chance.

Once in bed, Lily lay for a long time straining to hear any untoward sounds from the front room, but all was quiet and eventually she dozed off and slept soundly for the remainder of the night.

The next morning she woke to the sound of the milk cart trundling below the windows. She yawned and stretched, then remembering what had happened with Merry she hurriedly rose and after slipping on her robe went into the lounge where noises from the kitchen reached her.

'I've put the kettle on the 'ob fer a cuppa,' Merry informed her. 'An' I've done us some bread an' butter fer breakfast, but I've et mine.'

'Oh.' Lily was relieved. Everything in the place seemed to be where she had left it so it was a case of so far so good!

'I have to go out this morning. I have to take some sketches to my friend at the art gallery,' she told the child as they were drinking their tea. 'And you might like to come with me. On the way back we could call into the market and see if we could get you some decent clothes and some shoes.'

Merry nodded eagerly and soon after they set off with Merry looking considerably cleaner, although she was still barefoot and had had to put her old dress back on.

'Whoever is that?' Jean-Paul asked quietly when they entered the gallery. Merry had wandered off to admire the artwork and seeing the look of horror on his face, Lily grinned and told him about the offer she had made to Merry.

'You 'ave done *what*!' He shook his head. 'I fear you may well live to regret your kindness, *ma chérie*,' he fretted.

'Well, we'll see, won't we. But now I have to go. I'm taking Merry to get some clothes.'

Two hours later they returned to Lily's rooms with a bag full of second-hand but decent clothes for Merry. Some of them would be a little large but Lily knew that she could alter them to fit her and anything was better than the rags she was wearing. Merry insisted on trying on every single thing and sashayed about the place with a wide grin on her face, clearly delighted with her new clothes. Lily had even managed to find her a little pair of black leather button boots and Merry loved them so much she refused to take them off, even in the apartment.

Over the next few days Merry did all she could to do anything that needed doing as Lily sat by the window working and so eventually Lily bought a small brass bed from a second-hand shop and once it was delivered, they put it up together in the corner of Lily's bedroom.

One morning there was a knock at the door and when Merry hurried to open it she found Arabella standing on the doorstep.

'Ah, come in,' Lily called over Merry's shoulder, and to the child she said, 'Perhaps you could put the kettle on, Merry, and make us all a nice cup of tea?'

The child shot off to do as she was told as Arabella's eyes stretched wide. 'Whoever is that and what's she doing here?' she whispered.

Lily hastily told her and Arabella looked just as horrified as Jean-Paul. 'I'm not at all sure you've done the right thing,' she said worriedly.

'I'm sure I have; she's actually a great help. But tell me how your grandmother is and what's happening at home.'

'Grandmama is holding on but only by a thread,' Arabella confided. 'I don't think she'll be long for this world now. Louis' new stud business is doing splendidly and I called to see your mother and I'm happy to report she seems as happy as Larry. She and Ginny's mother are getting along really well and are wonderful company for each other. She asked me to send you her love and to tell you that it's time you went home for a visit. I think she misses you.'

A little pang of homesickness shot through Lily as she pictured the cottage at the top of the valley. 'I intend to do just that as soon as the exhibition is over,' she said.

Soon after Merry carried their drinks in, sloshing tea into the saucers but Lily didn't mind.

'Would you mind going to do some shopping for me?' she asked and Merry nodded obligingly as Lily handed her a small list and half a crown.

Merry's smile wavered and she blushed. 'Can yer just tell me what yer need?' she queried in a wobbly voice with an embarrassed glance at Arabella. 'I can't read, yer see. I ain't never been to school.'

'Of course I can.' Lily quickly told the child what she wanted, cursing herself silently for embarrassing her. She should have realised that being forced to live the life she had she would have had no schooling. 'And don't worry. I'll start to teach you your alphabet and you'll be reading and writing in no time.'

Merry hurried to fetch the wicker basket from the kitchen and clattered away down the stairs clutching the half-crown.

Arabella raised an eyebrow. 'I wouldn't mind betting that's the last you'll see of her now that you've given her money,' she warned.

'We'll see.' Lily sipped her tea hoping that Arabella would be wrong. Already she had grown fond of Merry and she would miss her if she were not to return, but all she could do was trust her instincts and wait and see.

Arabella was about to leave almost an hour later when the door swung open and Merry appeared lugging the heavy basket. 'I got everyfin' yer wanted an' you've got tuppence change,' she informed Lily proudly as she placed the money on the table. 'So I'll go and put everyfin' away in the kitchen now, shall I?'

'Yes, well done, thank you.' Lily grinned triumphantly at Arabella who shrugged.

'You can't be right all the time.' Her friend grinned. 'But I must be off. I'll see you at the exhibition. Mother and I are looking forward to it. Did you see the lovely article about you in *The Times*?

They were very complimentary about your work and I have a feeling it's going to go down really well.'

'Let's hope so.' Lily saw her to the door before going back to work. The demand for her work was such that she was spending every minute she could drawing or sketching, but she wouldn't have had it any other way. It certainly beat being a parlour maid. The only thing she missed about that place was Louis, and just the thought of him caused a little stab in her heart.

Chapter Forty-Four

At last the big night arrived and as Lily slipped into her new gown, which she had picked up from the emporium the day before, she was shaking with nerves. Merry was now like her little shadow and nothing was too much trouble for her.

'Eeh, yer look just like a princess,' she said in awe as she helped Lily to fasten the buttons on her gown. It was just as beautiful as Lily had hoped it would be, and it fitted like a glove. Lily had swept her hair high on her head and teased it into a cluster of curls and she had even treated herself to a new pair of satin slippers to go with her gown. She wore no jewellery whatsoever, but it was the pure simplicity of the gown and the lack of embellishments that made her look so stunning.

'I fink you'll be the prettiest lady there,' Merry announced proudly as she jumped around her in excitement. Lily was her saviour and she adored her.

'I doubt that'll be the case; Jean-Paul told me there are some very important people coming this evening,' she answered as she smoothed the lace at her neckline.

'Well, *you're* an important person . . . at least you are to me!'

Lily was so touched that for the first time she leant over and kissed Merry's cheek and the child allowed her to. Merry skipped to the window before racing back to tell her, 'Yer cab is waitin' downstairs, Lily. You'd best be goin'. 'Ave a good time.'

'I'll try.' Lily snatched up her bag and left. This was it! The night she had been waiting for.

Jean-Paul met her at the door of the gallery and she stared in surprise at the maids who stood about with crystal glasses of champagne and canapés on silver trays ready for the guests when they arrived.

One room had been given solely over to her work and she felt a little rush of pride to see it all displayed. Monsieur Levigne had come especially for the occasion and he smiled with delight at the sight of her. 'Why, *ma chérie* you look *superbe*,' he gushed, bending over her hand and kissing it gently. 'And I am going to forecast that after theese evening you will be the toast of the art world! But come, eet is almost time. We must stand by the door ready to greet our guests.'

They took their places and within minutes the guests began to arrive, Arabella and Lady Bellingham being amongst the first. Very soon the gallery was full and the first purchase was made for what Lily thought was an extortionate price.

'And that was only the first,' Jean-Paul whispered to her. 'It was bought by a duchess so everyone will want one now, you just see if I am not right.'

He did prove to be right and as the evening progressed the sold signs began to go up more quickly than Lily could keep up with.

'We are going to sell out at this rate,' Monsieur Levigne chuckled as he passed her with a lady who was keen to be shown one of her paintings. She noticed that Jean-Paul was enjoying a glass of champagne with Arabella and for the first time in many months her friend seemed to be glowing.

The atmosphere was light and as darkness fell Lily began to feel as if she was caught up in a fairy tale. Over the course of the evening, she had been commissioned to do two portraits, and although she was nervous, she was looking forward to the challenge. She was the star of the show and everyone wanted to talk to her. She wished that the evening could go on forever. But at last the first guests began to trickle away until she was alone with Jean-Paul and Monsieur Levigne. It was very late by then and Lily was tired but inordinately happy. She needed no one to tell her that the evening had been a roaring success and she couldn't stop smiling.

'I 'ave no idea 'ow much we 'ave made but I promise it will be counted up first thing in the morning,' Monsieur Levigne told her. 'Congratulations, *ma chérie*. The evening could have gone no better and no doubt when the reporter from *The Times* puts his piece in the paper tomorrow you will be the talk of the town and in very great demand. From now on the world will be your oyster and eet couldn't 'ave 'appened to a nicer person.'

The next morning Lily sent Merry out for a newspaper and the child crowed with excitement when they found a write-up about the exhibition on page three.

'Cor blimey, yer famous!' she gushed, beside herself.

Lily grinned happily, reading the review over and over again, unable to believe that she, a miner's daughter, was now being written about in the newspaper!

But there were still practical things to think of. 'That's all very well, but I think I shall have to get busy doing some more,' she laughed. 'I think most of my work sold last night and Monsieur Levigne can't sell it if it isn't there to sell. What I'm saying is, it's business as usual and back to work for me after breakfast, I'm afraid.'

It was mid-morning as Lily was taking full advantage of the light streaming through the window when Jean-Paul and Monsieur Levigne arrived bearing the most enormous bouquet of flowers she had ever seen.

'For you,' Monsieur Levigne said gallantly as he presented it to her with a little bow, while laughing at the smudge of paint on the end of her nose. 'As of today, you are the undisputed queen of the art world. And now to show you what you earned.'

He laid a large bundle of notes on the table and Lily gasped.

'There is over one 'undred guineas there, *ma chérie*,' he told her. 'Not bad for one night, eh? And theese is only the beginning, so I think per'aps it is time for you to move to more salubrious accommodation. Per'aps somewhere without all those stairs!'

She chuckled as he mopped his face and moustache with a large handkerchief. 'I may well do that but first I would like to return home for a few days,' she told him. 'It's time I paid a visit to my family.'

'Of course,' he agreed. 'And per'aps while you are gone Jean-Paul could start the search for somewhere a little more suitable for you to live?'

'I'd be very grateful,' Lily admitted. Although the top floor had suited her admirably, she certainly wouldn't miss all the stairs and having to cart the bath water up and down.

When the gentlemen had gone Merry stared down at the money in shock. 'Does this mean yer rich now?' she asked in a small voice.

'Well, I'm certainly rich compared to what I used to be. Why do you ask?'

'I were just thinkin' yer won't want me 'anging about now.'

Lily scowled. 'Whatever gave you that idea? I like having you around so when I move, if I move, you'll be coming with me if you want to.'

'An' wharrabout when yer go 'ome to see yer ma? Where will I go then?'

'It seems to me you have two choices, the first is, you can wait here till I get back, the second is you could come with me.'

'What . . . on a train, yer mean?' Merry's eyes seemed to be almost popping out of her head.

'Of course, but only if you want to. I'm sure my family would like to meet you.'

Suddenly without warning Merry flung her arms about her waist and hugged her, bringing a lump to Lily's throat. It was the first real sign of affection the child had ever shown her and it touched her deeply.

'I ain't never been on a train afore,' she muttered. 'Is it very scary?'

'Not at all. And before we go, I think perhaps we could run to a couple of brand-new outfits for you, what do you think?'

'I fink you're the kindest person I ever met,' Merry whispered with tears on her lashes. 'An' I luv you, Lily. Ever so much.'

'I love you too, sweetheart,' Lily whispered as she returned the hug and in that moment, she realised she meant it. This little girl had crept into her heart and she couldn't imagine life without her. 'There's just one thing though . . . if we're going to be staying together, I'd like you to go to school when we get back. Will you do that for me?'

Merry wasn't too keen on the idea but she nodded reluctantly. 'Awight, though why's we 'ave to know sums an' letters I don't know.'

Lily chuckled. 'The other thing is, if you are going to school you'll need to have a surname. What is it?'

Merry looked worried. 'What's a surname?'

Lily thought how best to explain it before answering, 'Well, my first name is Lily as you know, and my surname is Moon, so what's yours?'

Merry looked confused as she shrugged. 'I've allus been just Merry far as I know.'

'In that case you'll have to use mine.'

Merry frowned. 'So I'll be Merry Moon?'

When Lily nodded they both broke into peals of laughter. It was a very strange name admittedly, but now it was decided.

Three days later they set off for the train station with Merry looking very pretty in a new woollen dress and coat with a matching
bonnet. She was almost beside herself with excitement and she
hopped from foot to foot as they boarded the train, although she
went pale when the engine steamed into life and she clung to Lily
like a leech.

'It's all right,' Lily assured her. 'Look, you can watch out of the
window.'

Very soon, as the train steamed out of the station into countryside, Merry sat transfixed with her nose pressed up against the
glass. She had only ever known the teeming streets of London
and had never imagined that such wide-open spaces existed. They
passed fields full of horses, cows and sheep and her questions were
endless. Lily answered them all patiently as best she could and
with Merry to entertain her the journey seemed to pass quickly.

When they arrived at Trent Valley Station, Lily hailed a cab to
take them to the village and once again Merry sat with her nose
glued to the window, not missing a trick. A whole new world had
opened up to her and she didn't want to miss a minute of it.

When they reached the village, the cab dropped them at the
bottom of the valley and Merry skipped ahead wondering at the
many trees and the wild flowers. At last, the cottage came into
view and when Lily pointed it out, Merry gaped at in awe. It was
like something she had seen in picture books from time to time
but now she clutched Lily's hand feeling nervous about meeting
her family.

'Wharr if they doesn't like me?' she fretted.

Lily giggled. 'I like you, so why shouldn't they?' she told her
fondly.

As they drew nearer, Sassy suddenly appeared from the little
gate and seeing Lily she bounded towards them with her tail wagging furiously.

'Hello, Sassy,' Lily greeted her and Merry bent to stroke her. 'I've brought you a new friend to play with for a time.'

Sassy licked Merry's hand joyously, and the little girl's heart was lost. Then Sara appeared and seeing her daughter she raced towards her with her eyes shining. 'Aw, pet, it's so luvvly to see you,' she gushed. 'And who's this, eh?'

'This is Merry. I'll tell you all about her later but now come on, we're dying for a drink, aren't we, Merry?'

As they entered the cottage, Ginny's mother stepped towards her and gave her a hug and Lily was pleased to see how happy and content she looked.

'Hello, Mrs Davis,' Lily greeted her but the woman waved her hand at her.

'Oh, get away with you, it's Blanche,' she told her as she smiled at Merry. 'Now, would yer both like a cuppa?'

As the homely little woman bustled away to make the tea, Lily could see at a glance that the two women were getting along famously. Blanche's children were all at school now and with Ginny and Richie at work they were company for each other.

The next hour was spent telling them all about the exhibition and showing them the newspapers that had reported on it and Sara was glowing with pride. 'Who'd 'ave thought I'd 'ave a famous artist fer a daughter, eh? Eeh, if yer dad were 'ere he'd be as proud as punch. An' look at yer! Why, yer look like a real lady an' yer sound like one an' all.'

'Hmm, I don't know about that,' Lily chuckled. 'Now tell me what's been going on here. How are Bridget and the baby? And I notice there's another pig in the sty and a lot more chickens than there were.'

'Bridget an' the baby are fine. We've got a cow an' all,' Sara informed her. 'An' Blanche 'ere makes lovely cheese an' butter from the milk. We sell it down in the shop an' it brings in a fair little income. But things ain't so good up at the manor. Word 'as it the old lady is on 'er last legs.'

'Yes, Arabella told me she was ill,' Lily replied, wondering how Louis was feeling. She knew he was fond of his grandmother, despite the fact that she had caused so much trouble.

They went on to talk of other things, and Lily was delighted to see that both her mother and Blanche took to Merry, especially when Lily told them how she had found her. 'Poor little soul,' Sara said sadly. 'But what do yer intend to do wi' 'er?'

Lily chuckled. 'She's good company for me and very helpful. I'm going to send her to school when I go back and we'll take it from there.' And then she couldn't stop herself from asking, 'And how is Loui— Lord Bellingham?'

'Fine, far as I know. Our Richie reckons his stud business is really takin' off now.'

'Right, and any news on his engagement to Miss Thompson yet?' she pried.

Sara shook her head. 'Not that I've 'eard of. But 'ow long are yer stayin?'

'Just for a few days,' Lily told her regretfully. 'I've been commissioned to do a couple of portraits so I have to get back to make a start on the first one.'

Merry had already disappeared outside to play with Sassy and that set the scene for the next few days. The time passed all too quickly. Merry was obviously having a wonderful time running up and down the valley, playing in the copse and paddling in the stream – despite the weather being cool – but soon it was the afternoon before they were due to go home. Lily was sitting outside sketching as Merry and the Davis children played around her when a horse and rider approached, and her heart began to thud.

It was Louis.

He was dressed in beige jodhpurs and knee-length leather riding boots, and he looked so handsome that Lily ached for him.

'Good afternoon, Lord Bellingham,' she said softly when he drew close and dismounted. 'I wasn't expecting to see you.'

'It's Louis,' he told her shortly, then his voice softening he went on, 'Richie told me you were home so I thought I'd come and say hello and see how you were.'

'I'm very well,' she told him. 'But I'm sorry to hear your grandmother is so ill.'

He shrugged. 'She's had a good innings and between you and me I think she's ready to go now. She hasn't been right since Arabella had the baby; you know what a raging snob she is.'

Lily couldn't help but smile. He certainly had that right.

'Anyway, I'm told I'm now speaking to a famous artist. Congratulations on your success in London. Monsieur Levigne and Jean-Paul must be delighted.'

'Yes, I believe they are. And how is Miss Thompson?'

He frowned as he turned to stare at the children rolling about in the grass. 'She's well, I believe.' He clearly wanted to change the subject and went on, 'Richie informs me you'll be going back to London tomorrow so I came to see if you would like me to take you to the station in the carriage.'

'That's very kind of you but I've already arranged for a cab to pick us up,' she answered in a low voice.

'Oh, I see.' He tried to keep the disappointment from his voice but failed miserably.

Lily suddenly wished that he would just leave. They were clearly both feeling uncomfortable and didn't know what to say to each other so surely there was no point in continuing the conversation.

As if he had picked up on her thoughts, he turned back to the splendid black stallion he had arrived on. 'In that case, I'd best get on. It was nice to see you, Lily. Have a safe journey home.'

'Thank you . . . I will.'

He jumped effortlessly onto the saddle and rode away without a backwards glance and, watching him go, Lily's heart broke all over again.

Chapter Forty-Five

November 1877

Lily alighted from the cab outside her smart first-floor residence in Mayfair one dark afternoon, and after paying the cabbie, she pulled her scarf over her mouth to avoid breathing in the thick yellow smog that clouded the streets. The smog was so thick that she could barely see a hand in front of her. Behind her the street lighter was lighting the lamps, which cast glowing pools of dim yellow light on the pavements. Hurrying now, she went to the front door and inserted her key in the lock.

The past year had set her firmly amongst some of the most acclaimed artists in the country and she was now a very wealthy young woman. Even so, she still chose to lead a quiet life, although she and Merry now had a maid-cum-cook to look after them. Merry had been attending a local school for some time and had proved to be a very quick learner. Already she could read and write and her school reports were excellent. At Merry's request Lily had taken in yet another stray – a small gold-coloured dog with stubby legs and a bushy tail who they had named Honey, and the two were inseparable. Their new apartment boasted a good-sized garden where Merry and Honey could play to their hearts' content when the weather permitted, and life was good.

The elderly Lady Bellingham had passed away the year before shortly after Lily's visit to her mother but Arabella was now officially out of mourning and over the last months had become very close to Jean-Paul. Lily was pleased for them. Jean-Paul knew all about Annie's illegitimate birth and didn't seem to care a jot about it. In fact, it was clear that he was very taken with the child so Lily was hoping they might be announcing their engagement very soon.

She herself had been kept very busy, for as well as her sketches and paintings, she was now in great demand as a portrait artist and sometimes there didn't seem to be enough hours in the day.

As soon as she entered the apartment, she heard Merry and Honey pounding down the hallway to meet her. It was funny, Lily thought as she hugged them both, how different they both looked to when they had first come to live with her. Merry had filled out and her face now glowed with health, as did her long fair hair, and Honey looked nothing like the emaciated waif they had taken in off the streets as she wagged around her.

'There's a man 'ere to see you,' Merry whispered as Lily handed her coat to Abby, the maid, who had also come to greet her.

'A man? What man? I wasn't expecting anyone.' Lily frowned as she removed her bonnet and patted her hair into place in the hall mirror.

'It's Robbie who's married to yer sister,' Merry told her. 'An' Abby told 'im you wouldn't be 'ome fer awhile but 'e said 'e'd wait.'

'I see. Well, you go and help Abby with the dinner while I go and see what he wants, eh?' Lily smiled and gave Merry a gentle shove in the right direction and once the kitchen door had shut behind her, she took a deep breath and opened the door to the drawing room.

'Hello, Robbie. This is a surprise,' she said coolly. 'Is everything all right back at home? Are Bridget and the baby all right?'

He had been seated on a small sofa in front of a roaring fire but at her entrance he leapt to his feet and turned to face her, and immediately she saw that something was wrong. Despite the fact they now had a beautiful little girl, from what her mother told her in her letters, Robbie and Bridget weren't getting on any better.

If anything, they seemed to have drifted even further apart since Emily's birth.

'No, things ain't all right.' He shifted from foot to foot looking uneasy in such comfortable surroundings. 'It's Bridget, see? She's run off. Left the babby wi' me mam. I know where she is but she won't come back fer me so I wondered if you'd come wi' me to try an' persuade 'er?' Dressed in a coarse overcoat and clutching his cap in his hands, Robbie looked dishevelled, and there were dark circles beneath his eyes.

'*Me?*' Lily was shocked. 'Why would she listen to me? You know we haven't been on the best of terms since . . . Well, for some time.'

'You're still 'er sister though an' she admires you. *Please* say you'll come, if not fer me fer the baby's sake. She needs her mam!'

'Perhaps if you'd treated her better and not spent half your waking life in the pub it wouldn't have come to this,' Lily said sternly, but as his face crumpled she couldn't help but feel a bit sorry for him. 'So where is she?'

'Down by the docks in a little room she's rented,' he muttered. 'An' all I ask is that yer come wi' me to try an' persuade 'er to come 'ome. If she refuses again at least we'll both 'ave tried. I've begged 'er but she ain't 'avin' a bar of it an' I can 'ardly drag 'er 'ome kickin' and screamin', can I? I'd 'ave the scuffers on me neck in no time.'

Lily frowned as she bit her lip. This didn't sound like something Bridget would do at all, but then, she had been acting oddly for some time now. But so had Robbie, come to that!

'When do you want to go?' she said reluctantly.

'There ain't no time like the present, is there?' he said eagerly, screwing his cap into a ball. 'We could be there an' back in no time an' I thought per'aps if we could persuade 'er to come wi' us yer might put us both up 'ere fer the night. It'll be too late to get a train 'ome this evenin'.'

Lily hesitated for a moment longer before sighing resignedly. As he had pointed out, Bridget was her sister. 'Very well. Wait here while I go and tell Merry and Abby and then we'll get off.'

'But *why* are yer goin' out again?' Merry asked when she told them. 'Dinner's nearly ready an' we allus 'ave it together.'

'I'm sure you and Abby will be fine for just one night,' Lily soothed. 'My sister Bridget is staying down by the docks so I'm going with Robbie to see her before she goes back to the village.' She wouldn't give any more of an explanation because she didn't want to worry the child. 'And I shouldn't be gone for too long but if I'm not back for eight o'clock be sure to get yourself off to bed, it's school in the morning.'

Merry crossed her arms and pouted but she nodded all the same as Lily headed off to fetch her hat and coat again.

'Come on, let's go and get this over with,' she told Robbie and he followed her to the front door.

Merry had left the kitchen to join them as Lily pulled her coat on. 'It's really foggy out there,' she said with a worried frown as she eyed Robbie suspiciously. She had met him briefly once before when they had visited Lily's mother. She hadn't liked him then and she didn't like him now.

'I'll be fine and back before you know it. Now run along.' Lily dropped a kiss on Merry's head and shooed her in the direction of the kitchen.

As they stepped outside, the cold air almost took Lily's breath away and the thick smog made her eyes sting.

'Should we take a cab?' she asked.

He shook his head. 'No, I know where I'm goin' an' it shouldn't take long.'

He was walking so fast that Lily could barely keep up with him but at last they reached the areas surrounding the docks and she gazed about apprehensively. This was a bad area, not at all the sort of place anyone would want to be, especially after dark, but then she supposed she would be safe enough with Robbie with her. The shabby houses they passed were interspersed with tall factories and the gutters were running with raw sewage in places making Lily clutch her scarf more tightly across her mouth. Soon, the masts of ships could be seen above the roofs, flapping eerily in the smog.

'Is it much further?' Lily was getting seriously worried now. Whatever could Bridget have been thinking, taking a room in such a godforsaken place! But she supposed she wouldn't have been able to afford any better. Still, she would persuade her to come home with her and they could sort things there.

The nearer to the water they got the worse was the smell. The streets were deserted apart from the odd shady character who slunk by in the shadows against the walls but from every house they passed spilled the sound of people arguing, people shouting and babies crying.

At last Robbie stopped and taking her elbow he led her towards a house where the front door was hanging drunkenly off its hinges. 'This is where she is.'

A woman of indeterminate age was leaning against the wall with what looked like a bottle of gin in her hand and she eyed Lily's smart clothes enviously. She wore a ragged gown that was so low cut it was almost indecent and her pockmarked face was so heavily rouged that she looked like a hideous doll.

Lily was horrified. It was even worse here than she'd thought. They stepped into a dark hallway with noise coming from every room leading off it and she guessed that whole families must be packed in, sharing one room.

'It's up here.' Robbie started to climb the stairs and she followed cautiously, their steps echoing off the bare wooden treads. She felt as if she was caught in a nightmare and all she wanted was to see

Bridget and get her out of this terrible place as quickly as possible. She put her hand out and shivered as it connected with the damp wall. It was slimy and running with water; it was no wonder so many people died prematurely, living in such places.

'Spare a copper, mister?' A small boy clad in rags and sitting with his arms clasped about his knees on the first floor held his hand out hopefully, but Robbie merely snorted and booted him out of the way making the poor child yelp.

Lily gasped indignantly. 'There was no need to do that,' she scolded but he ignored her and started up the next flight of stairs leaving her no choice but to follow him.

'Only one more flight ter go,' he said encouragingly when they reached the next landing and once again they started to climb until at last they reached the top floor.

There were only four doors on this landing, although it was hard to be sure for it was almost pitch black up there.

Robbie paused and fumbled in his pocket for the key, which Lily found rather strange. Surely Bridget wouldn't have given it to him? But she had no time to think on it before he put his hand in the small of her back and pushed her inside, slamming and locking the door behind them.

'What do you think you're doing? And where's Bridget?' Panic was beginning to set in now as Lily narrowed her eyes and peered into the gloom. But it was no good, it was so dark she couldn't even see her hand in front of her.

'Just 'old on, I'll light a candle.'

Lily saw the match strike and seconds later the tallow candle that stood on an orange box began to dimly light the room.

'Where is she . . . what's going on?' she said as her eyes swept the room. There was no sign that Bridget had even been there.

He turned to her then and grasping her shoulders he soothed, 'It's all right, my pet. We don't need 'er. It's allus been you an' me.

An' now I've left 'er an' we're 'ere in London we can be together again.'

Lily's eyes blazed as she shook his hands from her and pushed him away. 'Have you gone completely *mad*?' she gasped. 'You're married to my sister and you have a baby with her. You and I were over a *long* time ago. When will you get that into your head? Now open that door immediately. I want to go home and I suggest you do the same and we'll forget this ever happened.'

As she moved towards the door and started to rattle the handle, he leapt forward and swung her about, almost overbalancing her.

'Sorry, I can't do that. I still love yer, see? An' till you realise yer still love me an' all, I'm gonna keep you 'ere.'

'You most certainly are *not*!' Lily was more angry than afraid now. 'Be sensible before this goes any further because I'll tell you now, I have no intention of staying here with you.'

He ran his hand distractedly through his hair. 'I'm afraid you ain't got a choice.'

Lily turned and began to rattle the door handle again. But it was no good and after a few minutes she turned back to him and said pleadingly, '*Please*, Robbie . . . this is madness. I don't love you. I'm fond of you but it's never been more than that. Even if you hadn't dropped me when I got back from Yorkshire, we would never have ended up together. Think of your wife and child!'

A solitary tear slid down his face and he shook his head. 'No, I were never good enough fer yer, was I? You preferred to be the mistress o' the lord o' the manor, didn't yer?'

'Don't be so ridiculous!' she spat. 'Louis will be engaged soon, if he isn't already, and there was *never* anything between us.'

'Oh no? An' what about yer fancy Frenchman?'

'The fancy Frenchman, as you refer to him, is walking out with Lady Arabella, if you must know,' she told him. 'In fact, I wouldn't be surprised if they didn't make a match of it soon.' Her hand flew to her forehead where the beginnings of a headache was starting to pound behind her eyes. The noises coming from the adjoining rooms were so loud that she could hardly make herself heard so she knew it would be no good shouting for help. No one would hear her. It struck her then that she was totally at Robbie's mercy and she felt sick. Deciding to try another tack she laid her hand on his arm and said softly, 'Look, this has all been a terrible mis-understanding. Why don't we just go back to my house now and have something to eat? We can talk more in the morning in more comfortable surroundings.'

He shook his head, reached behind him to snatch a length of rope that lay on the box beside the guttering candle.

'No, you're gonna stay right 'ere wi' me till yer see sense.'

Realising his intentions, she nodded. 'Very well, if that's what you want. But you don't have to tie me up.'

'Ha ha! I reckon I do cos the first time I turn me back or leave 'ere to get some food fer us you'll be off, won't yer? I ain't daft, yer know.'

Almost before she realised what he was going to do he took a foul-smelling piece of rag from his pocket and pressed it hard across her nose and mouth holding her to him. She gagged and kicked and tossed her head from side to side but her strength was no match for his and soon she dropped to the floor like a rag doll.

When Lily came round a short time later, she found her-self bound securely to a hard-backed chair. Her arms and legs screamed in protest when she tried to move them and her head was pounding. A quick glance around showed no sign of Robbie so she started to scream for all she was worth. After a short time she stopped – there was no point. The sound of shouting, children screaming and crashing and banging coming from the adjoining rooms made her realise that no one would take any notice. Despair washed through her, and tears gathered in her eyes. Where was

Robbie? Had he left her here to die because she had rejected him? She had no way of knowing and now all she could do was wait to see if he would come back. Thoughts of Merry made her tears flow faster. She would be so worried and afraid when she didn't come home. And worse still, what would happen to the child if she never did return? Would the poor little soul end up back on the streets or in the dreaded workhouse? Her chin drooped to her chest and she began to sob in earnest.

The hours slowly passed and the light in the room grew slightly brighter. Lily's arms were bound so tightly that they felt as if they were being ripped out of their sockets. She was terribly cold and she desperately needed the toilet, so she began to scream again, but once more no one came and she began to panic. What if Robbie didn't come back?

Just when she was beginning to give up hope she heard the key in the door and Robbie entered.

'Where have you *been*?' she hissed as she rocked the chair from side to side in a fury. 'I need to go to the toilet, untie me *at once*!'

He crossed to her and began to stroke her cheek and when she glared up at him her heart missed a beat as she realised that Robbie was ill. There was a blank look in his eyes and she saw the gleam of madness shining in them.

'Robbie . . .' she began in a gentler voice. '*Please* untie me. I need to go to the toilet and I'm in pain. You wouldn't want to hurt me, would you?'

He sank down to the floor. 'I've done everythin' wrong an' 'urt everybody!'

'It doesn't matter,' she told him urgently. 'We can put everything right, I promise you, if you'll only let me go!'

It was then that she felt a rush of warmth between her legs and she stared in horror at the stain seeping into the skirts of her gown; humiliation made her cry even harder.

Robbie was silent now, staring sightlessly into space as he rocked backwards and forwards and all she could do was sit and watch him helplessly. Robbie had locked himself away in a place where no one could reach him anymore; he didn't even seem to be aware that she was there and her hopes of ever escaping slipped away.

She would die here in this dirty rat-infested room – they both would – and there was nothing she could do about it.

Chapter Forty-Six

The maid in Kensington Place rushed to answer the furious pounding on the front door and as she opened it, Merry almost fell into the hallway.

'I . . . I need to see Miss Arabella,' she blurted out breathlessly. 'Sumfin bad's 'appened to Lily!'

The door to the drawing room opened and Louis, who'd arrived the day before for a visit, appeared. 'What's wrong?' he asked, seeing the child standing there shaking.

'It's Lily,' the little girl told him with a catch in her voice. 'The man, Robbie, what's married to Lily's sister, come to see 'er yesterday an' she went off wi' im but she didn't come back. 'E said that 'e were takin' 'er to see 'er sister but Lily's never not come 'ome before! She told me that she wouldn't be gone fer long an' I don't know what to do!'

Louis frowned as Arabella and her mother appeared behind him. One look at Merry's tear-stained face told them that something was seriously wrong and as Louis hastily explained what had happened, Arabella's hand flew to her mouth.

'Something must have happened to her,' she said shakily. 'She would never willingly leave Merry alone. She dotes on her.' Then addressing the child, she asked gently, 'Did Robbie say where he was taking Lily, Merry.'

Merry looked uncomfortable as she shifted from foot to foot. 'Well . . . I did listen at the door, though I weren't supposed to an' I 'eard 'im say that Bridget were stayin' somewhere down by the docks. That's where they were goin'.'

'But that could be anywhere,' Arabella said worriedly. 'Should we go to the police?'

Louis thought for a moment before shaking his head. 'Not yet. I'm going to try and find her myself first. *Someone* must have seen her. Lily would have stuck out like a sore thumb in those areas.' He turned to Merry. 'You stay here with my mother and sister and I'll start to look for her straightaway.'

Merry's mouth set in a determined line and she shook her head. 'Not on yer nelly, mate. I knows them docks like the back o' me 'ands an' you'll 'ave far more chance o' findin' 'er if I come along wiv yer. You don't even know yer way 'ereabouts.'

Seeing the sense in what she said, he nodded and started to put his coat on. 'Very well, but it could take some time.'

'I ain't cared 'ow long it takes so long as we gerr 'er back,' Merry said stubbornly.

Deeply touched by her loyalty to Lily, Louis took her hand and led her outside. 'So where do we start?' Louis asked when they were out on the pavement.

'This way.' Merry strode ahead and he followed her.

It was getting dark again and as something with red eyes and a big long tail skimmed across Lily's foot, she started out of the uncomfortable doze she had dropped into a short while ago. Thankfully she had lost all feeling in her tightly bound arms and legs so at least the pain had eased, but the smell of her soiled gown was disgusting and her mouth was so dry that her lips kept sticking together.

Robbie was still sitting in the same position and now she implored him weakly, 'Robbie, can I at least have a sip of water?'

He showed no sign of having heard her. It was now over twenty-four hours since she had eaten or drunk anything and she was starting to feel light-headed and weak. She looked about the room desperately. There was very little in it apart from an old table that leant drunkenly to one side, two hard-backed chairs and an old iron bedstead with a dirty blanket crumpled at one end of it. But then her eyes fastened on the table again and suddenly she was alert. There was a knife on it. If only she could get to it, she might be able to get hold of it and cut through her ties. With an enormous effort she began to rock the chair from side to side, keeping a close eye on Robbie. Each time she managed to balance the chair on two legs she threw her weight to one side, hotching it forward an inch at a time. It was hard work and soon she was gasping with the effort but she gritted her teeth and carried on, desperate to try anything now.

By the time the table was in reach the room was in pitch darkness apart from the faint light that crept in through the thin curtains. That was when she hit another problem. The table was higher than her tied hands so how was she to reach the knife? She chewed on her lip as she tried to concentrate and all the while Robbie sat motionless, seemingly unaware that she was even there. With a great effort, Lily painfully began to nudge the table with the top of her arm, which made the ties on her wrist cut even deeper into her skin. She could feel something warm running into her hands and realised it was blood, but she didn't stop trying and slowly the knife edged closer to her. Suddenly disaster struck when the knife clattered to the floor, completely out of reach now, and she sobbed with frustration. Dizziness claimed her and as a comforting dark-ness rushed towards her, she sank into it and knew no more.

'What do we do now?' Merry asked tearfully. It was very late at night and they had trudged miles round the docklands asking everyone they met if they had seen Lily. Thankfully Merry could remember what she had been wearing and had been able to describe it, but as yet no one had seen hide nor hair of her.

The child looked almost dead on her feet and Louis scratched his head as he tried to think what he should do next.

'I think it's time we involved the police,' he told her regretfully. 'And then I'm taking you home for a rest. It isn't safe for you to be out this late at night.'

'I'm all right!' Merry declared indignantly. 'I'm used to bein' out on the streets. I used to live on 'em till Lily took me in, remember?'

'I understand that,' he said soothingly. 'But even so I don't think there's much more we can do till it gets light again. Come on, we'll go to the police station and report her missing then I want you to get some rest. We'll start the search again first thing in the morning as soon as it gets light, although I think you should be at school tomorrow, shouldn't you?'

'I ain't goin' till Lily's back,' she told him with a determined thrust of her chin and Louis wisely didn't argue.

It was almost two o'clock in the morning before he delivered Merry back to Abby who was anxiously waiting up back at Lily's house, and he returned to Kensington Place with a heavy heart.

'The police will start the search for Lily and Robbie at first light,' an exhausted Louis told Arabella when he got home, and she tearfully shooed him off to bed to get a well-earned rest, although he tossed and turned all night.

Merry was back on the doorstep at the crack of dawn and the search began again, but as the day wore on Louis' spirits sank to a very low ebb.

They stopped the search briefly mid-afternoon to call into a café close to the docks for a drink and something to eat and it was in there that they saw a blowsy-looking woman with a pockmarked, heavily rouged face staring at them intently.

'What's an 'andsome gen'leman like you doing in these parts, dearie?' she asked Louis, as she sashayed up to him fluttering her eyelashes.

354

'We're looking for someone,' he answered politely. 'A close friend of mine. She was headed this way three days ago now but we haven't been able to find her. She was with a man.'

'An' she were wearing a burgundy gown wi' a dark grey coat over it an' a grey bonnet,' Merry piped up.

The woman narrowed her eyes. 'Oh arr . . . an' what's the reward if someone were to tell yer where they think she might be?' she wheedled.

Louis leant forward in his seat. 'Oh, I should think it would be worth a guinea at least,' he said a little too quickly.

She chortled with laughter showing blackened teeth. 'Wouldn't even be worth the walk to where anyone thought she could be fer that, duckie.'

'Then how about *two* pounds?' he urged.

Again she shook her head. 'All right, *five* pounds and that's my last offer!'

Now she was interested and she leant forward, her large bosom almost spilling out of her ragged gown. 'An' 'ow does I know yer've got the money to pay?'

Louis quickly extracted his wallet and took out a five-pound note and waved it at her, but when she went to snatch it, he pulled his hand away. 'Oh no you don't, not until we know you're not leading us on a wild goose chase.'

She pouted and crossed her arms. ''Ave it yer own way.' She licked her lips, her greedy eyes still on the note. 'Come on, then, if yer comin'. I reckon I might know where she could be.'

They followed her through a labyrinth of filthy alleys that smelled of rotting rubbish, dead dogs and urine and after what seemed like a very long time she stopped in front of a tall house.

'If she's the woman yer lookin' for she come in 'ere,' she told him.

Louis frowned. 'But it seems that lots of people live in here. How would I know which room she's in?'

'Yer speak to the landlord o' course,' she told him as if she was speaking to a child. 'Come out o' the way an' I'll do it fer you.'

Once inside she hammered on the first door they came to in the long hallway and eventually it was opened up by a wizened little man in a filthy waistcoat with straggly grey hair that stood out about his head like wispy snakes.

'Right, Bart, who yer been lettin' yer rooms out to lately?' she barked.

He looked suspiciously at Louis. 'Who wants ter know?'

'This toff 'ere, an' if yer tell 'im I'll see as 'e slips yer 'alf a crown!'

'Hmm.' He rubbed at his sparse grey beard. 'Me latest let were to a chap up on the top floor a few days ago.'

'That'd be 'im,' the woman said triumphantly and turning to Louis she said, 'There yer go – now cough the money up, squire.'

'Not until I've checked Lily is here,' he said, taking the stairs two at a time with Merry in close pursuit. The woman lifted her grubby skirts and followed them, huffing and puffing all the way until eventually they arrived on the top floor.

'Which room would it be?' Louis looked perplexed.

The woman shook her head. 'Listen an' you'll find out,' she told him. 'If yer can 'ear a family through the door you'll know it ain't that one, won't yer? Eeh, yer don't know much, do yer?'

It took a matter of minutes for Louis to check the rooms out and at last he stopped in front of the one from which there was no sound coming.

He rattled the handle and knocked loudly and when no one answered he told them, 'Stand back!' Then he threw himself at it and the flimsy door splintered and flew inwards. The smell and the darkness instantly hit them but as Louis' eyes adjusted to the gloom he gasped.

'Oh, my God. Merry, open the curtains. I think that's Lily.'

Within seconds Louis had released the ties that bound her and she flopped into his arms as he sobbed with relief.

'Go and find a policeman, tell them we've found her and that we need help,' he told Merry, and only too happy to oblige she shot away to do as she was told.

Chapter Forty-Seven

Lily blearily opened her eyes, suddenly aware that someone was gripping her hand. She tried to turn her head to see who it was, but for some reason it didn't seem to do as it was told.

'She's awake, fetch the doctor quickly, Merry.'

Was that Arabella's voice? And then there was another one. 'Thank God,' it said. Was that Louis? But it couldn't be, she was locked away in a grubby room with Robbie and Louis was far away back at the manor, surely?

She tried to move her arms but the pain was excruciating and then a man with a kindly face and a large beard was leaning over her. 'It's all right, my dear.' His voice was soothing. 'You're quite safe now and back in your own bed.'

'Robbie,' she said urgently as everything began to rush back to her.

'He's with the police, he can't hurt you now,' the man soothed.

She shook her head. 'N-no . . . you don't understand . . . he's ill. I don't want him punished; he needs help.'

'We'll talk about that when you've had a rest,' he told her.

She wanted to say, no, now! But the darkness was closing in again and she couldn't seem to fight it.

The doctor smiled at Louis. 'She'll be fine now,' he assured him. 'She'll be in pain from the wounds where she was bound, but I've dressed them and there should be no long-term problem. You say she comes from a village in the Midlands? If she has family there, I would suggest you send her back there to recuperate.'

'And what about Robbie, her brother-in-law?'

'Hmm.' The doctor shrugged. 'What happens to him will be up to Miss Moon when she speaks to the police. They can't charge him with anything if she doesn't wish them to, and I would have to agree with her, the man is mentally ill. He needs treatment rather than punishment. He appears to have had some sort of breakdown.'

'Thank you, Doctor.' Louis saw him out before returning to his vigil at Lily's bedside. He had barely left her side since bringing her home, where Merry and Abby were taking good care of her.

When everyone had left the room and he was alone, he gently kissed Lily's fingers. 'Oh, my darling, I don't know what I would have done if anything had happened to you,' he whispered. 'But we'll get you well again, never you fear.'

It was much later that evening before he left to return to Kensington Place and when he came back the next morning it was to be told that Lily was talking to the police.

He waited patiently until they left and when he went in to her, he found her propped up on the pillows, looking much more her old self.

'Thank you so much for finding me,' she told him with a smile.

He looked at her pale face and offered up a silent prayer of thanks that he had found her in time.

'I've just told the police that I don't wish for Robbie to be charged. He's not really been himself since he was trapped down the pit on the day we lost my father. He needs to go to the mental asylum, not prison. So I'm going to pay for him to be admitted to Hatter's Hall. Hopefully he can get the proper treatment there.'

He shook his head. 'You never cease to amaze me,' he said with a twinkle in his eye. 'After what he did to you most women would be baying for his blood.'

'But I'm not most women. The thing is, I think half of Robbie and Bridget's problem was that they were having to live in very cramped

359

conditions with Robbie's parents, so I'm going to buy them a little home of their own so when he gets better they can start afresh.'

'That's very generous. But what about you? Don't you think you should follow the doctor's advice and come home until you're fully recovered? I could take you back with me?'

'And Merry?'

'Her too, of course.' He chuckled. 'Not that she'd let me escape with you without her. She's a right little character and I suppose she'll want to take Honey too.'

'You're rather going to have your hands full.' She smiled. 'But actually, a little time off doing nothing does sound rather nice, so yes, I'd like to take you up on your offer.'

During the next days, Jean-Paul, Monsieur Levigne, Arabella and Lady Bellingham all came to see her and Lily felt blessed to have such good friends. Monsieur Levigne encouraged her to take as much time off as she needed to fully recover, assuring her that it wouldn't affect her blossoming career, and slowly Lily began to feel a little better. The trauma she had suffered at Robbie's hands had affected her both physically and mentally but she was painfully aware that had it not been for Merry and Louis things could have been far worse.

They travelled back to Nuneaton five days later and when they arrived at the cottage Sara almost covered her with kisses. Robbie had been taken to the hospital some days before and Lily was thrilled to hear that Bridget was spending as much time with him as she could.

'Seems she still loves 'im, so let's just 'ope he bucks 'is ideas up when 'e gets better, eh?' her mother said. Lily had told her about the little house she hoped to buy for them and Sara thought it would be the making of them. 'But now let's just concentrate on gettin' you better,' she said. 'I've 'ad strict instructions from the young lord that I'm to give you anythin' yer fancy. Money's no object. Seems like nothin' to do wi' you is too much trouble for 'im.' She grinned.

Lily flushed. 'Now don't get reading things into it, Mam,' she chided. 'He's just been really kind to me but if I need anything I'm more than able to pay for it myself.'

'Mm, yer can say that again!'

That afternoon Louis paid his daily visit armed with yet another beautiful bouquet of flowers from the hothouse at the manor and Sara chuckled. 'I shall be runnin' out of vases at this rate,' she teased him. 'This place is beginnin' to look like a florist's shop.'

Despite the chill, Lily was sitting in the garden wrapped in a blanket, enjoying the tranquillity of the place. She'd realised since being back home that as nice as it was living in London, she was a country girl at heart and she missed the wide-open spaces.

She smiled at Louis as he sat down beside her, and they sat in silence for a while, content just to be in each other's company.

'How is Miss Thompson?' Lily tentatively asked after a time. 'I've been expecting to hear the announcement of your engagement ever since the mourning period for your father ended.'

He grinned. 'I rather think Samantha got a little sick of waiting around for me,' he told her. 'And the last I heard she was walking out with a wealthy mill owner.'

'Oh!' Lily looked shocked. 'I'm so sorry.'

'Don't be, I'm not.' He bent to stroke Honey's ears before she bounded off to play with Sassy again – they were getting on famously.

'But . . . I thought you and Miss Thompson had an agreement?'

He shrugged. 'It was what my parents wanted but I think since losing my father my mother has realised that I would never have been happy with her. I also think that Samantha knew a long time ago that my heart belonged to someone else.'

Lily stared at him confused as he leant towards her and took her hand. 'I think you know who that someone is, don't you?'

'Don't start that again,' She flushed. 'We both accepted a long time ago that a lord could never marry a miner's daughter.'

'No? But he could certainly marry a famous artist, couldn't he? So, what do you say, Miss Lily Moon? I shall have to respect the six-month mourning period for my grandmother, of course, but then when it's over, are you going to marry me and make me the happiest man on earth? I reckon we've wasted quite enough time, don't you?'

When Lily still hesitated, he stood and drawing her to her feet, he took her in his arms just as Merry bounded around the corner. The little girl skidded to a halt, then with a wide grin she rushed off to tell Sara what was happening.

'But what will people say?'

He laughed. 'I don't give a jot. I'd have married you even if you hadn't had a penny to your name. One thing is for sure, if I can't marry you, I'll never marry anyone. I love you – I think I have since the first day I set eyes on you. I'll even have the room of your choice turned into a studio where you can paint to your heart's content if you'll be my wife. How does that sound?'

Lily leant into his arms and, looking up at him, saw all the love he felt for her shining in his eyes and she knew that she could fight her feelings for him no longer.

'In that case how can I refuse?' she giggled, quite oblivious to the fact that Sara and Merry were watching them avidly from the kitchen window.

There was no time to say more as his lips came down on hers. And despite all the success she had achieved and the happiness she had found, she knew nothing would ever compare to how she felt right at this moment, because at last she was exactly where she was meant to be.

Acknowledgements

Where do I start? There are so many people that I'd like to thank, not least my amazing Rosie Team at Bonnier. There are too many to mention; every one of them helps me to make each book as good as it can be and I hope they all know how much I value each and every one of them, so a huge thank you to you all.

Not forgetting my brilliant agent Sheila Crowley and my wonderful copyeditor and proofreader. Thank you all so much.

Thanks also to my wonderful family who support me every step of the way. I love you all millions.

And last but never least to my lovely friends and readers. I could never have done this without you, so thank you.

Rosie GOODWIN

BRITAIN'S BEST-LOVED SAGA AUTHOR

Want to keep up to date with the latest from Rosie Goodwin?

With exclusive content from the author herself, book updates, competitions and more, the Rosie Goodwin newsletter is the place to be if you can't get enough of Britain's best-loved saga author.

To sign up, you can scan the QR code or type the link below into your browser

https://geni.us/RosieGoodwin

Hello Everyone,

Well, here we are with Christmas behind us for yet another year. It doesn't seem like the blink of an eye since I was writing to you all at this time last year!

I hope Christmas was a happy time for all of you and that you got to spend it with your loved ones. I did and it was great! For me the lead up was the usual hectic last-minute rush to get everything done. It's the bit after Christmas that I don't like. It's always a bit of an anti-climax when all the decorations have been put away and it's too cold yet to get out in the garden. But now we have the spring to look forward to. I do love locking myself away with all my imaginary characters on dark winter nights, but I must admit I'm really looking forward to being able to get out into the garden again now. I always think there's something magical when you can watch everything come to life after the long cold winter.

And of course, I've been so looking forward to the release of *Our Fair Lily*, the first of three books in my Flower Girls collection. As with all my main characters I came to love this girl. She is such a strong person and so determined to make the best of herself despite all the setbacks she has. My hubby always tells me he thinks the dark side of me comes out whenever I start a story. Haha! I think he could be right because I do tend to give my characters a bad time, don't I? Anyway, I hope you all love Lily as much as I do.

I should point out that while the village this book is set in does exist, Oakland Manor, as far as I know, never did.

That's the great thing about being a writer, you can let your imagination run riot and invent people and places that never existed. The family who owned the manor are imaginary too, and certainly never owned the Haunchwood Colliery, so I hope whoever did own it will forgive me.

I'd like to thank you all for the lovely response to *The Lost Girl*. I really appreciate all your support, which is why I was so thrilled when I was given the chance to have my very own newsletter where I can write to you all on a regular basis and keep you up to date with what's going on. There's a link above to sign up if you haven't already. And for any of you that haven't yet, do join The Memory Lane Book Club on Facebook. They'll also keep you up to date with what all the other Memory Lane authors are up to and of course there are some great competitions and prizes up for grabs!

I can share that in the next book you'll meet Daisy in *Our Dear Daisy* and book three will be *Our Sweet Violet*. More on those soon, but they are both available to pre-order now. Meanwhile, I'm busily tapping away as usual getting more books written. Please keep your lovely messages coming, they really do make my day.

I'd just like to wish you all a wonderful spring and summer. Bring on the sunshine!

Take care everyone.

Lots of love,
Rosie xx

The Lost Girl

Can Esme lay the ghosts to rest to save
herself and find the life she deserves?

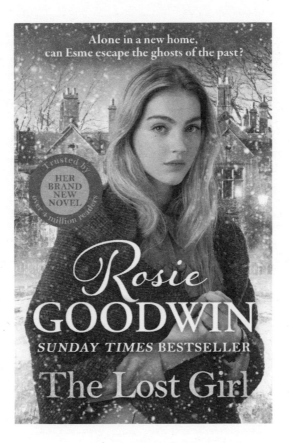

Available now

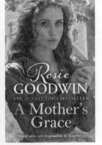
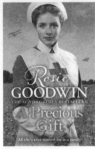

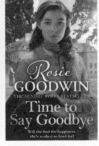

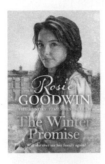

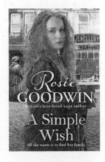
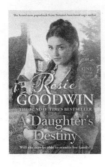

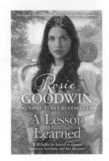

· MEMORY LANE ·

Introducing the place for story lovers – a welcoming home for all readers who love heartwarming tales of wartime, family and romance. Join us to discuss your favourite stories with other readers, plus get book recommendations, book giveaways and behind-the-scenes writing moments from your favourite authors.

· MEMORY LANE ·

www.MemoryLane.Club

www.facebook.com/groups/memorylanebookgroup